IF YOU

Want

ME

NEW YORK TIMES BESTSELLING AUTHOR
HELENA HUNTING

IF YOU (l)art ME CAST

HOLLIS HENDRIX
TERROR FORWARD
BEST FRIEND TO ROMAN HAMMERSTEIN

SIBLINGS
MICHA — MARRIED TO MIKE, DAUGHTER ELSA
EMILIA

TEAMMATES
DALLAS BRIGHT — BEST FRIEND TO ASH

ASHISH PALANIAPPA — HUSBAND TO SHILPA (TEAM LAWYER), BEST FRIEND TO DALLAS

FLIP MADDEN — BROTHER TO RIX, BEST FRIEND TO TRISTAN AND DRED

TRISTAN STILES — BOYFRIEND TO RIX, BEST FRIEND TO FLIP

PEGGY AURORA HAMMERSTEIN
(PEGGY, AURORA, HAMMER, PRINCESS)
DAUGHTER TO ROMAN HAMMERSTEIN, TEAM GOALIE

ROMAN HAMMERSTEIN
HAMMER'S DAD
HOLLIS'S BEST FRIEND, TERROR GOALIE

THE BADASS BABE BRIGADE

WILHELMINA REDDI-GRINST
(MEM, WILLY/WILLS)
PR FOR TERROR
FRIEND TO HAMMER
BEST FRIEND TO SHILPA

BEATRIX MADDEN
(RIX, BEAT, BEA)
ROOMMATE TO HAMMER
SISTER OF FLIP MADDEN
GIRLFRIEND TO TRISTAN STILES

MILDRED REFORMER
(DRED)
NEIGHBOR TO FLIP
PLATONIC FRIEND OF FLIP'S

TALLULAH VANDER ZEE
(TALLY/TELLS)
DAUGHTER OF TERROR COACH
INTERNED WITH MEM
CURRENTLY IN SENIOR YEAR OF HIGH SCHOOL

ESSIE LOVELOCK
HONORARY MEMBER
RIX'S BEST FRIEND
LIVES IN VANCOUVER

SHILPA PALANIAPPA
SHILPS
BEST FRIEND TO MEM
MARRIED TO ASHISH PALANIAPPA

ACKNOWLEDGMENTS

Husband and kidlet, I adore you. You inspire me every day and I'm so grateful for your love.

Deb, I adore you. Thank you for always having my back.

Becca, it is such an honor to know you, as a friend, as a badass fairy plotmother, as a strong, amazing businesswoman. Thank you for coming on this journey with me. I am forever grateful for that 3 am chat that brought you into my orbit exactly when I needed you.

Kimberly, thank you for coming on this journey with me. It's been an amazing decade and I'm excited for what's next.

Sarah, I honestly couldn't do this without you. You've been such a huge source of support and friendship and I'm so thankful to have you on my side.

Hustlers, you're my cheerleaders and my book family and I'm so grateful for each and every one of you.

My SS team, your eagle eyes are amazing, and I appreciate your input and support.

Tijan, you're a wonderful human and I'm blessed to know you.

Shaye and Lindsey, you are amazing and I'm so thankful for you and Good Girls.

Catherine, Jessica F and Tricia, your kindness and wonderful energy are such a source of inspiration, thank you for your friendship.

Jessica, Erica, Amanda, Julia, thank you so much for working on this project with me, I know it was a beast, and I'm so honored to be able to work with you and helping me make it sparkle.

Sarah, Gel, Kate and Rae, thank you for being graphic gurus. Your incredible talent never ceases to amaze me.

Beavers, thank you for giving me a safe place to land, and for always being excited about what's next.

Kat, Marnie, Krystin; thank you for being such incredible women. I'm so thankful for your friendship.

Readers, bloggers, bookstagrammers and booktokers, thank you for sharing your love of romance and happily ever afters.

To my amazing readers, thank you for trusting me with your heart,
even though I put it through the wringer every time.

CHAPTER 1
HAMMER

O f all the stupid things I could possibly do, this wins the gold medal. So, so stupid. Like what would ever possess me to do something so unfathomably idiotic?

I'm supposed to keep Hollis's cats company while the team is qn an away series, not succumb to my tried-and-true teenage fantasies.

I should be dating someone my own age, a nice guy from one of my university classes. But having a professional hockey player for a dad hasn't really helped my love life. Worse, my crush on his teammate started as a small, harmless thing that I tried to ignore. Tried and failed.

I knew better, *know* better, but I was weak and cuddled up, and my vibrator was right there in my bag. Brand new, and magical, and waiting to be tested…

What was I supposed to do?

Not test it out in Hollis Hendrix's bed.

But it's too late, the mistake has been made.

I, Peggy Aurora Hammerstein, masturbated in my dad's best friend's bed.

CHAPTER 2
HAMMER

"This is my literal nightmare." I slam my thumb against the button until the elevator arrives. It feels like my soul has left my damn body. I throw myself inside and struggle to calm my breathing as the numbers climb to the penthouse floor. My stomach is flipping, my mouth is dry, my palms are sweating. "You have time to get rid of the evidence. It'll be fine."

The team never comes back from an away series this early. Except today they are. I thought I'd have hours after my class meeting. The sheets still need to be washed. *I need to get rid of the evidence.* And I left my freaking vibrator behind. *How the hell could I have left it behind?* In all the months I've been taking care of Hollis's cats, I've always stayed on the right side of the infatuation line. Until now. And look at the mess I've gotten myself into.

I pace the tiny steel box as the elevator ascends forty-four stories. It takes an eternity. The doors finally slide open, and I launch myself into the hallway.

I will never do something this stupid ever again. The sensor on Hollis's door turns green as I pass the fob in front of it. I'm immediately accosted by Postie and Malone. I ignore them while I key in the alarm code.

Once that's taken care of, I give the needy orange tabby rescue cats a quick head scratch. "I need to take care of a few things, and then I'll give you a treat. Your dad will be home soon."

The floor creaks from somewhere in the penthouse. The cats' ears perk up. I freeze for a moment, then peer over the back of the couch as Hollis steps around the corner.

This is worse than bad. This is emergency-level holy shit. I cannot erase the evidence if he's already home. My eyeballs nearly pop out of my head and roll across the floor. Because he's fresh from the shower, running a towel over his face. Another towel is wrapped around his waist. It's ratty and smaller than the usual huge bath sheets he uses. Because the clean ones are in his laundry room. And so are the dirty sheets.

I should cover my eyes, or turn around, or announce my presence. But I'm too busy having a freaking panic attack. I can barely breathe. The rapid drumming of my heartbeat is all I can hear. Also, the possibility that I might die of embarrassment is real. Apparently, I can still appreciate the visual delight that is a mostly undressed Hollis Hendrix, though.

His jacked-up hockey body is a sight to behold. His biceps pop, highlighting his half-sleeve tattoo as he runs the towel over his dark, wet hair. It's a cool piece of art that's impossible not to admire. On his biceps, a hockey player skates across a frozen lake, the sun shining down on him. In the background, huge pine trees frame the edge of the water. As they rise to his shoulder, the winter scene changes to fall. The evergreens turn into maples with their boastful yellow, orange, and red leaves. Single vibrant leaves flutter over his shoulder and across his chest. Muscles flex and ripple, water droplets cascade over his drool-worthy pecs before he swipes them away.

I'm in so much trouble right now. So much trouble. From his spot across the room, I'm obscured by the couch. But freaking Postie, the noisy asshole that he is, gives me away by meowing obnoxiously.

I shoot to my feet.

Hollis startles and holds the towel in his hand to his chest. "What the fuck?"

"I'm so sorry!" I shout.

Postie meows and hurdles over the couch like an Olympian. Malone's tail puffs up, and he hustles his chonky butt across the room and disappears into Hollis's bedroom. The corner of the bed is visible from where I'm standing. I consider following him, but I'm not as fast as a cat, and there will be questions.

"What are you doing here?" Hollis growls as he adjusts his towel, securing it around his waist. I'm still shamelessly staring at his glorious chest and abs and bulging biceps, as well as the other exciting bulge hidden by the towel.

I attempt to avert my gaze, but my eyes keep darting in his direction. "I, uh—uh I...I thought I had time..." I can't be honest. "I didn't know you were coming back early. I need to throw your sheets in the wash. The cats were all over them. I meant to do it this morning. I can do it now." If I can get to the laundry room, I can wash away the evidence.

Hollis holds up a hand, and my gaze darts back down to the bulge at his waist. "I can take care of it."

I lick my lips, desperately searching for a reason to run to his bedroom that doesn't include throwing myself at him, which I would really love to do, but haven't, for obvious reasons. I come up empty. "Right. Yeah." I nod, and my eyes dart around the apartment before they come back to his naked chest.

I'm so hot right now. And sweaty. There are so many highly inappropriate thoughts running through my mind. Scenarios I've fantasized about more times than I'd like to admit—like Hollis closing the distance between us, taking me in his arms and kissing the hell out of me before he carries me to his bedroom, where he strips me naked and tells me exactly what he's going to do to me.

"I should go." I thumb over my shoulder and take a step toward the door. "I'm going to go." I'm still staring at him as I grope behind me for the doorknob. My fingers wrap around it. "I'm so sorry. So, so sorry. I should have knocked." I escape into the hall.

Hollis's confused expression and his hot-as-fuck body disappear as the door closes. I hustle over to the elevator and jam my thumb on the button until it opens. "Crap, crap, triple crap." I practically yeet myself inside and hit the button for the twelfth floor, gripping the back of my neck while I tap my foot furiously. "Maybe he won't notice. Maybe he won't do his laundry, and I can sneak in tomorrow morning and throw a load in and grab my..." I can't even finish that statement.

Maybe Postie or Malone knocked my vibrator off the nightstand, and it rolled under the bed. Those two are forever knocking shit off the counter. This is the one instance where their mischief would be welcome. The elevator stops at my floor, and I step off, my stomach churning with anxiety as I return to my apartment.

I let myself in and lean against the door, feeling like I might pass out, or vomit, or both.

My roommate, Rix, is in the kitchen. Her long dark hair is pulled up in a ponytail, and she's wearing a pair of leggings and an oversized hoodie. She's the sister of Toronto Terror's center, Flip Madden, and she's dating his best friend, Tristan Stiles, who also plays for the team. "Did you get everything sorted out?"

"Hollis is already home. I couldn't handle anything. And he was fresh from the shower. I saw him mostly naked," I say.

Her eyebrows shoot up and her mouth opens and closes twice before she asks, "How was that experience?"

"It was...he was...he has a significant bulge. Like, really significant. And I stared at it. Probably for longer than I should have." I run a hand down my face. "This is so bad. So, so bad."

"Shit happens. I'm sure it'll be fine," she assures me. "You've seen him in a bathing suit after he and your dad get out of physio. It's not much different, right?"

"Right. Yeah. Not much different."

"At least you didn't get an eye-full of dick."

"Yeah. No dick."

She tips her head. "Did something else happen?"

I bite my lips together to keep the truth in my mouth, but I blurt it out, anyway. "I forgot to put his towels and sheets through the wash."

Her eyebrows rise. "Why is that a big deal?"

I chew my bottom lip. She's my roommate and my friend. I can be honest about this. I can tell her what happened, and maybe she can help me figure out how to fix this.

"Did one of the cats poop on his bed?" she asks.

I shake my head. "Worse."

A slow smirk curves the right side of her mouth. "Did you have a nap in his bed while he wasn't there?"

I hide behind my hands. "It's so much worse than that, Rix. So, so much worse."

Her smile drops. "Worse than when your dad accidentally walked in on me and Tristan? Roman gave him dead eyes in the locker room for a week after that."

I drop my hands. "Actually, it might be pretty close."

"Oh, shit." She grips the edge of the counter. "What'd you do?"

"I tested out my new vibrator while I was there earlier. And I left it on his nightstand," I whisper. "And I couldn't get it back, and he'll find it." I throw my hands in the air. "I'll die of embarrassment. I'll never be able to look him in the eye again."

"Oh, girl."

My phone buzzes in my pocket, scaring the shit out of me. "Oh my God. What if he's found it? What if that's him and he wants to know why the hell I was masturbating in his goddamn bed?" I might faint from the mortification.

Rix snaps her fingers. "I knew you had the hots for him!"

"What? How the hell did you know that?"

She waves a hand around. "It was a feeling."

I don't know how to deal with that, so I let it go for now.

"What am I going to do?" I pull the phone from my back pocket. "Oh, thank God. It's just my dad." I open the message with shaking hands.

DADO

Pancake House in fifteen with me and Hollis!

Of course he's joining us today of all days. "Hollis is coming to the Pancake House," I tell her. "Maybe he hasn't seen it yet, and you can grab it for me while I'm there." Otherwise, things are about to get even more awkward.

CHAPTER 3
HOLLIS

I'm still standing in the hallway, staring at the door Peggy disappeared through. Postie winds himself between my legs. "The diner will be awkward."

Postie meows and trots over to his dish. He plunks his butt down and taps the bowl with his paw. Malone hustles out of hiding to join his brother. I shake out a few treats for my boys before crossing to my bedroom.

I should have warned Peggy that I was home early. Thank fuck I hadn't come out bare-assed. She looked shell-shocked enough as it was. She'll probably be embarrassed about the whole thing. She'll feel compelled to overcompensate by saying sorry a million times and texting repeatedly to make sure it's safe to come by. I don't want her to feel bad when it's on me to warn her. I know her routine. She stops by to check on the cats first thing in the morning and again when she gets back from class. I grab my phone from my bed, intending to send an apology message.

Malone hops onto the nightstand, and something clatters to the floor. He yowls and bounces like he has springs in his feet, tail poofed out as he races out of the room.

"What's got you so freaked out?" I frown as I bend to pick up the object. "The hell?"

It takes several seconds for me to process what I'm holding. And when it finally clicks, my brain almost liquifies. I'm holding a superhero vibrator. More specifically, I'm holding *Peggy's* superhero vibrator. It can't belong to anyone else because aside from her dad, she's the only person with access to my penthouse. And she's the only woman who's been here in a long, long time, apart from my younger sister and my niece.

So many questions arise. *So fucking many questions.*

Like why the hell is her vibrator in my goddamn bedroom? On my nightstand.

My mouth goes dry as I stare at my bed with the two cat-shaped dents near the pillows. Then I glance across the room at one of the two kitty cams I set up but didn't monitor while I was away. I forgot to even mention they were there.

Fuck. Fuck. *Fuck.*

Did she get herself off in my bed? *Why* would she get herself off in *my* bed?

Or did she leave it here on purpose to tempt me? No. She could have anyone. There's no way Peggy wants anything from me. And she can't know what has been going on in my head over the past several months.

For the past few years Peggy's been on the periphery of the hockey world, attending university, living in an off-campus apartment, around on weekends when she comes to visit her dad. I only saw her occasionally. She started watching my cats and kept me company during my injury last season, but even those things fit in very specific boundaries. We became friends. It was all fine.

At least until she took an internship position working under Hemi, the head of team PR in September. And then everything changed, even though I've tried not to let it.

I'll never forget the moment I rounded the corner and spotted her doing a hip shimmy down the hall, fist pumping the air. I hadn't realized whose curves I was admiring at first. Until she spun around, her wide smile aimed at me. It was such a damning moment. I'd been ogling my best friend's daughter. Since then, I've done my best to compartmentalize that event. To force myself to see her the way I'm supposed to. But now here I am, with a whole new battle to face.

Because this…is exactly what I *don't* need.

I try not to let any invasive, inappropriate thoughts root. I really do. But my imagination is a giant asshole. Not for the first time, an image forms of Peggy lying in my bed, lip caught between her teeth. Only this time, she's holding the superhero vibrator. I shake my head to chase it away.

Do I have footage of this stored on my cloud? My self-loathing is immediate and warranted. I let go of the vibrator like it's on fire. It drops to my bed and lies there. It looks so damn harmless. It's anything but. The rechargeable silicone device taunts me, a horrifying beacon of untenable hope.

She wants you. I shove that thought back down. That's impossible. "She's Roman's daughter, you fuckhead," I chastise.

I rub my bottom lip. I can't afford to indulge in these kinds of fantasies about her again—the kind where I replace the freaking superhero vibrator with my own goddamn body part. It's bad enough when it's outside of my control and happens in my dreams. I clench my fists, forcing those traitorous thoughts aside. I want to be wrong. I want this to be a bad joke. But the sheets have been changed. The dark blue ones were on when I left, and these are a lighter blue. They smell like my detergent.

I head for the laundry room. A basket full of towels and bed sheets sits on the floor in front of the machine. My throat tightens as I pick up the towel on top. It's damp. Did she shower here? *Do not picture her naked in your shower.*

Under the towel are my navy sheets. For reasons I don't understand, I pull them out. Maybe to prove I'm wrong? That this scenario I've conjured is all in my head? The top sheet is covered in cat fur. Postie and Malone like to burrow under the comforter and nap there like a couple of weirdos.

But then my fist closes around the damp fitted sheet. I frown at the very inconvenient semi tenting the front of the towel wrapped around my waist. My hand lifts without my permission, and I do something I'll probably regret for the rest of my life. I sniff the sheet.

And my knees nearly buckle.

I catch a hint of Peggy's distinctive shampoo, a combination of honey, banana, and coconut. But more prominent is a second distinctive scent that underscores what I already know to be true: she used my bed for self-gratification.

"Don't be a dirtbag." I angrily pull the previous load out and jam the sheets into the washing machine.

I need to deal with this situation. I set the sheets to wash, start the dryer, and return to my bedroom so I can get dressed. But my erection is excessive and highly inconvenient. Not to mention inappropriate. I need to keep my head on straight when it comes to Roman's daughter. Wanting her in secret is one thing, but actually entertaining the possibility that we could be anything more than friends is ludicrous. Any man would be lucky to love her, and it can't be me.

I put on jeans, a shirt, and a hoodie, ignoring my hard-on, then flip open my laptop and pull up the video feeds from the kitty cams. One is aimed at the living room couch, where the cats often nap. The second is on my dresser, focused on my bed. It only records when motion is detected. I'm unsurprised by the footage of my boys doing zoomies. I'm also unsurprised when it picks up Peggy entering my bedroom with the giant banana-duck purse I bought her last year for Christmas slung over her shoulder. I stop the feed immediately, move them both to the trash and hover my finger over the delete forever button. I'm disgusted with myself for even hesitating. I hit delete and close my laptop.

If I can talk to Peggy before the diner, it'll make this less awkward. I hope. I can even bow out of joining Roman and Peggy. Say something came up. Let them have their time together instead of tagging along. I don't want to admit to myself that it's been purposeful. A constant reminder that she's his pride and joy and whatever feelings I have should be kept to myself.

I send a single message, careful with my phrasing. It's hers. She knows it. I know it.

HOLLIS

I think you left something at my place.

The humping dots appear, then disappear, then appear again. This happens half a dozen times before they stop altogether.

It'll be an uncomfortable conversation, especially when I tell her about the kitty cams, but I can reassure her that any evidence is gone and we're the only two who will ever know it happened. I grab a gift bag from the closet in the spare room and one of my clean bath sheets, which she's apparently a fan of, folding it so it's narrow enough to stuff into the bag. I roll the vibrator inside the towel, turning it into an inedible Maki roll, then stuff it into the gift bag, adding tissue paper to cover the towel.

I'll set some very clear boundaries and then forget this ever happened. Or at least try to. But Roman is standing by the elevator when I step into the hall. Fuck.

"Oh hey, I thought you were already at the Pancake House," I say.

"I spilled coffee on my shirt earlier, so I came up to change first." His gaze drops to the gift bag in my hand. "What's that?"

"Uh…it's, uh…for Peggy." Double fuck. *Why didn't I lie?* "A gift for taking care of Postie and Malone." I thumb over my shoulder and reach for my door. "I'll drop it off at her place later."

"Nah. Don't do that. Bring it with. She's meeting us there." The elevator doors slide open, and he covers the sensor, waiting for me to join him.

It'll raise more questions if I don't bring it along, so I reluctantly follow. "How was your meeting with Coach?" I ask as he presses the button for the lobby.

"Good. They're assessing options for backup goalies next year, preparing for the inevitable, you know?"

"How do you feel about that?" I wouldn't love it, but goalies take a lot of training.

"I've had a good run, and there are other options to explore once I'm off the ice," he replies.

I just nod.

"I know you've got some time, but sportscasting would be a nice option for a good-looking guy like yourself," Roman says.

"I'm not sure my personality would be the right fit," I grumble.

Roman is in a much different headspace than I am about retirement. He's the oldest player in the league, and he's had a solid career and no serious injuries with one year left on his contract.

I, however, busted my ass after my knee injury last year so I could be back on the ice this season. Unlike Roman, who's pushing forty, I'm only thirty-three, and I'm having a great comeback season. If I can keep my stats where they are, Toronto could extend my contract for a couple more years.

We reach the lobby and step outside into the cold winter afternoon. It's mid-January, and snow dusts the sidewalk. Our breath puffs out in foggy bursts that disappear like ghosts. We cross the street to the diner. The familiar, comforting scent of fresh bacon and buttery pancakes makes my mouth water as we enter.

My stomach lurches as I scan the tables and spot Peggy, sitting at a four top. She's furiously typing on her phone, her bottom lip trapped between her teeth. She seems stressed. And I'm positive the contents of the bag I'm holding are the reason. I can relate. I squash the images that keep popping into my head. I know better than to want her.

I wish I'd left the bag at home, but I can't undo my stupidity. Roman would probably rip my head off if he knew what was inside and where it had been used. And rightly so, as I'm more than a decade Peggy's senior and she's my best friend's daughter.

Roman takes the seat across from Peggy, and I drop into the spot beside him.

Peggy's eyes bounce between me and Roman. Her cheeks flush, and a constipated grin forms—like she's trying to be friendly, but someone just dropped a green-fog fart. "Hey. Hi. How was the trip home?"

"Good. We got ahead of the storm. Looks like it'll mostly miss us here." Roman shrugs out of his jacket.

"I'm glad you didn't get stuck. I would have worried." Her gaze darts my way for a split second. Her cheeks burst with color again, and she tugs at the neck of her hoodie. It boasts the name of her university.

"Me, too," Roman says.

Rainbow, who started working here a few weeks ago, stops to greet us. Her hair matches her name. She presses her hand to her chest. "Oh, isn't this so sweet! I love that your dads take you out," she says to Peggy.

"We're just friends," I mutter.

"Of course." She winks. "What can I get you boys to drink? Coffee? Tea?"

We order drinks and food, and Rainbow flounces off.

"How was the first week of classes?" Roman asks.

"Oh, it was good." Peggy's voice is pitchy, and she keeps wringing her hands. "I like my courses."

"Are you sure? They're not too stressful? I know how much you loved working with Hemi on the internship last semester. I'm sure it's a shift being back in the classroom full time."

Peggy hides her hands under the table. "Oh yeah, it is. But I have a few friends in my classes. Plus, I'm the lead on the gala for my Event Management project. Hemi's been great about letting me take it over. Just one more semester and I'm done."

"I can't believe my baby girl will be a university graduate in a matter of months." Roman beams with pride.

"I'll also be twenty-one in a few months, Dad." Her eyes slide to me, and she bites her fingernail, then checks her phone again. She's jumpy as shit.

I cough into my elbow.

Roman holds up his hands. "I'm proud of you, honey. You're all grown up, you've almost finished school, you're living on your own with a roommate. Big steps. How is Rix? Tristan couldn't get out of the airport fast enough."

Rainbow drops off our coffees and tells us our food will be out shortly.

Peggy's roommate and our teammate, Tristan Stiles, have been dating for several months. He lives in the condo units above the Pancake House. "Uh...she's good." She checks her phone again. "And yeah, Tristan has no chill after away games. Hopefully Rix makes it to his place before his patience wears out." She grimaces. "I just need to..." She fires off a message.

Roman's expression shifts, eyebrows pulling together. "You haven't caught them going at it in the kitchen again, have you?" He crosses his arms. "He has his own damn place. It's not fair to put you in that kind of awkward situation. Is that why you're so antsy?"

She sets her phone down, eyes darting between us. "Oh, uh...yes. That's uh... They're really into each other. Like seriously into each other. He kind of forgets himself when he hasn't seen her in a while."

Peggy just threw Tristan under the bus. *Ice cold, Princess.*

"Well, he needs to learn how to control himself in front of other people." Roman turns to me. "Why don't you give Peggy her gift? I'm sure it'll make her feel better."

Fuck. I'd hoped he would forget I brought it along.

"Dad, seriously, can you not call me that? I'm not channeling my inner eighty-five-year-old. Call me Hammer or Aurora."

I'm pretty sure Aurora is her middle name ...

"Peggy is a nice name," Roman protests.

"Not when people expect me to have blue hair or use it to come up with horrible nicknames. Like when I broke my leg in grade seven and they called me Peg Leg Peggy, or when some asshole in grade nine called me Peg-Me Peggy for an entire semester." She rolls her eyes.

Roman holds up a hand and coughs. "Point made. Give *Aurora* her gift, Hollis." He elbows my arm.

It's my turn to sweat. I set the bag on the table. "You can open it later."

She stares at it like it's a bomb, not a glittery blue gift bag stuffed with white tissue paper. "What is this for?"

"It's a thank you for taking care of my cats. And making sure my towels made it to the dryer," I say pointedly.

Her gaze lifts, and her cheeks flush a deeper pink.

I attempt to backtrack, but it comes out as a grumble, "It's not a big deal."

"Go ahead, Pegs. Open it," Roman insists.

Peggy bites her lip and doesn't correct her dad again.

I suddenly feel like I'm going to vomit. There is literally no way to explain the contents of that bag to Roman. No good one, anyway. Which leaves a lot of room for jumping to conclusions. And until twenty minutes ago, I had footage of whatever happened in my bed. Thank fuck it's been deleted. I mentally prepare for the worst, which would be Roman killing me in a public restaurant for giving his daughter a superhero vibrator.

Peggy sets the bag on the seat beside her. "You didn't need to get me anything. You already pay me enough, and I love spending time with Postie and Malone."

A bead of sweat trickles down my spine. My worries about what happens after my contract finishes seem insignificant if my best friend beats me to death with a vibrator. Or his fists.

16

Peggy pulls the towel free from the bag. It's navy and gray striped. I hope it makes up for giving her what's hidden inside in front of Roman.

Her expression is a mixture of relief, surprise, and confusion. "I love it so much." She hugs it to her chest.

For a second I think I'm in the clear until she holds it up in front of her and it unrolls.

Her eyes drop to her lap and widen. "Thank you so, so much, Hollis," she chokes out. "Honestly, it's amazing. Just the best. So thoughtful."

She's mentioned in passing how nice the towels are, and how if she doesn't fold them right away, Postie and Malone will hop into the laundry basket and nap on them.

Roman frowns. "Is that a bath towel?"

"It's a bath sheet," Peggy and I say at the same time.

"What's the difference?" Roman asks. "Why is that one so great?"

"They're bigger than towels. I use the towels for my hair and the sheets for my body," Peggy explains. Her voice grows increasingly pitchy, and she hugs the terry to her chest.

I try not to let the image of her wrapped in only that bath sheet form in my head. My self-loathing is at an all-time high when I'm unsuccessful. Until today, I've done a decent job of keeping her in the don't-ever-go-there box. Mostly.

"Did we not have those when you were growing up? Was our towel situation lacking? Do I have bath sheets or towels?" Roman starts on a bad-dad spiral.

"We had great towels, Dad," Peggy—*Aurora*—reassures him. "These are huge and soft and really nice, but there's nothing wrong with your towels now, or the ones we had growing up."

If that was true, she probably would have showered at his place, not mine.

Rainbow arrives with our meals, and Peggy rushes to jam the towel back into the bag. Her eyes go wide at the low *thunk*.

Roman is too busy spiraling over his lack of towel game, and

17

Rainbow is all sparkle and sunshine, as Peggy and I duck under the table. We both grab the superdick at the same time, our fingers overlapping each other. *We are talking about this later*, I mouth. She yanks the vibrator free and practically snarls like she's channeling her inner Gollum.

She jams the device in her banana-duck purse and pops back up, her grin halfway to maniacal. "I kicked my purse over by accident." She grabs her rolled-up napkin of silverware, which clatters noisily on the table. "This looks delicious."

Roman passes her the maple syrup, which she pours all over her banana-nut pancakes and sausage links. She stabs one with her fork and bites the end off, groaning her appreciation. "These sausages are the best."

I give her a look.

She gives me one back.

Roman wants to know what brand my towels are.

Her phone goes off every few seconds, so she's highly distracted all through our meal.

And so am I. Because that superhero vibrator is inches away from my foot, and I can't stop thinking about the handoff that just occurred. Nor can I acknowledge that this feels a lot like Pandora's box has been jimmied open, and I don't know how to close it.

CHAPTER 4
HAMMER

My embarrassment is far from over as my dad and I take the elevator to my apartment. I hug him when we reach my floor, thank him for the pancakes, and tell him I'll see him later. He asks for the seven-hundred-and-fifth time if I'm okay. I tell him I'm preoccupied because I have a project due on Monday. This is not untrue, but it's ninety-five percent finished. I don't typically lie to my dad unless it's to avoid hurting his feelings, but in this case, I can't tell him the truth. Better for him to believe it's school stress.

I'm relieved when the elevator doors slide closed, allowing me the nervous freaking breakdown I spent all our meal fighting. I don't know why Hollis thought it was a good idea to bring my vibrator to the restaurant masquerading as a gift. I would honestly be fine with that remaining an eternal mystery, but avoiding him forever will be a challenge.

I try not to think about the fact that Hollis touched my Batdick when he rolled it in that towel. But now the idea is in my head, and my mind is sinking into the gutter. I wonder if he's ever fucked someone with their vibrator. I try to blink away the sudden image of me spread out on his bed, naked, and him wearing a too-small towel, holding it.

"Ugh, this needs to stop," I mutter as I let myself into my apartment.

Rix stopped answering messages about twenty minutes ago, so she's probably with Tristan. Getting laid. I sigh. I wish I had someone who sent me gifts all the time and wanted to be naked with me. Tristan worships the ground she walks on. It's been months since my last date. With a pro-hockey-player dad, university guys don't get my life.

"Fuck." I almost trip over Tristan's giant sneakers because he's left them in the middle of the floor.

I have just enough time to anxiety pee before Hollis knocks. I know it's him because he raps three times quickly, then pauses and knocks twice more. I wipe my damp palms on my jeans, take a deep breath, and throw open the door. Hollis's winter jacket is unzipped, revealing his black Toronto Terror hoodie with the angry Canada goose emblem. His jeans do an annoyingly great job of highlighting his amazing hockey thighs.

I wish he wasn't so hot. I also wish I hadn't left my vibrator on his nightstand like an idiot, because it says more than I'd like about my feelings for him. But I can't take it back, so the only way forward is to deal with it. It doesn't mean I plan to be honest; it just means we get to have this awkward conversation. Hopefully once it's over, I can forget about it for the rest of my life. *Not likely.*

This is probably the most mortified I've ever been. And that's saying something since I've accidentally seen my dad's wiener twice in the past six months.

"Explain." Hollis steps inside and crosses his arms.

His gruff tone and one-word order do all kinds of conflicting things to my body. I'm sweaty, I'm anxious, and now I'm horny. It's made that much worse by his deliciously furrowed brow and pouty lips.

I let the door fall closed and mentally will the flush making its way up my chest to stop before it reaches my cheeks. Based on the heat level in my face, I'm unsuccessful. "I didn't mean to forget Batdick at your place." *Or to refer to it as Batdick.* But I can't take either thing back.

"I fucking hope not," Hollis grumbles.

"You won't tell my dad, will you?" I throw up a little in my mouth at the possibility.

He stares at me but says nothing.

I get on my pro-self-exploration high horse. "I am an adult, and I do have needs." I immediately want to pluck those words from his ears and stuff them back into my ridiculous mouth.

His cheek tics. "Why are you taking care of them in my goddamn bed?"

He's so hot when he's angry. I cross my arms and spew more nonsense. "You don't know that for sure."

He tips his head.

If panties were made of sugar, mine would melt off my body from his expression alone. "Maybe it fell out of my bag while I was playing with the kitties."

He pokes at his top lip with his tongue. "Onto my nightstand?"

I swallow ten liters of anxiety saliva. "Postie likes to go in there and hunt for treats."

"And one of those treats was your vibrator?" He holds up a hand when I open my mouth.

"I need to tell you something important." His nostrils flare with his exhale. "I put up kitty cams in the penthouse last week and forgot to tell you about them."

"Kitty cams?" I parrot.

He runs a hand through his hair. "They're movement activated. Ash and Shilpa have them for their dogs. I thought it would be good for away games."

Ashish Palaniappa is one of my dad and Hollis's teammates, and Shilpa, his wife, is the team lawyer and one of my friends. I blink at him. "Where are they?"

"The living room and my bedroom."

My breath leaves me on a whoosh. I grab the edge of the counter for support. "You recorded me?"

"It was supposed to record Postie and Malone," he reminds me.

I tug at the neck of my hoodie. "Did you...did you watch it?"

He recoils. "Of course not! I deleted it immediately."

A tiny part of me is disappointed. The rest of me is relieved. Or maybe it's the reverse. I can't read his expression or tell if the idea disturbs him or what. "So you actually don't know if anything happened. That's you hypothesizing." This is good. I can deny it. "Maybe I went into your bedroom to get the boys."

His voice lowers to a growl that I feel in all the rightest-wrong parts of my body. "We both know that's a lie because you forgot to wash my sheets."

I open and close my mouth twice as we stare each other down. Another wave of humiliation washes over me. Which is very conflicting considering all the other things happening in my body. I try to keep my eyes on the floor, but they're disobedient assholes and lift anyway.

"It's the first time that's ever happened," I blurt.

"Elaborate," Hollis demands.

"You...want me to tell you what exactly I did?"

His teeth grind together. "No, Peggy. I don't want details. The first time *what's* ever happened."

"The whole thing. The everything." Explaining this is a lot like tripping around landmines. I cannot show my hand. The only thing worse than having a crush on my dad's best friend would be him finding out about it. "I was reading a spicy book and snuggling with the kitties, and I'd just gotten my new silicone friend, and one thing led to another, and I'm really sorry." I mash my lips together, but it doesn't stop the word vomit. "I meant to wash the sheets. You weren't supposed to know. It won't ever happen again."

He drags his tongue across his bottom lip. They're so full. So kissable.

22

I need to stop noticing these things. It's making my vagina ping despite how awkward this is, or maybe because of it? It's probably wrong that I half wish he hadn't erased the video. Definitely wrong.

"This doesn't explain why you ended up in my shower." His low, gravelly tone makes my stupid nipples tighten.

My anxiety takes over, and I blurt out more honesty than I mean to. "I was all sweaty after the…" I wave my hand. "And I should have gone back to my place, or to my dad's, but the shower was right there, and your jet placement is perfect for—" *Why can't I lie?*

He arches one dark, sexy eyebrow. Fuck him and his hotness. *No, no.* No fucking my dad's best friend, who is more than ten years older than me. The thought is already in my head, and my stupid imagination is forming a scene I'll probably use as fodder later, when Batdick and I are alone.

"Perfect for what?" he grinds out.

"It's just nicer." Thank God I wasn't completely honest for once.

His voice is raw silk dragged over bare skin. "And this is the first time you've done this? Taken care of your…needs in my bed?"

I run my tongue along my bottom lip. My mouth is so dry. I've already told him this. Maybe he's trying to catch me in a lie. "Yes."

His nostrils flare. His fists clench and release. His eyes close, and his words are barely audible when he murmurs, "If things were different…"

My breath leaves me on a whoosh. What does that mean? *If things were different,* then what? Would he want me the way I want him? Would the idea of me getting off in his bed turn him on instead of making things awkward between us? What if things *were* different?

"Hollis." His name is barely a sound.

He shakes his head, and his lids flip open. From one second

to the next, his entire demeanor shifts. "You have your own apartment. Why not take care of your needs there? Or your old bedroom at Roman's. That would have been better than *my* bed."

"You've seen my bedroom at my dad's. I outgrew Barbie when I was nine." I don't have the heart to tell my dad that, though. "It doesn't do a good job of setting the mood."

"What's wrong with your own apartment, then?" He's back to disapproving.

"I have a roommate, and sometimes it's nice to just let go and not worry about how much noise I'm making, or whether Rix can hear me through the door. It's hard to relax when she's home, and then it takes forever and there's chafing." Why can't I quit when I'm ahead? Why do I keep spewing exceptionally blunt honesty?

Hollis holds up a hand. His head looks like it's about to explode. "Stop."

At least I'm not the only one mortified here. "Oh, God." I raise my hand in front of my mouth. "Did those videos have sound?" I really let loose in every sense of the word when I did the unthinkable in his bed.

"No. At least I don't think there's sound. And like I said, I erased them without watching." His voice is stern when he declares, "That can't happen again. Ever."

I'm about to agree—even if I don't mean it—when a long, loud feminine moan filters down the hall. Obviously, Tristan and Rix are getting to the good part.

Hollis's eyes flare as he glances toward the noise. He's about to speak when another longer, louder moan interrupts. He clamps his mouth shut and waits until it's over before he says, "Tristan's here."

"Yup."

"Why don't they go to Tristan's?"

"To be fair, I went out for pancakes, and Tristan knows we do this, so he probably thought it was safe." Based on the sounds, they're getting close to the end. Of round one. Most of the time they do go to Tristan's, but occasionally I've come home in the middle of one of their exceptional fuckfests. "The walls are thinner than they realize." And they have phone sex every night when they have away games. I haven't told her how thin the walls are because I really don't want to make her feel bad. Usually, I just go up to see the kitties or clean my dad's place until they're done.

Hollis's eyes go to the ceiling. "Well, shit." He shakes his head and licks his lips. "Use my place if you need it."

"Seriously?" This is a twist I didn't expect.

He holds up a hand and eyes me from the side. "I don't want to know about it or see evidence of it."

My lady parts clench. "Yes, sir."

His eyes narrow. "And only the spare bedroom."

"Yeah, 'cause I guess a video of me touching myself is probably pretty conflicting," I mutter.

He purses his plush lips.

I cringe. "Sorry. Let's forget I said that. Do you want the towel back?"

"No. You keep that."

"Okay. Cool. Thanks. I'm sorry we had to have this super-awkward conversation."

"Never speak of it again."

"Sounds good." I don't know what to do with my hands, so I clasp them, then drop them at my sides.

"I'm gonna go," Hollis announces.

"Okay." I follow him to the door. "We're okay, right?" I bite the inside of my cheek.

His face softens. "Yeah. Of course, Princess."

"I need to hydrate before you turn me into a sex pretzel again!" Rix rounds the corner and comes to an abrupt halt. Tristan almost knocks her over.

"Oh, hey, Hollis. Hammer." Tristan's gaze flits between us.

"Tristan." Hollis salutes him and Rix and disappears into the hall.

Rix's eyes are wide. She turns to Tristan, who is currently wearing only a pair of black boxer briefs. "You need to get dressed and go home."

He gives her a disbelieving look. "But I just got here. We have five days to make up for. I've missed you."

"Hammer and I have something we need to deal with."

He stands there, looking unimpressed.

"If you go now, that thing we did two weeks ago is on the table later."

He turns around and disappears down the hall.

"So predictable." She waits until her bedroom door closes. "What just happened? Do I need to call a girls' summit?"

"Probably." I rub my temples. "That was so freaking awkward."

"Let me get Tristan out of here. Then we can talk."

A minute later, he reappears, looking a lot like a disgruntled bear.

"I'm sorry in advance for the conversation my dad is going to have with you tomorrow at practice. I kind of used you as a scapegoat, not on purpose," I say as he jams his feet into his shoes.

"Can't be easy to balance having your dad around all the time and in every part of your personal business." How he grunts that entire sentence is a wonder. He turns to Rix and wraps his hand gently around her throat as he leans in to brush his nose against hers. "Bea, your ass is mine later. Love you." He slips out the door. He's the only person who calls her Bea.

Rix slides her phone out of her back pocket. "Sorry I missed a bunch of messages. You know Tristan and waiting."

She thumb-types vigorously, and a few seconds later my phone buzzes with a text. There's a few minutes of back and forth before she slides her phone into her back pocket. "Does this call for nachos and margaritas?"

"Yes. Heavy on the margaritas."

Twenty minutes later, Hemi Reddi-Grinst, the director of

team PR who I interned with during my fall semester; Tally Vander Zee, the coach's daughter; and Dred Reformer, who lives in the apartment across the hall from Flip, arrive. Dred has recently become a regular fixture in our group. She and Rix's brother have also started hanging out, and much to our surprise, they're completely platonic. She has some kind of superpower that makes Flip a rational person.

Anyway, these ladies are my girl squad. It often also includes Shilpa, but she's out with Ashish tonight. I have school friends, but they don't really understand me like these women do.

"Okay. What in the sweet hell happened? You look like you're on the verge." Hemi makes a circle motion around her face.

I explain the situation—how I'd planned to go back later, but the team came home early. I leave out the kitty-cam part, though.

"Why didn't you go across the hall to your dad's place? You still have a bedroom there," Hemi asks.

"Because my dad decorated it, and I don't have the heart to tell him I've outgrown bubblegum pink."

Hemi cringes.

"It is sweet that he tried," Tally says.

He put so much effort into it and I don't want to make him sad that I don't like it anymore. It's one of those instances in which I won't be truthful with him. My dad is the most important person in my life.

"But you two are okay? He won't say anything to Roman?" Hemi asks.

"What could he say? Hey, buddy, your daughter got herself off in my bed. Want to talk to her about it?" Dred asks.

"Roman would murder him," Rix says. "With his bare hands."

"Hollis won't say anything." I probably shouldn't have said anything either. I run my hands up and down my thighs. "Maybe we should talk about literally anything else."

The girls exchange a look but roll with it.

"How about the guest list for the gala?" Hemi suggests.

"Yes!" I slap my thighs. The gala is my baby this semester and a way for me to prove I have the skills to organize and manage a large-scale event. It's an ambitious undertaking, but if I pull it off, it will be an incredible addition to my resume—and get me an A in Event Management. "I actually have a great idea."

"All your ideas have been great so far," Hemi praises. "I can't tell you how grateful I am that you're taking this on. It's been a rough transition going from two extra sets of hands to zero."

Tally and I both worked with Hemi last semester, and it was my dream internship. All I want is to work in the Terror organization again. "Do you need me to take on anything else? Besides the gala?" I'm all about channeling my nervous energy into something constructive.

"The gala is a full-time project on its own, but I appreciate the offer. I'll get things under control." Hemi sips her water. "You said you had an idea?"

"Right. Yes! So, Dallas and Flip attended the Hockey Academy, right?"

"Yeah. They went to the summer program when they were in high school."

"What if we extend an invitation to their staff? It's run by a team of legends. How cool would it be to have Alex Waters and Rook Bowman come to the gala? Or even better, Kodiak Bowman. He's on track to be the MVP this year. That might be shooting for the stars, but it would be amazing to have support outside of the team for this charity event."

"I love it. Do you want me to call?" Hemi asks.

"I can handle it. If I need any follow-up, I'll let you know." I need to prove I'm capable of handling this on my own. Otherwise it just looks like nepotism. My dad worked so hard for his career, and I don't want anyone to think I didn't do the work.

"Sounds good." Hemi smiles warmly. "This is shaping up to be our best one yet."

CHAPTER 5
HAMMER

I t's a home game tonight, and we're all in our box to watch Toronto play New York. Flip Madden, Rix's brother who plays center, has just gotten a penalty, which is unsurprising since his personal nemesis, Connor Grace, plays for New York. But one second I'm pissed about Flip's penalty, and the next I'm freaking out because Scarlet Reed, the actress, is sitting three rows back from center ice. She's with another movie star. I can't even.

"I heard she was coming out this way." Hemi taps her lip thoughtfully and pulls out her phone. "I wonder how long she's staying."

"Is she filming locally?" I ask. "I wonder if she'll come to more games while she's here. Wouldn't that be so cool?"

"What do I know her from?" Tally asks.

"She's been in a couple of movies lately, but *The Way We Weren't* was my favorite show during my teens." I watched it every week like it was my religion, and I was so disappointed when they ended it a year and a half ago. But I have all the episodes downloaded, so I can binge them whenever I want.

"Oh, yes! I started watching that this summer," Tally says.

Hemi's eyes pop as she scans her screen. "Oh wow. She's here filming through the beginning of June."

"I wonder where in Toronto they're filming," I muse. If the Terror makes the playoffs, she might come to one of those games.

"High Park for sure." Hemi's face lights up. "You know what this means, don't you?"

"That I might meet her and get a picture with her and fangirl like a complete loser and be embarrassed by my fangirling?" I ask.

"Yes, and also, she'll be in town for the gala," Hemi says.

I grab her arm. "Do you think she'd attend?"

"She's a hockey fan, and it's a charity event. It wouldn't hurt to extend an invitation," Hemi says. "Plus, we have the night with a hockey player auction, and you know that'll be a huge hit."

"I don't want to get my hopes up, but that would be so cool. How hard would it be to get a contact number for her?"

"I wonder if Hollis still talks to her. They used to date when he played for LA," Shilpa muses. "Maybe you could ask him to call in a favor?"

"Uh, yeah, but I don't know much about how that ended." I'm aware they dated, but he's never so much as mentioned her, and I've never asked. It's an unwritten rule. His life is already public enough, and I know better than to pry. He doesn't even know about my star crush on her. The media portrayed it as an amicable breakup, but who knows if that's true?

"I'll see what kind of strings I can pull for a contact," Hemi says.

"Can I try first?" I ask. "It's gala related, and I want to keep that off your plate since you have enough going on." Getting Scarlet to attend would be the icing on the gala cake.

"Absolutely. I love that you're making this yours." She squeezes my arm.

I refocus on the game, my mind spinning as I ponder this new twist. Hollis rotates onto the ice, and Tristan pats him on the shoulder, taking his seat on the bench. Hollis misses an easy pass. It's clear by his expression and the tight set of his shoulders that he's frustrated. Especially when New York ends up with the puck.

"Oh, shit. That's not great." We're already down by one goal. I bet my dad is pissed for letting it through.

Hollis heads for the crease, but Kodiak Bowman is on the same trajectory. Hollis spins, giving Bowman his left side instead of his right as they collide. Sticks go flying, and Hollis gets an elbow to the face. He goes down, his helmet hitting the ice with a crack that echoes through the arena. I stand, along with the rest of the girls, as the game is stopped.

"That did not look good," Rix says.

"That was a hard hit," Hemi agrees.

I cover my mouth with my hand. "I really hope he's okay."

My dad is right there, kneeling beside Hollis with his hand on his chest as the ref skates over.

The team doctor takes the ice, and after another minute of back and forth, Hollis gets to his feet and skates to the gate with the assistance of the team doctor and a ref. He disappears down the hall. I hope he's not out of the game completely.

Bowman gets a penalty, taking away their power play. But it's five on five, which means they're working extra hard on the ice. First period turns into second, but it isn't until the beginning of the third that Hollis is back on the bench. They don't rotate him in, though.

I shake my head. "I hope they're being cautious and he didn't mess up his knee again."

Last year was hard for Hollis. I was around for a lot of dinners with him and my dad talking rehab and next steps if he couldn't get back on the ice. He's interested in coaching college hockey, but my dad thinks he'd be a great sportscaster. I sincerely hope he doesn't have to make that decision now, though. Not when he worked so hard to get back on the ice this season.

Hollis getting benched also seems to impact team morale. They can't keep the puck away from the net, and Bowman scores a goal in the last two minutes of the game, giving New York the win.

While the arena clears, we hang in the box, all of us worried about Hollis and the loss.

"I feel like walking tomorrow will be a feat for the ages." Rix tosses a piece of popcorn in the air and tries to catch it with her mouth, but it drops into her shirt.

Hemi puts her hands over Tally's ears. "Nothing like a good old anger bang, huh?"

Tally rolls her eyes. "I can still hear you."

Rix shrugs. "Either that, or I'll have to use it to console him. Regardless, after a game like this, he'll be a monster."

"You are truly the leader of the corruption committee," Hemi says with a smirk.

"I enjoy making Ash feel better after a bad game," Shilpa says with a faraway look in her eyes.

"One day I hope I'll have someone who wants to make me happy after a bad day," Tally says with a sigh.

I pat her shoulder. "You and me both." I'd give my left tit to be the one to console Hollis after a game like this.

I glance across the rink to the fans in the one-hundred section filing out of the arena. I spot Scarlet and her castmate as they make their way down their row. The number 55 is emblazoned on the back of her jersey, and HENDRIX is stamped across her shoulders.

"Hmm... Maybe Hollis and Scarlet do still talk," Hemi muses when her eyes follow mine. "It might be easier than you think to get that contact info."

"Maybe." But that's a privacy line I don't want to step over with Hollis. I also don't love the tightness in my stomach, or the emotion I identify as jealousy. She's shown up to one of his games, wearing his jersey after more than seven years. Are they friends? Is he still interested in her?

Rix's phone pings with messages. "Looks like the guys want to go to the Watering Hole, which means you can come, Tally." The Watering Hole is a pub-style restaurant relatively close to where many of the guys on the team live. The locals who go there are respectful of the team, and the owners take good care of us. It's a lot different from the clubs Tally can't come to because she's underage.

"We should head there now. Grab a table and a round of drinks." Hemi stands. "You girls in? Tally, you want to check with your dad first?"

"Yeah, let me text him."

We leave the box and make our way to the staff lot where Hemi's SUV is parked. She's usually up for being the designated driver since she watches out for players like Rix's brother, who tend to make bad decisions on nights like these.

We arrive ahead of the team and grab a table near the bar. One of the regular servers who knows us all by name takes our drink order. But I'm still anxious about Hollis's on-ice hit. I send my dad a text, asking for an update, but he doesn't always remember to check messages after a game. I could text Hollis, who usually responds quicker, but things still feel weird. I hope he's okay.

Tristan, Flip, and Dallas show up first. Flip and Dallas head for the bar, while Tristan makes a beeline for Rix. As soon as he reaches her, his fingers slide along the edge of her jaw to the hollow behind her ear, and his thumb sweeps in the opposite direction. It basically looks like he's holding her by the throat— gently—and then he leans in and brushes his nose against hers.

Every time he does it, Rix turns into a giant puddle, and Tally looks like she's about to die. Hemi smirks. I watch in fascinated awe.

"That game was bullshit," he murmurs.

"It was bullshit," Rix agrees.

His nostrils flare, and he sighs. "One drink and we leave, Bea?"

"We'll see."

As soon as he releases her, I jump in. "How is Hollis?"

Tristan turns to me. "He has a mild concussion, but otherwise, I think he's okay. He and Roman went home straight from the game, though."

"They're not coming out?" I ask. Even after a bad game, my dad usually still goes out with the team.

"Nah. Hollis has a headache, and Roman offered to be on watch tonight, so they skipped."

"Was it that bad?"

"He was quiet in the locker room, but your dad probably knows what's what," Tristan offers.

"Okay. Thanks for the update." I don't want to overreact, but Hollis is good at pushing through pain. That he went straight home makes me question whether he's hurt worse than he's letting on.

"You girls need anything?" Tristan thumbs over his shoulder. "I'm gonna see if I can prevent Flip from making choices that will kill his endorsement campaigns."

"I appreciate you, Tristan," Hemi says. "I've got more than enough to manage without Flip adding fires to put out."

"Remember you said that when you need someone to dress up like a clown." He kisses Rix on the cheek and joins Flip and Dallas.

Rix sighs. "At least he's not out trying to conquer the world with his dick tonight."

"Why is he usually such a fuckboy?" I ask.

"Your guess is as good as mine," she says. "We have great parents, and our childhood was stable. He had a girlfriend through most of high school, but after he made the pros..." She shakes her head. "I don't know what he's been trying to prove, but it sure isn't great for whoever ends up with his heart. When he finally falls ass over head in love, he'll have to deal with the fallout of years of gratuitous, meaningless sex. I get the sense that it's less about him loving it and more that he's literally drowning himself in other people. We've both started therapy, but I don't want to bring it up with him. We're all on our own journeys, you know?"

"Hmm, that's an interesting theory," Hemi muses.

Tally pokes at the ice in her drink, looking sad.

My phone finally buzzes with a message from my dad.

DADO

Sorry, just saw this now. Hollis and I are unwinding, and I'm on concussion watch. So far he seems okay, but he's got one hell of a headache.

AURORA

Is it just a concussion?

DADO

Fingers crossed, but we'll see how he's feeling tomorrow.

AURORA

What time is practice in the morning?

DADO

Not until nine.

I have an early-morning class. I want to talk to my dad before he goes to bed.

AURORA

Heading home now. Can I come up and see you before you go to bed?

DADO

Of course.

AURORA

See you soon.

DADO

Be safe, love you.

35

AURORA

I will, love you back.

"I'm grabbing an Uber. My dad's on concussion watch," I tell the girls.

"I can drive you," Hemi offers. "Tally needs to be home soon, anyway."

I leave my drink half full and hug the girls. Rix ends up staying with Tristan because Flip is in full-on self-flagellation mode and also drunk—which isn't something he does often. He clearly feels like a giant bag of shit. As much as I don't want to play the blame game, if he'd kept his shit together and not let Grace get under his skin, maybe Hollis wouldn't have a concussion. But I don't know Flip's history with Grace. And there clearly is one. Two people don't hate each other that much for no damn reason.

Hemi drops me off, and once I'm in the elevator, I message my dad to let him know I'm on my way up.

He meets me at the door, dressed in his typical bedwear: a pair of plaid flannel pants and a white T-shirt. "Hey, kiddo. Sorry I missed your message earlier." He looks tired as he opens his arms and I step into them, wrapping mine around his waist. He's never had a serious injury in his twenty-year career, and until last year, Hollis had been the same way. It's terrifying to see someone I care about get hurt, especially a second time.

"How are you? How's Hollis?" I ask.

He gives me a squeeze, then steps back and runs his hand through his hair. "I'm fine. I hate to lose, but it's part of the game. Hollis though? The aches will hit him tomorrow. I rewatched that hit when I got home. He went down hard."

"What about the concussion? How serious is that?" If it's severe, it could impact more than being able to play. Not being on the ice with his team and having to stay back when they traveled after his injury affected more than Hollis's body last year. For a while, he was depressed. I spent a lot of time at his place, tidying up, making sure he was okay, that he was eating properly, and that he didn't drown in worries and what-ifs. Especially when he was stuck in his place, and the team was away. We were together more then. Spending all that time with him fueled my crush.

Dad rubs the back of his neck. "The team doctor suggested we wake him every few hours."

Concussions aren't as rare as we'd like them to be. "How long has he been out?"

"Not long. I'll check on him around three, and then again at six," he says.

"I can take the six o'clock check. I'll be out the door by seven-thirty, anyway. That way you can sleep a bit longer and check on him before you leave for practice," I offer.

"Are you sure that's enough sleep for you?"

"I'll be up around that time anyway, and I can stay in my old room tonight to make it easier." I can't wait until tomorrow evening to see for myself that he's okay, but I can't tell my dad that, especially not after what I did. I worry he'll see right through me. He has a strict no players rule, and I can't stand the idea of him being disappointed in me.

"If you're sure you don't mind," Dad concedes.

"Not at all. I'll run down to my apartment and grab what I need."

"Okay. Thanks, kiddo."

I return to my apartment, fill an overnight bag, and head back up to my dad's place.

"It's nice to have you here for the night, even if the circumstances are less than ideal." Dad hugs me. "We'll have dinner together tomorrow?"

"That sounds great, Dado. I can make my special homemade mac and cheese." It's his favorite after a big loss.

"That'd be amazing. Hollis would appreciate it, too."

I send him off to bed and stop in the kitchen to pour myself a glass of water and put the few dishes on the counter in the dishwasher. I peek in the fridge and note he's low on a few essentials. A list sits on the counter. I'm constantly trying to get him to use an app, but he can be old school about stuff like this. We're a team of two, even with his paper lists.

Once the kitchen stuff is handled, I pad down the hall to my old bedroom and sigh as I slide between the hot pink sheets. How upset would Dad be if he knew what I did at Hollis's? How angry would he be at Hollis for giving me permission to use his place for self-gratification? I don't even want to imagine his reaction. No hockey players is the only real rule he's ever enforced. We didn't really need them otherwise. I am his girl, and he is my dad. We've always been a unit of two. I take care of him, and he takes care of me. He's so protective. All his energy has been put into hockey and me. I love him, but sometimes I wish I wasn't the only woman in his life. He has a big heart, but sometimes all that attention can feel a little overwhelming. I'm compelled to be perfect all the time, always wanting to make him happy.

I set my alarm, then settle in to get some rest. At two fifty-two, I wake to the sound of the apartment door opening and closing, and the alarm being punched in. At six, my alarm goes off. I quickly brush my teeth and hair and head across the hall to Hollis's. Postie and Malone meow their excitement as I key in the alarm code. Before I check on Hollis, I give them both a generous helping of wet food.

My palms are suddenly damp and my mouth dry as I approach his bedroom door. My stomach rolls with shame, while my lady parts zing at the memory of what I did the last time I was in here. I'm frustrated that I can even think about that at a time like this. Hollis has a concussion. He needs to be taken care of, not ogled.

I open the door. He's lying on his back, and the comforter has been pushed aside, leaving one bare leg exposed. The sheets skim his waist, his bare chest and tattoos on display. While I've seen him in a bathing suit many times, he's usually the guy who pulls on a shirt once he's out of the water.

The last time I saw him shirtless, though, was last week when he was fresh from the shower, wrapped in only a towel. A line of light filters through a gap in the curtains and cuts across his stomach, highlighting rippling abs and his defined chest, marked with vibrant ink. I long to trace the outline of those leaves with my fingertips.

"Stop checking him out and make sure he's okay, you asshole," I whisper.

I take a deep, calming breath and cross the room, quietly calling his name. It feels illicit to be in his private space with him. I've taken care of him before, but what I did in here changes everything. Especially because he knows.

I call his name again, louder this time, but all I get is a little snort-snore. I sit on the edge of the bed to shake his shoulder. "Hey, Hollis. Wake up for a minute."

He groans and rolls toward me.

That makes it easier to jostle him. "Come on, Hollis. Wakey-wakey." His skin is warm and smooth, and I shouldn't let my fingers linger, but the zing that travels up my arm makes it hard to pull away.

He grunts.

"Come on, Hollis. Open your eyes for me, pretty please." Anxiety makes my heart race. I need him to be okay.

He rolls onto his back and grabs my hand. I'm forced to lean in as he settles my palm on his chest and holds it captive.

I exhale an unsteady breath at the unintentional intimacy. I miss how easy things used to be between us, but I can't turn back time. All these feelings I've kept buried have been unearthed, and they keep growing. His heart drums steadily under my hand. What I want most is to stretch out alongside him, rest my head on his chest, and tell him how scared I am—for him, for me, for what's happening to my heart. For the awful, wonderful hope winding around that single phrase, "*if things were different*." Those four little words have tilted my world. It's about more than getting off to thoughts of him. More than once over the past week, I've caught myself daydreaming about being his freaking girlfriend. About cuddling with him on the couch. Being his person. Taking care of him, like I am now.

"Hollis," my voice cracks with emotion.

His calloused hand smooths along my forearm and up my biceps to my shoulder. He's clearly not awake. He has no idea what he's doing, that he's playing directly into the fantasy I've woven. But I'm frozen as his warm fingers skim the column of my neck and slide under my hair.

Hollis makes a noise, this one low and deep.

"If things were different..."

His hand curves around the side of my neck as his eyes open. My breath catches as he blinks against the murky darkness. The sun is still an hour from rising, so only the ambient light from the buildings across the street cuts through the darkness.

The hand at the side of my neck moves, fingers drifting along the edge of my jaw. It's embarrassing the number of times I've wished for this. Longed to be wanted by Hollis the same way I want him. Imagined him touching me like this. To feel his lips on mine.

So much changed after his on-ice accident last year. He stopped being just my dad's best friend and a hockey star I lusted after in secret. We became friends outside of my dad. I saw Hollis vulnerable, uncertain of his future. The lines started shifting. He confided in me, expressed concerns about his future on the ice, how afraid he was of the unknown. He said he wanted to steal some of my enthusiasm and excitement for what was in front of me. He became more, and we became more. At least for me.

His unfocused gaze meets mine. "I need to stop dreaming about you."

My breath hitches, and my heart stutters. I catch his hand. "You're not dreaming. I'm checking to make sure you're okay."

"Princess?" His brows pull together.

I secretly love it when he calls me Princess. "Hey, hi. Sorry to wake you."

"You shouldn't be here." His gaze moves over my face and drops to my chest, eyes darkening before they lift again.

I let go of his hand, and it falls to the bed, his fingers skimming my knee. "You suffered a concussion last night. I have an early class, so I told my dad I'd check on you. Do you remember what happened?"

"What happened?" His tongue drags across his bottom lip.

"At the game. Do you remember?" I press.

He blinks a few times. "Scarlet."

"Reed? The actress? She was at the game." My stomach clenches. My fantasy dissolves. Maybe he invited her. What if he's interested in her again? She's beautiful, accomplished, and much closer to his age. I hate that I'm jealous.

He nods once and sighs. "It threw me. I didn't expect her to be there."

Relief is an anvil and a problem. "Do you remember what happened after you saw her?"

His eyes close. "I took a hit. Fuck." His eyes pop open, and he sits up in a rush. His hand goes to his temple, and he grimaces. "My head."

I hop off the bed and step back. I wring my hands, then cross my arms to hide my nipples. "I can get you a painkiller. Let me get you a painkiller."

He throws the covers off and slings his legs over the side of the bed. "It's okay. I'll manage." He takes a deep breath and pushes to his feet. He sways for a second, his hand at his forehead.

I put a steadying palm on his shoulder. He outweighs me by a good eighty pounds. I can't stop him if he goes down. "Please, Hollis. Let me help."

His fingers grip my wrist. The electric zip slams through my veins and turns my body into a live wire. He exhales harshly, and his gaze is slow to lift from the floor. It pauses at my chest, where my traitorous nipples perk against the thin fabric. His jaw tics, and his throat bobs.

His eyes close again. "I need you to go, Princess."

"But I—" My gaze drops, and my breath leaves me. "Oh." It comes out sounding halfway to a moan.

Hollis is wearing only a pair of boxer briefs. White boxer briefs. And they do absolutely nothing to hide the morning wood he's rocking.

"Now, please." His voice is rough as he releases my wrist.

"Yes. Right. I'm going. I'm sorry." I hustle my ass out of his bedroom. My hands are shaking as I rearm the alarm and quietly let myself out. I'm equally shaky as I let myself back into my dad's place. I don't rearm the alarm there. Instead, I get all my crap from my old bedroom and pull on a hoodie to hide my nipples. I take the elevator back to my apartment.

I should not get out Batdick. I should not get myself off to the fantasy of Hollis pulling me into bed with him. Kissing me. Touching me. Filling me. But I do.

CHAPTER 6
HOLLIS

"Warming the bench for two weeks over a mild concussion? Is that necessary?" I'm pissed this is even a conversation.

"I'd rather have you out for two weeks now than during playoffs because we didn't make the right call," Coach says. "Why don't we reassess next week?"

I rap on the arm of the chair. It's hard to argue with his logic, especially since it feels like I've been hit by a truck. "A week."

Coach's expression turns empathetic. "I know this is frustrating, Hollis, but I don't want to take unnecessary risks."

"I appreciate it." And I hear all the things he doesn't say. Me being on the ice right now is a liability. I don't want to screw over my team, but this is a giant step back. I've worked too fucking hard to come back this season in top form. "Shouldn't Doc have the ultimate say about when I'm ready for the ice?"

"He will."

"Good. I have physical therapy in twenty, and I want to make the most of it, so unless there's anything else, I'm heading out."

"We're good here."

I spend two hours in physical therapy, followed by a session with the massage therapist and acupuncturist while the rest of the team practices. I'm stiff, achy, and uncomfortable. My shoulder feels off, and my neck is sore.

After that, I run into Flip while I'm waiting for Roman. He looks like a bag of shit, and I'm probably the last person he wants to see, but he heads straight for me, anyway.

"Last night was my fault," he says immediately. "I let Grace get under my skin, and I should know better. I'm sorry, man."

I hold up a hand. "Your penalty isn't the reason I'm injured." It is a contributing factor, though.

"If I hadn't been in the box, you might not have been on the ice," he argues, determined to be the martyr.

"I was distracted." Thanks to my ex showing up as a surprise. "New York exploited a weakness. Whatever the deal is with Grace, get your head around it so it doesn't impact your game play in the future."

He rubs the back of his neck. "That guy runs his mouth all the time."

I nod. "You let it get to you. Block out the noise. Head down and focus on the game."

"He just knows how to hit my Achilles' heel. How long are you off the ice?" he asks, changing the subject.

"Hopefully only a week."

"You okay?"

"Yeah, I've had worse injuries." It's supposed to be a joke, but it comes out flat. This whole thing shakes me up. I don't want to panic, but it echoes last year.

Roman and Tristan show up, and we get invited out for a bite, but I'm tired and uncomfortable, so I decline. Roman follows my lead, and we head to the parking garage.

He catches the careful way I slide into the passenger seat. "You feeling the hit?"

"Yeah. You know how it is the day after. That's when things stiffen up."

"Wanna hit the hot tub when we get home? Might help with recovery," he suggests.

"Good idea." I slide my phone out of my pocket and frown at the new messages. My ex is the last person I want to deal with.

"You get some news you don't like?" Roman's concern is genuine.

"Scarlet messaged."

"Oh yeah? She's in town filming for a while, isn't she?"

"Apparently. It was news to me." I stopped paying attention to Scarlet and her career when I was traded to Toronto.

"When was the last time you spoke to her?"

"It's been some years." Three, according to the timestamp on the last message she sent.

"What's she saying?" Roman has no idea what happened with her, just that we dated, and our relationship ended when I moved here.

I give in and check the message. Avoiding her indefinitely will be difficult if she keeps showing up at my games.

> **SCARLET**
>
> I guess you know now that I'm in town. I'd planned to message before the game, but I lost my nerve. That was a rough hit you took. I hope you're okay. 💜 Maybe when you're feeling up to it we could grab a drink and catch up.

"She wants to catch up, whatever that means." Scarlet and I have a complicated and painful history that I'm not interested in revisiting. Her sudden reappearance in my life is unnerving. Especially considering how seeing her at the game took me out of it. Also, the way I woke up this morning—to Peggy sitting on the edge of my bed—adds another layer I don't want to examine too closely.

"When was the last time you saw her?" Roman asks.

"Not since I left LA." I made a point of never being available after an away game in LA, and she had a long-term boyfriend for several years, which made not seeing her easy. But they've since parted ways.

"Would it be so bad to grab a drink with her? It's been a long time since you broke up. You're both in different places in your lives. Might be cathartic to at least have a conversation instead of avoiding her while she's in your city for the next few months. You'll end up at the same place at the same time, eventually."

I let my head fall against the seat rest, carefully. He has a point. Leaving her hanging will make it more awkward when we finally do run into each other. I look back down at my phone.

HOLLIS

> Hey! Nice to hear from you. I'll be watching the next few games from the bench, but otherwise I'm fine. How long are you in town filming?

I send it before I have time to reconsider and change the last sentence, which leaves it open for a response. But I slide the device back into my pocket, unwilling to continue the conversation right away. I don't want to give her the wrong impression.

I feel like I already did that with Peggy this morning. I was out of it, convinced I must have been dreaming. It's been happening a lot recently—Peggy infiltrating my dreams in non-PG scenarios. Especially since I found what I found in my bedroom. But it's about more than my hormones. Sometimes I catch myself thinking about being with her in ways that are impossible. Innocuous as watching a movie together with her in my arms, or sometimes something more primal. I don't know how to deal with the way things have changed between us. I don't see her the way I used to before she started interning with Hemi for the team, and it's messing with me. I wasn't alert enough to stop myself from touching her the way I do in my subconscious. At least my brain came online before I did something really stupid.

"Hey, man. You okay over there?" Roman asks.

"Yeah. 'Sup?"

"We're home."

"Oh, shit." We're parked in his spot, next to my car.

46

After the hot tub, Roman invites me over for mac and cheese with him and Peggy, but I decline. It's my turn to dodge and evade.

Watching the next game from the bench sucks. But at least we win. Once again, Scarlet is here, wearing a jersey with my name on the back. It's a Saturday night, so when the guys suggest a club, I say yes. I've been cooped up for days, and I'm feeling more like myself again. I need to blow off a little steam.

We shower, change, and drop our vehicles at home, and then Roman, Tristan, Flip, Dallas, Ashish, and I take an Uber to one of the exclusive clubs downtown. According to Tristan, the ladies—which probably means Rix, Peggy, Shilpa, and Hemi—are already there.

"That's the second game Scarlet's been at in the past week," Roman says on the way over.

"Yeah." I already know where he's going with this, and I'm not in the mood.

"Rix watched that show she was in all through high school," Flip says.

"You mean *The Way We Weren't*," I offer grudgingly. It was a relief when the series finally ended and I didn't have to see commercials for it anymore.

"That's the one."

"Really? Wasn't that like a teen drama? She's more of an action-flick kind of girl," Tristan says, rubbing his bottom lip to hide a smile. "That's what we watch together."

"Fuck you. Wipe that look off your face." Flip punches him in the arm.

"Ow! What the fuck? I didn't say anything!"

"You didn't have to. You're wearing that smirk, and I know what it means."

Tristan shrugs, smile still on his face. "It's not my fault Bea picks action movies."

"Stop talking or I'll punch you in the balls." Flip turns back to me. "She and Essie watched that show every damn week. Took over the living room and screeched their way through every freaking episode. We used to get into fights over it because she'd want to watch it while a game was on, and we only had one TV."

"Peggy was the same about that show," Roman says.

"Really?" I never saw her watch it. Although, when Peggy was a teen she was mostly awkward and quiet, or holed up in her bedroom if she wasn't out with friends.

Roman shrugs. "There was a TV in the spare bedroom. She used to hang out there a lot when she hit her teen years. Scarlet was her favorite actress."

"Huh." It shouldn't matter that Peggy loved that show or Scarlet as an actress. It also shouldn't matter that I didn't know, but for some reason, the whole thing bothers me. Since my accident last year, Peggy had started to confide in me a lot more, especially when I was stuck at home while the team traveled. But lately we've had a few uncomfortable interactions.

When we arrive at the club, we bypass the line and find the girls in the VIP section. They raise an assortment of glasses as we approach. Hemi is probably drinking sparkling water since she doesn't let loose during the regular season. Shilpa sometimes indulges in a drink or two, depending on the night. Rix and Peggy, however, seem to have decided tonight is martini night. Peggy is built like an athlete and can usually hold her own just fine, but martinis have a narrow margin for error.

"Finally! Took you guys long enough!" Rix slides out of the booth, her martini sloshing perilously. She was wearing jeans and a jersey at the game, but she's traded the jersey for a crop top.

Peggy slides out after her. She's also undergone a wardrobe change, but hers is far more drastic. She was in jeans and a jersey, which I can deal with, especially since it hides her athletic body. But now she's wearing strappy heels and a slinky black dress that rides high on her thighs and accentuates every toned curve she has. Her eyes are rimmed with black liner, making them pop, and her lips are a sinful glossy pink. It's a real fucking problem that I notice how damn good she looks. It's even more of a problem that I want to switch up my role as bodyguard on the dance floor tonight. I want to be the man who holds her tight against himself. Seeing her dressed like this makes me want to take her home and put her in my bed.

"Hi, Dado." The heels mean she doesn't have to push up on her toes to kiss his cheek.

He purses his lips. "Where did this dress come from?"

"A store." She rolls her eyes. "And if you have nothing nice to say, don't say anything at all." Her gaze shifts briefly to me, but her eyes don't lift above my chin. "Hey, Hollis." She pokes Roman in the chest. "We're going to dance, and we don't need bodyguards." Not that it would matter because no one on the team would be ballsy enough to flirt with Roman Hammerstein's daughter.

Hemi slides out of the booth. She's wearing an ice-blue dress and matching heels, always representing the team. Hemi squeezes Roman's shoulder. "I'll keep an eye on her."

"Appreciate it," Roman says.

Hemi points a manicured finger at Flip. "Please try not to make tomorrow a PR nightmare for me. I really don't have time for it."

He looks up from his phone. "I'll be on my best behavior."

"That's my concern." She flips Dallas the bird as she passes him.

"Always nice to see your beautiful smile, Willy." Dallas is the only one who shortens Wilhelmina down to this instead of Hemi, probably because it annoys her.

"Eat your own dick, Dallas." Hemi disappears into the pulsing crowd of bodies.

"Is it just me, or does she hate you more than usual this week?" Ash asks.

Dallas slides his hands into his pants pockets. "I feel like she's warming up a little. Last week she told me she dreamed I contracted a case of genital herpes so severe my dick fell off. So telling me to eat it seems like a minor upgrade."

"Wow. That's a serious hate-on, isn't it?"

Dallas nods. "Yeah, but there's a fine line between love and hate, so maybe she'll eventually get tired of hating me."

Roman is still staring toward the dance floor, wearing a concerned frown.

I clap him on the shoulder. "She'll be fine. And with Rix out there, Tristan will be on guard."

We all look around for Tristan, but he's gone, probably doing exactly what I said. Thank God. If I see someone put their hands on her, I'll lose my fucking mind.

Roman blows out a breath. "I need a drink."

We slide into the booth, and the dedicated bartender immediately appears to take our order. Dallas isn't big on hard liquor, so he orders a pint.

This is the kind of club A-listers and sports figures frequent to avoid being swarmed by hordes of adoring, and sometimes overzealous, fans. I'm halfway through my scotch on the rocks when I spot Scarlet. She's with a costar who looks familiar.

"Did you post on socials?" I ask Flip.

"Yeah, why?" His gaze follows mine. "Oh, shit."

"Oh, shit is right," I mutter as her friend points in our direction and a wide smile breaks across Scarlet's face. I guess if I have to see her, it's better that I'm with friends and in a public place.

"You still interested in her?" Flip asks as she approaches.

I shoot him a look.

"Is that a no or a yes?"

I don't have time to respond, because she's right in front of us.

"Hi! Hey! I wondered if you'd be out tonight!" she shouts over the music.

I don't want to be a rude asshole, so I slide out of the booth to greet her. "Hey. How are you?"

She's stunning. That hasn't changed. But based on the way my stomach is roiling, I'm still not cool with the way things ended between us all those years ago.

"I'm good. It's so good to see you." Her eyes move over me in an appreciative way, and her expression turns coy.

I used to find it sexy, but now I feel nothing.

"You look great." Her hands settle on my chest, and she kisses my cheek.

"You too." I awkwardly pat her back and am grateful when she stops touching me.

It doesn't last long, though. She grabs my forearm, expression earnest. "I can't tell you how glad I am to see you. I just… I've wanted to talk for such a long time."

Ripping the Band-Aid off is the best way around this. "We were bound to run into each other, eventually."

"Especially with me watching you on the ice. Will you be back in the game soon?"

"Hopefully." God, this is awkward. "Why don't I introduce you to my teammates?"

"Oh! Yes! Please." She grabs her friend's arm. "And this is Candice Claymore. We're working together on a new movie."

"I've heard all about you," Candice says. "It's so great to finally meet you." I'm not sure I want to read too much into her smirk.

"It's great to meet you, too." My voice is wooden.

A round of introductions follows, and Flip, being Flip, tries to flirt with both of them. But Scarlet can't be bothered, and Candice seems more interested in Dallas, whose focus is on the dance floor, rather than her.

Scarlet pretty much glues herself to my side, asking how I've been, what I'm up to, if I'm dating anyone. The conversation feels stilted and uncomfortable. Not for the first time tonight, I find my mind and gaze wandering.

Eventually Rix, Hemi, and Peggy return to the table with Tristan in tow, glowering like he's ready to commit murder. Shilpa and Ashish might still be out there. No one exists outside of their bubble of two when they're on the dance floor together.

Hemi grabs Peggy's arm and leans in to say something. Suddenly her eyes widen and her mouth falls open. She lifts her hand to cover it as she scans the table. Rix notices Scarlet and latches on to Peggy's other arm. There's squealing from Rix, and Hemi is all smiles.

I expect Peggy to have a similar reaction after what Roman said, but her gaze locks on Scarlet's hand, which is currently resting on my forearm. Her legs are crossed, and she's leaning into me, which means her foot brushes my shin.

The sudden wave of guilt is jarring and unexpected. Peggy is as off-limits as it gets. I can't afford to have feelings about the expression on her face. But my chest still twists uncomfortably at the flash of hurt.

Telling her it's okay to use my place for privacy when I'm out of town feels like a line I can't uncross. So was putting my hands on her when she was in my bedroom the other morning. And the fact that I can't stop thinking about her is its own problem.

"Scarlet, that's my daughter, Peggy, in the middle. She's a huge fan." Roman motions to the girls.

Scarlet's eyes flare. "Daughter?"

"I was a hormonal teenager. Well, her mom and I were both hormonal teenagers who didn't read the fine print on combining birth control pills and antibiotics. Best oopsie-daisy ever, though." Roman smiles fondly at Peggy.

Scarlet presses her hand to her chest. "Aww... I love that you're out together. That's so fun."

"Peggy probably feels a bit differently about that."

Hemi and Rix flank Peggy, each holding one arm as they

drag her forward. Her eyes are wide, and the color has drained from her face.

Scarlet slides out of the booth and grabs my hand, pulling me with her. "Introduce me!"

I wipe my damp hands on my pants. "Scarlet, this is Hemi Reddi-Grinst, our team PR liaison."

"It's so lovely to meet you!" They shake hands.

"I love all the charities you support! I'm such a fan of your team promotion," Scarlet gushes.

Hemi, forever poised, graciously accepts the compliment.

"This is Beatrix Madden, Flip's sister. She's a financial planner, but she also preps meals for a few of us on the team. She's a wizard at creating a balanced diet, and we're lucky to have her," I say.

"Oh, I love that! That's amazing!" Scarlet says.

Rix flushes and waves the compliment away. "It's something I do for fun on the side. It's so great to meet you. I'm a huge fan. Like, so huge. I'm trying to keep it together, but it's a struggle. You'd think having all these hockey stars around would desensitize a girl, but apparently not."

Scarlet laughs. "Oh, I get it! I almost fainted when I met my unicorn actor last year at the awards."

"We all have a unicorn, don't we?" Rix and Scarlet share a laugh.

I swallow past the enormous lump in my throat as I make the final introduction. "And this is Peggy, Roman's daughter." I don't know what's going on with me, but this whole situation is beyond uncomfortable.

"Hammer. I'm Hammer. Most people call me Hammer except for my dad's side of the family," she corrects.

"Oh! Like Hammer, short for Hammerstein, because you grew up surrounded by hockey players?" Scarlet asks.

"Basically, yeah." Peggy's eyes dart to where Scarlet is petting my arm. "Didn't you and Hollis used to date?"

Scarlet's eyes flare in surprise, but she recovers quickly. "We did." She slides her arm through mine and leans her cheek on my biceps. "But I was young and stupid and didn't realize what a good thing I had. He's the one who got away."

"And now you're here. In Toronto. And so is he." Peggy's voice is almost robotic.

This couldn't be more awkward.

"I am." Her smile turns soft and hopeful. "It feels a lot like fates aligned."

"Yeah. Definitely." Peggy keeps nodding, her smile tight in a way only I would notice as she adds, "Especially since you're both single and ready to mingle."

"I wouldn't mind taking this guy off the market again." Scarlet squeezes my arm.

Or maybe it can get more awkward. I'm about to say something to end this moment when I catch Hemi's eye.

Hemi looks from me, to Scarlet, to Peggy, whose smile is so stiff it could be super-glued to her lips. "I need to use the ladies' room. Hammer, come with." Hemi threads her arm through Peggy's. "If you'll excuse us for a moment. It was so nice to meet you, Scarlet. I hope we'll be seeing you at another game soon."

"Oh definitely. I plan to attend as many as I can."

"Great." Hemi does a finger-curl wave and guides Peggy toward the bathroom.

Rix cringes and turns to Scarlet. "She was really excited to meet you. And nervous. You're totally her unicorn." She rushes after the girls.

Scarlet gives me a knowing smile. "I think someone might have a bit of a crush on you."

I laugh, but I feel like I'm going to vomit. "Peggy's basically family."

She pats my chest. "To you, maybe. How old is she?"

"Twenty." Almost twenty-one. Not that her being twenty-one will change how inappropriate it is for me to have dreams about her. Especially the most recent ones.

She bites her lip. "That's how old I was when we started dating. I was so stupid to let you go."

"We were young." That horrible lump in my throat keeps growing. "And you were right, it couldn't have worked. We live on opposite ends of the country."

"Hindsight, though." Her smile turns soft and apologetic. "I regret the way I handled things."

"It's water under the bridge." It's not really. What happened with Scarlet had a ripple effect that's framed my relationships. Only once in the past seven years have I been involved with a woman for more than a handful of months. Like all the rest, that one went up in flames, too. It just hurt a little more.

She tips her head. "Is it, though?"

"It was a long time ago, Scarlet."

"Maybe we could go for coffee. I'd love a chance to apologize. I know I hurt you."

"I have away games coming up." I'm all about avoiding painful conversations, especially with my head all over the place and my career feeling unsteady.

"When you get back, then. I'm here for a few months." She squeezes my arm. "Just think about it, okay?" She kisses me on the cheek, and she and Candice excuse themselves since they have an early morning on set.

Shilpa and Ash stop at the table. "Am I seeing things, or were you just talking to Scarlet Reed and Candice Claymore?" Shilpa asks.

"You're not seeing things." I down the rest of my scotch.

"Was she invited or did she just show up?" Shilpa's a little too good at reading people.

"She showed up."

She hums but doesn't comment further.

"We meeting up for morning yoga tomorrow?" Ashish asks.

"Yeah." I grudgingly added it to my routine after my physical therapist and chiropractor both suggested it.

"Excellent. I'll come your way." He squeezes Shilpa's arm, which is laced through his. "Ready to go, my love?"

"I am." She kisses him on the cheek.

They say good night and leave arm in arm. Sometimes I'm jealous of their easy bond. They're always so wrapped in each other, like the world outside their cosmos is inconsequential. The girls return a few minutes later to tell us they're heading home. Surprisingly, Flip doesn't pick anyone up tonight. Maybe he's turning a new leaf. The four of us grab an Uber home.

"What was up with Hammer tonight? She seemed off," Tristan says.

"I thought so, too." Roman wears his concerned-dad expression. "Maybe starstruck?"

"Probably. Rix said she nearly peed her pants," Tristan offers.

"Makes sense since she's her favorite actress," Flip adds.

I stay quiet.

On the way up to the penthouse floor, Roman crosses his arms. "Scarlet seemed happy to see you."

"Yeah."

"She ask to see you again?"

I rub my bottom lip and nod.

"You should go. Things are different now, Holl. She's older, more mature, and so are you."

I sigh. "There's a reason it didn't work the first time around." And someone who shouldn't be taking up space in my head is currently living there rent free.

"Because you were both basically kids. At least have coffee with her. Clear the air. Let go of some of the baggage you've been carrying around all these years. You haven't had a serious relationship since her. That must mean something."

I rub the space between my eyes. "Yeah, that I'm not a fan of heartbreak."

"Just think about it, Hollis. You deserve happiness and to have someone in your life. Maybe she's that someone."

I don't think she is, but the person I can't stop dreaming about isn't someone I can be with either. "Maybe."

CHAPTER 7
HAMMER

I stare at the message for an unreasonably long time before I muster the nerve to compose a reply. Do I want to see Hollis? Yes, and no. I absolutely want an eyeful of his hotness. And I miss him. Not just his smile, or how sweet he is with Postie and Malone when he can be so gruff with everyone else, or the way his face softens when he calls me Princess. Most of all, I miss how easy things used to be. I miss talking about hockey and school and classes and what I'm excited about after graduation.

And while part of me wants things to go back to the way they were, another part doesn't. This new version is awkward and uncomfortable, but it feels like something else, too.

I can't tell if it's all in my head, though.

So, as much as I want a Hollis hit, I do not want to deal with all the feelings that accompany seeing him in three dimensions. And I've been avoiding him again since I met Scarlet. I was super weird about the whole thing. For the past two nights, I've declined dinner with my dad, citing group study meetings. He's been understanding, but I still feel like shit about it. I've never been good at hiding things from him, but I wouldn't even know how to be honest about my feelings right now.

I'm so up in my head that it takes forever to compose a message.

AURORA

You can leave it at my dad's.

I hit send just as there's a knock at the door.

HOLLIS

I'm here now, so...

My shoulders sag, and my stomach does several somersaults as I flip the safety latch and open the door. I hate the way my heart rate picks up at the sight of him standing in the hall, dressed in a navy suit, looking gorgeous. "Hey." I smile, but it's forced.

His gaze sweeps over me, pausing at my shirt before rising to my face, one brow arched. "Hey."

Shit. I'm braless. I took it off as soon as I walked in the door because it was an underwire nightmare. I'm currently wearing a thin T-shirt. There's a fifty-fifty chance my nipples are saluting him. I hold out a hand. "Any special instructions?"

He glances at my open palm but doesn't make a move to drop his fob into it. "Can I come in for a second?"

"Sure." I reluctantly step back. He smells so damn good. Like aftershave, his body wash, and the product he uses to tame his thick, dark, wavy hair. I can't wait to huff his sweatshirts while he's away. *I seriously need help.*

"Is Rix home?"

I shake my head. "She's at Tristan's. Probably getting railed one last time." I cringe, because what the hell? "Sorry. I didn't need to say that last part. It's sort of a given."

He nods, eyes moving around the apartment. His gaze stops on the couch. My bra is hanging over the arm. "Do you want to grab a hoodie or something?"

I cross my arms over my chest to hide my nipples, which are stupidly happy to see Hollis. "I'm fine."

I'm not even remotely fine. It's become glaringly obvious, at least to me, that I have a lot of feelings about Hollis. They are real and inconvenient and a giant pain in my ass. The worst part is how fixated I've been on that phrase he uttered about if things were different and his admission that he can't stop dreaming about me. In my head, I've turned us into a thing. A couple. Boyfriend and girlfriend. Husband and wife, even. It's embarrassing.

His jaw tics. "Is that what you wore to school today?"

I frown. "Yeah. Why?" I'm wearing a cropped T-shirt, baggy jeans, and until I walked through the door, a bra. I also layered a hoodie over the top, plus a jacket and toque and scarf because it's winter, and I hate being frozen.

His nostrils flare. "It's February. You could get frostbite."

"What are you? Eighty years old? I'm in my apartment. Half of my classes feel like a trip to the Sahara and the other half feel like the inside of a freezer, so I layer accordingly—not that it's any of your business what I wear and where I wear it, Daddy Hollis." I'm enraged that the first thing he did was pull some kind of dad-style judgment card and make me feel like a little fucking girl. Which I am not. I'm a woman, and I won't be treated otherwise.

A thrill shoots down my spine at the way his eyes darken and his lip curls.

"You're a real button-pusher these days," he grumbles.

"What does that even mean?" He's the one passing judgment on my damn outfit. Like he has a right.

"Fuck." He runs a hand through his hair. "You've been avoiding me again."

"Why do you think that?" Oh yeah, I'm diving headfirst into Denial River.

"Because you've missed dinner the last two nights."

Which means he's been at my dad's if he knows this. "I've been busy." *Avoiding you.*

"You never miss dinners with your dad before an away series," he points out.

I'm building walls as fast as I can, trying to keep my truth from spilling out. "There's a first time for everything, I guess."

He flips his keyring around his finger. "We need to talk about the kitty cams."

"What about them?" Every time I think about them, I get a little sweaty.

"Are you okay with them, or do you want me to turn them off? Because I will. I don't want you to feel uncomfortable at all."

"They're fine."

"Are you sure? I feel bad that I forgot to mention them last time."

"I know now. And you don't need my permission to keep tabs on your pets." Although I guess now he can also keep tabs on me. That sends a little buzz up my spine.

"That's not—" He sighs. "I don't know what's going on with you, and I can't fix it if you won't talk to me."

"There's nothing going on." I hug myself tightly, as though it will keep the ache from building in my chest. It doesn't work.

"Liar," he fires back.

Being around him is like staring at my favorite cake through an unbreakable glass case. I miss talking to him and hanging out like we used to. I want him more than I realized. But I can't have him. And Scarlet already has. And she wants him back. I can't admit any of those things, though. I'd never survive the humiliation. "I'm not."

"You are." He paces the length of the kitchen before stopping in front of me. "Is this about Scarlet?"

"She seems pretty interested in shooting her shot again with the whole 'he's the one who got away' comment." I didn't mean to say that aloud.

He stops pacing and turns to face me. I can't look at him,

though. Can't see his expression because I'm afraid of how transparent I am.

"There's nothing going on with me and Scarlet," he says softly.

It's exactly what I want to hear, but his reason for saying it isn't what I want. I will my eyes to stay fixed on his polished black shoes, but they lift, drinking in the sight of him. He's wearing the tie I gave him last year for his birthday. That's our thing—I always get him a tie for his birthday, and he always gets me silly socks. This tie is both ridiculous and totally him. It features banana duck, who is also wearing a tie. Stupid seeds burst with tiny buds of hope, until my eyes reach his.

He gives me a pained look and motions between us. "But there's nothing going on here, either."

I *see* the lie on his face. That's the worst part of this whole thing. We know each other so well. Maybe too well. His denial makes it feel like he reached inside my chest and ripped my heart right out of it. I'm confused, and hurt, and angry, because it's abundantly clear that there *is* something going on here. Maybe he doesn't want there to be, but I feel the weight of attraction every time we're alone together lately. I felt it when I admitted what I'd done in his bed while he was away, and again last week when I checked on him after his concussion. And I feel it now.

"What did you mean when you said 'if things were different'?"

His jaw tightens. "Don't go there, Princess."

I hate that he's paired my favorite nickname with a command. If he's going to accuse me of being a button-pusher, I'll do my best to push his damn buttons. "You're the one who said it. I'm just asking for clarification."

He runs a rough hand through his hair. "Your dad is my best friend and teammate."

Light shines on that ridiculous bud of hope. "What if he wasn't?"

"You're still in university."

"For a few more months." Arguing this makes me feel stupid and pathetic, but I want confirmation that I'm not alone here, that I'm not imagining this new tension between us.

"You're twenty years old with everything ahead of you." His voice is low, gritty, but the words sound rehearsed, like a mantra he keeps repeating.

"And yet you're still dreaming about me." The words are out before I can call them back.

His eyes flare. "How the fuck do you—"

His expression shutters, and I know I've pushed the wrong button. I open my mouth to apologize, but he cuts me off. "I'm not playing this game with you. I'm sorry if you took what I said the wrong way, but whatever idea you have—" He motions between us. "—this isn't happening. Ever. The sooner you come to terms with that, the easier it'll be for both of us."

The humiliation is swift and cutting. My chest feels like it's caving in. I need to keep it together, but tears prick my eyes, and my chin trembles. "Got it." My voice cracks.

"Please don't cry." He steps closer, and his hand appears in my peripheral vision and for the briefest moment his fingers connect with the edge of my jaw. I want to lean into the touch, but it's for all the wrong reasons, especially with what he says next. "You have to know how impossible this is."

"Don't." I knock his hand away. "Don't placate me."

He looks so torn, like this whole conversation pains him.

I can't handle it. Not my own feelings, not his unwillingness to admit his exist, not legitimate reasons why this can't and won't work. "You're right, there's nothing. This is nothing." I wave a dismissive hand toward him.

"Listen, that's not—"

"You should definitely give Scarlet another shot. It's obvious she's still interested." If he's with someone else, maybe I'll stop wanting him. "You two make sense." And they would. They're evenly matched. Her world experience is far more extensive than mine. Still, saying it out loud makes me want to vomit. "Anyway, you should go."

He stands there a few more long seconds before he sighs and drops the fob on the counter. "I care about you," he says softly.

Hearing that makes it so much worse. He's mollifying, letting me down easy. Telling me without saying the words that whatever my feelings are, his don't match. It's the rejection I always knew would be there, but never wanted to hear. "Please, just go." I tip my head back and will my tears not to fall.

Thankfully, Rix bursts through the door. "Girl, I think Tristan legit just broke my vag—oh, hi, Hollis."

"Hi, Rix."

"Tris and Roman are waiting for you and Flip in the lobby." She thumbs over her shoulder, her gaze moving between us.

"I'm on my way down now." He turns to me. "I'll see you in a few days."

"Yup." I force a smile.

Rix waits until he's gone before she whispers, "That seemed tense."

"I need ice cream. And girl time," I blurt. And promptly burst into tears.

Rix wraps her arms around me. "What the hell just happened?"

"Nothing. I'm getting my period."

"Don't be a liar-face. You had your period last week." She pulls back, and her expression is all empathy.

It just makes me cry harder.

CHAPTER 8
HAMMER

"Who needs a top up on their drink?" I bring a fresh bottle of prosecco into the living room, along with another of sparkling grape.

A chorus of *me*'s follows.

I make a circuit around the room, filling glasses with the appropriate drink. Hemi, Tally, Shilpa, Rix, and Dred are over to watch tonight's game. It's a good break from all the angst up in my head.

"It's a strong start to the game," Hemi observes.

"Roman's killing it in net tonight," Shilpa adds.

"He was worried about this game, so I'm glad he's playing smooth." His goal has always been to go out on top, and so far he's been making that happen.

"How are we for snacks? Does anyone need anything else?" I survey the table. "Should I top up the chips?"

"You should sit down and chill out for five minutes." Rix pats the couch cushion beside her.

I set the bottles in the ice bucket and take the offered seat. The camera pans to the bench where Hollis is chewing on his mouth guard. I take a hefty gulp of my prosecco, relieved when the game goes to commercial break since I can't tear my eyes away.

I mute the TV. "How's everything going with your dance competition, Tally?"

"Good. It's a complicated routine, but if we can pull it off, it'll be a great finish to my senior year."

"You will, you're so dedicated," Hemi says proudly.

"Are there any guys on your dance team that you're interested in?" Dred asks.

Tally laughs. "For the most part those guys are interested in each other. But honestly, last year two of the people on my core troop started dating, and then there was drama and it just got awkward when they broke up. We spend so much time together, so we're all close, and I can see how easy it would be to give in to that temptation, but the fallout sucks for everyone."

"I relate to that awkwardness," Rix says.

"It's probably why Roman has always been on you about never dating the players," Hemi says with a chuckle.

"Yeah, that's part of it." I take another sip of my prosecco and fight the flush working its way into my cheeks. Having a thing for one of the players would be bad enough, but this thing I have for Hollis is on a totally different level. "Mostly he wants me to end up with someone normal, so I have stability. Which I understand, but the flip side is that normal guys don't really understand my life. I just want someone who will show up for me the way you all do." And I need to stop wanting that person to be Hollis.

"It goes both ways, doesn't it," Dred muses as her knitting needles clink soothingly against each other. She's making toques for the unhomed who frequent the library where she works. She's amazing. "You show up for all of us."

"And you really showed up for me." Rix hugs my arm.

"You're a badass babe," Hemi declares.

"This," Shilpa agrees.

"To badass babes." Hemi raises her glass, and we all follow.

66

"We should have Badass Babe Brigade shirts," I muse.

"I'll have them designed," Hemi replies.

"We'll be our own team," Tally says with a grin. "Officially."

"Yeah, we will."

I'm half in the bag, thanks to all the prosecco, and struggling to get my sleep shorts on when Hollis messages.

HOLLIS

Hey, checking in.

I forgot to feed the boys. They might be able to wait until morning, but it increases the risk of Postie taking an anger dump on Hollis's bed. Pajama situation sorted and phone in hand, I step into the hall. Rix's door is closed, and her light is off. I pause, rolling my bottom lip between my teeth. Part of me wants to use his spare bedroom to be a brat.

I return to my bedroom, stuff Batdick into my purse, shove my feet into a pair of fluffy slippers, and leave the apartment with Hollis's fob. Two minutes later, I let myself into his penthouse. A single light illuminates the living room. As predicted, he forgot to shut his bedroom door. I drop my purse in the hall outside his room and peek inside. Postie and Malone are curled up together on his pillow.

I scan the room for the kitty cam. I spot it on his dresser, across from his bed. It's tucked beside a small stack of books and a framed crayon drawing from his niece.

My stomach flips, and my mouth goes dry. The camera has a perfect view of the bed and the door leading to the hall. I believe him when he said he deleted the video without watching. Hollis is honorable and a rule follower. If his physical therapist tells him to sit in the hot tub for half an hour, he times it. If the team doctor says he needs to up his lean protein, he has Rix tailor his meals to hit that target. But I wish for once he could have let go of his rule-following ways and *watched* the video, instead of deleting it.

Postie stretches, and Malone's tail twitches. I glance from them to the camera. It's late. Hollis is probably in bed, already asleep. How much harm would it do if I joined the kitties for a minute or two? Just provide the cuddles they're missing before I give them a snack. Huff Hollis's pillow. Maybe even steal one of them for a possible self-gratification session in his spare bedroom. I climb up onto the bed. Malone lifts his head, and Postie gives me a head butt.

"Hi, boys. Sorry I'm so late for a little loving and a treat." I scratch under their chins.

My phone buzzes from the hallway, where it's tucked inside my purse.

I ignore it.

"You missing your daddy?" I rest my head on the pillow and inhale deeply. I'm not disappointed. Hollis's aftershave permeates the fabric.

My phone buzzes again. And again.

Postie trots to the end of the bed and hops to the floor. Malone climbs onto my chest and headbutts my chin.

My phone goes off again. This time with a call.

"Come on, buddy, that's probably your daddy losing his mind because I'm in his bed again." I move him off my chest and roll to the edge of the mattress, popping to my feet.

My heart thunders in my chest, and I'm suddenly anxious. I don't know why I'm acting like this. Maybe because I'm hurt? Maybe because he can't do anything about it while he's a flight away?

The call ends but starts again a few seconds later. I answer it on the second ring.

"You're pushing it," Hollis growls into the phone.

Everything tightens at his gravelly tone. "I was just petting the boys." *And huffing your pillow.* "If you closed your bedroom door, I wouldn't have to cuddle with them before I entice them out of your bed with treats."

"If you shake the treats, they'll come running," he says. "Apparently, there's a microphone in the camera."

I swallow past the lump in my throat and head for the kitchen. "Right, okay." I put him on speakerphone and set the phone on the counter while the boys meow their treat excitement.

"I'll regret telling you that," he mutters.

"You're the one putting kitty cams in your house without telling me, Hollis." It's easier to push him when he's not right in front of me.

"You're the one masturbating in my bed," he fires back.

My whole body clenches. I wish I'd recorded him saying the word *masturbate*. "I thought we weren't ever talking about that again."

"Yet there you were, rolling around in it *again*, while dressed in almost *nothing*."

I look down. "I'm wearing pajamas, not almost nothing."

"Were you dressed like that in the elevator? Did anyone else see you?" he snaps. "Men can be real creeps."

I can't tell if this is a dad-style reprimand or what. "Yes, Hollis. The elevator was actually full of people at eleven at night. In fact, a whole team of horny rugby players were on it with me. A few of them were super hot, too. They asked for my number, and I figured, why not, right?"

"Do not fuck with me right now, Princess," he warns.

My vagina gets excited and takes the reins. "Or what, Hollis? What are you going to do about it when you're all the way in Nashville and I'm in your kitchen, wearing *almost nothing*?"

I'm half drunk on prosecco. That's the only explanation for the crap I'm spewing.

"You need a lesson in respecting boundaries, little girl."

I flick on the kitchen light and rummage around in the fridge for the cats' food. I'm angry, horny, and hopped up on adrenaline, so my hands are shaking. I accidentally drop the can on the floor, causing Malone to jump and lumber down the hall. Postie isn't as easily dissuaded. "Is that what you want to do? Teach me a lesson?" I can't stop goading him. All this pushing will probably bite me in the ass.

He grunts. "Stop slamming things around. You're freaking Malone out."

"Stop spying on me like a dirty daddy." I wonder where mine is.

"A dirty…" He huffs. "What are you trying to accomplish, Peggy?"

"I came over to feed the cats before bed. That's it. You're the one using your spy cams and getting on my ass about my sleepwear. What are *you* trying to accomplish, Hollis?" I'm acting like a spoiled brat, I realize—behaving like the little girl he's accused me of being. Maybe because he's trying to keep me in the Peggy box when I want to be someone else to him. I spoon food into both dishes and move Postie to his bowl when he goes for Malone's food first.

"I want you to respect my boundaries."

I whistle and call Malone's name, but he doesn't come. Probably because I scared the shit out of him with all my banging around and the loud voices.

"Malone is under my covers," Hollis says.

"Do I have permission to retrieve him?" I'm all snark with a heaping side of attitude.

"Yes, you have permission to retrieve him."

I leave my phone on the kitchen counter and return to Hollis's bedroom. It only takes a moment to coax Malone out from under the covers. I carry him like a baby back to his bowl, pulling Hollis's bedroom door closed behind me. Postie, as expected, has already eaten half of both bowls. I top up Malone's dish and distract Postie with petting so Malone can eat his food in peace.

"Peggy?" Hollis's voice comes from the counter.

."Yup." I half expected him to hang up by now, since I'm being antagonistic.

"There are a couple of hoodies in the front hall closet."

"I'm not leaving yet. And literally no one was on the elevator when I came up here."

"Just grab one, please."

I scan the room, looking for the kitty cam. I spot it across the room by the TV. I roll my eyes dramatically, but cross to the front hall closet and open the double doors. Hollis has an exceptional collection of shoes and jackets. My knees turn to Jell-O as I inhale the scent of his cologne.

I choose a zip up, pull it from the hanger, and shrug into it. It's the one he wore the other day when we went to the diner. I turn toward the camera. "Happy now?"

"Immensely." His voice is guttural.

I grab my phone from the counter before I cross the room and pick up my purse from where I left it outside his bedroom door.

"What are you doing now?"

"What you said I could." I head down the hall to the spare bedroom. "Sweet dreams, Hollis." I end the call before he can respond.

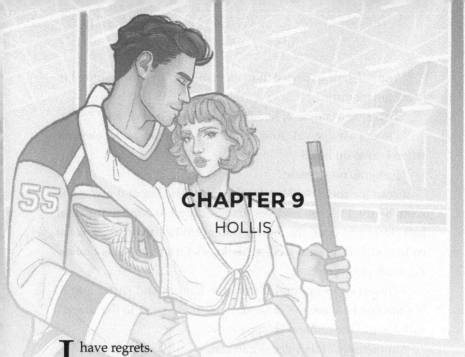

CHAPTER 9
HOLLIS

I have regrets.

I regret not turning off the fucking kitty cams.

I regret telling Peggy she could use my spare room as her personal pleasure space.

I regret calling her when I caught her in my bed again.

I regret telling her to put on one of my hoodies because her nipples were two beacons I couldn't stop staring at.

And I regret watching her disappear down the hall to the spare room as she hung up on me.

But most of all, I regret what I did after she hung up.

I vow to stay away from the kitty cams for the rest of our away series.

What I should do is turn them off. But I don't, and the motion alerts are a special brand of torture. It's a testament to my personal restraint that I don't even hover over the kitty-cam folder with my cursor.

My text conversations with Peggy are short and to the point after the most recent incident. Formal almost. Based on the extended evening visits and the pics of the boys on the couch while the game plays on the TV, Peggy spends at least an hour at my place each day.

When I return home, the spare room is spotless. But the sheets have been changed. It's what I asked of her, so I can't be upset. But fuck, it makes my head spin and my imagination dive into places it shouldn't.

She left my fob on the counter with a note that I'm running low on Postie's favorite treats in her pretty, neat cursive. She also brought up my meals for the week from Rix, so the only times I see her in the week that follows are during the Pancake House traditional meal when we return, and twice when she has dinner with me and Roman. Until my injury last year, I only came along occasionally. Now it's the only time I see her. When she and I are at the same table, she's polite and friendly, but she barely makes eye contact. I fucking hate it, even though it's for the best. Peggy needs to get it out of her head that there's more between us than friendship. And so do I. Every time we talk lately, I find myself hoping she'll push my buttons. Which is a fucking problem.

We're currently seated at Roman's dining room table in our usual spots, with Roman at the head and Peggy and me across from each other.

"What's next weekend look like for you? Do you think you'll have a lot of homework?" Roman asks.

"Just the usual stuff, taking care of Postie and Malone while you guys are away." Her gaze shifts my way for a second before returning to Roman. "It should be low-key. Why? What's up? Do you need me for something?"

"We're playing Vancouver on Saturday, and Tristan mentioned flying Rix out for the game so she can see her best friend, Izzy." He frowns. "Do I have her name wrong?"

"It's Essie. Yeah, Rix mentioned that yesterday." Peggy pokes at a carrot with her fork.

"Maybe you want to come along, too? You've been working so hard lately. It might be nice to have a weekend away—unless you already have plans, or a date, or something." Roman is totally fishing.

"Oh, uh, I don't have a date or plans."

"What about that Jameson boy? He's been messaging you a lot lately. Plus, he's a normal guy. It could be good for you," Roman presses.

That's news to me. I don't love the hot spike slicing down my spine. I hate the idea of her with anyone else, but what did I expect? Roman's rules on his daughter dating hockey players are pretty clear.

"We have group projects together. What about Postie and Malone? Who will take care of them?" Her eyes flip to me.

"My niece could probably handle it," I tell her. "She'd love a reason for a staycation at my place." I have two sisters, one older, one younger. There's quite the spread between us, and my older sister, Emilia, has a daughter close to Peggy's age, while my younger sister has a preschooler. My older niece is in her first year of her undergrad and is pre-med, so all she does is study. She's also an introvert, so her idea of a good time is watching a movie with a friend—or in this case, two cats.

"Maybe you should check first, to make sure?" Peggy pops a bite of pork tenderloin into her mouth.

"It's fine. If you want to come to Vancouver, I'll make sure the boys are covered." I refuse to acknowledge that I'd rather have her close in Vancouver than home alone.

"Let me talk to the girls and see what the plan is," Peggy says with a smile. "That would be a fun weekend."

The following weekend, we kick Vancouver's ass. It's almost unfair. I score two goals, Madden scores another two, with Stiles earning two assists, and Hammerstein freezes them out. It's one hell of a victory. Hemi brought Tally along for a girls' weekend, so we're celebrating at the hotel bar.

Everything is going great until a bunch of Essie's friends show up, a group of young twenty-somethings. Tristan acts like

Rix's personal bodyguard while Roman and I hang with Ash, Flip, and Dallas. Shilpa couldn't make the weekend work because she had a family function, and Flip is surprisingly low-key tonight.

We're talking about the game and where we think Vancouver went wrong when I notice one of Essie's friends talking to Peggy. At the game she was wearing a Toronto jersey and a pair of jeans. She's traded the jersey for a fitted shirt that does a fantastic job of highlighting her athletic curves. Her chin-length hair frames her face, and she's wearing gloss that draws attention to her perfect, pouty lips. I shouldn't be noticing all these things about her. And I definitely shouldn't be noticing how good her ass looks in those jeans.

What's worse is that this friend of Essie's is eating up her attention. He puts his hand on her back when someone squeezes by. He says something and her head falls back, eyes all lit up, her smile wide, her laughter warm. She's smiling for him. Laughing for him. He's touching her, and she's letting him. In fact, she looks like she's enjoying the attention. Which is exactly how it should be, except it's pissing me off.

Maybe because all I've gotten since that one phone call during our last away series has been syrupy smiles and excessive politeness.

We don't talk or text the way we used to. She can barely look at me these days, I make her so edgy. Logic says that's good, but I can't stand that I've hurt her. And I hate how much I miss her even though she's right across the room, hate that I have thoughts I can't control anymore. It eats at me that the way I see her has changed. She's the one woman I can't have.

I never should have opened a door I don't know how to close. And that phrase—"*if things were different*"—has been rolling around in my head ever since I stupidly said it aloud.

If she was five years older, if she wasn't still in university, if she wasn't my best friend's fucking *daughter*. If I wasn't more than a decade older than her with enough relationship baggage to fill a dump truck. But all those things are true. Unfortunately, it doesn't stop me from wanting to knock that kid's teeth out for touching her, for making her smile and laugh. Any guy would be lucky to have her attention. But I don't want it to be that kid —I want it to be me.

"Hollis, you okay, man?"

I drag my gaze back to the table.

"You all right?" Roman's eyes drop to my hand, which is currently fisting a coaster.

I drop it to my lap, letting the coaster fall to the floor. "I'm good."

Roman looks skeptical. "Maybe we should soak in the hot tub tomorrow before we fly out."

Of course he thinks it's pain related. Most of the time I do okay with the post-game aches. I spend a lot of time in the hot tub or the sauna and even more time stretching my knee. On top of all the workouts, training, and practice, I have at least two more hours a day of conditioning than anyone else on the team. But I'm back on the ice, so I'll take the extra work. "Yeah. Probably a good idea."

I look past Roman and watch as the guy tucks Peggy's hair behind her ear. I need to get out of here before I do something I regret. Like break all his fingers. "I'm calling it a night. Text me when you're up, yeah?" I knock back the rest of my drink and slide out of the booth.

"I'll stick around a bit longer," Roman says.

I pat him on the shoulder. "See you in the a.m."

Hemi and Essie flank Tally as I pass the girls, which is good. She's still seventeen, and they need to keep an eye on her. Peggy's eyes move my way as I cross the bar. She doesn't smile, doesn't look at me the way she did that day I came out of the shower in nothing but a towel. She'd been shocked, yes, but she'd been other things, too. *Things I shouldn't want or like, but do.*

Would everything still be the same if we hadn't taken an earlier flight out that morning? I wouldn't know what had happened in my bed while I was away. I wouldn't have that image burned in my brain, and I sure as hell wouldn't have offered my spare bedroom to her.

I make brief eye contact with the guy flirting with Peggy. His jaw drops, and he leans in to ask her something. She puts her hand on his arm and shakes her head.

I keep moving toward the elevators. I'm grateful when the doors slide open and no one else joins me. As soon as I get to my room, I strip out of my suit and change into joggers. I'm sweaty and agitated. Tomorrow we'll be on a plane to Winnipeg, and Peggy will be heading home. I'll have two more days before I see her again. It should be easier when we're on home turf. When Essie's friends aren't flirting with her. *At least that's all that will happen tonight*, I tell myself. Just some harmless flirting. She won't date this guy. But eventually she'll date someone. Fall in love. *But it won't be me.*

I pace the room, head spinning. I can't afford to feel this way. I can't afford to feel any kind of way. It would be good if she dated someone her age, someone who goes to her university. It would be better for her and for me. If she has a boyfriend, I can put her back in the box labeled *not for me.*

I hear someone moving around next door. Roman and I typically share a room, but this time we have connected suites, and we left the adjoining door open before the game. Maybe I should hit the hotel hot tub now. It might make it easier to sleep. Although, with Peggy sleeping on the rollaway bed in the living room, it might still be a challenge.

I move toward the door, intent on closing it, but I hear something move. It's Peggy. She's shirtless. Her back is to the door as she unclasps her bra. I freeze, unable to move, to blink, to speak as it slides down her arms and she tosses it into her suitcase before reaching for a tank and pulling it over her head.

"Why didn't you close the door?" I'm standing on the threshold, fingers curled around the frame.

She gasps, hands on the button of her jeans as she spins

around. "Shit. I didn't realize—" Her tongue drags across her lips as her gaze rakes over my chest.

I'm shirtless. Her tank says QUEEN OF DREAMS. The irony is not lost on me.

"You saw me get in the elevator." I'm all accusation and frustration.

Until this past year I've been on the fringe of her life. She's always been my best friend's daughter. Even last year after I messed up my knee, the boundaries were still there. But then I saw her in the Terror front office and recognized her as the woman she's become. That day sealed my fate. And the truth of it is messing with my head. I want things I shouldn't. Things I should erase from my brain, but I don't. I can't. Won't.

"Why didn't you close the door?" Her voice is soft as she moves toward me. "You could have closed it."

She's right. I could have. So why the hell didn't I? Why am I standing here with my heart hammering in my chest and a riot in my head? *Because I want what I can't have.*

"Does Roman know you're up here?"

"No, I snuck up while he wasn't paying attention because I want to stay with the girls tonight. I was leaving him a note."

"What about that kid you were talking to? Where's he now?" I try to keep my gaze above her neck.

"I don't know. He went to the bathroom, and I came up here." Her tongue drags across her bottom lip. "And now I'm here and you're here, and you look like you're about to blow a gasket. Why are you so upset?" Her hand rises, as if to touch me.

Which is a colossally bad idea.

I don't know what the hell I'm thinking when I grab both of her hands and step into her room. The electric hum between us is almost unbearable. Touching her when we're both half-dressed is dangerous. So is spinning her around and caging her against the wall, but I do it anyway—release her hands and crowd her space. She's all I see.

"Why do you keep pushing my buttons, Princess?" I should

give her some space. Get some perspective. Her eyes drop to my chest. If Roman walked in, this would look beyond bad. And yet I don't seem capable of making the smart, logical choice. Which would be to walk away.

I grit my teeth as her warm fingers skim my forearm. That gentle caress lights a fucking fire in my veins. I should stop her, but God help me, I don't *want* to.

"What's happening, Hollis?" Her throat bobs with a thick swallow. "I don't know what's happening anymore." Her fingertips drift along my arm, up my biceps. "This doesn't feel like nothing." As she lifts her head, our noses brush.

"What does it feel like, Princess?" This is a stupid, dangerous game to play. Wanting her is entirely selfish. Her star is rising, and mine is on the way down. She deserves better than me.

"I ache." Her fingers skim my collarbones. "You could make it go away."

I could give her that. Give in to the temptation. Take something for myself. Just one taste. One kiss.

She exhales a tremulous breath as she tips her head up. And that's when the smell of tequila hits me. She's been drinking. She's not thinking clearly. Tomorrow, when she's sober, she'll regret this. Be embarrassed. We'll have another awkward conversation.

Logic and desire battle in my head. I move a frustrated palm against the wall, and Peggy startles. "Go to bed, little girl."

I push away from the wall, my chest caving at the way her shoulders curl in. But I can't give her what she wants. It's one thing to have opened Pandora's box; it's another entirely to dive in headfirst. Especially when we've both been drinking.

I step around her and disappear into my room, locking the adjoining door behind me. That was close. Too close. I don't like how easy it is for me to lose my head around her. And I don't know how to fix it anymore.

CHAPTER 10
HAMMER

I t's been four days since Hollis caged me against the wall. Four days since I felt the warmth of his breath on my lips. God, he was glorious. Frustrated and sexy and looking a lot like he wanted to devour me.

In my fantasies, he doesn't tell me to go to bed. Instead, he takes my face in his hands and explores my mouth with his. Then he fucks me against the wall. I've had no less than ten orgasms to that particular fantasy. It's getting out of hand. But then, everything about this is.

"Aurora? You okay?" Jameson taps me lightly on the shoulder.

"Huh?" We met after class to work on one of our group assignments. The other two members left about ten minutes ago, since it's going on six thirty. I was close to finishing this section, so I decided to stay put. I'm also avoiding dinner with my dad and Hollis again.

His brows are pulled together, eyes concerned. "You're really flushed. Are you feeling okay?"

I press the back of my hand to my cheek. My skin is hot to the touch. "Oh. Uh, maybe I should head home." Here I am,

IF YOU WANT ME

sitting in the middle of the university café with my classmate, thinking about my dad's best friend. Again.

"I hope you're not coming down with something. One of my friends in res said there's this flu going around, and it's been a real nightmare." Jameson closes his laptop and slides it into his bag.

I shuffle my notes together. "Communal bathrooms and the flu sound like a special kind of hell."

"I lived in them during first year. That was enough for me." Jameson zips up his backpack while I do the same.

"I'm sure it was fun, though." I slide my water bottle into the exterior pocket of my backpack.

"You've always lived off campus, right?"

"Yeah. My dad worried about the constant party in residence."

"It could be that way, but mostly it was just fun to be around people my own age."

We shrug into our jackets, and Jameson passes me my backpack. We leave the café and head toward the subway. It's blustery today, but the cold air feels good on my overheated skin. When we reach the subway, Jameson takes his hat off and runs a hand through his hair. "Uh, a bunch of us are going clubbing downtown this weekend. I'm not sure if that's your scene or not, but you're welcome to join us, if you're feeling okay, anyway." He rubs the back of his neck.

"Sort of depends on the club, but you could send me the details?" I suggest.

"Sure." He shuffles nervously. "If it doesn't work out, we could meet for coffee or something next week."

"Yeah, sure. That'd be great. I'll see you tomorrow in class."

It isn't until I'm on the subway home that I question whether Jameson was asking me out for coffee independent of our study group. I think I totally missed that. I'm accustomed to being around elite athlete alpha males. Not uncertain university boys.

My phone buzzes as I'm waiting for my stop.

MOM

Hi honey! Checking in, how are you?

These are the moments when I wish she was the parent I told everything to, not my dad. It's like there's a block that stops me from spilling my guts to her. I'm not used to being so alone with my thoughts. I usually text my dad five times a day and vice versa, but we haven't done that as much the last few months.

AURORA

I'm good! Coming home from class. Probably going to make dinner tonight for dad.

MOM

He loves your Mac and Cheese. So do I! We're booking tickets for your birthday. Is there anything you want?

AURORA

I'm just excited to see you and North. Do you think he'll bring me that tea that he made last time?

MOM

I'm sure he will. I'll ask him for you. He says hi, by the way!

AURORA

Do you have plans this weekend?

MOM

We have a week-long camping retreat with some healers that I'm so excited about. I'll be out of cell range, so I wanted to text you and tell you how much I love you and miss you before we go.

AURORA

I love you and miss you too! Have fun! Just not too much hahaha I can't wait to see you in a couple months.

82

Loving my mom is easy. She's free and wild. It's one of my favorite things about her, but it also means we'll never have a normal mother-daughter relationship. My dad is my person.

I pull up his calendar on the ride home, checking his schedule. Tonight, he has a massage, which means Hollis also has a massage. It's part of their routine. They have someone come to the penthouse. Hollis always has his first and then my dad, followed by time in the hot tub. Maybe it's time to step out of avoidance mode.

Rix is washing dishes from her meal prep side hustle when I get home. A brand-new bouquet of peonies sits on the island. Tristan strikes again. She glances at the clock. "You're coming in late."

"I was working on a group project." I didn't tell her what happened with Hollis in Vancouver, but my coming in late all week says what I won't.

She tips her head. "I'm heading to Tristan's soon to cook dinner together, unless you need a little girl time?"

"You enjoy getting railed into next week. I was thinking about going to the pool for a swim." It's what I do when I need to think.

She rinses a mixing bowl and sets it in the drying rack. "Everything okay?"

"Yeah, just need to burn off some energy. All the sitting around is a lot." I miss the hustle that came with working in the office alongside Hemi and Tally. We were such a great trio, and we were always on the move. I go down the hall to my bedroom to change.

Rix gives me an appraising look when I reappear a few minutes later in my bikini, coverup slung over my arm. "That's quite the bathing suit choice for laps."

"Is it too much?" I'm feeling antsy and anxious, like my skin is too tight.

"If you're swimming with your dad, yes. If not, no."

"Cool." I slide my arms through my coverup. "Message me if Tristan's patience wears out and he comes here."

"Oh, that won't happen. I've already told him under no circumstances is he to come over here, or else."

"How'd he take that threat?"

"About as well as can be expected." She grins deviously. "Enjoy your swim."

"Thanks." I shoulder my bag, leave the apartment, and take the elevator down to the pool. It's empty when I arrive. Laps in a bikini aren't the most practical, but clearly, I had a plan when I made this poor wardrobe decision.

I'm not disappointed. Half an hour into my swim, Hollis walks in. When I reach the end, I flip over and start a backstroke. He walks the edge of the pool in time to my measured strokes. Just like in the hotel room, he's shirtless, all those defined muscles and his half-sleeve on display. He's standing in front of me when I reach the end.

I pull my goggles up, resting them on my smiling banana swim cap, and grip the edge. His toes are close to my fingers. I tilt my head back and let my gaze climb his thick, muscled legs. Heat blossoms in my belly, traveling up my spine and into my cheeks as I remember the way he caged me against the wall in the hotel room. How his nose brushed mine. His lust-soaked gaze. The intense ache in my chest and between my thighs.

It's a common theme these days, and it's only exacerbated when Hollis is physically around. He'd been glaring at me all evening while Essie's friend—Brandon? Brayden? I can't even remember his name—flirted with me. That guy was nice enough, but his wasn't the attention I'd wanted.

"How was the massage?" I ask.

"I'll probably be sore tomorrow, but it was what I needed." Hollis's gaze moves over my face, then dips lower, beneath the water. "How long have you been down here?"

I lift one shoulder. "Half an hour maybe."

"Not the most practical swimwear for laps," he observes.

"I like the challenge of trying to keep it from falling off," I reply.

His brow arches. "You're a fucking problem, Princess."

"I know." I extend a hand. The ladder is only a few feet away, but I don't even have to ask for help. His chivalry kicks in, and his fingers close around mine.

The electric zing makes my breath catch and goose bumps rise along my arm. The same reaction echoes across his skin. I brace a foot on the edge of the pool and a hand on his shoulder as he pulls me out of the water in one smooth motion. As soon as I'm steady on my feet, he releases me.

Neither of us moves. We just stand there, eyes locked, all the words I want to say stuck in my throat.

"Come on." He inclines his head toward the hot tub.

I cross my arms, as if it will protect me from whatever is coming. I bite the inside of my cheek, feeling young and stupid and like I'm wearing my heart on my sleeve.

Hollis and I have, by design, only been alone for a few minutes at a time since all this began weeks ago, and unless someone comes down to use the pool, we'll have a full forty-five minutes of me, him, and the giant elephant in the form of my out-of-control crush. He must read my uncertainty on my face.

"That's why you're down here swimming laps in a bikini instead of your one-piece, isn't it?" Of course he knows what bathing suit I usually wear for laps. We've been down here plenty of times together in the past. But the weight of the last few weeks makes the air heavy and the energy between us charged.

I remove my swim cap, running my fingers through my hair so I don't wring my hands.

He sighs softly, but his expression remains stoically neutral. "Come talk with me."

He turns and walks toward the hot tub. My gaze moves in a hungry sweep over his broad back. For a moment, I imagine what it would feel like to dig my nails into his rock-solid hockey

butt while he sank into me. Would he be a gentle lover? Possessive? Dominating? All the above?

I follow him, stepping into the bubbling water. It's deliciously warm. He stretches his arms across the edge, and I sit to
his left, a few inches from his fingertips.

"How's school?" he asks.

"Fine."

"Just fine?"

"I know what I want to do, and I'm ready to start my career,"
I say.

"Don't wish the semester away," he says gently.

"I'm not. I'm just done with university life." I could apply for
a master's program, but I want to be where I fit in the best, and
that's working for the league.

"University was some of the best years of my life," Hollis
says.

"Yeah, because you played for the university team and every
girl wanted to sleep with you. I'm the daughter of a professional
hockey player. It's a lot different for me," I remind him.

We've talked about this plenty of times, especially during my
first year, when I learned the hard way that my popularity was
tied to my dad's fame. I dated a guy who had friends on the
school hockey team for a couple of months. I figured it was fine
because he wasn't a player, until he started pushing to meet my
dad, and then I realized it wasn't me he wanted to date. It was
my last name.

"Has that been tough for you lately?" he asks.

"Dad's twentieth anniversary with the league is this year, so
he's gotten a lot of media attention. Most of the time my classmates are cool, but there's always some awkwardness when
someone gets all fanboy. Working with Hemi was great, because
she gave me free rein on community-outreach projects. But going
back to regular classes..." I drag my fingers along the surface of
the water and sigh. It's a reminder of how different my life is. "I
used to want to fit in with my classmates so badly."

"Not anymore?" he asks.

"It's not realistic. I don't know what it's like to grow up in a normal house with a mom and a dad who have regular jobs. My mom lives her nomad life and works as a healer. My dad has always been a professional hockey player. I've always lived this life, but most of my classmates can't and don't get it. I can't be my most authentic self around my peers, but when I'm with the girls, or you, or anyone else on the team, I can just be me."

"It's good to have people in your life outside of this world, though. It gives you perspective and helps keep you grounded."

"I know. And I have a few friends in my classes who are cool about everything, but we have a lot of group projects this year, and when everyone talks about their weekend plans, it's what club they're going to, or a party at someone's house, and I'm over here flying on a whim out to Vancouver with my friends for a game. It's not relatable."

At the beginning of the semester, I made the mistake of talking about the club we'd gone to for the new year. It's an exclusive place, and the tickets were expensive. That's all it took to change the way people see me.

"What about that guy your dad mentioned? James or something? He's interested in you, isn't he?" Hollis's eyes are on his fingers, which tap agitatedly against the edge of the hot tub.

I don't want to talk about Jameson. Not with Hollis. "All university guys want to do is hit the club, go to parties, or Netflix and chill. And when I say Netflix and chill, I don't actually mean watching a show and chilling."

Hollis narrows his eyes. "I know."

"So you can see why I'm not jumping at the chance to date university guys."

"It'd be better than my spare bedroom, don't you think?" Hollis clamps his mouth shut, like he didn't mean to say that. It almost makes me laugh.

I've done exactly as he's asked. I change the sheets, and I

wash and put away the used set before he comes home from away games. I leave no evidence behind.

"At least I know what I like and I can always get where I need to go."

Twenty-year-old boy-men have such fragile egos. They're not used to being directed, or guided, or a woman who asks for exactly what she needs. They watch too much porn and don't read enough romance.

He shifts, like he's uncomfortable. He brought it up though.

I change the subject and let him off the hook. "You've been playing clean, but I know you're working hard off the ice to make it that way."

His shoulders relax a little. "I know the importance of keeping my knee in good condition after that surgery. I've still got a year left on my contract, and I'm hoping for an extension."

This is the kind of conversation I'm used to. We've always talked about personal goals and career expectations. "You put in the work last summer."

"Thanks to you always dragging me down here to do laps."

I hated seeing him so down after his knee surgery, so I made it my mission to help as much as possible. "All my annoying you was effective. You're having an amazing season."

"You never annoyed me. You were the kick in the ass I need-ed." He smiles wryly, probably remembering how I'd steal his TV remote and refuse to give it back unless he got off his ass and joined me in the pool. Everything was different then. My secret crush was still a secret, and I wasn't hiding things from my dad.

"Well, you've had an incredible comeback. You keep playing like you are, and they'll definitely extend."

He nods. "That's the goal. I just need to make sure I don't re-injure."

"You follow all the rules, do all the work and then some. And even when you're ready to hang up your skates, you're more than a pretty face who's amazing on the ice, Hollis. Whatever direction you decide to go, you'll always have options."

He smiles a real, genuine smile, and it makes him so beautiful my heart can hardly handle it. "Always looking on the bright side."

"Can't go through life hiding from the rain clouds." I prop my cheek on my knuckles. "But I also understand the worry about what life could look like with a second serious injury."

He nods. "I'm not twenty anymore. Things don't heal the way they once did," he replies.

"You're only thirty-three, though."

"Says the twenty-year-old university student," he notes pointedly.

I sigh. I knew eventually we'd circle back to this. "I've watched rookies turn into star players. I've seen careers rise and fall. I get that I can't understand exactly, but I can empathize in a way a lot of other people can't." I feel like I'm trying to pitch myself to him, which is stupid, but still I add, "I'm not a little girl anymore, Hollis."

His eyes move over my face. "I'm well aware."

I don't want to be told, yet again, why I can't have what I want. I start to stand, but Hollis's fingers close around my wrist.

"Tell me something real and true." His voice is deep, gritty. Like this is a struggle for him, too. Like he hurts the same way I do. We used to play this game last year, but it feels different now.

I sink back into the water and shift so I'm facing him. "I miss how easy it used to be between us. But everything has changed, and there's no way to shift it back." And even if I could, I don't know that I'd want to. "I've missed this part of us."

His expression softens, and everything I feel reflects back at me. Before he can respond, I continue. "I'm changing. I have changed, and sometimes I don't know how to fit into my own skin anymore." I swallow my fears and say the things I want to, because holding on to them is starting to be painful. "My dad's family calls me Peggy, and the team and my hockey crew call me Hammer, which I get. It's a reminder that I'm Hammerstein's daughter, but neither of them feels like me. They're parts of me,

89

but they don't feel authentic. I've always felt like Aurora. And maybe it's silly, because it's just a name. But Peggy was my great-grandma, who we all loved, but I don't want to be an homage to someone else's memory. I don't want to be defined as the great-granddaughter carrying on a name, or as Hammerstein's daughter. I just want to be me, and I want that to be enough."

And when I'm with Hollis, that's how I want to feel. Seen. Like the me I want to be matters.

His eyes are knowing as he absorbs my words. "Do you want me to call you Aurora?"

"Or Princess. You're the only one who calls me that." Secretly it makes me feel special, but I worry if I say so, he'll stop. Especially now, with how uncertain everything feels. "It's your turn to tell me something real and true."

He rubs his bottom lip, eyes fixed across the room at the cityscape beyond the windows. "It's hard for me to separate you now from the teenager you used to be. I know you're not the same, that you're not that girl anymore—not at all. But I feel like that's supposed to be how I see you, and it's fucking with my head."

"I'm an adult. I have been for a while," I say softly.

"I know. I've been trying not to notice for a while." This time, his gaze lingers on my lips.

"I haven't made it easy for you lately." I bite the end of my fingernail.

"No, you really haven't," he agrees.

"I'm sorry about that."

"No you're not."

I shake my head. "You're right. I'm not. And I *am* sorry about that."

He tucks my hair behind my ear. I lean into the touch and turn my head, lips brushing his wrist. Not on purpose, but on purpose all the same.

"Princess." The word is guttural. Pained.

"Please, Hollis." I rest my cheek in his warm palm, and he doesn't pull away. An ache is heavy in my chest and pulsing between my thighs.

His eyes close, and for a moment, I fear he'll turn me away. Again. But when they open, there's such longing. And conflict. So much conflict. But he moves closer and leans in. "I shouldn't," he murmurs.

His calloused fingers are gentle against my cheek. His eyes move over my face, and my heart ricochets around in my chest. I don't dare move or breathe or say a word.

This is really happening. Hollis is going to kiss me. Finally.

His lips brush over mine, and I'm melting and on fire at the same time. That insidious ache flares between my thighs. Heat rushes through my veins as he pulls my bottom lip between his. He angles my head and parts my lips with a soft stroke of tongue. And I moan. God, I moan. At the velvet warmth of his lips, and the sure way he kisses me. My leg bumps his under the water, and his other hand cups my face as he pulls me closer.

No fantasy can compare to this. To him. Seductive strokes of tongue, his warm, soft lips moving against mine. It's so tender and sweet. So perfectly right. It's the kiss to end all kisses. I'll never be the same after this. His deep, needy groan sends a delicious shiver down my spine. I skim his ribs under the water with tentative fingers, afraid to break the spell but desperate to touch more of him. He angles my head further, tongue sweeping my mouth in rhythmic waves that make my toes curl. I've never been kissed like this. The rush of desire is dizzying.

I curve my hand around the back of his neck, needing him closer. I want to climb into his lap and wrap myself around him. I want his hands on my body, our bare skin touching. I want his fingers between my thighs, relieving the awful, glorious ache that expands with every passing second. I want more. Of him. Of this. I suck his tongue and whimper when he does it back. The sound he makes—part groan, part animalistic growl—makes my body hum with need.

I skim the back of his hand and trail the length of his arm. "Please, please." I don't know what I'm asking for, but I need something. I can't get enough of the pull of his lips, the gentle way he holds my face and yet commands my mouth with his.

I slide closer, leg pressing against his. I feel electrified, desperate for touch. For him to relieve this maddening, overwhelming throb that amplifies with every masterful stroke of tongue and nip of teeth. I'm seconds away from climbing into his lap.

And then suddenly his lips aren't on mine anymore.

My eyes open, and his expression makes my stomach drop. Lust and longing are still very much present, but the guilt is an anvil to my hummingbird heart.

"Fuck." His gaze moves to the side. "That was not—"

"It's okay, Hollis. We're not doing anything wrong." It doesn't matter if I'm right, that we're both adults who can make adult decisions. We're reading from the same book, but we're on different pages. He still sees me as his best friend's daughter, and I see him as the man whose bed and heart I want to be invited into.

"That was a mistake, Aurora." He pulls himself out of the water. "We can't happen. Not ever."

I desperately want to find a way to fix this, but as I take in his wet, tense form, and the very impressive erection tenting the front of his swim trunks, I already know I can't.

Worse though, is that any questions I had about my feelings for Hollis have been put to rest. I can't pinpoint how long I've felt this way, but the horrible, paralyzing pain in my chest confirms it. I'm in love with him.

I sit in the hot tub for several minutes after he's gone, trying to process what happened. It started as the best kiss of my life and ended as the worst. Not because of the kiss, but because of the way Hollis looked like he'd already stepped in a steaming pile of regrets within seconds of it ending.

CHAPTER 11
HAMMER

I pry my eyes open at the sound of my alarm. They feel like they have sand in them from all the crying. I woke more than once last night in tears. I cringe when I get a load of my reflection in the mirror. My eyes are ridiculously puffy. In my dreams, Hollis got back together with Scarlet, and he kept kissing her in front of me.

That had better not be a premonition.

Rix has already left for work, so I drag my ass into the shower. It doesn't help with the puffiness. While I'm lying on the couch with tea bags on my eyes—the online recommendation to alleviate my issue—my dad lets himself into my apartment. It's a bad habit of his.

"Hey, kiddo, what are you doing?"

Shit. I can't tell him I spent last night crying over his best friend. I scramble for a plausible lie. I remove one tea bag and blink him into focus.

Dad frowns. "Are you okay? Did something happen? You've been crying."

"I'm fine," I croak. I'm a terrible liar. "I went on a *The Way We Weren't* rewatch kick, and you know how emotional that show makes me."

"Oh, yeah. You scared me for a second there. I thought I was going to have to kick someone's ass."

Just your best friend's because he called kissing me a mistake. "No. No asses need to be kicked, Dad."

"Okay. That's good. I was thinking we could order Thai for dinner tonight from your favorite place. Does that sound good?"

"Yeah. Sure. That'd be great."

"Perfect. I'll get all your favorites. Six thirty work for you?"

"Yeah, six thirty is fine."

"Great. See you then, sweetheart." He bends to kiss me on the forehead. "Have a good day."

"You too, Dad."

After he leaves, I check my phone. I have messages from my school friends and another from Rix asking how my swim went.

> AURORA
>
> Things happened.

> RIX
>
> What kind of things?????

> AURORA
>
> Un-take-back-able things.

> RIX
>
> Please to be expanding on that.

> AURORA
>
> Lip things.

> RIX
>
> ● ● ● ● ● ●

My phone rings. "I'm about to get on the subway, but tell me what happened and whether I need to pick up fresh limes and the makings for nachos for tonight," Rix says.

"Maybe yes on the limes, but for later tonight, I'm supposed to have dinner with my dad." I rub my temple, wishing I'd said tomorrow. What if he invited Hollis? "That guy I like kissed me and then told me it was a mistake. It was the best kiss, Rix. The best kiss of my entire life, and then it was the worst."

"Oh, muffin. I'm sorry he can't deal with his feelings."

"He admitted that he feels like he should still see me as the teenager he knew when he first came to Toronto, but he doesn't, and it's messing with his head."

Rix sighs. "I can see why it would. He's watched you grow up, and now you're this gorgeous, driven woman he's attracted to. He obviously cares about you, but he's in the guilt-spiral phase."

"What if he never gets out of the guilt spiral?"

"Then he doesn't deserve your heart."

The bigger problem is, he already has it, so how the hell do I take it back?

CHAPTER 12
HOLLIS

I sleep like garbage. It serves me right for being a selfish asshole.

I kissed my best friend's daughter.

I knew better than to put myself in the path of temptation. Especially with how strained things have been between us. Instead of fixing the problem, I made it infinitely worse.

Giving in was the worst mistake. Because now I know what her lips feel like. The memory is etched into my brain for the rest of my fucking life. She was so soft, pliant, and the sound she made… The way her fingers felt on my skin. Like they belonged. Like I'd never get enough. Like she should be mine to keep. Utterly perfect.

I clench my fists. My cock strains. My balls ache. I refused to take care of my situation last night, but I'm reaching critical mass. If I don't do something soon, I'll end up having a wet dream like a teenager.

I cross to my bathroom, but Aurora is stamped all over this space. Maybe I'll have better control over where my thoughts go in my spare bathroom. Decision made, I stalk down the hall.

But I pause when I reach the threshold. I swear it smells like Aurora. Peggy ceased to exist after that kiss. Nothing I do will make me see her the way I used to. I swallow past the guilt and step inside. I'm halfway across the room when I spot something on the floor. I bend to pick it up and groan when I realize what it is. A hair tie.

"It's called a scrunchie, Hollis."

I rub it between my fingers. It's made of soft fabric with a banana print. She only pulls her hair back when she's cooking, or sometimes when she's working on a project and doesn't want her hair in her face.

As I clutch the scrunchie, a horrible idea forms. It's sick. Fucked up. But I cross over to the bed and yank back the comforter anyway. The sheets are fresh. The spare set is in the linen closet. It's the only evidence that she uses this room.

I grab one of the decorative pillows and bring it to my nose, groaning at the faint hint of her perfume. It was a gift from her ex-boyfriend, and she considered throwing it out after they broke up, but decided against it because it's expensive and also her favorite. And he only bought it for her because Roman mentioned it to him.

I hate that I want to bludgeon her ex with my hockey stick for having had her in a way that I can't.

Instead of jumping in the shower and trying to drown out images of Aurora naked in my spare room, I stretch out on the bed. Pushing my boxers down, I slip the scrunchie over the head of my cock, eyes falling closed as the soft fabric slides down my shaft.

"Dirtbag asshole." Even as the guilt rolls through me, I don't fight the memory of kissing her. God, her lips were perfect. She let me lead...at first. Tentative strokes of tongue as we learned each other's mouths. And then she bit my lip and sucked my tongue and showed me that saucy side I love so fucking much. I wanted to wrap her legs around my waist and carry her back to my penthouse so I could make that ache she complained about disappear.

I regret leaving her there, looking so lost. But if I hadn't, I would have done something infinitely stupider. Something impossible to come back from. Maybe I already have.

Out of control, I let the fantasy play behind my eyelids, reinventing the kiss, turning it into more. Instead of pushing her away, I pull Aurora closer as our tongues slide against each other. She straddles my thighs, fingers running through my hair and over my shoulders as I grip her hips and pull her tight against me—skimming all that warm, smooth skin as I rock her against my cock. She consumes me as I thrust into her. Her soft moans in panted warm breaths against my lips.

The orgasm slams through me, and I come all over my hand and Aurora's scrunchie. Guess I'm not giving it back anytime soon.

I'm still trying to catch my breath when Roman's voice comes from inside my apartment. "Hey, Hollis? You ready to go, man? I texted. We need to get a move on!"

"Shit." I roll off the bed, hand still covered in jizz. "Yeah! Give me two!" I rush to the bathroom and slam the door, flipping the lock.

Turning on the shower, I step out of my cum-covered boxers, toss the scrunchie on the vanity, and step under the still-cold spray. I don't bother with soap as I rinse off guilt and bodily fluids. My stomach twists and rolls as I reach for the towel hanging from the bar. It smells like Aurora. And now every shower has a memory of her naked attached to it. And every bed.

I'm so fucked. So, so fucked.

I wrap the towel around my waist, try to breathe around the nausea, and walk down the hall.

Roman stands in my kitchen, his frown deepening as he takes me in. "Everything okay, man?"

"Yeah. I, uh… Give me a minute." I dress in a rush and return to the kitchen, grabbing the container of almond-flour muffins. "I might need to stop for coffee on the way."

"You off this morning, too?" he asks.

"How do you mean?" I shove my feet into my trainers, shrug into my winter jacket, and tuck my wallet, fob, and phone into my pocket as I follow him into the hall.

"Peggy was lying on the couch with tea bags on her eyes this morning. Said she watched too much *The Way We Weren't*, and it always makes her cry." He rubs his chin. "I don't know. Something's off with her lately. Was she at the pool last night? She mentioned she might go for a swim."

I already feel bad about the kiss, and for masturbating with Aurora's scrunchie to images of her straddling me, but this news is crushing in ways I don't know how to deal with. I feel like I can't fucking breathe. This is what happens when I'm a selfish dick.

Over the years, I've seen Aurora cry a handful of times—once when she took a rogue puck to the chest as a teenager during a pickup game, which scared the shit out of me and Roman. Hell, last year, the little shit she was dating broke it off right before Valentine's Day, so I consoled her, and we ended up hanging out and watching Batman movies. The team was away, and I was stuck at home nursing my injury. I had all the makings for brownie sundaes delivered, and she nearly made herself sick on top of being sad. But *being* the cause of her tears—that's a gut punch.

"Uh, she was on her way out when I was on my way in." Lying to Roman's face is a new low on top of my epic betrayal.

"She looked okay when you saw her? She didn't seem upset?" he asks.

"Maybe a little on edge." *Because I kissed her and told her it was a mistake.*

If ever I wished for a do-over, it's that fucking kiss. I know Aurora. I know exactly how she'll react to my reaction. She'll pick herself apart over it.

Tristan, Flip, Dallas, and Ash meet us at the gym for a morning workout.

"Everything okay with Hammer?" Tristan asks Roman once

we've set up our routine and everyone is at their designated station.

Roman frowns. "Why are you asking?"

Tristan continues his biceps curl-overhead press combo as he speaks. "Bea is supposed to stay over tonight. We were planning to make a new recipe she was working on together and I was really looking forward to spending time with her, but she said she might have to cancel because Hammer is going through some things. She wouldn't elaborate, though."

Roman's concerned gaze flicks to me. "I thought you said she seemed fine when you saw her at the pool last night. I wonder what she's been going through."

I shrug, my gut churning. "Like you said, she's been off lately. Maybe it's school related."

I glance at Tristan out of the corner of my eye. He's frowning in my direction. What if Rix knows about the kiss? Would Aurora tell her? Would Rix tell Tristan? One mistake could blow up nearly a decade of friendship.

The fact that I'm worried about myself in this makes me even more of an asshole. Because not only am I lying to my best friend, Aurora's lying to her dad, too. They have a great relationship. Sure, he can be overbearing and overprotective, but they're close. And now I'm coming between them. She deserves so much better than this. Than me.

"Hemi really misses having her and Tally around," Ash says.

"She hasn't even taken the extra desks out of her office." Dallas grunts through a squat.

"Shilps sometimes does her paperwork at Hammer's old desk to keep Hemi company," Ash adds.

"I didn't realize that." I add ten pounds for the next set of lunges.

"Hemi went from having two assistants to no assistants. And Hammer was incredible, especially with the way she took Tally under her wing and helped manage the endorsement campaigns," Flip says. "Hammer is a scheduling wizard. I bet

Hemi's feeling the pressure without her, and those girls are together all the time outside of work, so I'm sure they're missing each other."

"Shilpa says the office feels empty without them," Ash agrees.

Roman adds plates to a barbell. "Maybe that's what's going on with Peggy. She's been distant lately. She's missing dinners more often." He turns to me. "You've noticed it too, right?"

I keep my eyes on my weights. "I chalked it up to coursework." The problem with a web of lies is that eventually, I'm bound to get trapped in it. And then what will happen?

"It's too bad her internship wasn't this semester. Especially with the gala coming up in April," Dallas says.

"Hemi wrangle you into the auction again this year?" Flip asks.

"Last year she didn't even ask," Dallas gripes. "But she put Hammer up to it this year, and I wasn't going to say no."

"I'm glad I get a pass this year," Tristan mutters. "And hopefully for the rest of my life."

"I had fun last year," Flip says dryly.

The "night with a hockey player" auction is usually pretty family friendly. Often it's meant to be an opportunity for the winner to hang out with their favorite player. Sometimes it consists of some ice time, giving back to the community in a meaningful way, and a private dinner with a small group, but last year Flip's date went in a less PG direction.

Dallas shoots him a look. "I'm putting it out in the universe that I'd like to have an evening with someone less than three times my age this time."

Last year I opted out because of my injury. This year I didn't have a reason to say no. I still don't. But I wish I did. It's a lot of being personable, which I'm not always good at.

After our workout, we go for lunch. We have practice early this afternoon, so I have an hour of downtime. I debate my options. Part of me wants to call my younger sister for advice.

She met her husband when she was working on her master's. He's a professor and fifteen years her senior. At the time it was scandalous, and we were a little wary of Mike, but it was clear after we met him that they were meant for each other. This isn't the same, though. Roman's my best friend and teammate. Aurora's not even done with university. It doesn't matter how perfect that kiss was. She's not for me. I can't fix this, but I can apologize.

I send a single message:

> **HOLLIS**
> I'm sorry.

Aurora reads it almost immediately but doesn't reply for half an hour.

> **PRINCESS**
> Why apologize when it was a mistake?

> **HOLLIS**
> I didn't mean to upset you.

She replies as I'm sliding my feet into shoes.

> **PRINCESS**
> Let's forget it ever happened.

I don't think that will be possible. But for her, I'll try.

That evening, Roman won't let me off the hook for dinner. We stop at Aurora's favorite Thai restaurant. He also stops at the bakery and buys her an assortment of desserts. While he's inside, I call my older sister Emilia just to say hi and catch up. Roman returns and I take the pastries from him, setting them in my lap so they don't get jostled on the ride home.

My stomach is a twisted-up mess when Aurora walks through his door at six thirty. It sinks further when her gaze meets mine and her expression goes flat.

"I got all your favorites from Spicy Thai! And desserts! You can take the leftovers home with you." Roman pulls her in for a hug, then holds her at arm's length. "Are you okay? You look tired. Is it school-related?"

She smiles, but it seems forced. "I'm okay. I didn't sleep the best. Probably too much caffeine."

We take our seats at the dinner table and pass around the takeout containers. Aurora slides a pink-and-yellow, banana-patterned scrunchie off her wrist and pulls half her hair up on top of her head.

"That looks new," Roman observes.

"Yeah, I can't find my blue one. I hope I didn't lose it. It's my favorite."

I choke on my sip of water and cough into the crook of my elbow.

"I can get you another one," Roman offers.

"There are a few places I need to check first. It's just the perfect scrunchie."

She avoids eye contact with me and pushes her food around her plate, barely touching it.

"Aren't you hungry? Did I get the wrong thing? I thought tamarind curry was your favorite," Roman fusses. "Are you feeling under the weather? That might explain why you were crying last night. You always got teary when you were sick as a kid, and universities are hotbeds for seasonal illness."

She cringes and glances at me. "*The Way We Weren't* always gives me the feels." She pokes at her mango salad. "And Tristan sent Rix another cake, and it was on the counter when I got home from class. I figured a slice wouldn't hurt, but then I went back for seconds, and yeah... I'll totally enjoy this as leftovers." She eats a small bite of tamarind curry.

I look away, because watching that fork disappear between

103

her lips makes me think about what happened last night. And despite knowing it's wrong on so many levels, I selfishly want to do it again.

I wonder if this is what it was like for Tristan and Rix when they were hiding what was going on from Flip. Did it feel like the guilt would swallow him whole because he was lying to his best friend? As I sit across the table from her, with Roman spiraling over the tears I made her cry, I desperately want things to be different. And for a moment I consider blurting out the truth. But then what? I blow up years of friendship and create an irreparable rift? That's not fair to Aurora either.

"So it doesn't have anything to do with classes?" Roman asks. He cannot let this go.

"They're a lot of work, but so far, they're good," she assures him. "I'm just preoccupied, and I have a group meeting tonight."

"Is that boy who was interested in you last year in your group?" Roman presses.

"Uh, yeah." Her eyes rest briefly on mine. "Jameson's in my group."

"Is he still interested?" Roman asks.

"Um, yeah. He, uh...he asked me for coffee the other day," she mumbles.

Is this the kid who wants to Netflix and chill with her? Jealousy leaves a bitter taste in my mouth. Which is another problem. She should be all over Netflix and chill with her classmate.

"Did you say yes?" I ask.

Surprise and hurt cross her face before her gaze returns to her plate. "I... This week has been too busy."

"Coffee is what? An hour commitment?" I press. Every word feels like a razor blade. I need to put what I want aside. It's better this way. She should be dating, and this guy has been interested for months. It shouldn't be me she's thinking about, and I sure shouldn't be thinking about her.

"Do you like him? Is he nice? He doesn't play hockey, does he?" Roman asks.

"He's nice and no, he doesn't play sports. He is going into sports management," she confirms.

"That's good. Pro sports careers aren't stable. An accountant or manager is a much better side to be on. So what's holding you back?" Roman sets his fork down and gives Aurora his full attention.

She pokes at her rice. "I, uh, I sort of... I liked someone else, and uh, it's not... He doesn't..."

The crack in her voice makes me want to stab myself in the eye.

She takes a deep breath, eyes on her plate. "He's not interested in me the same way."

"Sounds like his loss if he can't see what an amazing person you are," Roman says gently. "Maybe coffee with Jameson is exactly what you need. I just want to see you happy with a normal guy, living your life."

"Yeah." She sighs. "I should probably say yes. At least he's not afraid to go for what he wants."

That sword cuts deep, because she's right. And isn't that what she deserves? Someone who will take risks for her. Someone who doesn't kiss her and tell her it's a mistake when it feels like the opposite.

Roman grins, completely oblivious—thank fuck—to the horrible tension. "That's my girl. Don't wait around for some guy to realize what he's missing. You go for what you want."

"Thanks, Dad. I think I will." She smiles, but it looks pained, at least to me.

She excuses herself a few minutes later, her plate still half full, to go set up for her group meeting.

Roman waits until she's gone before he turns to me. "I knew there was more going on. I don't know why she felt like she had to keep that from me. I've always tried to keep an open-door policy between us."

"Maybe she was processing, especially if she found out this other guy wasn't interested in her as recently as last night." That

I'm able to keep my voice even is a miracle. Lying to Roman feels almost as shitty as pushing Aurora into the arms of someone far more age appropriate.

"Yeah, that could be it. We don't keep a lot from each other." He taps the edge of the table. "Speaking of dating, have you given any more thought to seeing Scarlet?"

I rub my bottom lip. My ex is the last person I want to see. "We're on the road half the time."

"It's just drinks, though. Like you said, it's an hour commitment. It could give you some closure at the very least. You don't know if you don't try, right?"

"Yeah. I guess."

"Send her a message. See if she's available. She's only in town for a few months. Get closure, if that's what you need, but take the opportunity for what it is."

I pull my phone from my pocket, annoyed that his rule about no phones at the table seems to be out the window recently.

HOLLIS

Hey. Still interested in grabbing that drink?

I press send and feel like I'm going to vomit.

"Happy?"

"Yes, I am. Thank you."

I'm about to slide my phone back into my pocket, but it buzzes. Roman gives me a chin tip, so I reluctantly check the screen.

SCARLET

Absolutely. Are you free tonight?

I exhale a lungful of guilt and dread. I don't want to do this, but I know I should. Not because I have any misgivings about ever getting back together with her. She's not the one I want.

"She say yes?"

"She asked if I'm free tonight."

He nods. "Tell her yes and get out of here."

106

"I'm getting closure, Roman. That's all this is." Scarlett has already done enough damage. I won't give her the power to do more.

It makes me wonder if this is how Aurora will feel about me one day. And wouldn't that be exactly what I deserve?

CHAPTER 13

HOLLIS

"I'm so glad you said yes." Scarlet ushers me into the penthouse apartment she's renting.

"I figured it made sense with you in the city for a while." I shrug out of my coat and toe off my shoes. I'm not entirely comfortable being in her personal space, but after a short back and forth, this seemed the best location to avoid ending up in the tabloids. I can't handle hurting Aurora more than I already have by being seen with my ex the night after I kissed her. Being with Scarlet feels all kinds of wrong already.

"Hard to escape me when I'm everywhere, huh?" Her smile is both wry and impish.

"It must get old, being followed wherever you go." The local tabloids have a daily feature, and lately, it's been Scarlet getting her morning coffee, or highlighting her designer jacket or shoes, or who the fuck cares what else. I'm used to the fame of being a pro hockey player, but no one tails me from my home to the arena.

She waves a dismissive hand. "You sort of sign on for it in my line of work." I follow her into the kitchen. "What can I get you? I have wine, scotch, and beer."

"Beer is good." I'm driving, and anything stronger would be a bad idea.

"Sure." She opens a bottle of my preferred brand, obviously prepared. "Would you like a glass?"

"The bottle's good."

Her fingertips graze mine when she passes it to me. It doesn't spark anything except more guilt.

"Thanks." I take a long swig. "How are you handling the Canadian winter?" Yup, definitely struggling for conversation if I'm already talking about the weather.

"It's so cold here! I don't know how you stand it."

"It takes some getting used to. But I travel during the worst months, so I get a lot of breaks. Can't be easy on a California girl."

"I shouldn't complain. This role is incredible, and I'm thrilled to have the opportunity. Plus, I get to watch you play." She pours herself a glass of white wine. "It's good to see you back on the ice. How are you feeling?"

"Good. The concussion was a minor setback."

She leads me to the living room. I sit in the corner of the couch. She takes the middle cushion and angles her body toward me. She's wearing jeans and a cropped sweater that falls off one shoulder. Her hair is curled, and her makeup is done. She looks like she's ready for the camera. She probably is, I realize, in case we leave her apartment together.

"You have another year left on your contract with Toronto, don't you?"

She enunciates each syllable in the city's name. I used to do it when I was first traded to the Terror, and Aurora found it hilarious. My chest tightens when I think about what she's doing right now. Did she make plans with that James kid? How hurt would she be if she knew I was here?

"Hollis, are you okay?" Scarlet puts her hand on my knee.

"Just, uh...up in my head a lot lately." I shift positions and cross one leg over the other to sever the contact.

Her smile turns empathetic. "I'm sure it must be hard, coming off an injury and then being out of the game again. But you're back and better than ever, right? Who knows what could happen at the end of next year. Maybe you'll wind up back in California. Or Vegas even."

That's unlikely. "I'm hoping Toronto will renew for a couple more years."

"Don't you miss the sun and the year-round nice weather?" she asks.

"I have family close by, and I'd like to finish my career here." I love my team, I'm comfortable, and the people I care about most are close.

"It's kind of exciting, isn't it? You'll only be in your mid-thirties and starting your second career. Have you given any thought to what's next for you?"

I shrug. "I'm more focused on the game than what's after it. How about you? Your star keeps rising."

"The last seven years have been a whirlwind," she admits.

"It must be a challenge having your life on display all the time." But even as I say that, I'm not sure it is for her. Our differing views on this topic were a big part of the reason she broke it off. She welcomes the media attention. She constantly posted pictures of us when we were dating, putting our relationship on display in ways I wasn't comfortable with.

She smiles and drops her gaze. "It can be difficult on relationships, as you know."

"I know." My stomach twists. Our end was public and painful. Our final fight caught on camera for the world to speculate over. It's the reason I'm so intensely private now and also why I've avoided serious, public relationships.

She sets her wineglass on the table and runs her hands over her thighs as her eyes lift. "I'm sorry for the way things happened, Hollis. So sorry. I wish I'd handled it better."

I'm about to tell her it's fine, but then what the hell was the purpose of coming here? "I thought we were on the same page,"

I say instead. "I thought we wanted the same things." We'd talked about marriage and settling down. More than once.

Her fingers drift over her lips. "Everything was happening so fast. *The Way We Weren't* was taking off, and you'd just been traded. I didn't think I could handle that kind of distance, especially with you wanting so much secrecy around our relationship."

"I just wanted some privacy," I counter. "I didn't want us under a microscope all the time." I'd been positive we could handle the distance. Sure, it would've been hectic with our careers, but I'd been so fucking in love. So ready to love her for the rest of my life. And she'd ripped my heart out. At least I hadn't actually proposed. But she'd learned my plan after the fact.

She rubs her bare ring finger. "I know that now. I was so young then. There isn't a day that goes by that I don't wish I'd done things differently."

"But you didn't." She interpreted my lack of interest in being media fodder as being unsupportive and ended us.

She moves closer and takes my hand. "I know I hurt you, Hollis, and I can't take it back. But it's the biggest regret of my life. I should have realized you were trying to protect our relationship by keeping it out of the media spotlight. I was scared of all that distance and what it would mean for us. I know one conversation won't fix things, but I'm here for a few more months. Maybe we could spend some time getting to know each other again."

It would be the right thing to do—date someone closer to my age. But the idea of having a relationship with the world watching, again... I still don't want my life any more available for public consumption than it is. And the idea of putting my heart back on the line, especially with someone who's already shredded it once, seems like a stupid thing to do. But beyond any of that, I don't want the woman sitting in front of me.

Not to mention what it would do to Aurora. My being here

feels like a huge betrayal to a woman who isn't even mine. I'd never be able to fix what I've broken if I went down this path with Scarlet again. And judging by the weight in my stomach, it's not something I could live with.

I lick my lips, my mouth dry and my chest tight. "We're very different people now, Scarlet. What you did to me, how you left things—you're right, one conversation won't fix that. And I don't know if spending more time with you will either. You're fresh out of a relationship—"

"Things weren't good there for a while," she interjects. "I was supposed to wait until we started filming here, but it just... We weren't working."

"You were still together for two years, according to the tabloids anyway, which is how long we were together. I wasn't over the end of us after three months." I push to a stand. "I appreciate the opportunity to talk, and I'm grateful for your honesty, but I don't know if this is what I need." But I do know. Unfortunately, the person I want, I can't ever have.

CHAPTER 14
HAMMER

"How do I look? Should I change? I don't know about this shirt."

I snap a selfie and send it to my mom. She's back in the land of internet and sent me some photos of the mountains. They're supposed to bring serenity whenever I look at them. She's right though, they do calm me.

"If you were attending a church gathering with seniors, that shirt would be fantastic. I suggest a V-neck and the bra you usually wear to the club for this date," Rix says.

"I agree," Hemi adds as my phone buzzes.

MOM

I love this color on you, but I feel like you're not comfortable in it. If you don't feel your best, you should put on something else that helps your energy.

PS. He better treat you right or I'll tell your dad to give him his scary face.

PPS. Send me his star sign if you think he's
worthy!

AURORA

Thanks, mom! Fingers crossed it goes well!

"I've never seen your club bra, but in a little more than a year, I'll have one of my own," Tally announces.

"I've also never seen the club bra, but I trust Rix's shirt recommendation for highlighting the assets." Dred is always up for the Watering Hole and hanging at our places, but the club is not usually her scene.

"Hell has a special place for us." Rix hands me a margarita.

That I need a drink before a coffee date says a lot about my expectations for the impending hour. It shouldn't even be a big deal. I see Jameson all the time. We have classes together, and we're always working on group projects, but for some reason labeling this as a date has me all angsty and flustered. He's the kind of guy my dad wants for me.

"Hell will roll out the red carpet for you, my dear," Hemi says dryly. "Tristan was in a particularly good mood today, which I assume means some produce met an untimely end last night."

"This morning, actually. RIP cucumber." Rix grins.

"I thought you were joking about the produce." Tally looks horrified.

"I am."

"She is."

Hemi, Rix, and I are in perfect harmony.

Dred arches an eyebrow.

"Oh my God. You're not." Tally looks to Hemi. "Can I have a sip of that?"

"No." Hemi sets her margarita on the table and looks away.

Rix and I do the same. Sort of on topic and with my confidence up, I take the opportunity to tell her the truth about how thin the walls are.

"Speaking of your sex life, I didn't want to tell you, but I feel like if I don't..." I whisper in her ear.

"Oh God." Her eyes go wide. "What did I do?"

"So, uh, it turns out, the walls are thinner than we thought. During away games—" I cough. "I can, uh, I can hear you get to the good part."

"No." She slaps a palm over her mouth.

"It's not a big deal."

She grabs my arm, and I'm shocked to see she's close to tears. "But it is. My brother used to—" She gives her head a quick shake. "I am so, so sorry, Hammer. You've been dealing with this for months."

"I went up to my dad's or Hollis's. It gave me time with his cats."

"Never again, though." She pokes her chest. "I'll wait for you to be out. Or be quieter. I'm just so sorry."

I hug her. "It is absolutely okay. I wasn't upset at you at all. But I want you to have your privacy and to feel free."

"If we ever make you uncomfortable, you have to swear to tell me," she whispers.

"Swear." And link pinkies. "I just want you to be happy. Proud of you." I bump her shoulder.

Tally sneaks another sip. The joke's on her though, because Hemi's margarita is like Tally: a virgin. But it makes her feel badass when she thinks we let her sneak sips of alcoholic beverages. Bless her adorable, sweet, seventeen-year-old heart.

"I'll change my shirt." I head to my bedroom.

"Just change your bra. I have a great shirt you can borrow." Rix disappears into her bedroom.

A minute later I return to the living room, wearing only my favorite bra.

"Oh, wow!" Tally's eyes go wide.

"That bra is a winner, and I need six." Dred gives me a double thumbs-up.

"The bra makes them look more substantial. I'm a modest B-cup. Except when I have my period; then I'm a serious B-cup," I explain.

Tally taps her lips. "Can we go bra shopping one day? I only have sports bras and plain black and nude bras."

"Absolutely. We'll plan a trip." I'm built very much like my mom with my dad's ridiculous metabolism. It means I'm lean, without a lot going on in the boob department. When I was in high school, some of the girls made fun of me because I was skinny and a late bloomer. I'd really hoped puberty would help a girl out, but my boobs never grew into my body. I do have a butt, thank God.

"You're built like an athlete. There's nothing wrong with that," Hemi says. She has curves for days.

"Our bodies are beautiful exactly as they are." It's what my mom always says. I know she's right, even when it's hard. The bra does a good job making what I have work for me. And I can always go braless, if I want. Except when it's really cold and my nipples can cut glass.

"I have two options." Rix does a double take. "Holy hell, that bra is truly magical."

"I know. It's my favorite forever." I should stockpile a few in case they stop making them.

Rix tosses her shirts over her shoulder. "Can I?" She raises a cupped hand.

"Oh yeah, go for it." I motion for her to go ahead.

She pushes at the fabric. "Oh, that's nice. It's soft padding."

Tally raises her hand. "Can I also feel?"

"Yeah. For sure. Hemi? Dred? You want in?"

Dred shrugs. "Might as well."

"Damn, there's nothing better than a soft supportive bra that seriously fits." Rix's eyes are wide in awe.

"Girl, I'm trying to rein these babies in on a regular basis." Hemi motions to her ample rack.

Dred comments on the excellent support while checking out the straps.

Tally hops off the couch and gives my bra a tentative poke.

"Knock! Knock! Checking in to see how things are going pre-coffee date!" My dad comes barging into the apartment.

Tally, Rix, and Dred freeze with their hands by my boobs.

"What the—" My dad turns around and heads for the door.

"Dad, you need to wait until I say it's okay to come in."

"I don't know what's going on, and I don't want to know. I'll message later." The door closes behind him.

Rix, Hemi, and Dred burst out laughing. Tally covers her mouth with her hand and giggles. Then her eyes widen. "Do you think he'll tell my dad?"

"No. Definitely not. Also, he literally has no idea what he walked in on. And I've told him at least half a dozen times not to let himself in."

"I'm glad we were having normal kitchen sex when he walked in that one time," Rix says.

"You'd think he would have learned his lesson."

"Seriously." Rix hands me a shirt, and I pull it over my head. It's a long-sleeve, loose knit, black V-neck sweater.

"You don't need to try the other one on. This is perfect. You look sexy and cute and like the perfect date," Rix assures me.

My phone buzzes. I check the screen. "Oh, God. He's here. I'm nervous."

"Don't be. Forget about the other guy who's too stupid to see a good thing when it's right in front of him and have fun," Rix says pointedly.

"Purse." Hemi hands it to me.

"Shoes." Rix guides me to the front door where my cute, impractical-for-the-weather flats wait.

I message that I'm on the way down and buzz Jameson in so he can wait in the lobby.

"We'll all be here when you get back, unless you tell us to GTFO so you can have some private time. Then we'll be over at Tristan's. Or text if you need saving and we'll be there," Rix assures me.

"You got this. Have fun." Hemi pulls me in for a hug.

"It's going to be great." Tally gives me a thumbs-up.

"That bra is really kick-ass." Dred high-fives me. "Have a good time."

I leave before I do something stupid, like change my mind. My stomach is full of butterflies as I take the elevator to the lobby.

Jameson is sitting on the couch when I step off the elevator. He's a nice-looking guy. Hot, really. He has dark brown hair, lightly tanned skin, and dark brown eyes framed with thick lashes. He's over six feet, lean, and a runner. He doesn't play hockey and is involved in a lot of extracurriculars. He's definitely one of the good guys.

"Hey." He runs his hands over his thighs as he stands. His eyes light up and a wide smile forms as his gaze moves over me. It's an appreciative look.

"Hey." I return the smile and adjust my purse.

He comes in for a hug, which I awkwardly return.

"You look really good," he says after he releases me. His gaze darts down for a second before returning to my face. "I like your sweater."

"Thanks. You look good too." He's wearing a university hoodie, a pair of jeans, boots, a winter coat, and a baseball cap. So he's dressed like any regular student.

"Oh, uh, I came straight from campus." He motions to the lobby. "This place is nice."

"Yeah. The pool and workout room are pretty sweet. And there's loads of shopping and restaurants around." I don't know what to do with my hands, so I shove them in my pockets. "We can go across the street to the diner, if that's cool with you."

"Yeah, absolutely." The right side of his mouth tips up. "I'm really glad you said yes to coffee, Aurora."

God, he's sweet. And he likes me. There's no hot and cold with him. He's consistent, unlike one guy I know. "Yeah, me too."

But my stomach tightens as the front doors open and *that guy* walks through them, bringing a swirl of cold air and a furl of snow with him. Hollis removes his toque and runs a hand through his thick, dark waves. He's wearing a pair of jeans that hug his hockey thighs in all the right places, the ridiculous banana duck hoodie I bought him two years ago for Christmas, and his winter jacket. His outfit and Jameson's are pretty much the same, but for some reason Hollis makes it look effortlessly sexy.

"Holy shit," Jameson mutters.

I should have met Jameson at the Pancake House.

Hollis's expression softens when he sees me, until his eyes shift to Jameson, whose hand is currently pressed against the small of my back. Hollis's gaze turns murderous, and my vagina gets stupidly excited.

"Is that Hollis Hendrix?" Jameson asks.

Hollis tucks his toque into his pocket and heads for us. "Hey, Princess." He shocks the hell out of me when he pulls me in for a hug.

I stand there, stiffly, trying not to appreciate the way he smells, or how right it feels to be in his arms—even though I'm highly confused and justifiably pissed off. Eventually, I get it together and poke him in the ribs.

He releases me. I give him a look. He smiles.

"Aren't you going to introduce us?" Hollis asks expectantly.

"Right. Yeah." I glance between them. "Jameson Grover, this is Hollis Hendrix. He plays right wing for Toronto, and he's my dad's best friend. Hollis, this is Jameson, one of my friends from school."

Hollis extends a hand. I seriously hope he doesn't crush Jameson's.

"It's so amazing to meet you," Jameson gushes and pumps his hand. "I'm such a huge fan. I have your jersey at home. And your rookie card. I've been following your career since I was a kid."

"Oh yeah? You play hockey?" Hollis asks through a tight, made-for-TV smile.

"For a few years, as a kid, but I uh…liked watching better. You're having such a great season. That hit you took was such bullshit. Man, we were worried you'd be out again, but you showed them, huh?" Jameson finally releases Hollis's hand.

Hollis runs his hand through his hair. "Mostly they were worried about the concussion."

"Oh yeah, I can totally see that."

I need to get us away from Hollis. "Well, Jameson and I should probably head out."

"It was so great to meet you, Mr. Hendrix," Jameson says. "Good luck tomorrow night."

"Thanks. I'll see you later, Princess."

"Sure, Hollis."

I grab Jameson's arm and drag him toward the lobby doors. *Fucking Hollis.*

Jameson waves over his shoulder as I push through, and we step outside into the cold February afternoon.

"Holy shit. You just introduced me to Hollis Hendrix."

Jameson is a nice guy. Kind, hardworking, polite. It totally makes sense that he's starstruck. I was when I met Scarlet Reed. "I did."

"It's one thing to know your dad is a pro hockey player, but the reality didn't set in until that." He thumbs over his shoulder. "Was that weird for you? I mean, I guess you're used to being around pro hockey players all the time." His brow furrows. "He called you Princess. He and your dad are bros, right? Like tight? That's how the media makes it look, anyway. You must know him really well."

I know what it feels like to have his tongue in my mouth. I've also fantasized an unreasonable number of times about being fucked by him. But I seriously doubt that's what Jameson means. "I've known Hollis since I was in high school."

Jameson nods thoughtfully. "He's kind of like family then, right? Like an uncle or something?"

I choke back a hysterical laugh. "Yes and no? Mostly it's this giant friend group who all have each other's backs."

When the light changes, we cross the street to the diner.

"Right, yeah. It's kind of like having a bunch of older brothers. Like a lot of brothers who could kick some ass."

"They can be protective like brothers."

"I kind of caught that vibe from Hendrix. I hope I made an qkay impression."

"Don't worry about Hollis. He's grouchy on a good day." I keep looking over my shoulder, half expecting to find him trailing us.

I can't believe he hugged me. He's the one who said kissing me was a mistake. He told *me* I should go on a date. He's sure as hell getting an earful the next time we're alone.

"Dating must be pretty tough, huh?" He holds open the diner door for me.

I murmur thanks and wave to Rainbow, heading for a booth near the back. "Sometimes. I'm used to being surrounded by high-level alpha dudes who are driven and super competitive." I belatedly realize he probably meant it was hard to date with so many guys looking out for me.

Rainbow comes over to take our drink order.

"Hey! You ditch your dads today?" she asks.

I don't bother to correct her. I think it's hilarious that she believes my dad and Hollis are a thing. "Sure did. Rainbow, this is my friend Jameson. Jameson, this is Rainbow. It's Jameson's first time here."

"Oh, you are in for a treat. I highly recommend any of the milkshakes, and the cookies-and-cream waffles are to die for."

"I can attest to this," I say.

We both order coffee and water, and Rainbow leaves us to look at the menu. "Don't feel compelled to eat if you're not hungry, but the waffles and milkshakes are really awesome."

"I'm always hungry," Jameson says with a grin.

"That's a phrase I'm used to hearing."

"I hope I didn't fanboy over Hendrix too bad. I wanted to be cool about it, but I'm a hockey fan, and a Terror fan, and I didn't expect to meet him. Or anyone, really, except for you." He smiles shyly. "Thanks for saying yes to coffee."

"Thanks for asking." His expression should make my heart all melty and my girl parts all excited. Instead, I find myself comparing him to Hollis. Which isn't fair. They're not even playing in the same league, let alone on the same field.

I want to be attracted to him. I want to like him as more than just a guy in my class who's shown an interest in me. But my head is across the street with Hollis, even though I'm pissed at him for pulling that bullshit.

Rainbow drops off our drinks. I order banana pecan pancakes with sausage links, and Jameson decides on waffles with a side of bacon.

"So what are your plans after graduation? Did you apply to any graduate programs?" Jameson asks.

I shake my head. "I'm kind of done with school. I've wanted to work for the league since high school, and there might be a public-relations-assistant position coming in the spring." Hemi mentioned a few days ago that she'd submitted a proposal with Shilpa's help. I'm crossing my fingers it goes through. The Terror are like family. I can't imagine a life where I'm not at the arena or part of that team in some way, especially with my dad retiring soon. Working for them makes sense. It's where I belong. "What about you?"

"I applied for a few master's programs—two in Toronto, one in Ottawa, and two out west."

"The West is beautiful." Although I've mostly seen it from the inside of a hockey arena.

"It is," he agrees.

"So you could be living in BC this time next year."

"Or I could be here."

"Or Ottawa."

He nods, and just like that, the door on whatever this might have become closes. If Jameson's moving across the province, or the country, there's no point in trying to start something with him. At least that's the excuse I make for myself. That this revelation isn't followed by a pang of disappointment, but rather relief, is telling.

Rainbow stops by to top up our coffee cups and let us know our food will be out soon.

Jameson taps the edge of the table. "I'm going to use the bathroom before our food arrives."

"Sure."

As soon as he leaves the table, I pull my phone out and send a message to the girls and then my mom.

> **AURORA**
> Not sure there will be a date two.

My mom responds first.

> **MOM**
> That's too bad, honey. The right someone is out there. You'll find them when they're ready for you!

I shift to my private messages with Rix.

> **AURORA**
> 20-year-olds don't do it for me.

My group message goes off first:

> **RIX**
> Does he push food onto his fork with his fingers instead of his knife?
>
> **HEMI**
> Did he order liver and onions? You know secretly he's a grandpa inside if he does.

DRED

Can he even grow facial hair yet?

TALLY

Why is liver and onions on the menu at the diner?

Maybe he's nervous.

My private messages with Rix buzz.

RIX

I don't know if it's fair to compare him to a professional hockey player.

AURORA

Side eye He's applied to grad school all over the country.

I move down to my messages with Hollis:

AURORA

WTF was that bullshit?

The bell above the door dings, and I glance up, then slide over in the booth until I'm practically eating the wall. This can't be happening.

CHAPTER 15
HAMMER

"Peggy? I thought you were going for coffee." Dad approaches the table. "Where's your friend? Did he leave already?"

Hollis lags behind, his phone in his hand. He frowns and slips it back in his pocket without responding to my message. My stomach flip flops with fresh guilt over the secrets I'm keeping from him, but my anger overrides it.

The girls are still pinging the hell out of me.

"He's in the bathroom."

"So he left you out here on your own," Hollis says.

I give him a look. *How else was he supposed to go to the bathroom, Hollis?* He has the gall to still be gorgeous while also smug.

"Maybe you two should go somewhere else," I suggest, but I'm too late.

"Oh, man. Roman Hammerstein." Jameson wipes his hand on his pants and extends it. "Jameson Grover. I'm friends with Aurora." His smile is fairly manic. "Sir, it's an honor."

Oh my God. This isn't happening.

Hollis's eyes slide to Jameson, and if looks could kill, my coffee date would be nothing but a pile of ash.

"Jameson, it's a pleasure. Peggy has such nice things to say about you."

"Dad," I warn.

"What? You've talked about Jameson plenty of times at the dinner table. Always nice things to say. Isn't that right, Hollis?" Dad elbows him in the arm.

"Uh-huh." Hollis pokes his cheek with his tongue.

"Do you want to join us?" Jameson asks. "There's more than enough room."

"Yeah, sure, why not?" Hollis slides into the booth across from me.

"Great. Awesome. This is just—wow." Jameson is about to jizz in his pants.

Hollis looks like he's plotting murder and evil things, and I'm so pissed—but also he's so fucking hot, and I hate it. My dad seems genuinely pleased to meet my date and completely oblivious to how awkward it's all become.

I fire off another text to the group:

AURORA

My dad and Hollis crashed my date.

And my date invited them to join us.

And they said yes.

I kick Hollis's shin under the table. We are so having words after this. Angry words. What the hell is he playing at?

He shrugs out of his jacket, drapes it over his lap, and smirks.

Rainbow comes over with our meals. "Oh! Your dads are here! How cute is this?"

"We're just friends," says Hollis and my dad at the same time.

"Of course." Rainbow winks and turns to me, dropping her voice to a whisper. "They're so cute together."

I make a heart with my fingers. "Aren't they, though?"

Rainbow makes the heart back. "I ship your dads so hard."

I'd like to ship my dad's best friend hard.

Jameson looks super confused.

"I'll bring you coffee and menus," she tells them. "Unless you both want the usual."

"The usual is good," Dad and Hollis say in unison.

"I'll take a beer instead of coffee, though," Hollis adds.

"Make that two," Dad agrees. He gives me a disapproving look after she leaves.

I roll my eyes. "Let her have her fantasy."

"I didn't know you two were..." Jameson trails off.

"We're not," Dad says.

"I love pussy," Hollis says flatly.

"Hollis." Roman elbows him.

I nearly spray him with my coffee. I swear, Hollis is entirely unhinged right now, and I don't even know what to do about it.

I kick him under the table, hard. Except I'm the one who flinches because I wore a stupid pair of cute flats and not practical winter boots as the weather would suggest.

He doesn't so much as blink. "That was crass. I'm a cisgender, heterosexual male. I can't speak for Roman, but we've been friends for a long time."

"Right. Yeah. It would be totally cool if you were gay, though. I have a younger brother who is. And my aunt is married to a woman," Jameson says helpfully.

"Hemi has two moms," I add. Just to be part of the conversation, I guess.

"You two should dig in. Don't wait for us." Dad grins and reclines in his seat.

Hollis stretches his leg into my space. I'm about to kick him again, but then I remember it's the right one, and he often does this because it's more comfortable post-surgery.

"Do you want some waffle? We can get extra plates, so you don't have to wait," Jameson offers.

He's so excited about eating with Roman Hammerstein and Hollis Hendrix. This further confirms that Jameson and I are destined to be friends only. He's not surly enough, or old enough, or Hollis enough.

I'm so screwed.

My dad and Jameson start talking hockey, of-fucking-course. It's not that I don't love hockey talk, but now my date is fawning all over my dad. It's annoying.

And my phone is blowing up. I have twenty-seven new messages in the Badass Babe Brigade chat.

Several of them are surprised and dying GIFs.

Rix messages in our private texts:

RIX

If he's going to fuck with you, you should fuck with him back.

She makes a good point.

Hollis is ruining my date. Probably on purpose.

AURORA

He can't take a bite out of his cake, tell his cake it was a mistake, and refuse to let anyone else eat it.

RIX

Agree. What are you going to do about it?

What *am* I going to do about it?

My dad and Jameson are still yammering away. I dump maple syrup all over my sausages and stab one with my fork.

Hollis eyes me with amusement. I take an angry bite.

"Honey, your knife," Dad mutters, then goes back to talking to my date about first draft picks this season. Normally I love draft talk, but right now I'm beyond frustrated. Because I'm hiding things from my dad for one, but also, the hockey player sitting across from me is the one I'd love to be on a date with, and instead Hollis's sabotaging the one he explicitly told me to go on.

As anticipated, my dad's and Hollis's meals appear a minute

after their beers. They're regulars, and everyone loves them, and Rainbow ships them. Hollis digs into his poached-egg breakfast hash, while I cut my sausages into tiny bite-sized pieces and occasionally offer my thoughts when they're asked for by my dad or Jameson.

Hollis agrees with everything I say, especially if it contradicts Jameson. It's irksome.

I drop my shoe on the floor and slide my foot up his calf. His gaze lifts from his plate. I keep going up the inside of his thigh. And all the while, my date and my dad keep blabbering on about who knows what. Part of me wonders if Jameson actually wanted to go out with me, or if it was an excuse to meet my dad and maybe score tickets to a game. It wouldn't be the first time.

My big toe brushes against Hollis's jacket, which is still draped over his lap. And I keep going. I don't know what the hell I'm thinking, but I'm committed to this stupid, dangerous course of action.

Hollis's gaze shifts to my dad and Jameson—neither of them is paying attention to us—and moves back to me as his hand disappears under the table. I fully expect him to shove my foot away, but that's not what happens. At all. Instead, he moves it between his very warm, very thick, very strong thighs and presses it against the exceptionally prominent bulge behind his fly.

His coat covers his lap. We're tucked into a booth in the very back corner of the diner. No one can see what's happening under the table.

I can't believe what's happening under the table.

Hollis better not have a foot fetish. At least I think I hope he doesn't have a foot fetish. I mean, I'm not opposed to foot rubs, but I don't want to give him the foot version of a handy. Or have him try to stick his foot in my lady business. That's definitely not my kink. But having him hold my foot against his hard cock under the table with my dad and my date right beside us might very well do it for me based on the way my nipples tighten and everything clenches below the waist. Also, my toes curl.

"What do you think, Pegs?"

"Huh?" My gaze snaps to my dad.

"Bowman's having a great season with New York, but so is Grace. Who's a more likely trade?"

"Grace. He's a hothead on the ice, and Bowman is methodical and levelheaded. If they're willing to trade one player, it'll be Grace, but only if it's evenly matched."

"But Grace has more years on the ice," Jameson argues.

"That's one factor." Hollis gives his two cents. "But it's about more than experience. Bowman is all about the team, and Grace has been known to pull stupid moves because his ego demands it." Hollis's thumb slides between my foot and his bulge, and he runs it firmly along my instep.

I cough into the crook of my elbow to cover my moan. His hands feel huge.

"Hollis makes a good point." Dad glances at my plate. "Is your appetite still off, honey?"

I look down. All I've managed to eat is one maple-syrup-drenched sausage. "Oh, uh, no. Just savoring today, I guess."

Hollis taps the top of my foot. His hand reappears as I drop my foot and slip it back into my shoe, but not before my toe lands in a wet spot on the floor.

I spend the rest of my date trying to eat while my stomach flip-flops all over the place. There is definitely a conversation coming with Hollis. My dad pays for the entire meal and, because he can't help himself, invites Jameson to a home game. Jameson is all smiles and excitement. As we finish up, Hollis stands off to the side with his hands in his pockets, looking as annoyed as I feel.

When we get back out to the sidewalk, Jameson hugs me, but thankfully doesn't go in for any kind of kiss on the cheek with my dad and Hollis standing guard.

"I'll text you later, okay?" He's all shy smiles again.

"Yeah. Sounds good."

I wave as he disappears down the stairs to the subway.

"He's a nice young man," Dad says.

"Yeah, you two got along like a house on fire." He's oblivious to my irritation, and everything else apparently, but I have bigger issues to deal with. Namely, his best friend.

"I have to run to the store and pick up a few things. Do either of you need anything?"

"Nope," Hollis and I reply at the same time.

"Okay. If you think of anything, just message."

He strides down the street, and Hollis and I walk silently back to our building. He holds the door open, and we don't say a word until we're alone in the elevator.

"What in the actual fuck, Hollis?"

He leans against the rail. "I didn't know you were going to the diner."

"This is about way more than the diner." I cross my arms. "You don't get to kiss me, tell me it's a mistake, and shove me into the arms of someone else you deem more age appropriate, then act like a territorial ass and ruin the fucking date you sent me on!" I snap.

"You're—"

I hold up a hand. "I'm not done." The elevator stops, and the doors slide open.

An adorable elderly couple gets on with us. As usual, we talk about the weather. When we reach my floor, I give Hollis a pointed look, and he gets off the elevator with me.

"Do you have a foot fetish or something?" I whisper-hiss once the doors close behind us.

He raises an eyebrow. "Do you?"

"What? No. You were the one rubbing my foot on your dick, not the other way around." I hate how good it felt to have him touching me though.

"You were playing footsies with me under the table," he reminds me.

"You crashed my date, Hollis!" I'm so furious, and turned on, and confused. "You either want me or you don't."

The smirk slides off his face. "It's not that simple, Princess."

I stalk down the hall, and he falls into step beside me.

"Isn't it, though? You can't play head games with me. It's not fair."

"That's not what I'm trying to do."

"You're saying one thing and doing the opposite. I'm pretty sure that's the working definition of head games."

"You don't want to date that kid," he grumbles.

It annoys me that he calls him a kid when Jameson and I are the same age. "You mean *you* don't want me to date him." I stop when I reach my apartment, then remember the girls are still there, waiting for a report. I can't invite Hollis in to continue an argument that's probably going nowhere good.

Hollis crosses his deliciously thick forearms across his equally thick chest. "You're right. I don't want you to date him. He's too fame-smitten, and not smitten enough with you."

He's not wrong. Jameson spent the entire meal talking to my dad and not me. He didn't even try to include me in the conversation much. That was all my dad, and only occasionally. Meanwhile, Hollis sat there, being gorgeous and doing bad things under the damn table with his best friend right beside him and my date across from him. The fucking nerve. "So what's your plan? Are you going to vet every guy I date until you deem one worthy of my attention?"

"If that's what it takes to make sure you don't end up with an asshole, then yes."

I prop my fist on my hip and lean in, eyes narrowed. My anger is made that much worse when I'm forced to rage-whisper because we're still in the damn hall outside my apartment. "There's one sure-fire way to ensure that."

He gives me a dark look. "You know that can't happen."

I throw my hands in the air. My frustration is boundless.

"You can't keep saying that and then pull the shit you did today!"

His expression shifts, and his arms drop to his sides. Shame lurks behind his eyes. "I know."

"Then why did you do it in the first place?" My heart aches so badly. He's right here in front of me, but he's so far out of reach. Sure, I'm lying to my dad and hockey players should be on my date-never list. Hollis just looks so earnest as he regards me. And I'm so angry at him for putting us in a box labeled *don't open* when it's clear he feels some type of way.

"I don't fucking know, okay?" He runs a rough hand through his hair, messing it up, and kneads the back of his neck. "I saw you with that preppy little shit, and he was touching you, and you looked like this." He flings a frustrated hand in my direction.

"Look like what?" He better not outfit-shame me. I look good, and my boobs are magical.

"Seriously?" His lip twitches. "You need me to spell it out for you?"

"Apparently."

His eyes rake over me, hot like molten lava. "You look like every sin I want to commit, Princess. So, yeah, I acted without thinking."

Of all the things I expected him to say, that wasn't anywhere on the list. But all it does is fuel my anger-fire. "Is that supposed to make me feel better about you ruining the date *you* sent me on?" He wants me, I want him. Why can't it be as simple as that?

"Yeah. No. I don't know. I'm trying to be honest without blowing up my fucking life." His nostrils flare. "You gotta stop making me admit this kind of shit. It's not doing us any good."

He's shutting down again, and I know better than to keep pushing when he gets like this, but my half-broken heart won't allow me to stay silent. He's the worst man for me to be falling for, but this is where I am. I know we can't be anything, but that doesn't change what I want. "You can't keep sabotaging my dates and saying shit like this, Hollis."

"We're at very different points in our lives, Aurora."

And here comes the rationalizing. "That sounds like another bullshit excuse. What are you so afraid of?" I take a step closer. "I'm right here, telling you I want you."

"It's what you think you want right now." He sighs.

There is nothing more infuriating than having him use the life-experience card like he knows what's best for me. "And what about you, Hollis? What do *you* want?"

His eyes move over my face like a caress. "You're killing me, Aurora."

"Good, because this is agony, Hollis." My voice cracks. To want someone so desperately but have them so far out of reach. Why can't a nice boy like Jameson be enough?

"Please, don't cry. Please." His hand lifts, hovering for a second before he caves and his fingers brush my cheek.

I lean into the touch and raise my own hand to skim the back of his. Every part of me hums with desire and longing. It hurts to want him. "Do you feel this the way I do?"

"Yes," he whispers.

"Then why are you fighting it?"

He leans in, and my heart stutters as his breath breaks against my lips. He changes course and skims my cheek with his mouth on the way to my ear.

His voice is a pained whisper. "I'm trying really hard not to screw shit up more than I already have today, and trust me when I say I know I fucked up in a lot of ways. I'm struggling here. And I know it's not fair to you. It's killing me, Aurora. But I'm losing the battle with my self-control. So please, before I do or say something to screw things up even more, or worse, say something that makes you cry again, I need you to go inside your apartment."

"But—"

He drops his hand, and it grazes the length of my arm, his thumb skimming like a phantom kiss.

I lean back enough that I can see his face. His jaw tics. "Hollis?"

"Please." His gaze shifts away. "I need this from you."

The look on his face is the reason I stop pushing. Because I see all the things I feel—the frustration, the longing, the fear, the desire. And the echoing agony. At least I'm not alone.

"Okay. I'll go inside." I fumble for my key fob.

Hollis doesn't move, just balls his hands into fists and watches me with an intensity that makes my knees weak.

I swipe it over the sensor and open the door.

"Be a good girl and stay home tonight," he murmurs darkly.

"Yes, Daddy Hollis." I slip inside, but not before I see his eyes trace my face one last time.

Rix, Tally, and Hemi are sitting in the living room. Dred has a shift at the library, so she'll need to be filled in later. I hold a finger up and spin around, pressing my eye to the peephole.

I'm not disappointed. Hollis grips the doorframe, glaring back at me. He shakes his head, and my body lights on fire from the inside. He takes a deep breath and pries his hands free, nostrils still flared. Eventually he steps back and disappears down the hall.

God, that was intense. I turn to my friends.

"So? What the hell happened?" Hemi asks.

"My dad loves Jameson, and he loves my dad, and I think it would be better if they just dated each other at this point."

Rix tries not to laugh. "So no second date?"

With a shake of my head, I sigh.

"Who was at the door?" Tally asks.

I scramble for a plausible fib. I don't want to lie to Hemi and Tally, but I can't tell them the truth about the Hollis situation. Not when everything is so...uncertain. So I give them the censored version. "I had it out with Hollis for crashing my date."

"You got angry at Hollis?" Tally's eyes are huge. "He's kind of scary."

"Not when you've known him as long as I have."

"Did he feel bad?" Rix asks.

"Not bad enough to get a clue and leave." I flop down on the couch. "I should have gone anywhere but the Pancake House."

"Maybe you subconsciously went there because there was a chance your dad would do what he did, and you already knew this date would be a bust," Hemi suggests.

"Fuck." I hug the Puck Yeah! pillow on the couch. Hollis got it for me. Fucking Hollis. Fucking complicated bullshit. "I don't know why I try to date university guys. It never works out."

Tally bites her fingernail. "Because your dad and Hollis always crash your dates?"

"I wish that was the reason." I sigh. "I don't think Jameson had bad intentions, but he was so starstruck. And now he'll look at me differently, and I'll look at him differently."

"You'll find a guy who likes you for you," Hemi says.

We all relax for a little while, but Tally still has homework, and she needs to be up early for dance practice, so Hemi takes her home.

Rix flops down on the couch beside me once they're gone. "Should I ask what really happened, or is this one of those situations where the less I know the better?"

"I don't even know what's happening. It feels a lot like we're planets orbiting each other, but the trajectory is off, and we're either doomed to miss each other or crash and burn up."

She nods. "Did he have an explanation for why he crashed the date?"

"He said I looked like every sin he wants to commit."

"Damn. He's fighting some real demons."

"I want to be worth the risk because what if it worked out," I admit.

"You are. Don't ever doubt that. Men and fear are a tricky combination."

"Isn't that the truth?" I feel like I'm on a roller-coaster ride that won't end.

We decide to watch a movie—a comedy with no romance, because I can't deal with hearts and feelings—but my mind is all over the place.

Jameson texts to tell me he had a great time. I leave it unread. I need to let him down easy. That he has possible plans to move several hours away is a good reason for us to stay in the friend zone.

Later, as I'm getting ready for bed, my phone buzzes with a new message. My stomach flips as I open it.

HOLLIS

Walking away from you is the hardest thing I've ever done.

CHAPTER 16
HOLLIS

W e're playing against Florida tonight, and it's been a rough game. We're down two goals, and we're already five minutes into the third period. With only six weeks left in the regular season, we're looking for wins and goals, not this shit.

The arena is packed, the girls are sitting in the box, and it's getting harder not to notice how good Aurora looks these days. It doesn't matter that weeks have passed since our kiss; it's on a constant loop in my head. I drag my eyes away from the box, grateful Hammerstein is in the net, so he can't see me watching his daughter.

Stiles and Madden rotate off, and I rotate on with Bright. We gain control of the puck a few seconds in, but Florida is on their game, making it difficult to get within shooting range. Bright skates into the crease, passing to Spencer. I get into position, and he fires the puck my way, but it bounces off the end of my stick before I can protect it.

It's a mad scramble as Florida closes in, sticks slapping against each other as we fight for possession. I lose the puck, and Spencer chases it down the ice, gaining control again. It's another thirty seconds of high-speed skating, me and Bright passing the puck back and forth, Florida on our heels. I take the shot, but I'm facing right, instead of left, so I'm half a second too slow making the turn in the crease and a Florida player slams into me.

It shouldn't be the kind of hit that does damage. I hear the pop and feel the snap, followed by agony that steals my vision. I land on my back on the ice. The roar of pain is all-consuming as the whistle blows. The crowd screams and boos.

Breathing feels like an impossible task. It hurts so much.

"Hendrix, man, hey, hey, look at me. Look at me." Bright is right there, his huge body creating a barricade between me and everything else.

I blink him into focus and try to sit up.

"Stay down." He puts a gloved hand on my chest. "I heard it. I heard the pop." He shakes his head. "Don't try to stand up. You don't want to make it worse."

"It's the same fucking knee," I grit out as panic takes hold.

"I know, buddy. I'm sorry." He turns to the ref. "Get medical. He can't walk off the ice."

I'm surrounded by my teammates. The game is paused while they stabilize my leg—that induces more vision-stealing pain. I'm moved to a stretcher and carried off the ice. Numbing fear settles under my skin. This could be a career-ending hit. I don't want to believe that tonight was my last game. I won't.

I'm taken to the hospital and rushed in for X-rays and scans. My phone is blowing up with messages from my family. But I can't respond yet. Not when I have no idea what's going on. The doctors murmur to each other, examining the X-rays. I can tell by the looks on their faces that the news isn't good. "I need surgery again," I say through gritted teeth.

I'm grateful the team doctor came with me, because I'd rather hear whatever needs to be said from him than some guy I don't know. "I'm sorry, Hollis."

"Fuck. *Fuck.*" I run a hand through my hair. "How bad is it this time?"

"The good news is it's a straight reattachment," he says.

"The healing time is better on that, right? Quicker." I could be back on the ice in a matter of weeks.

"Technically, yes. But you've already had one surgery, and we don't know how your body will handle this. We'll know more once we get inside and fix you up."

"I'll be able to play again, though, right?" I'm not ready for this to be the end. It can't be.

"We'll do everything we can to make that happen, Hollis."

I hear what he doesn't say—that I need to be prepared for any outcome, including the end of my career. "How soon is surgery?"

"They're prepping a room now. So within the next hour or so. You want to make a few phone calls, reassure your family you're okay, now is the time."

My sister Micha has called three times already. She's five years younger than me and has a daughter named Elsa. She and Mike live a couple of hours away in Niagara. She picks up on the first ring.

"Are you okay? Please tell me you're okay and that hit looked worse than it is." Micha's voice shakes.

"I'm okay, but I'm heading into surgery soon." My stomach twists and rolls as I verbalize it.

"No. Oh no, Hollis. I'm sorry. Should I come up? I can get a sitter and come up. You need someone with you for this."

"It's okay. Roman will be here. You've got a kid and a husband to take care of, and I've got a whole team."

"Is it the same knee?" she asks softly.

"Yeah."

"Oh, Hollis, what does that mean? Will you be able to play after this? Should you?"

"First surgery, and then we'll go from there."

"Will you call me when you're out?"

"Yeah, of course. Or I'll have Roman text. But we'll let you know how it goes."

"I'm so sorry this is happening again."

"Me, too."

"Do you want me to fill in Emilia?"

"Yeah. She's on nights this week, so she probably doesn't know yet. And we can hold off on telling Mom and Dad since they're on a cruise." Our older sister is a NICU nurse out in Bobcaygeon.

"They're supposed to be in the Cayman Islands tomorrow, so we can try to touch base then," she suggests.

"Yeah, better to wait until I'm out of surgery."

"Agreed. I hope it goes smoothly."

"Same. I love you, sis."

"I love you, too, Hollis."

I end the call, and the worry is all-consuming. It's a blessing when they come to put me under.

They keep me overnight after surgery. The procedure went fine, but the doctors have warned me to take it easy. My knee is swollen to twice its size, and my pain levels make me short-tempered and prone to snapping.

I'm sent home the following morning once I've seen the team physiotherapist and have been cleared for release by the doctor. All I want is my own bed, and my cats, and to escape from the relentless beeping and the smell of sanitizers. Roman wheels me out and helps me into the back seat of his car, since bending my leg is off the table for the next while.

"This was the one thing I didn't want to happen," I say once we're on the way home.

His gaze meets mine in the rearview mirror. "I know, man. I'm sorry."

At least he isn't feeding me bullshit about things being okay. The doctors are *cautiously optimistic*, a phrase I hate. I thought I had time to prepare for retirement, and now it might be here.

Getting from the vehicle to the elevator is a chore, and the ride up to the penthouse makes my head swim. I close my eyes and lean my head against the mirrored glass.

"You okay?" Roman holds the doors open for me, and I crutch the short distance to my penthouse.

"Just tired." I want to sleep for the next several weeks—until my knee is healed and this mental shitstorm is over. *You're only a handful of hours post-surgery*, I remind myself. I might be fine. It's a big might, though.

Roman helps me into my place. The throw pillows Aurora added to the couch last year after my first surgery are in the corners. The blanket neatly folded in the center boasts two cat-shaped dents. I'm pretty sure that's not how I left things.

The boys trot out of my bedroom, meowing loudly. I stop in the middle of the room while they wind around my legs. I can't even bend to pet them. "Hey, Postie. Hey, Malone. Sorry I left you so long. I hope you didn't shit on my bed."

"Peggy stopped by last night and again this morning," Roman offers.

"I'll have to thank her for that." Malone rubs himself against my leg. "You mind giving them a couple of treats? First cupboard on the right, the one with the yellow lid. Just a few, though."

"No problem. You want to lie on the couch or your bed?"

"Bed. I'm beat."

"It's been a rough twenty-four." He finds the treats, and Postie and Malone bumble over to their dishes and plunk their butts down.

I hobble the short distance to my bedroom. The covers have already been turned down, and the sheets changed. Two bottles of water sit on my nightstand, with the book that was on the side table in the living room beside it, along with two hockey magazines. She's so damn thoughtful, and I'm over here sabotaging her dates because I can't control myself. And fucking her scrunchie like a creep because I can't have her.

I look over to my dresser. I put her scrunchie there after I washed it, and now it's gone. *Fuck.*

That's a conversation I don't want to have.

I set my crutches against my nightstand and gingerly sit on the edge of my bed. I pull my hoodie over my head and toss it aside as I stretch out on the fresh sheets.

Roman appears in the doorway. "You need anything before I go?"

"I'm good. Thanks for getting me home."

"No problem. I'm heading to practice, but if you need anything, just message. And Peggy said she'd stop by after her classes to check on you and the boys."

"She doesn't need to do that," I say.

"She's worried. She had a rough night. She wanted to be here when you got home, but she has a meeting with one of her professors. I don't think she slept well, so you know, maybe let her do what she does."

"Okay." Last year when I had my first knee surgery, she cried on me in the hospital. But I haven't been alone with her since I ruined her date. Such an asshole move.

Roman taps the doorframe. "I'll be back later to check on you."

Postie and Malone jump on the bed and curl up beside me as Roman leaves. Their warm little bodies feel like the only thing anchoring me right now. Postie is constantly peeping his head up then scooting closer as if to make sure I'm okay. He always has a sixth sense for when I'm fucked up.

I drop a message in the family chat to let everyone know I'm home and I'll call them later. Micha has been great about keeping everyone updated, and I messaged her late last night when I got out of surgery to let her know things had gone well. I'm wiped, so it doesn't take long for me to pass out again. I wake up several hours later to a horrible throb in my knee and the sound of Aurora talking to the boys.

"I brought your favorite, boys. I know we ran out, and you had to settle for chicken instead of salmon. I'm sure it was rough," she cajoles softly. A giggle follows. "I love you, too, Postie, and you, Malone." Excited meows accompany the sound of a can being opened.

I need to take the prescription anti-inflammatories and get this pain under control. I sit up and push the covers aside. I'm forced to take a few deep breaths before I shift my legs over the edge of the bed. The pain flares with the movement, and my stomach rolls uncomfortably. I breathe through it. I don't want to vomit on myself. All I've eaten is buttered toast today.

When the nausea abates, I reach for my crutches, but I'm uncoordinated. They clatter to the floor, out of reach. "Fuck."

"Hollis? Are you okay?" Aurora rushes in.

I raise a hand. "Fine, just clumsy."

She picks up my crutches. "What do you need? What can I get you?"

I glance at her for a second, but my head is swimming, and the nausea is overwhelming, so I go back to staring at the floor. She's wearing loose-fitting jeans and socks with cats on them. I gave them to her last year for her birthday.

I hold out a hand. "I need my crutches."

I hate that I'm right back where I was less than a year ago. And it feels worse this time, the pain more intense. I'm fresh out of surgery, though, and the first few days are always the worst. I hate not being able to manage shit on my own. I don't want Aurora to see me like this again.

"Do you need to use the bathroom? I can help you get there," she says softly.

"I don't need the bathroom, and I don't need help." I'm a snappy asshole.

"You're sweating, your face is green, and while you're always hot as hell, you also look like actual hell, Hollis. I'm standing right here, asking you what you need. Let me help you, please." Her voice cracks.

I slowly lift my eyes. She's on the verge of tears. "I'm sorry. I'm in a lot of pain."

"There's a prescription on the counter. Can I get it for you?" she asks.

"Yeah, that'd be great," I concede. Other than my sisters and Roman, I haven't had someone look out for me—try to take care of me—like she does. I should get her to leave, setting more boundaries I wish I could barrel through.

She leaves me sitting on the edge of the bed and returns a moment later with my prescription. She opens the bottle and shakes two pills into my open palm, then twists the cap off a bottle of water and passes it to me. I down the pills and half the bottle of water.

She wrings her hands. "Are you hungry? Can I get you something to eat?"

"I don't need you to play nursemaid, Aurora."

"You just had emergency knee surgery again, Hollis. I'm sure the last twenty-four hours have been pretty awful for you, but they've been awful for all of us on the other side, too. I watched it happen, and then they took you to the hospital, and I had a stupid presentation, and a meeting I couldn't miss today, and they obviously wouldn't let anyone in last night at the hospital. Not that you wanted me to come visit you, but I was worried." Her bottom lip trembles, but her eyes are alight with frustration and fear. "I know my feelings for you are inconvenient, but I can't just turn them off. They're mine and they're real and believe me, I wish I didn't feel the way I do. But the last twenty-four hours really freaked me out. So if you could let me take care of you a little, even if it's just to make some toast you won't eat, that would be great."

I should give her a task. Something to occupy her. Instead, I beckon her closer. "Come here."

"What do you need?"

I extend a hand. "I need you to come here."

She tentatively slips her fingers into my palm. The hairs on the back of my arms rise. This didn't happen before the kiss, but now, every time we touch, it feels charged. Like we're

145

channeling an electrical current, but it's calming at the same time.

Her hands are much smaller than mine, and she has long, slender fingers. Her nails are painted pale blue with little hockey logos. I tug her forward and part my legs so she can fit between them. It's the wrong thing to do. I know this. I know I'm sending more mixed signals, but I'm powerless against her tears, and the sheer *need* to console her overrides the conviction that we should maintain boundaries.

"What are you doing?" she whispers.

"Hugging you, because I think you need it, and so do I."

She nods. "I would like that."

"Just careful of my knee."

She closes the distance between us. I wrap my arms around her, and her hands settle on my shoulders, tentative at first. "This is okay for you?" she asks.

I nod and give her a gentle squeeze. My whole body relaxes with her in my arms. Having her so close is what I need. For a moment I almost believe we're different people and this can be real.

She moves her arms around me and curls forward until her face presses against my neck. Her soft sigh wakes up parts of my body that have no business being involved.

It shouldn't feel this good to hold her. Shouldn't feel this *right*. But it does. I've hugged Aurora over the years. No...I've hugged *Peggy*. Celebrated her wins and consoled her over her losses. But this is different. It doesn't feel like me consoling her. She's a balm, a haven, something secure when everything else feels the opposite. I don't know how to handle the shift between us. I want her, I want this, but there's so much at stake. I've already made the mistake of giving my heart to someone who didn't want it. She's young. She might want me now, but in two years, five? What will I lose if she changes her mind?

"I was so scared," she whispers, lips moving against my skin.

"It'll be okay." I rub circles on her back.

I don't know how true that is, in any capacity. It feels like my life is unraveling. Everything I thought I knew is shifting faster than I can handle. I breathe her in, wishing she was five years older, that my career wasn't hanging in the balance, that her dad wasn't my best fucking friend. That I hadn't pulled her into this deception. That I didn't have the memory of that kiss.

That fucking kiss.

The taste of her. The feel. The desperate need to have more of it. All of it. All of *her*. I'm over here thinking about forever, and she has no idea how much baggage I'm carrying around.

The longer I hold her, the harder it is to let go, but eventually I pat her back and she takes the cue, putting space between us.

She wrings her hands, then crosses her arms, like she doesn't know what to do now. "Can I make you something to eat?"

"I'm pretty nauseated from the pain."

"A few crackers would help. You'll get gut rot from the meds if you take them on an empty stomach."

She's right, and it makes her feel better to be helpful. At least that's the excuse I make in my head. "Okay, yeah. That'd be good."

A half smile tips the corner of her mouth and makes the dimple below her right eye appear. "I'll be right back."

I lie down and focus on breathing and blocking out the pain.

Aurora returns a minute later with buttered soda crackers. She slides another pillow behind my head to prop me up and pets Postie, who has come up to see if I have anything interesting.

"I have some stuff to work on. I could hang out with the boys in the living room for a while," she offers when I'm done with the crackers. "And if you get hungry, I could make you something else."

She did the same thing when I was injured last time—hung out with the cats, made me food, and took care of my laundry when I couldn't. She dealt with my shitty attitude when I was depressed and dished out snark and sass to keep me from wallowing. But things have changed between us since then. Turning her away now will hurt her. And I want her here, despite it all.

"Yeah, okay, that'd be good."

She smiles again, looking relieved this time. "Okay. I'll be in the living room. Holler if you need anything." She pulls the bedroom door mostly closed on the way out.

I must doze off again, because when I open my eyes, it's dark outside, and it's closing in on dinnertime. The meds are working, and the pain is manageable. I sit up and grab my crutches, carefully making my way to the bathroom to relieve myself before I go to the living room.

Aurora is sitting cross-legged on the couch, her hair pulled up into a short ponytail on top of her head with her scrunchie. The one she reclaimed. Postie is stretched along the back of the couch behind her, and Malone is snuggled up beside her. She looks like she belongs here.

"Hey, hi." She sets her laptop aside, stands, and runs her hands down her thighs. "How are you feeling?"

"Okay. Better now that the pain is under control again." I don't understand how it can feel simultaneously right and wrong to have her here.

"Can I make you something to eat? Rix and I made that breakfast hash you love. I know it's dinner, but there's never a bad time for breakfast hash, and it might be easier on your stomach."

"That'd be great. I can help."

"Just keep me company or hang out on the couch with the boys."

"I need to stand for a bit. I've been lying down for a lot of hours."

I follow her to the kitchen and lean against the counter while she pulls out a pan and the container of breakfast hash.

She's so fucking beautiful. And smart and talented. Instead of being on a date with some guy in her class, she's here, taking care of me. I doubt she realizes what an honor it is to be wanted by someone like her, even if it shouldn't—can't—go anywhere.

"My dad said the doctors are hopeful," she says.

I blow out a breath. "We'll see how rehab goes."

She adjusts the temperature on the burner and turns to face me. "I'm so sorry, Hollis. I wanted anything but this for you."

"Me too. I might have to start looking at what's next, and I thought I had more time."

"Are you worried about how this injury will affect you in the long run?" She pulls the scrunchie free and runs her fingers through her hair. "A lifetime of pain management for a couple more years on the ice is a hard tradeoff."

"Not a lot of people understand this the way you do." Most young players don't even realize how hard this job is on a body. Even without serious injuries, it's intensely physical. But with them... I can't afford another knee surgery. Two inside a year will have a lifelong impact. And then there was that concussion. Sure, it was mild—this time.

"I've seen the way injuries take players out of the game," Aurora says, shaking her head. "Especially if they try to rush recovery. Look at Alex Waters." She turns back to the hash, flipping it and adjusting the heat again. "He was at the top of his game. He could have gotten back in after that concussion, but if he'd taken another hit like that..."

"He's a legend. But leaving the game when he did was a smart move." Waters shocked the hockey world when he hung up his skates. I watched his interviews afterward, talking about the impact of his concussion and how his priorities had shifted. He had a wife and a family. I don't have that yet, but I want it. Maybe more than I'm willing to admit. Especially in current company. "Another concussion could have changed his life forever. I don't want to risk not being able to walk so I can play a few more seasons, but I don't want to give up my career prematurely either. It's a real mindfuck, that's for sure."

Aurora's sad smile is full of empathy. "One day at a time, though, right?"

"That's all I can do."

Aurora asks me to pass her the butter, and I struggle not to step in and help just so I can touch her. I make an excuse about my knee aching and move to the living room while Aurora finishes the hash. Malone, being the weirdo he is, starts kneading the blanket beside me, and then the air hump starts. He's fixed, but he makes love to that blanket every night. I ignore him and turn on the TV for background noise.

Aurora brings over a lap tray when the food is ready and nudges Malone out of the way. He grudgingly curls up with his back to us on the chair across from the couch. Our fingers brush as she passes me silverware and again, I'm struck by how different it is this time around. How much I like being taken care of by her, how much I wish I could do the same. I ask her about school while I eat. I want to know what happened with that Jameson kid, but bringing that up is inviting more problems. I've given her enough mixed signals today.

When she sits on the couch next to me, Postie climbs into her lap and nudges her chin with his nose, then stretches out. He puts a paw on either shoulder, and his motor starts running.

"Dude, you have no chill," I mumble around a mouthful of hash.

She holds his paws and laughs as he headbutts her chin. She turns toward me, her smile wide and so beautiful. Her expression softens, and her voice is barely a whisper. "I missed this."

"Me too." Such a simple thing to say. But it's too much honesty. Too much truth. Especially when being with her like this is so easy. It makes staying inside the lines so fucking hard.

I consider what it would be like if I gave in to the craving that seems to grow with each passing day. We could be good together. She's smart, sassy, and she doesn't put up with my shit. She's easygoing, and she loves a good movie night as much as I do. My cats adore her. I adore her. Me starting my second career while she's starting her first could work in our favor. It might be difficult at first, but the people we're close to could get past the gap. She's been part of my life for years. But would Roman ever come around? I don't know. She's his world.

Sports highlights come on, along with news about my accident on the ice.

"I can change this," Aurora says.

"No, it's okay. I'm used to the fodder."

But I don't expect to see Scarlet splashed across the screen. I hadn't realized she was at the game again. Her horror-struck expression comes first, and her back with my number and name embroidered on the jersey appear next, followed by a slideshow of images from more than seven years ago, back when we were dating. She was twenty-two, and I was twenty-six.

Reality is a sharp blade. Aurora is younger than Scarlet was when she ended things and broke my fucking heart. I'd been so sure we'd work out. The life I'd been planning with her was suddenly gone, and with it went my ability to trust someone. I never wanted to feel that vulnerable again. I'd be an idiot to invite that kind of pain back into my life, especially when it's already turned upside down. Aurora is young, and I might seem like a good idea now, but eventually she'll find someone better. Someone's already changed their mind about me once and the scars from that have impacted me in ways I can't even begin to unpack. Aurora has her whole life ahead of her and I don't need to put either of us through that kind of hell.

"You know what, I'm really bagged. I need to lie down again. You don't need to stay or clean this up. I'll take care of it later." I turn off the TV and grab my crutches.

"Are you sure? I can put the dishes in the dishwasher." She wrings her hands.

"No. You should go. You've got assignments to work on.

Thanks for stopping by and for the hash. I appreciate it." I can't look at her as I turn toward my bedroom.

"Did I do something wrong, Hollis?" she asks.

"No, Princess. You're not the problem. It's just better if you go." I can't keep doing this to her. To myself. I hate that I keep hurting her, but I can't put myself through that again. I'm an infatuation. That's all. If I stop indulging it, she'll move on. I'm sure of it.

CHAPTER 17
HAMMER

"I need another martini." I tip my glass back and drain the last of it. I'm making bad choices tonight, like drinking too much. The past few days have been a lot of wallowing and dissecting what's happened between me and Hollis.

I've deduced that we're hot for each other, but Hollis is apparently a masochist with poor impulse control since he keeps doing things he says he shouldn't. These boundaries he enforces and then steamrolls are pissing me off.

"I also need another drink." Rix peeks over the back of the booth, presumably looking for her boyfriend.

"What kind of drink do you think I'd like?" Tally muses.

Rix looks back at Tally with a somber expression. "Don't rush to grow up, Talls. It's okay to enjoy your life in the phase you're in."

"Plus, drinking isn't that cool and the hangovers are stupid." Dred pats her on the shoulder.

"I always add club soda to my drinks to avoid the hangovers," Shilpa says.

"Water is the elixir of life." Hemi nods.

I spot Hollis by the bar with Dallas. "I'll get us another round."

"Aren't you the sweetest?" Rix gives me a knowing look.

"Everyone want another one?" I slide out of the booth.

Dred taps her bottle. "I will take another beer."

"I'm good." Shilpa shakes the ice around in her half-full glass.

"I'm also good," Hemi replies.

"One of these days you will have more than one drink," I tell her.

"Your birthday is coming up, isn't it, Hemi?" Tally asks.

Hemi gives her a look. "How did you know that?"

"Dallas mentioned it last week."

"Freaking Dallas," Hemi mutters.

As if he can hear us talking about him, he looks our way, gives us a chin raise, and winks at Hemi. She flips him off.

Tonight is the first time Hollis has been out of his penthouse since the accident. We haven't talked about what happened the other day, when Scarlet came on the TV and he promptly sent me home. But since then, I've done an unreasonable amount of research on them as a couple. It doesn't take a genius to see that relationship left him with scars on his heart. Not when one minute he's giving me long hugs that feel like there's so much more than simple comfort wrapped up in them and letting me take care of him, and the next he's telling me to leave. *Conflicted* seems to be his primary emotion when it comes to me. It's making me angsty, and I'm also inclined to be bratty—AKA the button-pusher, as Hollis likes to call me.

Tomorrow the team has an away game, so tonight they're out talking game strategy at the Watering Hole. My dad is deep in conversation with Ash, and Dallas has just gone to the bathroom, which means Hollis is currently on his own at the bar. I slide into the spot beside him and order a round of drinks.

He gives me a sidelong glance. "You look like trouble tonight."

I know this already. I picked my outfit for maximum button

pushing. I don't look at him when I reply. "You can't say things like that and not expect me to read into them."

He sips his beer. He must be off the pain meds. "You can't come to a bar braless and expect me not to notice."

My sweater is off the shoulder, which is bare. "You seem to be paying an awful lot of attention to my wardrobe choices lately."

"I'm trying to stay on the right side of the line, but it's hard when I want to gouge out every set of eyes that notices how good you look the same way I do," he grumbles into his glass.

I fucking love grumpy Hollis. I love it when he looks like he's thinking about doing naughty things to me. "So you admit you like my tits, Hollis?" It comes out way breathy.

"You're pushing it, Princess."

I think I love keep-doing-that-and-there-will-be-consequences Hollis even more than grumpy Hollis. "Bet you'd love to teach me a lesson or two about that, huh?" God, I'm skating the edge here.

He grinds his teeth.

The bartender sets a margarita, a martini, and a beer in front of me.

"I've got those." Hollis passes his card over.

"Thanks." My shoulder brushes his when I lean in close, dropping my voice. "By the way, broody and sexually frustrated is a good look on you. I look forward to fucking myself later to the memory of that exact facial expression." I wink, gather the drinks, and leave him glowering after me.

I'd like to say I don't know what the hell is wrong with me. But I'm horny as hell, probably getting my period, annoyed by how hot Hollis looks, frustrated by his unwillingness to budge from the we-can't-go-there stance, and maybe a little drunk. Definitely a little drunk since this is my third martini in less than two hours.

"Why does Hollis look extra intense?" Tally asks as I set the drinks on the table.

"The team doctor said he needs to stay home and rest during the upcoming away series," Hemi says.

"Really?" That's news to me. "When did he find that out?" I ask.

"Just before he got here tonight," Hemi explains. "It was not the calmest conversation from the little I could hear."

"Isn't the coaches' office at the other end of the hall?" Rix asks.

"Yeah." Hemi sips her water.

"Sitting on a bench for three hours in the cold probably isn't the best for a healing knee," Dred muses.

"I feel bad for him, even though he scares me. He's just so intimidating and serious all the time. I swear I've only seen him smile like five times ever," Tally says. "He was having such a great season."

"It hasn't been easy for him." It's like he's reliving last year all over again, and here I am being antagonistic. "His bark is worse than his bite, though." I steal a look his way, and he narrows his gaze before turning back to Dallas.

"I can attest to this. He's always been pleasant with me," Shilpa agrees.

"I totally crushed on him as a teen," I admit. And that sure hasn't changed.

"Really?" Tally's eyes light up. "I used to have a huge crush on one of my dance instructors. But I was thirteen." She folds her hands on the table and looks at me expectantly. "I want to know more about your crush on Hollis."

I shouldn't have said anything. Fuck me.

"How come this is the first I've heard of this?" Hemi asks.

We worked together every day for three months. We shared a lot of stories, and I learned a lot about the guys on the team, including how extensive her hate-on for Dallas is. But I did not share this. I would never share this.

"I don't know. I'm in drunk-blab mode, I guess." I shrug. "I pretended to be bad at algebra once because I found out Hollis was good at it."

"You *pretended* to be bad at algebra?" Rix makes it sound like I've committed a heinous crime.

"Yeah. I intentionally failed a test in grade nine and everything. I had this entire plan." At the time I thought it was genius.

"We need to hear about this plan," Hemi encourages.

Am I really going to spill the beans on this? "He'd been over one night while I was working on homework and I'd asked my dad for help. Math wasn't his jam, but apparently it was Hollis's. In my head I'd come up with this master plan that he would be my tutor and I'd get to sit with him for uninterrupted hours while he explained the Pythagorean theorem. And he did help me. But only once."

During that one session I got to stare at his profile and imagine what it would be like if he kissed me. And now I have firsthand knowledge. I would give my left nipple to feel his lips on mine again. To hear him groan, to have his tongue sweeping my mouth.

"Why only once?" Tally asks.

"My dad hired an actual tutor who was not cute or fun."

"That backfired in the worst way!" Rix chuckles.

"Totally. I brought my marks up in a hurry, but it took a month of twice a week sessions before my dad let me off the hook." And I never did something that stupid again. Until BDF —Batdick Fiasco, anyway.

"Does Hollis know this?" Hemi asks.

"That I faked being bad at algebra? Of course not."

"What about your teen crush? Does he know about that?" Dred asks.

"Oh, God, no." It's bad enough he knows I have the hots for him now. He doesn't need to know about my teen crush, or that it never really went away. I mostly admired him from a safe distance. But he was always nice to me when I was a teen. Kind. Gentle. Soft, when he could be the opposite with everyone else. I was always Princess. But like everything else, that nickname has shifted lately.

"I wonder what he'd say. I bet he'd be flattered. You're so beautiful, and fun, and smart," Tally says.

"Thanks, Talls. You're stunning and sweet and brilliant, and you should be told that often. Also, I would prefer to never find out how he feels about my teen crush."

"How who feels about your teen crush?" Tristan asks.

"That's not information you need," Rix says.

"Bea had a crush on me when she was fourteen, but I was too much of an idiot to see it, thank fuck, because I would have screwed that up hard back then." He inclines his head. "You're a goddamn saint, and I love you."

Rix smiles. "I love you, too."

"I need you to sleep over at my place tonight, so I can show you how much I love you with…" His gaze jumps to Tally for a moment before returning to Rix. "All of my body parts."

"Someone hide the cucumbers." Tally slaps a hand over her mouth and sinks down in her seat, eyes comically wide.

Shilpa looks confused and leans over to whisper something to Hemi, who shakes her head and mutters, "Later."

Tristan's mouth opens and closes. His cheeks flush. It's the first time I've ever seen him blush.

I pat his arm. "We already know we're going to hell; at least the trip will be fun."

He walks away and I swear the tips of his ears are bright red.

"Oops, sorry," Tally whispers.

Rix waves off the apology. "He'll survive his embarrassment."

"You know what we should talk about…" Hemi gracefully changes the subject.

"Not my sex life?" Rix offers.

"I disagree. I think we should definitely talk about Rix's sex life," Shilpa argues.

"Some things are better left to your imagination." Hemi rests her chin on her steepled fingers. "Let's discuss the gala."

"I got your email this morning. I'm staying on top of every-thing," I assure her. We have weekly planning meetings. I pull my newest checklist up on my phone. "I'm checking in with the Hockey Academy this week."

"Are you sure you don't want me to call? Or even Phillip or Dallas?" Hemi offers.

This will be the second follow-up call, but I want to be the one who secures attendees. I need this to be my baby, and I need to be the one who makes it amazing. "I can handle it, but I'll let you know if I need your backup."

"No problem. Usually, I'm on an intravenous coffee drip at this point with all the juggling. And it's proving more than anything that I need an assistant. My role has morphed so much over the past two years."

"That's because you're efficient, and you love the challenge of taking on new things," Shilpa says.

"This is accurate." Hemi sighs. "What about the date pack-ages? Do you need help with any of those?"

"Nope. I'm almost finished creating the packages for the auction, and all the restaurants are comping the meals." It's been fun setting up these experiences and tailoring them to the player.

"You are amazing. And having this all set up before the auction will make my life so much easier once the event is over. Hopefully an organized agenda will keep Flip from sleeping with whoever buys a night with him," Hemi grumbles.

"I mean…he's been better lately, so we can hope for the best," Rix says, probably cautiously optimistic.

Tally pokes at her lime.

"How much did he go for last year?" I ask.

"Seventy-four thousand," Tally offers. She looks around the table, cheeks flushed. "I think, anyway. And Dallas went for fifty-two."

"That was damn well magical to watch Fielding's great-grandmother kiss him full on the lips." Hemi laughs evilly.

"Your hate-on for him is vast and unyielding," I muse.

"Like the desert, brutal and unrelenting," Shilpa mutters.

"That's an excellent comparison." Hemi sips her water. "Is Hollis still on board?"

I asked him months ago, before...everything. I wasn't super excited about him going on a date back then, but I'm even less excited now. Especially since the date I designed for him is my personal fantasy. "He hasn't said anything about backing out."

"Great." Hemi leans in and drops her voice. "And you extended the invitation to Scarlet and her castmates?"

"I did, and I'm following up again this week." I felt like I was going to vomit the entire time, but I talked to her assistant.

"If you don't hear back, I can follow up. If she says yes, we can do some really cool cross-promotion. It'll elevate the event."

Part of me secretly hopes there will be a scheduling conflict and Scarlet won't make it. But the part that wants this to be the best gala we've ever had knows it would be fantastic if she could be there. I pull my scrunchie free from my wrist and finger the fabric. I found it the other day in Hollis's bedroom when I fed the cats. It smells faintly of his laundry detergent and body wash. I slip it back on my wrist before I give in to the urge to sniff it in front of my friends.

Rix grabs my wrist. "You found your favorite scrunchie! Where was it?"

"At Hollis's. It must have fallen out of my pocket." I wonder when he found it. And why was it on his dresser?

Tally's phone buzzes on the table, and she checks the screen with a sigh. "I have to go home."

It's a school night, and it's closing in on ten. She has a ten-thirty weeknight curfew.

"I'll drive you," Hemi offers.

"Are you sure? I know it's early."

"Absolutely. I have a coffee date tomorrow morning."

"Coffee date?" I ask as we all perk up. "With who?"

"Just some guy I met online. I need a date for this thing in the summer, so I'm starting on the mission early." Hemi shrugs into her jacket.

"Summer? But that's months away," Rix says.

"Ash's cousin could be a good option," Shilpa offers.

"I love you, and I love the offer, but I'm a lot of woman, and I don't want that kind of awkwardness if he decides I'm not his type." Hemi hugs Shilpa's arm.

"I think you're the perfect amount of woman, but I also understand." Shilpa's gaze shifts across the room to where Ash and Dallas are chatting.

"I need a good head start. Online dating is a nightmare," Hemi says. "Zero out of ten, don't recommend."

"I tried it once. Epic fail." Rix also grabs her jacket. "Speaking of potential nightmares...Tristan has been boring a hole in the side of my head for the past half hour. I should probably get him home before he drags me into the bathroom."

"Would he really do that?" Tally asks as we slide out of the booth.

"I'd like to think he wouldn't, but I can never be sure."

Tristan, who was on the other side of the bar three seconds ago, is suddenly at Rix's side. "We're going home, baby?"

She pats his chest. "Yes, we're going home."

"Thank fuck." He kisses her cheek then helps her into her jacket. "Ladies, have a nice night. Tell the guys I said bye." He takes Rix's hand before she can go in for good-bye hugs and drags her out the door.

"I want someone to want me that much." Tally has a dreamy, faraway look on her face.

"We all want that." Hemi pats her on the back.

"I have that, and it is glorious," Shilpa declares.

We say our good-byes, and Hemi's about to offer to drive me, but my dad is on his way out, too. Apparently, Hollis left a while ago. Before BDF, he would always stop to say good night to all of us before he took off. But like everything else, I guess that's changed.

I'm tipsy as I follow my dad to the elevator back at home—not so bad that I can't walk a straight line, but my brain is sloshy, and all I can think about is Hollis and that kiss.

"You'll keep an eye on Hollis this week?" Dad asks.

"Yeah, of course." The team leaves in the morning for the away series.

"Thanks, honey. He's doing better, but I think he's hurting more than he's letting on." We wait for the elevator to arrive. "I don't want him alone and stewing all week."

I swallow the sudden wave of guilt and wonder how much worse it must be for Hollis. He kissed me. I wanted it to happen more than I wanted my next breath. But the fallout isn't anything I planned for. Or how awful it feels to keep this secret from my dad. I force a smile, but it feels heavy. "He really wants to finish this season."

Last year was hard on him. My heart hurts thinking of the dark places his mind may go this time.

Dad nods, his expression softening, maybe misreading my guilt for empathy. "He might be able to get back on the ice if we make it to the playoffs."

"We can cross our fingers." I switch the subject. "Do you need me to tackle anything besides groceries and laundry while you're away? And did you leave me a list?"

"The list is on the counter."

"Should I pull out your spring wardrobe?"

"I know you've got a lot on your plate with school and everything else."

"I don't mind." If I don't rotate his wardrobe, his closet is a nightmare.

"Only if you have time. We still have some weeks with snow left. Before I forget, how's that Jameson kid? You planning a second date?"

"I think we're better off as friends." Even though he's the kind of guy my dad wants for me.

He kisses the top of my head. "That's too bad, kiddo. You deserve the best. Don't ever forget it."

I hug my dad and wish him luck when the elevator stops at my floor. The apartment is empty when I come in. Rix will spend the night at Tristan's. Unless they have early practice, it's where she sleeps when he's not traveling. It's only a matter of time before she moves into his place.

I flip the latch and lock the door behind me, heading for my bedroom. Since I have the place to myself, I can make as much noise as I want. I strip out of my clothes, shivering as the cool air caresses my bare, overheated skin. I retrieve Batdick from my nightstand drawer and my bottle of lube—I doubt I'll need the latter, but better to be prepared than fumbling around for it when I'm halfway to an orgasm. I also grab Hollis's hoodie from my dresser and lay it over my pillow.

I'm a little obsessed.

I climb into bed and pull up one of the folders on my phone. It's labeled STUDY MATERIALS. It's actually full of pictures and video footage of Hollis from games. I made a video compilation of all my favorite Hollis moments a while back. In many, he's squirting water into his mouth. I run my hand over my stomach as I settle in, then realize I still have my scrunchie on my wrist and free it.

As my video compilation plays, I run the soft fabric over my lips. The Hollis scent is slowly fading. As I watch him wipe sweat from his face and chew on his mouth guard—it should not be hot, but it is—I again wonder when he found the scrunchie and why he hadn't given it back. Especially when he knew it was my favorite.

I pause my video, and before I can rethink it, I hold the scrunchie in front of my bare knees, take a picture, and send it to him.

> **AURORA**
>
> Why was this on your dresser?

I hold my breath as the humping dots appear.

> **HOLLIS**
>
> Why were you in my bedroom? Again.

> **AURORA**
>
> Kitty love.

I'm being intentionally suggestive. The dots appear and disappear a few times.

> **HOLLIS**
>
> I thought we agreed that my bed wasn't your pleasure playground.

I bite my lip and press my knees together.

> **AURORA**
>
> I was referring to Postie and Malone. Good to know where your head is though.
>
> I've been a good girl and only used your spare bedroom. And I never leave evidence.

> **HOLLIS**
>
> Untrue. You left your scrunchie, and the constant change of sheets tells me all the things you don't, which is its own special brand of mindfuck.

His honesty is unexpected, and it emboldens me.

> **AURORA**
>
> What did you do to my scrunchie, Hollis?

> **HOLLIS**
>
> I washed it.

> **AURORA**
> Why did it need washing?

HOLLIS
I found it on the floor.

> **AURORA**
> Why did it end up on your dresser?

The dots appear and disappear several times.

> **AURORA**
> Did you do naughty things to my scrunchie?

HOLLIS
Go to sleep, little girl. You have class in the morning.

That's as good as a yes.

> **AURORA**
> Can you say that again in a voice message?

I hold my breath as I wait to see if he'll respond. A minute later, a voice memo appears.

His rasping command sends a shiver down my spine. "Stop pushing my buttons, Princess."

I listen to it on repeat while putting Batdick to use. And come twice.

CHAPTER 18

HOLLIS

> **PRINCESS**
>
> Do you need anything from the store?

> **HOLLIS**
>
> It's late and dark. Why are you going to the store?

> **PRINCESS**
>
> It's a two-minute walk. I need chips.

> **HOLLIS**
>
> What kind of chips?

> **PRINCESS**
>
> The kind I don't have in my apartment.

The team left for their away series two days ago, and Rix flew out to North Carolina this morning, which means Aurora is on her own this weekend. I don't love the idea of her walking to the store in the dark.

> **HOLLIS**
>
> I might have what you need.

I send it before I consider how it reads.

The dots appear and disappear several times before a message pops up.

PRINCESS

I think we've already established that, but in terms of chips, do you have all dressed or smoky bacon?

HOLLIS

I have both.

They're her favorite, so I always keep some in the pantry for when she takes care of Postie and Malone.

PRINCESS

I'll be up in a few.

I check to make sure my deodorant is doing its job and my hair isn't a mess. I shouldn't care how I look or smell. I should also not be this excited to see her. But she's been busy with school the past two days, so any interactions have been brief— and fraught with so much sexual tension, I feel like I'm choking on it.

Less than two minutes later, she knocks. Postie and Malone follow me to the door. Aurora stands in the hall with her banana duck bag slung over her shoulder, looking like the problem she is. She's wearing slipper boots and a pair of sleep shorts that are barely visible because she's wearing my favorite hoodie. She's had it for weeks.

"Hi." Her gaze moves over me. I'm wearing a T-shirt and jogging pants.

I try and fail not to allow the memory of how those lips felt on mine to surface. I clear my throat before I speak. "Hey. Come on in." I move aside. I'm still on crutches for at least another week.

"I brought up a few meals from the freezer. I can put this stuff away and grab the chips and be out of your way." She averts her gaze and tucks her hair behind her ear.

I hate that I've made it this way between us. I'm the one who keeps crossing the line and stepping back. We can hang out for a couple of hours. I can manage my hormones and my impulse control and avoid doing something that would result in Roman digging me a shallow grave.

"I was going to watch a movie, if you want to stay and keep me company," I say. "Unless you have other plans." The possibility that she might go out with that James kid again makes me want to punch something.

Her eyes flare. "I don't have plans."

My relief is instantaneous and problematic, but it's too late to backtrack, and anyway, I don't want to. Fighting the draw is exhausting. I'm tired of trying to keep all these walls up when it's so damn easy for her to break them down. "Good. Come on." I crutch my way to the kitchen. "Let's raid my snack cupboard."

Aurora puts the meals in the freezer, except for two, which go in the fridge. She follows me into the pantry. It's big enough for the two of us, but my crutches make it a tight fit.

She surveys the shelves and pokes at a half-empty container of salted-caramel chocolates. "Looks like someone's been eating his feelings."

"I won't be on the ice for a while, so I loosened the reins on my diet."

She unscrews the lid and nabs a chocolate, biting it in half before she offers the rest to me. "These are so good, but they're a lot."

I pop the other half in my mouth as she puts the container back on the shelf.

She grabs a bag of smoky bacon chips and another of gummy worms. "Anything else look tempting to you?"

My gaze rakes over her. Yeah, tonight is going to be an exercise in restraint.

"You shouldn't look at me like that if you don't want me to get ideas, Hollis."

"And how am I looking at you, Princess?"

She brushes by me. "Like *I'm* the snack."

Lately I live for these moments, when all the uncertainty and awkwardness disappear and Aurora is her saucy, beguiling self.

Then she turns back, and her expression shifts. She looks worried. "I'm sorry. I just...don't know where the lines are anymore. They keep moving, and I feel like I'm always two steps behind."

"You're not alone, Princess. I keep trying to stay inside them. It's pretty fucking impossible."

"Because I'm pushing your buttons," she whispers.

"Yeah." She doesn't realize she doesn't need to try to get my attention. She always has it. I grip my crutches, so I don't reach out and tuck her hair behind her ear. "But I like it when you do."

Her eyes lift, with hope I shouldn't want lurking in them.

"Let's just hang out and watch a movie and not pick apart whatever this is," I suggest.

"Okay. That sounds good."

Aurora pours a bowl of chips and fills another with gummy worms. Then she peers in the fridge, surveying my beverage options.

"There's a bottle of riesling in there," I say.

"Oh! My favorite." She retrieves it. "Do you want a glass?"

"I'll have a beer." I prefer red to white, but again, I usually keep a bottle on hand for Aurora.

"Are you completely off the pain meds?" she asks as she retrieves a wineglass and uncaps a bottle of beer.

"Yeah. Just the occasional anti-inflammatory when I've been on my feet too long." My knee is achy and sore, but I'd rather use cold compresses to manage the worst of it.

"That's good. You started physical therapy this week, right?"

"Yeah. I'll be hitting the pool a lot." Low-impact workouts are the best way to get my range of motion back and strengthen the muscles around the injury.

"Do you want me to avoid the pool, then?"

"I should."

She eyes me from the side. "Sounds like there's a but attached to that."

"I don't want you to avoid me." I miss my time with her. I miss her. She's become one of the most important people in my life.

"I don't want to avoid you, either." She picks up the tray of snacks and carries it to the living room.

Last year when I couldn't travel, she'd come over and watch the games. She'd tell me how excited she was to work with Hemi and the team, and how I'd be back on the ice by then, playing like the injury had never happened. For a while, she was right about all of it.

I lean my crutches against the back of the couch and take a seat. Aurora steps in with a pillow and tucks it under my injured leg.

"Would you like a cold compress?" Her hand rests on my shin.

The touch burns through my joggers, awareness waking up the rest of my body. "I'm good for now." I pat the cushion beside me.

Aurora leaves a foot of space between us, crossing her bare legs. The shorts disappear under the hem of my hoodie.

I force my eyes away and grab the remote, scrolling to the movie channel. "What are you in the mood for?"

She runs her hands over her thighs, fingers curling over her bare knees. "Um...action would probably be safest. Or maybe horror."

"You can't stand horror movies. They give you nightmares."

"Not all of them."

I tap the back of the hand closest to me, where her nails dig into her knee. "You're already bracing for jump scares. Let's scroll and see what's appealing."

"Sure." She keeps running her hands over her thighs. It's hard to keep my eyes off them. I'm hyper aware of the space between us, of the way she smells, of how close I was to giving in to the urge to kiss her after I ruined her damn date.

We finally settle on an action movie—lots of car chases and revving engines. But it's been a long time since I've watched this one, and I'd forgotten how much sex there is. So much fucking sex.

Every time another spicy scene, as Aurora calls them, plays across the screen, she crosses and uncrosses her legs. She also gulps her wine. And goes back to the kitchen for a second glass. I accept her offer of a second beer so I have something to hold on to.

Postie and Malone hop off the chair and follow her, expecting treats.

While she's refreshing our drinks, I rearrange myself, tucking my erection into the waistband of my joggers and adjusting my shirt so it hides my problem. I stretch my arm across the back of the couch, trying to relax. I should probably stop the movie or change it to something else. But then I'd have to admit she's getting under my skin.

When Aurora returns, the hoodie is unzipped, revealing a fitted T-shirt with *Princess* scrawled across the front. It's a wonder she still has it since I bought it for her years ago. She drops down beside me, closer this time, and stretches her legs out, resting her slipper-covered feet on the coffee table. The back of her head rests against my forearm. She reaches over her shoulder, fingers grazing mine.

"Is my arm okay there?" I ask.

"It's fine."

Postie and Malone join us, but Malone decides to pull his air-hump move on the arm stretched across the back of the couch.

"No, dude. Why can't you just be normal?" He bites me when I try to move.

"Must be something in the air tonight," Aurora murmurs. She hops up, moving the blanket to his chair and pats it. "Come on, Malone. Your sexy girlfriend is right here, waiting for your love."

"He's such a weirdo."

"At least he's not humping his brother," Aurora says with a smirk.

Malone takes the bait, and Postie climbs onto the arm of the chair, unfazed by Malone's antics.

Aurora returns to her spot beside me. Every time one of us moves or passes the snacks, we gravitate closer. My fingers brush her shoulder. Hers graze my thigh when she reaches across me for the remote to adjust the volume. Every accidental brush makes me want more.

A better man would put some space between us. Someone less selfish would end this and tell her to go home. But I am not that man. Instead, when she tucks her hair behind her ear and our fingers brush again, I link mine with hers and pull her closer. Her skin is warm against mine, and I feel every shaky inhale as she settles against me. I don't want to leave this moment where she's suddenly mine. I could do this with her every night— cuddle on the couch, watch movies, talk. I could be the person she comes home to. The one she sleeps beside.

I turn my head and breathe in her honey, banana, and coconut shampoo.

"Are you sniffing me?" Aurora whispers.

"Shh... Just watch the movie."

I catch her smile out of the corner of my eye as she snuggles deeper into my side. She fits so perfectly against me. I'm crossing all kinds of lines, but having her close like this makes me want to forget everything else.

Yet another sex scene flashes across the screen. They're frantic hands and mouths, tearing at clothes, pushing, pulling, heavy breaths and desperate kisses.

Aurora slides a hand between her thighs. "Did you remember there being this much sex?"

I clear my throat. "I haven't seen it in a long time."

"Me neither. Probably not since high school."

It's on the tip of my tongue to make a joke, but she pokes me in the ribs.

"No snide comments about how that probably feels like yesterday. I've been a high school graduate for almost half a decade."

"I've been a high school graduate for more than a decade and a half."

She makes an annoyed sound and starts to move away, but I wrap my arm around her shoulders and pull her against me. The movement catches her off guard, and her hand lands on my thigh. I drop my lips to her ear, relishing the closeness. "I'm not trying to be a dick, Aurora. I'm just stating facts."

I loosen my hold, but her fingers wrap around my forearm. I've lost the will to fight it.

Her fingers glide along my forearm, and I break out in a wave of goose bumps as they drift over the back of my hand. "Is this okay? Are we okay?" she whispers.

"We're okay." I curl my fingers around hers.

The movie ends, and the streaming service previews the second in the series.

Her lips brush my wrist. "The movie's over."

I stroke the edge of her jaw. "You can stay for another one, if you want."

She exhales a shaky breath. "I don't want to push so much that you do something you regret and tell me it's a mistake again."

"I shouldn't have said that." I drop my head. "I'm responsible for my own actions."

"What does that mean?" She tips her head, offering me access to her skin.

And I take it. I feel her pulse hammering against my lips. She smells so good, feels even better tucked against me like this. So I give her the truth, even if it's damning. "It means I could have made a thousand different decisions, but I chose to kiss you."

"Because I pushed you." Her breaths come faster, unsteady.

"Because I let you." I had every opportunity to walk away, but I didn't. I kept telling her no, but everything I've done contradicts my words. The electric draw is impossible to deny.

I sweep the contour of her bottom lip with my thumb, and her tongue peeks out.

The next movie has started, but neither of us pays attention to it.

Part of me realizes if I don't stop this, I could be exploding nearly a decade of friendship. But my career is circling the drain, my body is a fucking mess, and Aurora is the only thing that makes sense. And she's right here—so warm, and alive, and beautiful. I want this one good thing. Fuck what's right. Fuck blowing up my life.

I slip my thumb between her parted lips as her eyes lift.

I'm so screwed.

We both groan as her lips close around my thumb.

My cock kicks in my joggers. Her nails dig into my thigh.

She sucks, running her tongue over the pad. I remember every moment of that kiss. Remember how soft she was. How perfect she was. *Is.* I doomed myself by kissing her. I'll never forget it, and there will never be another who can compare.

She moans my name as I sweep my thumb along her plush bottom lip.

I press my lips to her temple. I've rejected her too many times already. Hurt her more than I've meant to. I can't do it again. I don't want to. "What do you need, Princess?"

"I don't know." Her hand slides between her thighs. "I'm so achy."

"Do you want me to help you with that?" *Fuck the conse-quences. I'd give anything to touch her right now.*

She sucks in a breath. "Hollis?"

I shift, dropping my feet to the floor. My knee is stiff from being straight for so long. I pat my lap. "Come here."

She turns, eyes wide and uncertain, like she doesn't quite trust me. It makes sense considering how hot and cold I've been.

I skim the outside of her left thigh. Her skin pebbles under my touch. "Is this okay?"

She nods, eyes searching mine.

I pat the space beside my right hip and wrap my hand around the back of her leg, above her knee, tugging gently. She follows the cue, straddling my lap.

"Am I okay here?" she asks.

I nod. "You're perfect, and so fucking beautiful." I tug the zipper the rest of the way down on the hoodie.

"So are you." She shrugs out of the hoodie and drops it on the couch beside us. "What about your knee?"

"It's fine," I assure her. I can only feel her right now. Nothing else.

She's braless again. Her T-shirt is tight, conforming to every curve, and threadbare, her peaked nipples visible through the pale, worn fabric. I run my hand up her bare leg and settle it on her hip. "Tell me where you ache."

She trails a finger over her breast. "Here."

I brush over the tight bud through the fabric. Her eyes flutter closed as she moans. It's the same sound she made when I kissed her. And it's fucking addictive. I want to be the only person she ever moans for like that.

"Anywhere else?"

Her eyes open, and she drags a shaking finger down her stomach, stopping at the apex of her thighs. "Here."

I pull her forward until she settles over my straining erection.

"Oh." Her eyes flare. "I feel you."

"Don't ever doubt that I want you, Aurora." It's as much apology as it is honesty. "Let me get rid of that ache for you."

She nods. "Please."

Our eyes drop as I move her up and down my cock through the barrier of our clothes. It should not feel this good, but hell if I don't want more of her little whimpers and moans.

"I can't believe this is really happening." She runs her hand through my hair as we find a rhythm. "I don't think I've dry fucked since high school."

My fingers dig into the soft, fleshy part of her ass as I level her with a glare. "Don't talk about other dicks while I'm rubbing you on mine." I am out of my mind with possessiveness when it comes to her.

A coy grin tips one side of her mouth, and she leans in until her lips are at my ear. "I like when you're jealous."

She has no idea. I slide my fingers into the hair at the nape of her neck, tugging as I rock her over me. "Such a little brat, aren't you?"

Aurora leans back until our eyes lock. "You love it."

"I fuckin' do."

"It's better than I imagined," she whispers.

I make a noise in the back of my throat as she drags her nails down the side of my neck and braces her hands on my shoulders. I could die with her hands on me, knowing it's me she wants.

"I think about you all the time. About you touching me," she admits. "In the shower, on this couch, in your bed, on your kitchen counter."

"What else do you think about?"

"About your mouth on me." She slides high, and the head pushes against her through layers of clothes. "How good it would feel to have your fingers inside me." She rolls her hips. "What it would feel like to be fucked by you."

If only she knew all the things I've dreamed of in the quiet dark of night.

She grabs her breast and tugs her nipple.

I cover the other with my mouth, sucking the tight bud through her shirt.

"Oh my God, yes." She grips my hair at the crown and moans. "Please, oh God, I think—I think...I'm so close, Hollis. So close."

She tries to move faster, so I tighten my grip, maintaining control. "Let it build." I bite her through the wet fabric, and she groans.

"It's so good," she breathes. "How can it feel this good?"

I know what she means. I shouldn't be close to any kind of edge, but the way she looks is unraveling me. Her cheeks are flushed, my hands molding to her soft curves, the heat of her pussy grinding all over my cock, her fingers in my hair. Her warm breath washes over my face with every moan. *She's mine. She belongs with me.*

"Does it feel good for you too?" she pants.

"Better than good, Princess."

She smiles at the praise.

"You're a goddamn vision." *Mine.* I adjust my grip, cupping her ass, fingertips meeting hot skin, close to all that warm and wet.

Her eyes roll up as her thighs start to shake. "I need, I need…" Her rhythm falters, and I take over, moving her faster and harder over my length. Adjusting my position so my good leg takes the weight.

She grinds down and throws her head back, one hand still fisting my hair, the other aggressively gripping her breast.

"That's it. Chase it." There's no coming back from this. It's so much bigger than stepping over the line. I'm obliterating it. I slide a hand around the back of her neck and press my thumb against her chin. "Look at me. Eyes on mine."

They roll down, hazy and unfocused as they find my face.

"That's it. Good girl."

Her mouth drops open, and a deep moan tumbles from her lips as she jerks and trembles. I feel the pulse of her pussy as I slide her up and down my cock.

And I'm right there with her, just holding back because I want to soak up every moment of this—commit it to memory in case this is the only time it happens. Because it should be a one-time thing. A never repeat. But she feels so damn good, so damn right. I don't want anyone else to see her like this.

Her gaze sharpens. Her eyes search mine, and it's as if she can sense how close I am. She grinds down on my cock, my face cupped between her palms. Her hair is damp at the temples.

Her breath breaks across my lips. But neither of us makes a move to kiss. Or take this any further.

"Do you think about me when you fuck your hand, Hollis? About what I did in your bed, and your shower?"

"All the fucking time. I can't get you out of my head," I admit. Months of images and filthy fantasies wash over me.

"Me neither, so I stopped trying."

The orgasm slams through me, stealing my breath and my vision. My hips jerk, and my fingers dig into her skin.

Aurora grips my chin in her hand. "Let me see you."

My eyes open. Her lips are a breath from mine. But still, she doesn't claim my mouth. Her gaze roves over my face, drinking me in the way I did her. All the tension leaves my body, and I melt into the couch. Aurora sags against me, both of us breathing hard, the movie still playing in the background.

Reality filters in.

I just dry fucked my best friend's daughter. And came in my pants. Like a teenager. I should feel like a giant bag of shit. And part of me does—the part that worries about what Roman would do if he found out. But a bigger part wants to do it again. Minus all the clothes. Take her. Claim her. Keep her.

Aurora is the first to move. She sighs and strokes my cheek as she leans back. "Thank you."

"Au—"

She puts a finger to my lips. "Shh... Don't say anything." She pinches my lips together. "I'm going to leave so you can manage the mess you made." She's so pleased with herself as she pats my chest and carefully climbs off me.

She grabs the arm of the couch to steady herself for a second. "Is your knee okay?"

"It's fine." It aches, but that's on me. "You should take the hoodie."

Her eyes follow mine to her chest. Her left nipple is visible through her shirt, thanks to the huge wet spot. "I'll grab one from the hall closet on my way out."

I start to push up off the couch. "I can walk you."

She raises a hand. "It's better if you don't. We both know you'll open your pretty mouth and say something to ruin my afterglow."

I rub my bottom lip and fight a smile.

"Thank you for the movie, Hollis." She crosses to the closet and flips through my hoodies until she finds one she likes. She sniffs the fabric before she shrugs into it and zips it up.

I like how it looks on her. So much. I also like that she wants to marinate in my smell. She pauses at the door and rolls her scrunchie off her wrist, sling-shotting it across the room. I catch it out of the air.

"I bought an extra, so you can do naughty things to that one until it stops smelling like my hair." And with that, she turns around and walks out of my apartment.

Opening Pandora's box has nothing on the massive crater I've just made for myself.

CHAPTER 19

HAMMER

Hollis and I dry fucked. Like a couple of high schoolers. If it weren't for the state of my panties the other day, I might believe it was a fever dream. Hollis didn't even really touch me anywhere illicit, apart from sucking on my nipple through my shirt. God, it was so hot. He looked so good, jaw set, eyes dark with lust, hands on my hips moving me over him. And then he ordered me to look at him when I came. Every time I think about it, my vagina feels like it's about to explode.

And then there's the fact that I made Hollis come. In his damn pants. Without even putting my hands on the parts that count.

Honestly, my ego is enormous. My head is an inflated balloon. And I'm so distractible these days. Yesterday I handed in a paper and forgot to attach my works cited. I resubmitted the assignment, but I hope it doesn't impact my grade. With everything that's been going on, a couple of my grades have slipped, and if I'm not careful, I won't have the average necessary to make the dean's list.

"Are you sure you're okay?" Hemi asks for the tenth time, affirming my distractedness. We met at a restaurant between school and the arena so we can eat and discuss the gala.

I blink myself back to the present. "Yes. I'm fine. Great. Awesome."

She leans back in her chair, crosses her arms, and gives me the face she usually reserves for Flip when he's done something to put him back in her bad book, or Dallas for being Dallas. "Your face is all red, and you're kind of sweaty. If you're coming down with something, please let me know. I don't want to run you into the ground, especially not with the gala coming up. Also, I don't have time to get sick."

"I promise I'm not sick." I roll my shoulders back. I can't let Hemi down, not when I'm the one who asked to take the lead on this event. "I'm here and focused."

"You're sure you're feeling okay?" she asks skeptically.

"Totally positive." I turn to my spreadsheet. "Donations for the silent auction are all accounted for, and all the guys have signed off on their date packages."

"Even Dallas?" Hemi asks.

"Even Dallas. Oh! And the Hockey Academy got back to me this afternoon." That this wasn't the first thing out of my mouth when I sat down proves how distracted I am. I can't afford to be a lovesick fool right now. "They're attending, and Kodiak Bowman and his wife will even be able to make it."

"That's fantastic! Why didn't you lead with that, you boss babe?" She high fives me.

"I don't know. In my head I'd already mentioned it maybe?" I shrug. "Anyway, Alex Waters and his wife are also coming, and possibly his son and his son's girlfriend. We have an entire table reserved for them."

"You're making it so easy for me to tailor a position just for you." She leans back in her chair, all smiles.

"I don't want it handed to me." *Or I'll forever be worried I don't deserve it like every whisper in the break room was true.*

"It won't be handed to you, Hammer. You've single-handedly taken over the entire gala while attending school full time. You have an impressive resume, and anyone who saw what you've accomplished would pick you up in a heartbeat." She snaps her fingers.

"That's good to hear." Proving that I'm not just the team princess, that I can work with the league and be an asset, was something I needed—for me, if not for anyone else.

"All we need is Scarlet to attend, and we'll have an all-star guest list," Hemi says.

"I have a follow-up call this week."

"Excellent." She leans in and makes a circle motion around her face. "Now can you tell me what's going on, because you're flushed again."

"I need to work on my poker face," I mutter.

She holds up a hand. "If you don't want to talk about it, that's totally okay. Just know I'm always here if you need me."

Hemi is a full-on badass. She's no-nonsense and takes no shit from anyone. But she's also a great friend, and we've gotten close since I interned with her. "I have a situation." I gather myself a moment. "It is not unlike Rix's. Minus the hate-fucking. And I'm not intentionally keeping it from you, but I don't know what's going on, and it's been a bit of a cluster."

Hemi's eyes narrow and then widen. "Oh. Oh, shit. Oh, holy shit. If this is about who I think it's about… Holy fuckballs."

We stare at each other for a few long seconds.

"I'm clarifying that you don't have the hots for Flip, right?"

I make a cringey face. "Oh, God, no. I mean, he's a nice guy, but no thank you to the nightmare that would be running into the endless string of women he's been with. I feel bad for him and the girl he eventually falls in love with. His regrets hole will be deep and horrible to climb out of."

"Okay. I didn't think so." She blows out a breath. "And it's not Dallas, right?"

"No. It's definitely not Dallas." Besides, I'm pretty sure Dallas has a hard-on for Hemi that rivals her hate-on. Sometimes I catch him looking at her the way I look at Hollis.

"I figured that was unlikely. Dallas is afraid of clowns, you know." She says it like he's committed an unforgiveable crime.

"Clowns can be creepy." I'm with Dallas on this one.

"I guess," she says grudgingly.

"You really can't stand him," I muse.

"I don't trust him as far as I can throw him. I've known him a very long time. He's habitually late for every endorsement campaign, and he blew one off completely. I tell him to be there at least an hour earlier than required so he isn't ridiculously late every single freaking time."

"I didn't know that."

"It's part of the job." She drops her voice to a whisper. "It's number fifty-five, isn't it?"

I nod.

She slaps the table. "I knew it!"

"Shh!" I flick her in the arm. "Keep it down."

"Sorry. So are you two like..." She makes a circle with her thumb and finger and pokes the index finger of her other hand through the hole.

I shake my head.

"But something is going on?"

I shrug. "I think so. But it's so complicated."

Hemi's back straightens, and she pales. "This has been going on for some time? You've had a crush on him for years."

Suddenly I understand Hollis's conflict in a way I didn't before. "Wherever your head went, that's not what's happening here. He's always, *always* been nothing but appropriate with me. He's tried to stay on the right side of the line. But it's like...I opened a door, and we both stepped through it, and now I don't know if we can ever close it again. And I don't want to, but I worry he's still several steps behind me."

She exhales a relieved breath and nods. "He's a good guy. A little bit of a black cloud at times, but I never picked up on any vibes between you until this season."

"You mean after the BDF." Batdick Fiasco.

Hemi shakes her head. "No, I mean since last year in the beginning of the season, when you started interning with me."

It's my turn to straighten. "How do you mean?"

"It was little things. I caught him looking at you like…he was seeing you for the first time." She gives me a small, empathetic smile. "It makes sense. You were dressed for business. You're smart, savvy, a natural in this industry. Everyone saw how competent you are. Him included. He's watched you turn into this self-assured, ambitious woman."

"It's messy." I rub my bottom lip.

She nods. "It is." She taps on the edge of the table. "Look, I'm not saying this to make things harder, but I want to be honest with you. If I were in your shoes, I would be careful. Dating players is highly frowned upon. Head office takes it very seriously. I know you don't want anyone to think your dad is the reason you get the assistant job and that's one of the reasons you've stepped in and taken over the gala. Proceed with caution, okay? The heart wants what the heart wants, but I would hate for you to have everything blow up in your face. Just because I know how hard you work, doesn't mean everyone else is going to see you for who you are."

"Why do you two look so serious?" Rix slides onto the empty stool and cringes.

"You're sitting down rather gingerly," Hemi observes.

"I actually bruised my ass, and not for the reason you think," she says before either of us can interject. "I was climbing on the counter to get something from the top shelf, and I literally fell, but I knocked one of those giant Post-It paper blocks on the floor in the process and landed on top of it. It really freaking hurt. Hurts. Still."

"I told Hemi about the situation." Keeping it to myself has been a pain in the ass anyway. Hemi is like a vault. Do I feel a little bad that Tally, Shilpa, and Dred don't know the details? Yes, but I think less people knowing is better for the time being.

Rix's eyes flare. "Did something else happen while we were away?"

"Something else? So things *have* happened?" Hemi is back on alert.

"I knew something was up. Spill the beans." Rix makes a go-on motion.

I glance around to make sure no one is paying attention, then lean in and whisper, "We dry humped."

Hemi and Rix's brows both try to touch each other in the middle of their foreheads.

"I didn't know it was possible for me to get off on a dry hump." I swear the look on Hollis's face tipped me over the edge. He seemed ready to eat me alive.

"I have no experience with this, but now I kind of want to try it," Hemi admits.

Rix's eyes light up. "What about Hollis? Did you leave him hanging?"

"I probably should have, shouldn't I?"

"He deserves it after the whole date-sabotage nonsense and the kiss business." Rix rolls her eyes.

"Kiss business?" Hemi asks, then raises a hand. "Don't feel obligated to tell me. I totally understand if you don't want to rehash everything."

"It's fine." I give her a rundown with all the ups and downs.

"Oh, you totally should have left him hanging. I mean, dude needs to shit or get off the pot." I appreciate Hemi's annoyance on my behalf.

"While accurate, that phrase isn't very visually appealing," Rix observes.

Hemi's eyes light up like she stumbled across a shoe sale. "I think we need to properly appreciate your badassery for a moment."

"In what sense?" I ask.

"You made a professional hockey player come in his pants

like a high school boy, while fully clothed. You're a fucking queen." Hemi smiles with pride.

"I was pretty shocked, to be honest." I grin. "And as soon as it was over and I could walk, I left. I didn't want to give him the chance to ruin my afterglow."

"Yeah, you did." Hemi high-fives me.

"Have you talked to him since? How long ago did this happen?" Rix asks.

"We haven't talked, and it's been two days." Normally we meet up at the diner when my dad returns from an away series, but he arrived while I was in class, so he came to campus and we ate there. Without Hollis. "But he texted today."

"What did he say?" Rix asks.

"That he had a doctor's appointment so he couldn't make the Pancake House."

Hemi nods. "That's true. Coach Vander Zee and Fielding were meeting with him after. It was on their calendar."

"Yeah, my dad said as much. I sent him a good luck GIF."

Hemi leans back in her chair, nodding. "Good on you for playing it cool. He has no control when it comes to you."

Rix taps her lips. "He's a rule follower, and he's used to being in control all the time, but you're making him lose it consistently. Just keep doing what you're doing. I think you two would be good together."

I don't know if my heart can handle it if we keep taking one step forward and two back.

"I do think we can help move things along, though. In your favor, of course." Hemi thinks a minute. "So I'm aware management is planning a birthday party for me."

Rix and I exchange a look. "That's supposed to be a surprise."

"It's hard to get things past me when I'm responsible for scheduling promotion around games. To be fair, they tried to use code words on the calendar, but my birthday falls on a Saturday this year, and it's between games, so it was pretty obvious." She waves a hand. "I haven't told them I know. From my sleuthing, I believe we're having a catered dinner so Tally can be part of the festivities. You don't need to confirm or deny anything, but this would be a good opportunity to go dress shopping."

"Yes to dress shopping," I agree.

We pull out our phones, and Hemi fires off a message to Tally, Dred, and Shilpa for a full-crew shopping trip.

A clip of Scarlet getting into a car flashes across the screen on the TVs across from our table. My buoyant mood deflates like a popped balloon, and I quickly look away.

Hemi tilts her head. "How will you feel about it if she's able to come?"

I exhale an anxious breath. "It'll be great publicity for the event." And good for my resume, but probably not for the welfare of my sweaty palms.

"That's not a real answer."

"I know." I bite the inside of my cheek. "She's already been invited. We can't take it back, and I don't even know what's going on with me and Hollis. I guess we wait and see?"

That isn't an answer either, but I can't admit to being jealous of his ex. It's clear we both have feelings, but that doesn't mean we'll end up together. Not if he can't get out of his own way. Or worse, if he decides Scarlet is worth a second chance.

CHAPTER 20
HAMMER

I t's late when I get home. Rix is staying at Tristan's, as is typical when he's not traveling. The end of the season is coming, which means I'll be minus a roommate soon. And I only have the apartment until November since it's a sublet, unless the owner decides to extend her stay.

On cue, my phone starts ringing. It's like my mom knows when I need to hear from her. "Hey, mom."

"Hey, honey. I'm missing my girl. How's school?"

Balancing classes and everything else has been hard, but I don't want her to worry. "It's been great, my projects are going well, and all my group members all pull their weight this year."

"That's so good to hear. I know it isn't always the case. Do you need anything? I can get you an appointment with the sound bath healer you like, just to center you and help with some of the stress," mom offers.

This is one of the ways she shows me she loves me. "I could probably go next week in the afternoon if he's available."

"I'll make the appointment. I can't wait to see you. I'm sorry our last visit didn't work out." I hear the sincerity in her voice.

That's the thing about my mom, she always tries her best, but it's hard for her to be a constant in my life when she's always on the move. I learned long ago the importance of accepting people as they are, though. She loves me the best way she can. "It's okay, Mom. North was sick and then you had that trip to the mountains, it was outside of your control."

"Still, I don't want to be away from you for this long. I can book a flight if you need me sooner than your birthday."

"It's okay. I just have a lot on my mind. And you'll be here soon enough."

"If you need to talk anything through, I'm always here," she says.

"I know, Mom. I promise I'm okay."

"Okay. I love you, honey."

"Love you, too, Mom. Talk soon?"

"Absolutely. I'll text you the appointment details."

I check my mailbox on the way up and find a package. I don't remember ordering anything, so the contents remain a mystery as I take the elevator to my apartment. Once inside, I flip the safety latch—Rix will go straight to work from Tristan's in the morning. I drop my keys in the bowl, toe off my shoes, and hang my coat in the closet before I tear open the package and dump the contents on the counter. Inside are three identical scrunchies. They're the same as the one I left with Hollis the other day, navy blue with a yellow banana print.

I press my fingers to my lips. It's well after eleven. Hollis is regimented about his sleep and usually doesn't stay up late, especially since he's spending a lot of hours on rehab.

I still send him a pic of the scrunchies along with a message:

AURORA

Are these from you?

He responds immediately.

HOLLIS

Yes. So you have spares in case one goes missing again.

AURORA

You're up late.

HOLLIS

So are you. Don't you have class in the morning?

AURORA

Don't you have physical therapy?

I startle when my phone rings and nearly fumble it as I answer.

"I know what you sound like and look like when you come, and it's all I can see and hear when I close my eyes." His voice is a seductive rasp.

"It's the same for me," I admit.

"You've been quiet since the other night," he says.

My conversation with the girls gives me the confidence to be honest. "I felt you needed the space, and I didn't want you to tell me it can't happen again."

His swallow is audible. "It probably shouldn't."

"But you can't stop thinking about it either," I finish as I cross to my bedroom.

"I really can't." He sighs. "Are you in bed?"

"I just got home. I was out with Rix and Hemi, but I'm on my way there. Are you?"

"Yeah. Is Rix at Tristan's tonight?"

"She is." I put my phone on speaker and drop it on my bed.

"So you're all alone." His voice is gravelly.

I almost suggest he come over and dry fuck on my couch, but it's too soon. Hollis can't handle a repeat yet. "Yup, it's just me." I lower my voice to a sultry whisper. "No one around to hear me moan."

He groans. "You can't say shit like that to me, Princess."

"If you can't stand the heat, Hollis, get out of my bedroom." I pull my shirt over my head. I fully anticipate another chastisement—secretly they're becoming my favorite—and then him hanging up on me.

"Are you getting undressed?"

"Do you really want to know?" I pop the button on my jeans, but I grab my phone from the bed and hold it close as I drag the zipper down.

"Fuck. You are." He exhales a harsh breath. "What have you taken off already?"

My nipples tighten. "Just my shirt."

"You wearing a bra?"

"Yes."

"Is the bralessness mostly for my benefit, then?"

"And to get a rise out of you."

"Such a bratty girl."

"I probably need to be taught a lesson." I press my fingers to my lips and wait.

"I should come down and spank the naughty right out of you."

"Yes, please."

He makes a sound in the back of his throat. "Not tonight. Take your pants off." I step out of my jeans and toss them in the hamper.

"What do you want me to take off next?"

"Pull your covers down first and get into bed," he orders.

I turn down my comforter in a rush, pillows tumbling to the floor, and clamber onto the mattress. "I'm in bed."

"Good girl. What do you have left to take off?"

"My bra, panties, and socks." I rub my thighs together. I'm pretty sure we're about to have phone sex.

"Hmm... Tell me about your bra and panties." His voice is deliciously compelling.

I look down at myself. I could lie and tell him I'm wearing a matching lace set, but honestly, I don't think that's what he wants to hear. "I'm wearing the same bra I had on the day you crashed my date."

He exhales heavily. "I still don't regret that. What about your panties?"

"They're boy shorts. Seamless with a blue and white cheetah pattern."

"And your socks?"

"Team colors."

"Take off the bra and panties but leave the socks on."

I give the phone a look, which he can't see, but I do as he asks. "I'm naked apart from my socks. Now what, Hollis?"

"Where to start?" He hums softly.

It sounds like he's moving around in his bed. I picture him shirtless, one hand tucked behind his head, the other fisting his generous erection.

"Where are your hands?" he asks softly.

I look down at my naked body. "The right one is cupping my breast."

"And the left?"

"Is fisting the sheets."

"I want you to bring that one to your lips."

"Which set?"

He chuckles. "The ones above your neck."

I follow the order. "Now what?"

"Drag them gently down your throat."

I do, shivering at the sensation, a soft moan leaving my lips.

"Such a good girl," he praises. "Now follow your collarbones until you reach your breast."

I do as he asks. "I'm there."

"Are your nipples hard?"

"Yes."

"I couldn't resist them the other night," he admits. "Circle the left one with your fingertip and pinch the right."

I suck in a gasping breath as the sensation ripples through my body.

"That's it. Do it again. That's the fucking sound I can't get out of my head," he growls.

I pinch and tug, circle and moan. "I need more."

"Trail your right hand down your stomach," he orders. "But slowly."

I groan and follow his command, sliding my fingers over my stomach, eyes closed, imagining it's his hands on my body, his fingers pulling at my nipple, skimming my stomach.

"Stop before you touch your pussy."

"I'm so achy, Hollis."

"I know, Princess. We're going to fix that," he cajoles.

I'm vibrating with anticipation. I can't get enough of his voice in my ear. My breath comes faster as I wait for the next directive.

"Drag one finger through your slit, but just one." His breathing is labored now.

I groan as I graze my clit. "Should I get my vibrator?"

He chuckles darkly. "Baby girl, you came from rubbing yourself on my cock fully dressed. You don't need your vibrator to get off."

He has a point. It's just a lot easier with assistance. "But you're not here to help."

"Don't worry, we'll get you there. Circle your clit, nice and slow, and tell me how it feels."

I rub lazy circles around the wet, swollen flesh. "Good. It feels good."

"Is it helping with the ache?" His voice is so soft in my ear.

"I need more," I whimper.

"Slide two fingers into that sweet little pussy."

I moan at the low timbre of his voice and his words. I curl my fingers, and it makes a liquid sound.

"Ah, fuck. I can hear that," he grunts.

I curl my fingers again.

"Yes. That's it. Good girl. Now rub your clit again, before you add another finger."

"I wish it was you. I want it to be you," I whimper as I circle my clit, harder this time, faster, chasing the wave of bliss. I'm panting now, my body covered in a sheen of sweat as sensation builds and spirals.

"Three fingers, Princess. Fill that pussy for me," he grinds out.

I start with two, curling once, twice, before I add the third. I bite my lip, used to muffling the noises I make.

"Stop trying to be quiet. I want to hear you."

I can picture him, muscles tight and corded, expression severe, his hand sliding up and down his cock. And I imagine what it would be like to be filled by him, to have his hands on my bare hips, moving me over him. Fucking me. Filling me. I gasp as I find that spot inside that makes fire rush through my veins. I press the heel of my palm against my clit and roll my hips while I curl my fingers. And I moan, long and loud as the orgasm gathers like a storm.

"That's it. That's the sound I want more of."

"I-I-I—" The words are lost as bliss washes through me, weighing me down and making me feel like I'm floating at the same time. I'm chanting *oh, God*, my body shaking, my hips rolling.

"Ah, fucking hell." Hollis's breaths come fast and hard. "Sweet dreams, Princess."

"Wait, what—"

He ends the call.

I'm still panting. My fingers are still inside me. My clit is still pinging.

I use voice-to-text to message him.

AURORA

Did you come?

It takes a minute before he responds.

HOLLIS

No.

AURORA

Why did you hang up then?

No response. It's not a surprise. I put on my brat hat and send two more before I leave him alone.

AURORA

Try not to be too hard on my scrunchie. Or yourself.

Sweet wet dreams.

CHAPTER 21

HOLLIS

I t's Hemi's birthday, and the entire team is out celebrating. Management took us to dinner so Tally could be part of the festivities, but now we're at a club so the rest of the girls can get their dance on. Aurora looks like temptation personified tonight. Her dress is killing me. *Fucking killing me.* So is the incessant boner I've had since she floated through the door, looking like the sexiest fairy princess I've ever seen. Her gauzy pale blue gown skims the floor. The bodice is intricate with lace and beading, and based on the thin straps I could snap with my fingers, she's braless. There's a slit up the right side, showing off her creamy, athletic thigh. That I've had my hands on, that has straddled my lap while I rubbed her cotton-covered pussy all over my cock.

As if her being fully clothed somehow made what I did less of a betrayal.

And now I can't get the other night out of my head. Can't erase the memory of her soft whimpers and deep moans, of the wet sounds, of my name on her lips when she came.

I thought I was fucked after the kiss. Then I thought I was even more fucked after the dry fuck. But the phone sex. *God, the fucking phone sex.*

"You all right, man? You seem a little out of it tonight. Pain levels okay?" Roman asks, like the good friend he is.

"Doing okay." My knee aches, but not unmanageably. I'm used to the stiffness when I first walk, to the familiar ache that fades after a couple of minutes. With four hours of physical therapy a day, regular massages, chiropractic, osteopathy, and a lot of time in the pool, my range of motion is returning. Does it mean I'll be able to get back on the ice anytime soon? Who knows.

"Something else eating at you then?" Roman presses.

I dry fucked your daughter while you were away and then had phone sex with her three nights ago and can't stop thinking about how much I'd like to do it again. But not over the phone.

She hasn't messaged me since, and it's eating me alive. She seems to be handling this a hell of a lot better than I am. I don't know what to say, and it feels like every conversation digs my hole deeper. But I don't want to climb out of it. "Just preoccupied is all."

"Fingers crossed you'll get the all-clear in time for playoffs." He claps me on the shoulder.

A woman recognizes us and invites me to the dance floor, but I politely decline.

"Why'd you turn her down? She seemed...fun."

"I'm not really looking for fun." The only woman I want, I shouldn't have.

"Does that mean you changed your mind about a certain starlet?" He's clearly on a fishing expedition.

Of course that's what he thinks. "No, my feelings on that haven't changed." She's texted a few times since I saw her. Once she suggested I visit her on set. Roman was around when I got that message and has been pushing me to give her another shot. He has no idea that I am obsessed with his daughter and already have my hands full. I'm definitely vying for the shittiest best friend of the year award.

"You worried about the gala?" Roman asks.

"Why would I be worried about the gala?" I've participated in the auction enough times to know what to expect. Although I feel conflicted about it this year. Usually, these dates end up being with someone's grandmother, or a couple who just want to talk hockey. The way Flip's date ended last year is an exception, and not the rule.

He gives me a look. "Didn't you read the email from Hemi? She sent it this morning."

"Uh, no. Why?" I had physical therapy this morning, followed by a barrage of other appointments, all meant to help me heal.

"Scarlet and a bunch of her castmates are attending."

My grip tightens on my scotch. I needed something stronger than beer tonight, with Aurora looking like temptation personified. "I didn't realize." That is not ideal at all. I don't want Aurora and Scarlet in the same room together, and now that's unavoidable.

I look over at the dance floor, where Aurora and the rest of the girls are. They're all dressed like princesses. Aurora must already know about Scarlet coming to the gala. Maybe that's why she's been quiet this week. I don't know how to define what's going on with Aurora. But I do know it's getting harder to stay away. She's breaking me, little by little, without even trying.

"Are you sure you don't have some unresolved feelings? You're pretty tense about it. I don't want to push you." Roman sips his bourbon.

I run a hand through my hair. Roman and I became fast friends when I was traded to Toronto seven years ago. He wasn't into the party scene the way so many of the players my age had been. He had a teenage daughter, no partner, and a lot of responsibility. I was nursing a broken heart and had no interest in a string of meaningless flings. Using sex to get over having my heart ripped out seemed like the worst possible idea.

I'd always been private about my love life, but even more so after Scarlet and I split. Mostly because the world had a front-row seat to that breakup. We'd been out for dinner when it happened, and the argument was caught on camera. Two days later she gave a statement saying we'd broken up, and it had been amicable, but more pictures of that argument circulated, along with speculation. My lack of comment only fed the rumors. Then I moved to Toronto. Put my head down and channeled all my energy into hockey.

"I don't have unresolved feelings about her," I correct. "I have unresolved feelings about how things went down when I was traded to Toronto."

The worst part had been seeing her on the arm of someone else less than two months after I moved. The breakup was enough of a gut punch, but that she'd gotten over us so quickly…that was a shot to the heart I hadn't expected. Knowing I loved her so much more than she'd ever loved me.

"You were young. You're in different places now."

"She's here for a few months, and then she'll move back to LA." Besides, there's already enough chatter on the hockey sites about her coming to games. She's always in the public eye, and with this new movie, that won't change. Not that it matters since I'm not interested in rekindling our failed relationship.

"Okay, I'll drop it." He sips his drink. "I need to plan something for Peggy. Her birthday is just around the corner. I can't believe she's turning twenty-one. It feels like she just graduated high school."

I wasn't at her convocation, but I celebrated afterward with her family. She'd already been accepted at her university of choice, with a scholarship. Things had been different back then. She was still a kid.

"She give you any hints about what she wants to do to celebrate?" Whatever it is, she'll want Tally involved.

"Her mom's coming to visit, but I'm keeping that a surprise —unless Zara can't contain her excitement and ends up telling her. It's been a few months since she's seen her."

"Is she coming on her own, or bringing North with her?"

"Pretty sure he's coming," he says.

"Are they staying with you?"

"If it's just the two of them, yeah."

"It still blows my mind that your ex and her partner stay with you when they visit."

He shrugs. "It's easy because she and I weren't meant for each other. If we hadn't had an amicable split, it would be different. She's a great mom to Peggy, and we get along better as friends than we ever did as a couple. Besides, her lifestyle and mine don't mesh. I'm not the sharing type."

"Yeah, me neither." I sip my drink.

Zara is a total free spirit. She's been in an open relationship with North for as long as I've known Roman. Sometimes when they visit, they bring an extra friend along and stay at a hotel. I don't pretend to understand the dynamics since half the time the extra "friend" is a woman and half the time it's a man, but it seems to work for them. Personally, the idea of sharing Aurora with someone else makes me feel homicidal. Not that she's mine.

Dallas drops into the chair beside me and chugs a bottle of water. The hair at his temples is damp with perspiration, and his dress shirt is open at the collar. "Roman, you look like a bodyguard. Hammer is safe out there. The entire team knows better than to hit on her."

"She would never date a player anyways. I would never allow it," Roman adds.

I choke on my scotch.

Roman claps me on the back. "You all right?"

"Just went down the wrong pipe." Six months ago, I was playing bodyguard along with Roman.

Tristan is out there with Rix, grinding her body against his. When she tries to spin around, he grabs her hip and drops his mouth to her ear. She melts against him. I look away and my gaze snags on Shilpa and Ash. They're slow dancing even though it's a high-energy song, oblivious to everyone around them. What I wouldn't give to be able to touch Aurora like that.

"Why aren't you two out there?" Dallas asks, pulling me out of my head.

I point to my leg. It's the only excuse I have right now to keep me from doing something I shouldn't.

"I don't dance." Roman polishes off the rest of his drink.

"Untrue. I've seen you out there before." Dallas finishes his water.

"Amendment: I don't dance unless I'm drunk, and we have practice tomorrow, so getting shitfaced is off the table."

"Suit yourself." Dallas hops up and heads for the girls.

Roman pulls his phone from his pocket and frowns. "Shit. I missed a call from my agent. I need to check my voicemail. You mind watching Peggy's purse thing?" He pushes the tiny, pale blue clutch across the table.

"Sure, no problem. Take your time."

He heads toward the exit, and I settle back in my chair, scanning the dance floor as Aurora's favorite song comes on. Her gaze catches on her dad's empty chair as she looks my way, and she crooks a finger, inviting me to join them.

I shake my head. It doesn't matter that it's all I want—to go to her. To touch her freely.

She leans in and says something to Hemi, who nods. And then she's slipping through the crowd, weaving between bodies as she heads for me. Her hair is damp at the temples, her skin glistening. She's just so fucking beautiful.

She leans down, lips skimming the shell of my ear. "Why are you all alone?"

I turn my head, our cheeks brushing. "Your dad needed to check a message. His agent called."

"Come dance with us." She leans back, eyes moving over my face. She's been drinking, but she's not drunk.

I drag my tongue across my bottom lip. "It's not a good idea, Princess."

"I'm not asking you to fuck me on the dance floor, Hollis. Just come dance for one song. Have a little fun. You know if it's his agent, he'll be a while. You always used to dance with us. It's my favorite song. Pretty please." She bats her lashes.

I'm so weak for her. "Just this song."

She grabs my hand and pulls me out of my seat. It's something she's done in the past. But the innocence of it is gone, replaced with an awareness that didn't exist before. We move through the pulse of hot bodies, sweat and perfume and cologne mixing, but I can still smell her shampoo. I put a protective hand on her waist as we weave through bodies. She pauses, fingers lapping mine as she looks around. Even with heels, she's not quite tall enough to see over the heads of others.

I bend until my mouth is at her ear. "They're about twenty feet to the right."

She shifts until her back is flush with my chest. "Can they see us?"

"If they were looking this way, they could." My heart is thundering in my chest. I should step back, but I don't want to lose this connection, even though it's a dangerous game we're playing.

"But they're not?"

"For the moment."

She moves my hand to her hip, her ass pressed against my growing erection. My fingers grip her automatically. I can feel the heat of her through her dress.

"It's too public a place, Princess. Whatever you're thinking, it's not a good idea." But fuck if I don't want it to be. I want to kiss my way up the column of her throat. I want to take her home and peel her out of this dress and make her come again. I want to make her mine and never let her go. But Roman's words dig at me. *She would never date a player. I would never allow it.*

"If you'd get out of your own way, it would be a perfectly excellent idea." She releases my hand. I follow as she slips through narrow gaps and try to catch her wrist, but she's just beyond my grasp.

When we reach the group, Aurora pulls Rix away from Tristan, and the two of them start dancing together. It's borderline obscene. Which is the point.

Tristan stands beside me with his arms crossed. "I can't decide if this is payback or foreplay."

"Probably both. You two are good, though, yeah? And you and Flip are back to normal."

He glances at me out of the corner of his eye. "Yeah, to all of the above. It's easier now that me and Flip aren't living in the same space. We're both in therapy so that's good. He and I aren't all the way back to normal yet, but it's better that I can't see what he gets up to. Mostly it's conflicting, you know?" He turns to me. "Actually, you probably don't, since you and Roman haven't done the kind of shit me and Flip have." He sighs and rubs his bottom lip. "It's a tough situation to navigate. Flip knows more about me and what I like than he should, and I know more about him than I should. But I love Bea more than anything, and he knows that, so the rest we try to either ignore or look past."

"It's good you're working things out."

"Yeah, it is. I was my own problem. Sometimes I still am."

"We all are." Isn't that what Aurora meant when she said I should get out of my own way? Maybe she's right.

I watch as Rix and Aurora sway to the music, laughing, Aurora's hands on Rix's shoulders and Rix's on Aurora's hips. What I wouldn't give to trade places with Rix. I want to believe Roman would get over it the way Flip has, but I don't know. In some ways, Rix ending up with Tristan is more fucked up, considering his history with Flip. Those two have seen sides of each other that complicate things. But Aurora is so young. What she wants now could change, *should* change with time and experience. I don't want to complicate her relationship with Roman.

"Oh, fuck, dude."

I look over at Tristan. He's staring at me with something like understanding, empathy, and pity. The last time I saw this look on his face was when they carried me off the ice a few weeks ago. "What's going on?"

"Now it all makes sense."

"What makes sense?" Maybe he's drunker than he looks.

"Don't make the same mistake I did. I caused a lot more hurt than I needed to."

Panic makes my throat tight. Back when Tristan and Rix were still hiding what was going on, Roman called him on it. I didn't find out until after shit hit the fan that he already knew, but I hope this isn't Tristan telling me he thinks he knows what's going on with me and Aurora. I don't even know what's going on. Only that it's become impossible to stay on the right side of the line. "What are you—"

I startle when Roman's hand lands on my shoulder. "Hey, man, do you have Peggy's clutch? Is everything okay?"

I hold up the clutch, then point to Aurora and the girls. "Yeah, just keeping an eye on things."

"Thanks for making sure she stays out of trouble." Roman makes a constipated Kermit the Frog face when Aurora starts twerking in her princess dress. "I gotta head out. I'm meeting with my agent in the morning."

"Is everything okay?"

"Yeah, just a couple of things we need to discuss. You staying a bit longer or you want to come back with me?"

My knee is starting to ache, and sticking around means Tristan can grill me. I don't want to do something stupid, like actually confide in the guy. And being this close to Aurora without putting my hands on her, kissing her, is pushing me to the edge. The wave of guilt is more than I can deal with. I'm screwed all the way around. "I'm ready to go," I say, though it's not really true.

We say our good nights and leave Tristan, Flip, and Dallas to watch over the girls. Roman tells Aurora to text him when she's home. He passes out on the ride back to our place, probably because of the bourbon. He's bleary eyed on the ride up to the penthouse, mumbling good night as he lets himself into his place.

I feed Postie and Malone as soon as I walk through the door. Then I hit the shower and whack off to thoughts of Aurora, feeling guilty as fuck when I come. I change into a T-shirt and joggers, turn on the TV, grab an ice pack, and sit on the couch, flipping channels until I find the news. Postie kneads my legs until he deems them appropriately tenderized, while Malone humps his blanket and I scroll through social media, checking Hemi's feed. Half an hour ago, she posted a picture of her and the girls at the Pancake House across the street.

Rix will stay at Tristan's tonight. Aurora's probably home by now. I war with myself to stay where I am. To not give in. To not be weak.

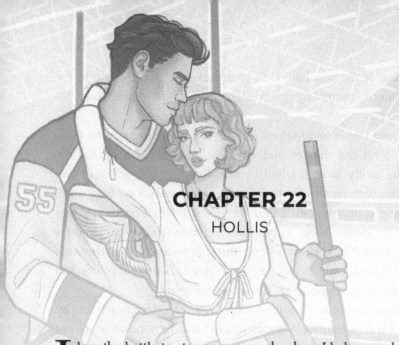

CHAPTER 22

HOLLIS

I lose the battle to stay on my couch where I belong and grab my fob. I'm not thinking about consequences as I step into the elevator and push the button for Aurora's floor. If she doesn't answer, I'll go back to my place, jerk off again, and go to bed.

But she does.

The door only opens a few inches because the safety latch is engaged. She's still wearing the princess dress. "Hollis?" She looks up at the latch. "You better not be here to give me a speech about why what I did on the dance floor was a bad idea. No one could see me."

I shake my head. "That's not why I'm here." Of course that's what she thinks. It's what I've done every single time I've lost control—let her feel like she's responsible for my inability to handle myself around her. It's her way. To own things that aren't hers. I need to remember that.

"Hold on." She closes the door and opens it all the way. "Is everything okay?"

I grip the jamb. "Yeah. No. I don't know." I close my eyes for a second. "You can tell me to go."

"It's okay." Her expression softens, and she steps back. "Do you want to come in?"

"Is Rix at Tristan's?" I'm teetering on the edge. Rix being here would save me from making more decisions I can't undo.

"For the night, yeah."

I'm still standing in the doorway, still trying to do the right fucking thing. I should tell her I wanted to make sure she made it home okay and leave. I shouldn't complicate her life like this. I want her to turn me away; I want her to ask me to stay more.

She gently pries my fingers from the jamb. "Please come in."

The wave of relief is damning. I cross the threshold, and she closes the door behind me, locks it, and re-engages the safety latch.

"Talk to me."

And despite everything I've put her through these past weeks, she strokes the edge of my jaw, her touch tender, and exactly the balm I need. "Not being able to touch you, kiss you, be near you is torture."

Her breath leaves her on a surprised exhale, and she moves closer, until our bodies almost touch. "I'm right here."

I cup her cheek in my palm, the contact electrifying and soothing. "Is this okay?"

"Of course it's okay. This is what I've been waiting for." Her fingers drift along the side of my neck. "Aching for."

"You look so beautiful tonight. Staying away from you is wrecking me." I brush my lips over hers, and like the first time, my entire body breaks out in a wave of goose bumps.

Aurora spears her hands into my hair and tips her head, parting her lips for me as I stroke inside. I mean for it to be soft, but the moment our tongues meet, we both groan. It's weeks of pent-up tension, desire, and need colliding. Hunger takes hold, and the desire to devour, own, and claim rules me.

I spin her around, pressing her against the door. My good knee finds its way between her thighs, and she rolls her hips on a wanton moan. It shouldn't feel this good, this right. But God help me, I want her, want to watch her unravel for me again, want the sound of my name on her lips when she comes. Want is all I am when I'm near her.

The kiss grows frantic, heated, volcanic. One of Aurora's hands leaves my hair and moves over my shoulder, fingertips gliding down to my forearm. She moves it to cup her breast, arching into the touch as she rubs herself on my thigh.

"Please, Hollis," she whimpers as she finds the hem of my shirt and eases a hand up my side. My skin burns in the wake of her touch.

I can't get to her breast without doing damage to her dress, so I skim the curve of her hip until I reach her thigh, which is hooked around my leg. I slide up and under, squeeze her bare ass, and run my hand back down until I reach the bend in her knee. I tug, but she's determined to stay wrapped around me, possibly trying to get herself off on my thigh with the way she's riding it.

I break the kiss, my thumb pressing into the soft spot under her chin until she tilts her head up. I brush my lips over hers. "Let me take care of you."

Desire makes her eyes heat. This time she doesn't resist when I tug on her knee, bringing her foot to the floor again. I drag my fingertips up the outside of her bare thigh.

"You in this fucking dress." I suck her bottom lip, dragging it through my teeth. "Has been breaking me all night."

"You like it, then?" Aurora's palm slides up my back.

I stroke the edge of her jaw. "Like is an understatement. You're too much to resist. You steal my breath." I skim the inside of her thigh with my other hand until I reach the apex and brush over satin.

Her eyes flutter closed. "Oh, please."

I cup her through her panties. "Tell me what you want, Aurora."

"What I've always wanted. You." She pulls my mouth to hers, tongue pushing past my lips, greedy and desperate.

I rub her through her panties, barely there caresses that light her up, but won't send her over the edge. The fabric grows damp, and her nails dig into my skin.

"Please touch me." She bites my tongue and sucks. "Please. Oh, God." Her hips roll and jerk again.

I shift the fabric aside, skimming smooth, soft, wet skin until I find her swollen clit. Aurora's eyes roll up, and her knees buckle. She scrambles to grip my shoulders as I wrap my other hand around her waist. Once she's secure, I tap the outside of her other thigh. "Wrap this around my waist, Princess."

"What about your knee?" she asks, even as she complies.

"Don't worry, it's fine." Layers of satin and gauzy fabric slip over my arm as I adjust her stance, cupping her ass to keep her in place and open her for me.

Her protest dies as I stroke between her thighs and her head falls back, eyes fluttering closed. "Oh, God, it feels so good. I knew it would."

I kiss a path up her throat. "Open your eyes. I want to see you."

Her hazy, lust-soaked gaze meets mine.

"Good girl." She shudders when I drag my fingers lower and circle her entrance. "Tell me how it feels."

"Like...like..." One hand curves around the back of my neck and the other moves over my shoulder and down my arm again. "Please don't stop. I need more."

"I'll give you more." I keep circling her entrance. I've dreamed about what she would feel like under my touch. "Just tell me how it feels and what you need."

"I'm on the edge already, and you've barely even touched me. I'll never get enough of your hands on me. I want them everywhere. I want you inside me, filling me, fucking me."

"Like this?" I ease a single finger inside, groaning at how soft and warm and wet she is. She's so snug around that single digit. How tight would she feel stretched around my cock? I've never wanted anyone the way I want Aurora.

Her nails bite into the back of my neck and her mouth drops open as I curl—once, twice, a third time. "Oh my God, yes."

I ease out, and she clutches my wrist. "Don't stop. Please, don't stop," she whimpers.

"Not until you're coming all over my fingers." I circle her clit again, gentle caresses that drive her wild. I want to own her pussy.

Her hold on my wrist tightens. "More. Harder."

"So demanding." I slide two fingers inside her and curl them, finding the spot that makes her legs tremble while I press my palm against her clit. "Is this better?"

"Better," she pants. "But I still want more."

Her face is flushed, her eyes hot with need. I need this as much as she does. Maybe more. I love seeing her like this, completely uninhibited, demanding, needy. I drink in the sight of her—the way her chest heaves with every panted breath, the way her gaze moves between my face and the hand working between her thighs. How good would it feel to be inside her? To be surrounded by her? How fucked would I be then?

Her head lolls against the door, but her gaze stays locked with mine.

Her tongue drags across her bottom lip. "More, please."

"Such a greedy girl." I add a third finger, and she moans, grinding on my hand, her juices dripping into my palm. It makes me wonder what else she'd let me do to her. How she'd bend and whimper just for me.

"Oh, fuck, that's—" She sucks in a breath as I curl my fingers. "It feels so good, Hollis."

She pulls my mouth to hers and releases my wrist. The sound of a zipper being dragged down follows, and then she tugs at her bodice, freeing her breast. I break the kiss, eyes dropping as she pinches her nipple roughly.

I dip down and suck the tight peak.

Her hand slides into my hair, gripping tightly. "Oh, God...

Oh my God... I can't... I'm—" The words get lost in a moan as she trembles and clenches around my fingers. Her eyes fall closed as her body quakes.

I squeeze her ass, fingers dangerously close to that space between her cheeks. "Eyes on mine, Princess."

They open, pupils dilated with desire. She claws at my arm, sinking into my hand as she gives herself over to the sensation. I adjust my grip, taking her weight as she rides it out and then sags against me.

"Holy fuck." She pulses around my fingers, the orgasm slowly waning. "That was..." She licks her lips. "Not an experience I've had before."

I brush her clit with my thumb, and she jerks. "I can't—"

"Can't what? Come again?" I release the thigh around my waist and let it slide to the floor. "I think you can. Let's see who's right." I wrap my arm around her and start again.

I circle her swollen clit, gathering more of her wetness. Teasing her and driving her wild with every purposeful caress.

"Arms around my neck," I rasp with shredded control.

Her smell is everywhere. She bites her lips and gazes up at me like I rule her entire world.

"Don't drop your hands. Don't move them. Do you understand?" I love the subtle nod, like she can't do anything except feel my hands on her. Fire licks at my chest as if it can burn us both from the inside out.

I run my tongue up her neck and whisper in her ear, "This pussy is mine. Do you feel the way my fingers fill you?"

Shivers wrack her body with every word. Rubbing her clit in strong focused strokes, I up my intensity. My breath comes harder.

"Can you imagine how hard I'd fuck you? How I'd cage you in and hold you tight so you couldn't squirm away from every orgasm I want to give you? How no part of you would be left untouched?" Thoughts of licking her, caressing her, owning her cascade through my mind. Her bent over with her wrists held behind her back. Her underneath me as I pound into her like it's the only thing I've ever cared about.

"Oh my God." Aurora's eyes flare, and she claws at my shoulders, trying to find purchase as I finger-fuck her to a second orgasm. Mostly because I want the satisfaction of being right.

She's a ragdoll in my arms as I gently ease out from between her thighs, wipe my hand on my jogging pants, then dip down and slide my arm behind her knees.

She clutches my neck. "What are you doing? Put me down! Your knee."

"My knee is fine." And Aurora isn't particularly heavy. She's close to five-nine, lean, and athletically built, but I can bench heavier. Would my physical therapist be annoyed if she found out I'd been lifting a hundred and fifty pounds? Probably, but my fucks-to-give meter about that is at zero.

"You're limping. I can totally walk to wherever you're taking me. Down. Now."

I set her feet on the floor. She maintains her hold on my shoulders as she tests out her legs. She wobbles and stumbles into me.

I settle my hand on her waist. Half of her right breast is still exposed, a hint of nipple peeking out. "What were you saying about being able to walk?"

"I'm getting my bearings." She gives me a look and pokes my chest. "Stop looking so impressed with yourself."

I take her face in my hands and slant my mouth over hers. She sways into me and moans when she feels my erection pressing against her stomach. She pulls back, eyes heavy with lust all over again. Her hand slides down my chest, and she cups me through my joggers. "I want that."

I gather both of her hands in mine and bring them to my lips. "Not tonight."

Her face falls. "Why not?"

I kiss her fingertips. "Because tonight is about making *you* feel good." And if she gets her hands on me, I'll embarrass the hell out of myself. "Let's get you into bed."

She drops her head and peeks up at me through her lashes. "Are you leaving?"

Sleeping here isn't a good idea. Not when Roman could let himself into my place and realize I couldn't have gone far with my car keys and phone sitting on the coffee table. That isn't how I want him to find out about this. "I can stay until you fall asleep. How about that?"

"Okay." She links our pinkies and leads me to her bedroom.

I've seen the one in her dad's place. It does look like Barbie decorated it while on an LSD trip. Her current bedroom couldn't be more different. She has an abstract painting of a woman looking over her shoulder on the wall across from her bed. Her furniture is dark wood, and the color scheme is blue and pale gray. It's feminine and sexy.

She closes the door and reaches behind her, unzipping her dress the rest of the way. The fabric pools around her feet, leaving her in pale blue panties that match it.

She's a fucking vision. Toned and strong and curvy. I don't know what happened to the uncertain girl I was dealing with back in January, but she's transformed, and in her wake is this self-assured woman I can't get enough of. She closes the distance between us and fingers the hem of my T-shirt.

"What are you doing?"

"Getting ready for bed." She tugs my shirt. "And I want to sleep in this." I raise my arms and she steps forward, bare breasts brushing my chest.

It takes every ounce of my restraint not to pick her up, wrap her around me, and get naked along with her. But I'm in way deeper than I ever meant to be. And I don't want to give in to the draw, only to have to sneak out in the middle of the night, leaving her to wake alone.

That I'm acknowledging this, already planning a way to get a whole night with her, is telling. I want this. I want her. And not just for a night, or a week, or a month. I'm past casual relationships. I want someone I can rely on. Permanence.

But she's too young to be saddled with what I'd have to give her. A heart and body covered in scars with no idea what the future holds. And then I'll be right back where I was when I was traded to Toronto. I'm not ready to face that reality when everything else is still so unsettled.

So instead of telling her what I want, where I'd like to see this go, I let her take my shirt off and pull it over her head. She's swimming in fabric. The sleeves nearly reach her elbows, and the hem ends above her knees.

I arch a brow. "You expect me to leave here shirtless?"

She bites her lip and crosses to her closet. A moment later, she returns with another T-shirt. This one has the team logo on it. "You can put this on." She hugs it to her chest. "But not now. Before you leave."

"You want me to wear one of your dad's shirts?"

She ducks her head, her cheeks flushing. "It's not my dad's."

"You've been stealing my shirts." Fuck. That does something to me, makes me crave the fantasy world where she wears just my shirts every night.

"I always bring them back. After they stop smelling like you."

I close the distance between us and tip her chin up until her eyes meet mine. "How long have you been doing this?"

Her gaze darts to the side. "A few months."

"Before or after I found out you were getting off in my bed?"

"Before. And that only happened once—me getting off in your bed, I mean."

"You've been naughty, haven't you?"

She nods, her grin coy.

I exhale harshly, trying to keep a leash on my hormones. One of these days I'll break and give her what she's asking for. I take the shirt from her, swat her ass, and give her a nudge toward the bathroom. "Brush your teeth and get ready for bed, little girl."

"Okay." She rushes across the room, pulling the bathroom door closed behind her and turning the lock.

Smart girl.

I move across the room to her dresser. There's a small bowl with a collection of scrunchies. I pick one up and bring it to my nose. It doesn't smell like Aurora, but my fingers sure do. I put it back and glance at the small cluster of framed photos. There's a recent one of her and the girls at a game, and another of Aurora with her mom and Roman. I took the photo last year on her twentieth birthday. The third is a picture of me, her, and Roman at the diner. This one was taken pre-Batdick. I'm hit with a crushing wave of guilt.

It's about more than hiding shit. I'm in so deep, and these feelings... I have no idea if I'm just an infatuation for her. Finding out how she really feels is like jumping off a cliff and I'm fucking terrified. No clue if we're on the same page. Hell, I'm still struggling with the page I'm on. If I could give her the stability Roman wants for her, would he be okay with it? Or am I fooling myself into believing the impossible?

Aurora wraps her arms around me from behind, cheek pressed against my back. "Please, please, *please*, don't tell me this was a mistake."

I turn around and cup her face in my hands. She lets me tip it up, but her eyes are closed. "Please, Hollis." Her voice is a broken whisper.

I would rather have my heart ripped right out of my chest by the woman in front of me than make her cry again. It's a damning realization. There's no way out of this without someone I care about getting hurt. But I'd rather it be me than her.

I stroke her cheek and press my lips to hers. "Baby, look at me."

She opens her eyes, and the fear in them makes my heart feel like it's been put in a vise.

So I give her as much honesty as I can. "This should feel like a mistake, but it doesn't. At all." It feels exactly right. And that scares the shit out of me. I kiss her softly, slowly, but break it before we can get too carried away. "Bedtime, Princess. You have a meeting with your group in less than eight hours, and we both know you're grouchy when you've had less than six hours of sleep."

"I knew I shouldn't have given you access to my calendar," she gripes.

She did that when she started taking care of Postie and Malone. She turns off the lights, except for the lamp on her nightstand. I pull back the sheets, and she climbs in, me following. I set the timer on my watch for an hour, turn off the light, and stretch out on my back. Aurora snuggles into my side, head on my chest, hand resting lightly over my heart.

I curl my fingers around it, in case she gets any ideas.

She kisses the back of my hand, then settles her cheek on my chest. "Hollis?"

"Yes, Princess?"

"Your hand smells like my pussy."

I laugh. "I know."

"You're not going to wash it, are you?"

"No."

"You're a little dirty, aren't you?"

I smile in the dark. "Yeah."

"Good. Me too." She shifts around, and her lips find the edge of my jaw, working their way up to my lips. "Thanks for finger-fucking me against my door."

"You're welcome. Now go to sleep."

"Okay." She settles against my chest again and a few seconds later whispers, so quietly I almost don't catch it, "Old man."

"You're pushing it, Princess. G'night."

"I know. G'night, Hollis."

She throws her leg over mine and tries to free her hand, but I thread our fingers together. It doesn't take her long to fall asleep. I lie there for a long while, staring at the ceiling, listening to her steady breathing, wishing I could see into the future and know for sure that this path is the right one. This doesn't feel fleeting, but I've been wrong before. And there's so much at stake for both of us. But I can't stay away anymore.

CHAPTER 23
HAMMER

"Oh, my God! Yes!" I pump my fist in the air, then realize exactly what this means. "Oh, shit."

"What's going on?" Rix asks. "First, you looked thrilled, now you look like someone stole your favorite vibrator."

"Ha ha. Hollis has the go-ahead to travel with the team again."

"Which is great for his morale but not so great for finger-bangs and make-out sessions," she finishes.

I love that she understands, and that I can tell her things. And even if she tells Tristan, he's good at keeping his mouth shut.

There was a zero-percent chance that I could keep what happened to myself. Plus, my buoyant mood was a real tipoff. And Hollis must have gone to the twenty-four-hour grocery store at stupid o'clock in the morning, because he left my favorite muffins on the counter. Without a note. But still. It was sweet.

I flop down on the couch. "I was kind of hoping we'd have four days with no one around so I could finally get my hands on his cock."

"I still can't believe you haven't touched it. Like…" She makes the mind-blown gesture.

The apartment door opens three inches, startling the shit out of us, but the safety is engaged. "Want to let me in, Pegs?"

I hop off the couch and push the door closed, flipping the latch before I open it again. "You know knocking is a thing, right, Dado?" Then I see Hollis, standing behind my dad with his phone in his hand. Spending time with the two of them is hard these days. Part of me just wants to get it over with and tell him, but the other, bigger part is so scared of how hurt he'll be. Mad and disappointed too, probably. How much it could change things.

"Sorry. Yeah. I keep forgetting. We got some good news, and Hollis and I were heading to the Watering Hole for dinner to celebrate. Maybe you want to join us?" Dad is all smiles.

"What kind of good news?" I pretend like Hollis didn't send me a text message five minutes ago. Which means he told me before my dad. My heart gets all mushy and my nether parts all zingy while my bucket of shame over all the broken rules and lies we're telling him gets a little heavier.

"Hollis is cleared to travel with the team. He's not back on the ice yet, but this is a step in the right direction." He claps Hollis on the shoulder.

"That's amazing!"

"Isn't it? It'll be nice to have my roommate back." Dad grins at Hollis.

He nods. "It'll be good to get back to a normal routine. Or as normal as it can be, for now."

"So, what do you say? Coming for celebratory nachos?"

"Yeah. Of course." I haven't been with my dad and Hollis together for any length of time since the fingerbang and him holding me to sleep. Which, oh my God, was literally my favorite way to fall asleep in the history of my almost twenty-one years. But I have no idea how to manage this situation now that his fingers have been inside me.

"What about you, Rix? Want to join us?" Dad asks.

"Uh..." She glances from my dad to me.

"Yes, please. Join us." If ever I could use some freaking backup, it's now.

"Cool. I'll change into something that isn't this." Rix motions to her ratty sweats and old tank top that clearly belong to Tristan, based on the size.

I look down at myself. I'm braless and wearing jogging pants and an old shirt. Thankfully not Hollis's. I sleep in that. "I'll do the same. Do you want us to meet you there, or..." I let it hang.

Hollis checks his watch. "We'll grab a table."

"Cool. Yeah." I give them the thumbs-up. "We'll be right behind you."

"Great. Don't take too long, though," Dad says.

"See you soon," Hollis adds with a tight smile.

Once they're gone, I flip the lock and the latch and turn to Rix, who is still standing in the kitchen. "Oh, girl." She shakes her head.

"Is it obvious? Am I being obvious?"

"You're being a little weird, but to be honest, you've been a little weird for the past few months, so your dad will probably chalk it up to working for the team so hard and school stress?" It comes out more of a question than a straight answer.

I run my hands through my hair. "How the hell did you do this with Tristan for two freaking months while living in the same damn space as your brother?"

Rix gives me an empathetic smile. "It wasn't ever easy. We were hate-fucking each other for weeks before that hate had turned into not-hate. You two are kind of already in love and have been fighting off the feelings."

"He's not in love with me," I say. I don't deny that I probably am though.

She opens and closes her mouth a couple of times, then crosses the room and takes me by the shoulders. "Do you need to believe that to make this easier to handle?"

I purse my lips. "I don't know."

"I see the way he looks at you when he thinks no one is watching. We'll have four days to dissect all of this while they're away."

"Thank you for being such a good friend." I pull her in for a hug.

She squeezes me back. "You'd do the same for me. You *have* done the same for me." She takes my hand and pulls me toward my bedroom. "Come on, let's put you in something sexy so he's rocking an uncomfortable boner all evening."

The entire crew ends up at the Watering Hole, so the potential awkwardness is diluted by all the other people. Rix and I stuff ourselves into a booth with the girls and discuss the gala. I'm even more nervous about Scarlet attending now that this thing with Hollis has moved to another level. But I play it off like it's fine, because having her attend is another checkmark on my resume, and what else can I do?

It isn't until I'm home and getting ready for bed that my phone buzzes with a new message.

HOLLIS

Dinner tomorrow night at my place.

AURORA

A date? With my dad across the hall O_o ???

HOLLIS

He has a dinner meeting with his agent.

He's had a lot of those lately. When his contract ends, he plans to hang up his skates and move on to the next phase of his career.

AURORA

What time?

HOLLIS

You have class until five thirty, right?

AURORA

Yes.

HOLLIS

Roman's dinner meeting is at six, so come up
any time after that.

AURORA

Can I bring anything?

HOLLIS

Just your beautiful self.

CHAPTER 24

HAMMER

The next evening, Rix is already at Tristan's by the time I head up to Hollis's. I text three times to make sure my dad has really left for dinner. He was disappointed when I said I had too much homework to go with him, but he was understanding —especially with exams around the corner and final projects coming due. My shame bucket is getting close to overflowing, but telling him now…it's more pressure than I can handle. Not that I'll admit that to anyone but myself. Sure, he's a little over-protective and sometimes he struggles with boundaries, but he's spent his whole life putting me first, and I'm plotting and lusting after his best friend. A man who is so expressly out of bounds. I've heard *'don't date hockey players'* my entire life. It's shitty, espe-cially because I don't have any intentions of stopping, or being honest. Not about this. Not yet.

I zip the hoodie over my outfit. I'm wearing black, high-waisted dress pants, a spaghetti strap camisole with lace accents, and a gauzy pale blue blouse over the top. No bra, because my lack of one really seems to set Hollis off. I'll never get over knowing he wants me. I grab my purse and the glass baking dish, check my reflection one last time, slide my feet into my flats, and leave the apartment. My heart is racing by the time I reach the penthouse floor. I glance at my dad's door. A pang of guilt makes my stomach churn. I take a deep breath and knock on Hollis's door. I half expect my dad's to swing open and catch me in the act. But Dad's door stays closed, and Hollis opens his. My mouth goes dry. He's wearing black dress pants, a crisp white button-down that hugs every one of his deliciously defined muscles, and the tie I gave him for his birthday last year.

"Hi," I breathe.

"Hi, yourself. Come in." He takes the dish, closing the door behind me. "You didn't need to bring anything."

"It's dessert and a decoy in case I ran into someone on the way up. Just covering all the bases. Oh, wow." I look around the penthouse. The lights have been dimmed and the dining table set for two. Wine chills in a bucket and candles flicker. "So you brought your A game?" My hands shake as I unzip the hoodie.

His gaze heats as it moves over me. "Something like that."

Postie and Malone bumble over, meowing their excitement. I crouch to pet them while they wind themselves around my legs. "How are my favorite furry boys? I'm so excited to watch the game with you next week."

They abandon me and head for the kitchen, conditioned to believe I'm here for love and treats. When I stand, Hollis is right in front of me. I don't know what to do with my hands, or any part of me. I'm vibrating with nerves, and my vagina is all achy again.

I exhale some of my anxiety and remind myself that we share a very real mutual attraction. Hollis would not have gone to the trouble of setting up this date if he wasn't interested in seeing where this could go.

I run my hand down his tie, wrapping the soft fabric around my hand. "You look great."

His hand settles on my hip, gently pulling me closer. "So do you."

I lift my chin, and he drops his head until our lips meet. The familiar zing courses through me at the gentle contact, and I sigh into the soft, unhurried kiss. It's a dance of tongues, a promise of what's coming.

Unfortunately, he ends it before it can escalate.

He laces our fingers and kisses my knuckles. "Dinner's almost ready."

I follow him to the kitchen, where two glasses of wine sit on the counter.

He passes me one. "To first dates."

My stomach flip-flops as we clink. "To first dates."

We sip our wine, and Hollis presses a chaste kiss to my lips.

I set my glass on the counter, worried he'll see the tremor in my hands. I'm also ridiculously parched thanks to the nerves, and liable to chug it. I move toward the cupboards, but he holds up a hand.

"Whatever you need, let me get it for you."

"Just some water, please."

He fills a glass and when he passes it to me, I wrap both hands around it to hide how unsteady I am. I try to sip it but end up downing the entire thing.

Hollis takes the glass and inspects my trembling hand. His concerned gaze meets mine. "What's wrong?"

For the first time, I truly feel the age gap. He has so much more dating experience. My classiest date has been dinner out at Earl's, a local pub chain. I wore jeans and a nice shirt.

Hollis knows how to seduce. And take care of a woman's needs. The front door fingerbang is proof of that. My sexual repertoire is limited to university boys. What if the dry fuck was a fluke? What if all the sex in the movie made me more appealing? What if this was all just my own fantasies and built-up teen angst?

"Princess?" He cups my cheek in his hand. "Talk to me."

I'm on the edge of emotion. I better not cry. "I'm so nervous."

"About what?" He leans back against the counter, posture open. "Is this too much for you?"

"No. I want this." So badly. I've wanted this for so damn

225

long, and now that I have it, I'm terrified. I wrap his tie around my fist. The fabric slips through my fingers over and over. "I just... I don't know what I expected, but I guess...I thought we would order in dinner and then we'd—" I gesture to his bedroom. That was a whole lot of truth I didn't mean to tell.

His thumb sweeps along the edge of my jaw, soothing and igniting. "I don't have any expectations about what happens after dinner, Aurora. I just want time with you. That's all."

"Okay," I whisper.

He parts his legs, wraps his arms around my waist, and pulls me between them. "What aren't you telling me?"

"It's kind of annoying that you can read me this easily." But also, so, so nice.

He runs his palms up my back and down my arms, moving my hands so they link behind his neck. "You used to share everything with me. It goes both ways, though, doesn't it? Tell me what else has you worried."

I sigh and look up at the ceiling. Am I really going to admit this? "You have a lot more experience in certain areas than I do."

"That goes without saying, Aurora. Be more specific."

I huff, eyes on his chin, while I blurt, "You have a lot more experience with sex."

He takes my face in his hands. "Look at me."

My gaze lifts.

"One, we have wicked chemistry, the kind that's pretty fucking impossible to ignore. Two, you ask for what you need from me, and I listen, and three, I know how to read you, Aurora. Frankly, I pay far more attention to you than I should. Whatever you haven't been getting out of sex in the past is not because there's something wrong with you. Do you understand?"

I nod. My entire body hums with pent-up sexual tension. We're already three knuckles deep into this conversation. Might as well lay it all out for him. "It's not your experience or your ability to make me feel good that I'm worried about. It's my ability to please *you*."

"I came in my jogging pants from a dry fuck," he says dryly.

"But that was all friction, and you wouldn't let me touch you after the fingerbang." I want to stuff my words back in my mouth and swallow them.

His jaw clenches, and the hand on my hip flexes. "I wouldn't let you touch me after the—" He clears his throat. "—fingerbang because I didn't want to embarrass myself. Again."

I blink at him, and he blinks back at me. It takes me a few seconds to process his admission. "You didn't want me to touch you because you didn't think you could…stay in control?"

"That's a nice way of putting it."

"Oh." *Well, that's one hell of an ego boost.*

He narrows his eyes. "Don't make me regret being honest."

I finger the end of his tie. Which is close to his belt buckle. "I'll try not to."

"You're a real problem, you know that?"

I look up at him through my lashes. "So you keep telling me."

"Fuck, Aurora. Why do you have to be so damn tempting all the time?" He spears his hands in my hair and claims my mouth in a searing kiss. It makes my knees weak, and heat floods my center. But it's over as quickly as it began.

He exhales a steadying breath, which calms me. At least we're struggling to keep ourselves in check together. "Just like you told me what you needed, I'll tell you what I need. When we get to that point. Which isn't now, because what I need is for you to let me make you dinner and treat you like the princess you are, at least for the next two hours, okay?"

"I'll do my best."

He hands me my wine and takes a hefty gulp of his own.

"Can I do anything to help with dinner?" The sooner we eat, the sooner we can get back to him telling me what else he needs.

"You can keep me company while I finish up."

"What are we having?" It's the first time I've processed how mouthwateringly delicious it smells in here.

"Fresh rolls from Best Buns Bakery, a mixed green salad with that balsamic dressing you and Rix make, pan-seared sea scallops, and fettuccine Alfredo—and whatever you brought for dessert."

"Those are all my favorites." Every time we go for dinner at Greystones, I order the scallops or their peppercorn fettuccine.

"I know what you love." He kisses me softly on the cheek.

I'm at risk of melting into the floor. Dates with university guys aren't like this. At all.

"What's in here?" He taps the dish I brought.

"Rix and I made individual lemon meringue cheesecakes."

"Lemon meringue is my favorite."

I smile. "It's like we know each other."

He sets his cast iron frying pan on the stove and pulls the scallops out of the fridge, along with the butter. I lean against the counter, happy to watch him work.

"Are you excited to be traveling with the team again?"

"Being with my teammates is good, but sitting on the bench, watching the action and not being able to participate, is a tough headspace to manage."

He did that last year, too. I don't know what was worse, watching from the couch with me or from rink side. "Do you think you'll be cleared for the playoffs?"

"I hope so. I'm healing well and mobility is good. But my physical therapist is focused on what's down the line, and play-offs are different than the regular season."

I nod. "They're way more intense."

"They are, so I need to be in peak physical condition to be valuable to my team the way I'd like. It's one day at a time for now."

Hollis drops a generous pat of butter into the frying pan and rolls his sleeves halfway up his forearms while it melts. This is an image I'll never forget so long as I live.

I groan. "Seriously, Hollis, how am I supposed to survive two hours when you're pulling out the forearm porn?"

He arches a brow. "Forearm porn is a thing?"

"Uh, yeah, it's totally a thing." I've been obsessed with Hollis's forearms for a long time. See the STUDY MATERIALS folder on my phone for evidence.

"Interesting." He swirls the butter in the pan, adding two crushed cloves of garlic. "How are classes? You have final projects coming up and exams."

"Most of my final projects are presentations, which is good." Even though it was only one semester with Hemi full-time, I'm out of practice with written exams, and my concentration lately hasn't been the best for memorizing facts. "I learned a lot about how to create dynamic ones, trying to get the Terror front office to do or approve things."

He smiles. "That's great. You know, whatever you set your mind to, you can have. The stars are yours. You just need to reach out and grab them."

"What if I've already picked my star? The team is my family. This is where I want to be. Working with Hemi and Tally proved that. Tally and I get each other. We've spent our lives next to the ice."

"It has its perks and pitfalls, doesn't it?"

"Everything does. My life would've been so different if I'd lived with my mom." I went to three different schools for junior kindergarten. My mom tried to settle down in one place when I started senior kindergarten, but she wasn't happy being tied to a location, so it only lasted a handful of months. It was hard as a kid to understand, but having my mom be that unhappy and stressed while trying her absolute best to make it work for me wouldn't have ended up going well. Our relationship would have been toxic, and she would have crumbled. Now, I have someone vibrant who loves me at her best, even if sometimes I long for what other people have.

"Not a lot of stability for you with the way she moves around."

"No. I refused to decorate my room for the first year I lived with my dad. I think he believed it was because I didn't want to be with him. But I didn't want to get too comfortable in case it didn't work."

"You weren't used to being in one place." Hollis flips the scallops.

I'm glad he has something else to focus on. "I wasn't. But after the first year, I settled in and it was better, for me at least. My mom is an infinitely healthier person now. My dad put me ahead of everything and everyone." It still took two years before I stopped keeping a packed bag in my closet.

Hollis's gaze meets mine, and I catch a momentary flash of guilt. "You've always been his first priority."

"He's put his own needs aside because of what I went through as a kid."

"Do you mean relationship wise?" he asks.

"Yeah. But also everything too. My parents are opposites. My dad has had two girlfriends my entire life, at least that I've met. One was when he was playing for Calgary. But then he was traded. That was hard on both of us. He tried to date another woman about a year after we moved to Toronto, but it didn't work out. He's not even forty yet. I've been his whole world other than hockey. It'd be great if he would date."

"He's said the same thing about you," Hollis says.

I roll my eyes. "The last time I tried to go on a date, someone crashed it."

He looks guilty, but not that guilty.

"I only went because you told me I should, and I thought this would never happen." I motion between us.

His expression softens. "It wasn't because I didn't want this, Aurora." He tucks a single finger under my chin and brushes his lips gently over mine. "I do, but it's complicated."

230

"I know." I still worry the complications could outweigh his desire for this to work. There are real stakes for both of us.

"And I honestly believed I was doing the right thing when I suggested you go out with that kid." His eyes darken.

"I was so pissed at you." I sip my wine to hide my smile.

"I was a territorial asshole."

"You absolutely were."

"You didn't seem to hate it," he observes.

Jealous and possessive Hollis is hot though. "Is that you telling me to go out on another date?"

"Fuck no." His lip curls. "What happened with James, anyway? Did he ask you out again?"

"You mean Jameson. And no. I put him in the friend zone where he belongs."

"Good. He seemed way too into Roman that day. He should have wanted you all to himself."

Postie hops up on the counter and headbutts my hand. He's not supposed to be up here, but I pet his silky fur, anyway. "Half my dates end up with guys asking about my dad and his teammates. It's fame by proxy, I guess. And I get the fascination. But it highlights how much I'm *not* a regular university student. I tried to be one, Hollis. I really did. I tried to date university guys and do the keg-party thing, which is a hotbed of terrible decision making."

Hollis chuckles. "I remember those days."

"I always ended up being the designated sober person, because one." I hold up a finger. "I hate beer." I raise a second finger. "And two, the last thing I wanted was to end up in some random guy's bed with a hangover and a ton of regrets." I've seen enough of my friends do it, and I'm good without that experience.

He frowns. "Did that ever happen?"

I give him a look. "Where did I spend my weekends?" I allocated one weekend a month to staying at my off-campus apartment, mostly to appease my dad, who thought it was a good life experience. I was just grateful the complex was mostly pre-med, and all most people wanted to do was study.

"At hockey games or with Roman."

"I like being with the team. I love Hemi and Shilpa and Rix and Tally—and even Dred doesn't get all googly eyed about hockey players. I always felt protected and cared for. Especially by you," I admit.

He nods. "I like taking care of you."

He spears a scallop half with a fork and lifts it, holding his palm under it to catch the dripping butter. "Would you like a taste?"

"Please."

He slips the fork between my parted lips, and I free the scallop with my teeth, groaning as the flavors hit my tongue. "It's perfect."

His thumb sweeps along my bottom lip, wiping away a drip of butter. I wrap my fingers around his wrist and bite the end of his thumb, swirling my tongue around it. Last time I did this, we ended up dry fucking.

Hollis's eyes darken, and the grin that spreads across his face is downright lascivious. He wraps an arm around my waist and pulls me closer. "Careful, little girl. You're giving me ideas about that sweet mouth of yours."

I run my hand down his chest and bite the edge of his jaw. "Hopefully you mean your cock, Hollis, because I would love to get on my knees for you."

He turns off the burner and moves the pan off the heat. Then he grabs me by the waist and spins me around, pressing me against the counter. He pins me with his hips, and his erection nudges my ass. I moan and arch, pushing back against him. The arm around my waist moves up until it's barred across my chest. He bites his way up my neck. "You want to get filthy, Princess?"

"You know I do."

He shifts, swats my ass once, twice, a third time. Not so hard it hurts, but the sting makes my clit ache and pulse. He moves back into position, grinds his cock on my ass, and pulls me away from the counter. His hand snakes between my thighs and cups me, fingers pressing against my entrance through my pants. His other hand slides over my collarbones and along the edge of my jaw. He turns my face toward him, claiming my mouth.

When he pulls back, his eyes are heavy with lust. "Can you be a good girl and behave yourself through dinner?"

"What do I get if I'm good?"

"Good girls get to come all over my fingers again." His lips brush my cheek. "And if you're really good, maybe even my tongue."

The throb between my thighs intensifies. "I'll be good. I'll be the goodest girl ever."

"We'll see about that." He releases me, unfortunately, and adjusts himself. "Can we please eat dinner without you trying to get me to fuck you every five minutes?" But I hear the laughter he's trying to hide in his voice.

"That was more like twenty minutes, but sure."

He gives me a look.

I smile.

He turns back to the stove.

Hollis plates our dinner and brings it to the table, pulling out my chair before he takes the spot beside me. He refreshes our wine, and I set my serviette on my lap, waiting until he's done the same before I take a bite.

I groan my appreciation. "This is as good as the dish from Greystones."

He smiles a real Hollis smile. It's the smile of myths and legends. "I don't know if I'd go that far, but I'm glad you like it."

"Thank you for making my favorites. I know this is hard," I say as I spin noodles onto my fork.

"Being with you is easy, Aurora. It's all the other stuff that's difficult." Hollis focuses on his plate. He reaches out and tucks my hair behind my ear, fingers lingering on my skin. He looks so torn. "I don't know what I believe anymore. But I can't stay away from you, no matter how hard I try. I wanted time with you before I leave for the away games. It's selfish and self-serving."

I leave it for now. I don't want to ruin this beautiful dinner. "I kind of love it when you're selfish."

He leans over and kisses me again. I curve my hand around the back of his neck, parting my lips. He indulges me for a few strokes of tongue before he settles back in his chair.

I blow out a breath. "This feels like foreplay."

"That's because it is." He catches my hand and kisses the tips of my fingers. "I'd like you as worked up as possible by the time we're through with dessert."

Malone tries to jump onto the table, and Hollis extends his other arm to thwart him.

"Looks like my pussy isn't the only excited one," I mutter.

Hollis snorts a laugh. I love seeing him unguarded like this. I feel special, getting to see what no one else does. Most people only know serious Hollis, but I get these sacred pieces of him.

Dinner is the most exquisite torture, full of light touches and gentle kisses. And I get a glimpse of what it could be like to date Hollis. Under that gruff, quiet exterior, he's devastatingly romantic, and I can only imagine how that translates in the bedroom. Will he be gentle? Commanding? Will he whisper dirty things in my ear while he fucks me sweetly? Or sweet things while he fucks me dirty? Both?

I help Hollis bring the dishes to the kitchen. His fingers brush the dip in my spine and his lips skim the edge of my jaw as he reaches around me. I feel his erection against my hip when he leans in to grab the dishcloth. There's no way I can sit through dessert without spontaneously combusting. I grab his tie and try to pull his mouth to mine, but he tips his chin up, looking down at me with hot, knowing eyes.

His salacious smile makes everything below the waist clench. "We still have dessert."

"Let's save it until after." I shift so his leg is between mine.

"Until after what, exactly?"

"Getting naked. Then my list is pretty endless."

He tugs me closer. "I'd like to hear more about this list."

"I'll tell you all about it if you'll take me to your bedroom."
I'm not above bargaining.

"Is that right?"

"I'll even show you."

The alarm beeps, startling us.

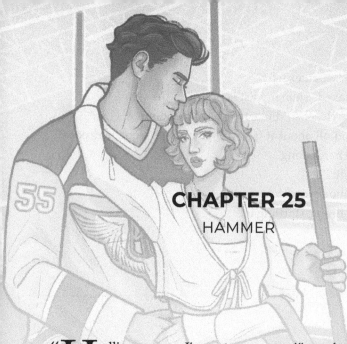

CHAPTER 25
HAMMER

"Hollis, my man, I've got some news!" my dad shouts.

He has the worst habit of showing up without knocking or texting in advance and waiting for a reply.

We freeze for half a second, my panic echoed in Hollis's eyes. But his hold so many other emotions, too, like guilt and shame. My stomach sinks.

"Go to the spare bedroom, now," he orders. He strides across the kitchen, shouting, "Hey, man. We've talked about this."

I rush around the corner and down the hall. My heart is in my throat, my stomach in knots. We were seconds away from getting caught. If we'd been in the dining room, we would have.

"Oh, shit. Are you on a date? Did you change your mind and decide to see Scarlet again?" Dad asks.

The knot in my stomach becomes a brick.

Heat climbs my spine at the mention of Hollis's ex and my former favorite actress. And then the words register. *Again*? He's seen her? Since when?

"Yes, I'm on a date. Not with Scarlet. You think we can do this later?" Hollis's tight voice filters down the hall.

"Right, yeah. Absolutely. Sorry, man. Good for you. You should've told me."

"How about I text you later?"

"Or I'll just see you in the morning. We can talk on the plane. Have a good night."

I'm shaking with anxiety and anger. Sweat trickles down my spine, and my heart thunders in my chest. He was right. We *used to* tell each other everything.

Hollis appears in the doorway. "He's gone, and I put the safety latch on."

I cross my arms. "See Scarlet *again*?"

"It's not what you think."

"How do you even know what I think? When did you see her? Before you kissed me? After?" He knew about Jameson. He was there for the entire dumpster fire. This is why I always feel off center with Hollis.

A million emotions cross his face, but it's the remorse that makes my stomach and heart sink.

"Aurora."

"Before or after, Hollis?"

"After." He runs a hand through his hair.

He might as well rip my heart out. "What the hell?" I try to step around him, but he blocks the door.

He raises a hand, like he's trying to calm me. Like I don't have a right to be upset. "Can you let me explain?"

"Do not barricade me in this room so you can feed me some bullshit story about why you went to see your goddamn ex-girlfriend after you kissed me and told me it was a mistake!"

"That's not what I'm doing." He moves aside, though, and I step out into the hall.

He follows.

"Did you fuck her?" I'm on the verge of tears.

He blanches. "Of course not."

I spin to face him. "Did you kiss her?"

I can't read his expression, but he looks almost...disappointed that I would ask that.

"No."

I hate the wash of relief and how desperate I am for there to be a good reason why he kept this from me. "Why should I believe you?"

"Because you're here and she's not."

It's a simple answer. Direct. "Why didn't you tell me? Why did I have to hear about it from my dad?" I should be more upset about almost getting caught, but this is a twist I didn't see coming.

His eyes soften, and so does his voice. "Because I didn't want to upset you."

Because he didn't think I could handle it. And maybe he's right, but we'll never know for sure. "When did you see her?"

"After I said you should go on a date with that James kid."

My mouth drops, and I swear I'm at risk of throwing up my meal. I don't even bother to correct him on the name. "Why would you send me on a date and then go see your ex? What were you trying to accomplish?"

He steps forward.

I hold out a hand. "Do not touch me right now."

His expression is pained. "I was trying to do the right thing and not fuck up my life and yours. I didn't want to see her—not the way she wanted to see me. But I had all these feelings for you that I couldn't get a handle on. And then she started showing up at games. I needed closure. She broke my fucking heart when I moved out here. I have no desire to go down that road again. It was a long time ago, but I needed to deal with it. The only way I could do that was to have a conversation. Nothing happened, Aurora. We just talked. That's it. I haven't seen her since."

I wrap my arms around myself, like it will keep me from falling apart. "Have you talked to her since?"

"She messaged after the last accident to see how I was doing, but that's it. There's nothing going on. I promise."

I believe he's telling the truth, but it still stings. It makes me feel out of my depth all over again. "I don't want to be some convenient distraction to help you get over whatever happened with her." I realize, though, that whatever did happen must have really hurt him. And maybe that's part of the reason for his hesitation with us. But it doesn't make it okay that he kept this from me.

"You're a lot of things, Aurora, but you're not a distraction from someone else. What can I do to fix this? Tell me what I need to do." He looks so uncertain. Vulnerable.

"This hurts." I rub my temple. "I need time to process. Alone." But how the hell will I get to my apartment without running into my dad? What a mess of a night.

"I can go over to Roman's. Give you some time on your own. Then we can talk?"

"I'd like to process in my own space. I'll text you when I'm ready to have a conversation."

"Okay. I understand." He nods, crosses and uncrosses his arms. "I'm sorry. The last thing I wanted was to hurt you again."

"Are you sure you weren't trying to protect yourself instead?" I wait for him to take the opportunity to open up, to share what made that breakup so painful, but all he does is sigh.

"Maybe. I'll go check in with Roman so you can have time."

He walks away, leaving me wondering how the most amazing date turned into the worst one, and all because of his ex.

CHAPTER 26

HOLLIS

I should be shitting my pants that I almost got caught on a date with Roman's daughter. And part of me is. I feel like a giant bag of garbage. I'm deceiving him every day. But the bigger, more telling part of me is worried about how Aurora is handling this. Because on top of the stress I'm putting on her relationship with her dad, I withheld information.

For a while now I've been living in the land of denial, believing I could lock down these feelings. Telling her I'd seen Scarlet, and assuring her that the feelings I once had are long gone, would have meant admitting I want something more with Aurora. I hadn't been ready to do that, and now I've upset her. Again.

Hurting her feels like stabbing myself. When she's in pain, I itch with the need to fix everything for her. Seeing her smile, being part of what makes her happy, holding her close? Those are the things I want to spend my days and nights doing.

I leave my phone at my place and go over to Roman's. When he asks what happened to my date, I tell him she has to work early, and he's so preoccupied with his news, he doesn't question it. I end up staying for an hour and a half while he explains his post-retirement options. I try to remain engaged. Try to be a good friend and share his excitement, but my stomach is churning. Aurora's words keep rolling around in my head. Who was I really protecting? Her or me?

It's late by the time I finally leave. Postie and Malone meet me at the door and follow me into the kitchen, meowing insistently. I ignore them and check my phone, stomach sinking at the lack of message from Aurora.

I don't want to force her into a conversation she's not ready for. But I also want to own my mistakes.

HOLLIS

> I know you need some time, but please don't shut me out. Even if I can't fix it now, I don't want to get on that plane without seeing you before I go.

I wait a few minutes, but I don't get a response. I change and get ready for bed, pack my bag for tomorrow and pick out my suit, then clean up the rest of dinner and put the cheesecakes in the fridge. Aurora hasn't messaged by the time I'm ready for bed, so I take it as a sign that she's still processing.

I sleep like garbage, tossing and turning. Postie keeps trying to reposition near me. At five thirty in the morning, my phone buzzes on my nightstand. My anxiety spikes when I see a text from Aurora.

PRINCESS

> Message when you're awake.

HOLLIS

> I'm awake now. Can I come down?

The humping dots appear and disappear twice.

PRINCESS

> Yes.

241

I'll be down in five.

I roll out of bed, give my teeth a quick brush, and pull on a pair of joggers and a hoodie. I grab the extra key fob and wish I'd done something smart last night, like buy Aurora flowers. But that's only occurring to me now.

My stomach is in knots as I knock. A few seconds later, the door opens. Aurora looks the opposite of happy to see me, but her red-rimmed, puffy eyes are the biggest gut punch. I want to reach out and pull her against me, but she steps back and crosses her arms, communicating that contact isn't welcome.

Everything feels too tight. "Thank you for agreeing to see me."

"You needed to give me your key, anyway." Her eyes stay focused on my chin.

We both know I could have left it at Roman's. "I should have told you I saw Scarlet. My split with her wasn't amicable. It wasn't just because I ended up here and she was in LA. I wanted to make the distance work, but she didn't feel supported because I didn't want our relationship to be public fodder, so she ended things." There's more, but that conversation needs to wait.

"Do you still have feelings for her?" Aurora's voice is low and raspy.

I shake my head. "No. Not romantic ones. I saw her because she's in my city for a few months, and I needed to try to clear the air between us."

"But she still has feelings for you," Aurora says softly.

"She has memories of what we were, but there are a lot of years between then and now. I'm not the same person." I'm definitely more cautious with my heart, maybe too cautious. "And I'm pretty hung up on you. When I get back, if you still have questions, whatever you want to know about my relationship with Scarlet, I'll tell you—if I haven't fucked this up beyond repair."

"You haven't fucked it up beyond repair." Her chin trembles as she lifts her head. "It's just a lot for me to manage. You have history with her. She's accomplished and polished, and she's had you in ways I haven't, and I hate it. Especially because it would be so much easier for you to be with her than it is for you to be with me."

"But she's not who I want, Aurora. You are." I wish I could tell her how deep those feelings are. How she's all I have been able to think about for months. That I've risked more of myself for her than anyone since Scarlet.

I've confided in Aurora so much since my accident last year, but never about Scarlet. And that needs to change. "Can we talk when I get back?"

She nods.

"Can I hug you?" The need to comfort her is a physical compulsion.

"Please." Her voice cracks.

I open my arms, and she steps forward. Her hands slide around my waist, and mine curve around her shoulders, one hand cupping the back of her head as she rests her cheek on my chest.

I press my lips against the top of her head. "I slept like shit last night, Princess."

"Me, too. I should have messaged you before bed, but I looked a wreck," she mutters.

"You're always beautiful. Fuck. I hate when I upset you," I admit.

"I have a lot of emotions when it comes to you," she says softly.

I take her face in my hands, studying every flutter of her lashes. "It's the same for me, Aurora. I wish last night had gone differently. Maybe when I get back, we can have a do-over."

"I'd like that. Except we should probably put on the safety latch, so my freaking dad doesn't come busting in like the Kool-

Aid Man. How did that go? Do you think he suspects anything?" She pulls her lip between her teeth.

I shake my head and tamp down the guilt, not wanting her to see how heavy this weighs on me. Not when I have to leave her after the clusterfuck that was last night. "He was too preoccupied. He barely even asked about my date." Which I was grateful for. I felt like I was in one of his spirals, aware I'd hurt Aurora. If he knew the truth about how last night was supposed to end, he'd probably unalive me. And he'd have a right. "He wanted to text you, but I reminded him you have an early class this morning."

"Crisis averted," she murmurs.

"For now, yeah." That's another conversation we need to have. But it all depends on what she wants out of this. I'm terrified about what that could be and what it would mean.

She sighs and fiddles with the string on my hoodie. "I need to get going. I'm meeting with my group before class. We have a presentation this morning, and we want to go through it one more time."

And now I feel even worse. It's fine for me to sleep like trash. All I'm doing is sitting on a plane and a bench, but this could mess with her grades. "I'm sorry you're going into this underslept."

"I'm in university, Hollis. I can function on five hours of crappy sleep."

"It's my fault it was shitty, though."

"It could have been less shitty if I'd texted last night instead of worrying about puffy eyes." She pats my chest.

I cover her hand with mine and bring it to my lips.

She taps hers with a finger. "I'd like those here, please."

I cup her face and brush lightly over her lips.

It only takes one soft stroke of tongue before her nails are digging into the back of my neck and I'm pulling her tight against me. She breaks the kiss and covers my mouth with her palm when I try to reclaim hers. Her mouth is heaven.

"I still need to get ready, and I have to leave in less than half an hour."

"I'll message you tonight?"

"Yes, please."

"And I'll make up for the crappy date when I get back."

"Also yes, please."

I kiss her one last time, and she pushes me out the door.

I'm stepping off the elevator as Roman opens his door. He frowns when he sees me. "Where have you been?"

"I was dropping off my key for Aurora." It's not a complete lie, but I still feel like a bag of shit. Especially since I can taste her mint toothpaste on my tongue. What if he'd arrived two minutes earlier? How quickly would he put it all together? How would I explain? How could I leave Aurora with the fallout of that?

His brow furrows. "She's up already?"

"She has a group presentation this morning. She's heading to campus early so they can practice. I would have dropped my key off last night, but we were up late talking."

"Right, yeah. She's still home, though?" He pulls his phone out and starts thumb typing.

"She was getting ready when I dropped off my key a minute ago." A bead of sweat trickles down my spine.

"I'll head down and say good-bye now, then."

"Sounds good." I take a step toward my door as he moves toward the elevators. "I should be ready to roll in twenty."

He nods, his eyes still on his phone as he steps into the elevator. I disappear inside my penthouse, the weight in my chest growing with every lie I tell my best friend.

CHAPTER 27

HOLLIS

I send Aurora a bouquet of gerbera daisies, wishing her luck on her presentation, before Roman and I leave for the airport. I sleep on the plane and watch practice from the bench. They've started rotating in our backup goalie during practices to prepare for the inevitable shift when Roman hangs up his skates.

Coach takes a seat beside me as the team skates. "Doc said your knee is healing well."

"The strength is coming back faster this time." I'm crossing my fingers it means I'll be back on the ice sooner.

"I know it's frustrating to be out with another injury," he says.

"It's important to give it the time it needs to heal." I know this is the right answer, though I hate it. "I'm doing everything I can to get back on the ice before the playoffs."

"One step at a time, Hendrix. Hopefully, you'll be cleared for practice soon."

When they're finished on the ice, I join the guys in the sauna and grab lunch with the team. Roman and a bunch of the guys plan to rewatch Seattle's last couple of games when we return to the hotel. But my kitty-cam alerts show activity in my penthouse. And I have new messages from Aurora.

"I need to call my sister, but I'll catch up with you in a bit, if that's okay," I tell Roman when we get back. The lies feel like quicksand these days. But I want to check on Aurora, make sure she's okay, and I need privacy for that.

"Everything okay there?" Roman asks, always the concerned dad.

"Oh yeah, just our weekly call." We have a standing date we rarely miss. It's just not right now.

"Okay. We'll be in Dallas and Ash's room. Sixteen-thirteen."

"See you in a bit." I flip the safety latch after he leaves and check my messages.

> **PRINCESS**
>
> Someone sent me flowers today. Without a card. They're beautiful.

It's accompanied by a picture of them on her dresser.

> **PRINCESS**
>
> Too bad you're at practice because I'm about to visit the kitties.

Another picture, this one of her lying on my bed with my cats, follows. Postie is stretched out on her chest, and Malone is snuggled up beside them, looking disgruntled. It was sent half an hour ago.

I keep scrolling, jaw clenching as I scan the next messages.

> **PRINCESS**
>
> Now that you've had your fingers in my pussy, am I allowed to use Batdick in your bed?
>
> Guess I'll find out later.
>
> Might want to check your kitty cams.
>
> You're missing all the fun.

I fire off a reply.

> What bad things are you doing in my bed without me, Princess?

No response.

I retrieve my laptop and flip it open, popping in my earbuds as I pull up the video feeds. My living room is empty. And I'm momentarily confused when I check the camera in my bedroom. I'm looking at my shower instead of my bed. The glass is foggy, but Aurora's naked outline is visible. Her hands are pressed against the wall, and her head hangs low. The sound of the spray hitting the tile muffles her words until she moans loudly. "Fuck, yes. Right there. So damn close."

What I wouldn't give to be there with her. But since I'm hours away, all I can do is watch and wish. Things should have gone differently before I left, but at least Aurora seems to have forgiven me. I spot her phone on the edge of the vanity and message her again.

> Someone's a very naughty girl.

> Getting off in my bed and my shower again.

> Remember I'm keeping track.

I hear the *ping, ping, ping* as each message registers on her phone.

Aurora's lips turn up in a coy grin as she slides the door open and hops out of the shower. I drink in the sight of her naked body, slick and wet, all her curves on display as she drips water on my bathroom floor. She wipes her hands on a towel and holds her phone up, unlocking it.

She says something I don't catch, but a second later my phone pings.

248

PRINCESS

You better mean that.

You're watching right now?

HOLLIS

You're naked in my bathroom.

That's how our date should have ended.

PRINCESS

Want to see why I love your shower so much?

HOLLIS

Show me.

She grins again, sets her phone down, blows the kitty cam a kiss, and steps back into the shower, leaving the door open. She spreads her legs wide, braces a hand on the tile and adjusts the angle of the wall jet. And now it makes perfect sense. Her head falls forward, and she plants both palms on the wall. When she moans, I slide my hand into my joggers and stroke myself in time to the roll of her hips.

"So close, so close." She catches her bottom lip between her teeth and grabs the handrail. Her legs tremble, and I quicken my pace, aggressively stroking my cock as her back arches and her head falls back.

Judging from the pitch of her moan, she's about to come. And I'm right there with her. She drops to her knees and twists away from the jet so it hits her back. Her hand slides between her parted thighs as she rides out the orgasm. She slaps her clit repeatedly, moaning my name as her hips jerk. It isn't until she sags against the shower wall that I let go. But I grab a handful of tissues first, so I don't have to change my freaking shirt. Or pants.

She slowly pulls herself to standing and turns off the water, then grabs a towel from the rack and wraps it around her gorgeous body.

What I wouldn't give to be there toweling her off, taking her to bed, kissing every inch of her, touching her in all the places that make her moan my name.

I grab my phone and call her.

She answers on the first ring, slightly breathless. "Hi."

"We're showering together when I get home." Aurora wet, naked, and soapy? Fuck yes.

"We'd better be doing a hell of a lot more than showering, Hollis."

"Oh we will be, I promise." I pull one of my earbuds free, making sure all is quiet. "But first, I think I need to spank that naughty little ass of yours for all the bad things you get up to when I'm not home."

Her eyes light up as she moves toward the kitty cam.

"Now I really can't wait." She carries the camera back to the bedroom and aims it at the bed. Then she crosses to my closet, finds a T-shirt, and pulls it over her head. "How was the flight and practice? How's your knee?"

Beyond the unbearable sexual tension that's growing exponentially, my desire to confide in her again is also on the rise. "The flight was fine. I slept for most of it. Aside from watching from the bench, practice was good. Fingers crossed I get cleared for the ice next week. Might not have to wait for the playoffs after all. And my knee was a bit achy from all the sitting, but I spent some time in the sauna, and the pool, and the hot tub, so it's better now. How was your presentation? Did you do well?"

"Uh, we had a PowerPoint glitch, but I had a printed version, so I talked through the points and used the whiteboard while they sorted it out."

"That's my girl, always on top of things."

"I'd like to be on top of you—or under you."

I chuckle. "Both can be arranged when I'm home."

"God, I'm so horny it's ridiculous, Hollis. I've already made a mess of your sheets and your shower, and I'm still all achy."

"You need me to talk you through another round?" Tell her exactly how I'd hold her hips as she straddled me. How I'd pinch her clit and fist her hair to keep her close.

"What I need is you pounding me into a mattress. Rix will be at Tristan's all weekend." She runs a brush through her hair. "She's halfway moved in already."

"So I could come to yours." When it's just her and I it's easy to forget how complicated this all is outside our bubble of two.

"It would be easier than me sneaking up to your place." She bites her lip.

We need to talk this part through. All the sneaking around, hiding shit—it can't continue indefinitely. Unless she's not at the same place as me. Even if she is now, nothing is ever guaranteed.

"Hollis?"

"Sorry, yeah, I agree. It would be easier."

The door to my hotel room opens, but only a few inches, thanks to the safety latch.

"Hey, Hollis, can you unlatch this? I gotta grab my iPad."

"Shit," I mutter. "Coming! Just a sec." I slam my laptop shut, but not before I catch Aurora's panicked expression.

"Is that my dad?" she whispers.

"Yeah. Talk tomorrow." I end the call before she can reply and roll off the bed, shoving the tissues under my pillow before I rush to let Roman in.

He gives me a questioning look.

"Sorry. I didn't mean to lock you out. You heading back to Dallas and Ash's room?"

"Yeah. Everything okay?"

"Yeah, all good. Let me grab a sweatshirt real quick." I turn away and take a few deep breaths, calming my heart rate. That's two close calls. I pull a hoodie over my head while he grabs his iPad, then follow him into the hall, so grateful I'd flipped the latch.

"You look so much more rested than you did before I left." Roman holds Aurora at arm's length at the Pancake House, inspecting her.

I'm itching to wrap my arms around her, breathe her in, and tell her how much I've missed her. Instead, I shove my hands in my pockets and feel guilty for wanting what I want.

"I'm fine, Dad, just a lot on my plate with the gala and finals coming up." She pats his arm, and he releases her.

"Do you need me to take anything off your plate? I can order my own groceries and handle my laundry when I get back from away games," he offers.

"I do your groceries when I do my own, so it's not a big deal. And we both know how you are about laundry." She slides back into the booth. She's already ordered for us—probably as eager as I am to get this meal over with. But I'm not sure our reasons are the same. All the things I love about our diner tradition are now a reminder of the lies I'm steeped in.

"I could get better at it." He frowns. "I should get better at it. You can't do my laundry forever. I could get a housekeeper."

I drop onto the bench across from Aurora, as does Roman.

Her gaze shifts my way, and she smiles like it's any other day, like we don't have plans to go back to her place after this.

"Or you could start dating," Aurora says cheekily.

Roman rolls his eyes. "Stop sending me apps."

She sips her coffee and shifts gears. "You really kicked some butt this week. Two solid wins, and against high-ranking teams. How are you feeling about the game against LA on Monday?"

While they talk game strategy, I try desperately not to think about all her messages from the past few days.

PRINCESS

> I'm rearranging my dresser so my mirror catches the bed, in case you want to watch yourself fuck me.

> I should probably be on top for the sake of your knee.

> Unless you're more inclined to fuck me against the front door. I guess we'll see how far inside the apartment we make it.

Aurora's foot bumps my shin under the table. I glance at her. We're not playing footsies again. Her eyes dart to the table. My food is sitting in front of me.

"You're preoccupied today," Roman observes.

"I have an appointment with my doctor tomorrow." It's true, but not why I'm distracted.

"Do you think you'll be cleared for practice?" Aurora asks.

"That's the hope."

"Have you given any more thought to sportscasting, or are you still considering coaching as an option after you hang up your skates?" Roman asks.

I rub my bottom lip. "I have at least another season before I need to think about that."

"You'd be great leading a team." Roman pats me on the back.

"You'd be a great coach," Aurora agrees. "You're a patient teacher, and you're great at giving direct instruction."

I sure as fuck know she's not talking about hockey. "I'm not out of the game yet," I grumble. Roman shifts the topic, probably mistaking the tension for career stress.

We finish our meals and leave the diner. It's warming up, the snow turning to brown slush.

"I need to grab a couple of things from the grocery store. Either of you need anything?" I ask once we've crossed the street.

"Not that I can think of," Roman says.

"I went shopping yesterday, so I'm good, too," Aurora replies.

"Okay. I'll see you later." They push inside the building, and I make the short trip to the store. I pick up Aurora's favorite candies and stop at the local florist on the way back.

By the time I return to the building, Aurora's already messaged to let me know the coast is clear.

My palms start to sweat when I step into the elevator. The line we're stepping over today will change things again. For half a second, I question whether I should go through with this. But I can't deny her after all the shit I've put her through. It's about more than how it affects her, though. It's me, too. I can't keep sitting on the fence with her. I don't want to.

The elevator dings, and I step into the hall. I half expect Roman to be standing outside her door, but it's bodyguard free —and it opens before I can knock. Aurora pokes her head out, looking both ways before she grabs the front of my shirt and yanks me into her apartment. The door falls closed as she tries to pull my mouth to hers.

I tilt my head back. "Hi."

"Hi, please kiss me before I die." She pushes up on her toes and puckers her lips.

I laugh and drop my head, parting when she strokes the seam of my lips. Her hands are already on the move.

I break the kiss and murmur, "Safety latch."

"Right. Yes." She releases my shirt and secures the door.

When she turns around, I hold out the flowers. "For you."

Her expression softens as she brings them to her nose and inhales deeply. "They're beautiful. Thank you."

"Just like you, and you're welcome."

"I'll put them in water later." She sets them on the side table, takes the grocery bag, and doesn't bother to look inside before she drops it on the floor. "I know we have a lot to talk about, but I would really like to save the whole important-conversation part until later."

"Feeling impatient, are we, Princess?" I stroke her cheek.

"Extremely, yes. And even though I wanted to jill off this morning, I didn't, because I knew you would be worth the wait. But then I had to sit through that meal with you looking yummy." She pushes my jacket over my shoulders and runs her hands down my arms as it falls to the floor.

"You think it was any different for me?" I trace the edge of her jaw and skim her cheek with my lips. "I wanted to wrap you in my arms, like this." I pull her against me. "And tell you how much I missed you." I take her earlobe between my teeth. "And that I haven't been able to stop thinking about all the ways I want to make you feel good."

"I want all those things, too," Aurora whispers.

"We'll get there, eventually." I bite my way along her jaw. We have uninterrupted hours ahead of us. This is my chance to show her exactly how much I want her, to give her what I've denied us for the past several weeks. I want to be exactly what she needs. "But I plan to savor every single moment of this. No rushing."

I tip her chin up and take her in—eyes rimmed with liner, lashes long, full lips glossy. She's wearing one of the many shirts I've bought her for various occasions over the years, and jeans I've complimented. If I looked down, I would find her wearing socks I gifted her.

"Please kiss me," she whispers.

I slant my mouth over hers, and she softens against me. For a minute, she lets me lead. But then her hands begin to wander, fingers traveling lightly down my spine until she reaches my ass and squeezes. "I can't wait to do that when we're naked and you're inside me."

"You're getting ahead of yourself, don't you think?"

"Thinking is all I've done for months, Hollis." Her fingers travel along my beltline. "About getting my hands on you, exactly like this." She pops the button of my jeans.

"Tell me what else you've been thinking about." This is not just about distracting her and slowing us down; I want to learn what makes her tick in the bedroom. But more than that, I want to figure out if we're in this for the same reasons. I don't want to be a passing fantasy for her.

"So many things." She tugs the zipper down. "About how good it will feel to touch you." Her fingertips dip inside my waistband, gliding from one hip to the other. "How much I loved it when you fucked me with your fingers, and how much better it will be when it's your cock filling me."

"That's a dirty little mouth you have, Princess."

Aurora's hot gaze meets mine as her hand slips into my boxer briefs. Her fingertips graze the head and gently skim the length. "I think you like my naughty mouth."

"Fucking hell," I groan as her warm, soft palm wraps around me. I spin us around until her back meets the door and brace my left forearm above her head.

"You feel so good in my hand." Aurora's thumb sweeps over the head.

"Your hand feels so good on me," I grind out.

My eyes roll up, and my teeth snap together as she reverses the motion. I cup her chin in my hand so I can kiss her again. Her strokes are slow, a gentle exploration. Every time she reaches the crown, her thumb runs over the slit and circles the head before she drags her fist back down. It's fucking bliss.

Her free hand slides under my shirt, fingertips gliding over my abs and up my chest to circle a nipple. She's all sultry sweetness as her tongue drags across her bottom lip. "Can you take your shirt off for me please, Hollis? I don't want to stop touching you."

"That makes two of us." I can't get enough of the feel of her hands on my skin, of her sweet, breathy sighs and her lust-heavy eyes. I pull my shirt over my head and toss it to the floor. Her greedy gaze rakes over me, making me feel like a fucking god—especially with the way her fingers trail over my inked skin, her eyes tracking the movement.

She frees me from my boxer briefs, and one side of her mouth kicks up. "I knew it."

"Knew what?" My voice is all gravel.

Her grin turns impish. "That you'd have a boyfriend dick."

I grunt when her thumb circles the crown. "Explain that, please."

"It's pretty, like the rest of you." Stroke up. "And thick." Circle the crown. "And big." Stroke down. "I'll want to ride it all the time."

"You mean you'll want to ride *me* all the time." My fingers twitch on her hip. I want to put my hands on her, get her naked. But I'm afraid I'll lose control and we'll end up fucking on the living room floor. Which is not how I want this to go.

She moves my hand to cover hers. "Show me what you like. I want to learn."

"Ah, fuck, Princess." And like a neanderthal, I want to castrate every single guy she's ever touched before. Thankfully, that thought stays in my head.

I lace my fingers with hers, tightening our grip. Her gaze flips between my face and our twined hands as they move over my cock. She squeezes with every downward stroke, loosening her grip as she reaches the head so she can smooth her thumb over the crown. It feels too good. Every stroke taking me higher. Too soon, I'm teetering on the edge.

"I won't last much longer," I warn.

"But you can go again, right?" she pants.

"Yeah. Of course." *What kind of question is that?*

She nods. "Okay. Good."

I untwine our fingers. "I need you to stop or I'm—"

"I want to see. I need to see what I do to you," she pleads.

That's all it takes. My body goes rigid as I thicken in her hand, and my hips jerk, chasing her touch. I grab the doorknob so I don't end up on my knees.

When my vision clears, I'm staring at Aurora's cum-covered hand still wrapped around my cock. "Well, fuck." I finger the hem of her shirt, which didn't escape this event unscathed.

Her eyes light up, and her smile is radiant.

"So proud of yourself, aren't you?"

She holds her thumb and forefinger a hairsbreadth apart. "Maybe a little." Her smile turns shy. "I want to be what you need."

"You are, Princess. You're everything and more." This woman brings me to my knees.

"Is it my turn now?" she asks as my lips brush hers.

"I think we might need to clean you up first." I tuck a finger under her chin. "Why don't you show me all the naughty things you get up to in the shower when you're thinking about me?"

CHAPTER 29
HAMMER

It's really happening. This is really happening. I finally, *finally* got to put my hands on Hollis. The feel of him in my hand, the look on his face, the sounds he made, the incredible rush that came from knowing I was the reason—I made him feel that way. I pushed him over the edge. And now we're going to get naked together and shower. And then we're going to have sex. Fuck? Maybe have sex *and* fuck. Hopefully. I feel like both are possible with Hollis.

I pull my shirt over my head and wipe my hand on the fabric. Hollis's gaze drops to my bare chest. And suddenly his hands are on me, caressing, squeezing. He drops his head and covers the tight peak with his mouth. His lips are soft, his tongue warm and wet as he laves my nipple. And then his teeth sink in and he sucks, hard.

I spear my hand into his hair and grip the satiny strands, as if I'll actually be able to keep him there. His fingers circle my wrist, finding the pressure point that makes me loosen my grip.

He kisses my nipple, then bites the swell again, like he can't help himself. Hollis straightens, eyes hooded. He points toward my bedroom. "Into the shower with you."

My knees go weak at the fire in his eyes. Nervous excitement

259

makes my mouth dry and my palms and panties damp. I've fantasized about this countless times, thought about being with him this way. And now he's here. And he wants me the same way I want him. I rush across the apartment, and Hollis follows at a leisurely stroll, tucking his erection into his boxer briefs on the way.

I disappear into the bathroom and turn on the shower. Mine isn't nearly as awesome, hence the reason I used his. This one has two wall jets, but the placement isn't ideal. It does have a removable showerhead, though. I turn on the water and adjust the temperature. Then I get to work on unbuttoning my jeans with unsteady hands.

Hollis steps up and covers them. His expression is intense, eyes brimming with need. "I'll do that."

This is what's been missing. *He* is what I've been missing. Hollis knows exactly what he's doing. More than that, he knows *me*. He can read me. He's commanding but gentle as he moves my hands aside. Completely in control.

It's one thing to get myself off in his shower while he's watching on the kitty cam, but this is so different. The walls are down between us. At least for now. It's part of the reason I wanted to wait until after to talk. I'd rather be in the dark if he doesn't want the same thing I do. I can hold on to the fantasy of us a little longer.

I push those thoughts aside. I want to stay in the moment. I want to remember every second of this first with him.

"Hey." Hollis cups my face in his wide palm. "Just say the word, and I'll stop. If I do something you don't like, you tell me, okay?"

I nod. I trust him implicitly, with my heart, with my body. "Can you kiss me, please?"

"Of course." His lips brush over mine. Soft, sweet.

I move closer until we're skin to skin from the waist up. He keeps one hand on my cheek and the other snakes around my waist. I sink into the kiss, into the feel of his arm wrapped possessively around me, his body pressed against mine.

"Show me what happens when I'm not here to take care of you," he says when we break.

His fingers dip into the waistband of my jeans, and he pops the button, tugging the zipper down. He skims the edge of my blue lace panties. They're the same color as his team jersey. Which also happens to be his favorite color.

"These are pretty." He sinks to the floor on his good knee and tugs my jeans over my hips and down my thighs. "Let's hope they survive me."

My heart is at risk of beating out of my chest. I've worn a bathing suit in front of him plenty of times, but being undressed by him is intimate. He's never looked at me this way before; like he wants to cherish me and devour me at the same time.

I brace a shaking hand on his shoulder and lift my foot so he can slide one leg out and then the other. Then he takes off my socks, leaving me in only panties.

He runs his hand from my ankle to my hip, fingers drifting along the waistband. "Would you like me to take these off for you, Princess?"

I'm shaking with anticipation. "Please."

He hooks his fingers into the fabric at each hip and slowly drags it down my thighs, eyes never leaving mine. I step out of my panties, which are so unreasonably damp it's almost embarrassing. All he's done so far is kiss me and suck my nipple.

Without looking down, he leans in and presses a kiss at the apex of my thighs.

I'm pretty sure I'll spontaneously combust before we even get to the sex part. His hands move to my hips, eyes falling closed as he inhales deeply. Is he steadying himself? Breathing me in? Trying not to take me to the floor? It's incredibly humbling to have this huge, intimidating man on his knees for me. I run a trembling hand through his hair, grounding myself as I wait to see what he does next.

He rises slowly, lips dragging over my stomach, between my breasts, and along the column of my throat until he's looming over me, eyes dark with lust. My hand, which has been fisting his hair, loosens and falls to his shoulder. My legs are halfway to giving out. My breathing is as unsteady as the rest of me.

But I can't look away. He's so gorgeous, and fierce, and he looks like he wants to eat me alive.

The hand on my right hip moves inward, and I stop breathing. The backs of his fingers sweep over my bare skin, and then his index finger slides between my folds. I'm so wet. So ready for him. I moan—wantonly, unabashedly, loudly.

His mouth curls up in a salacious smile that makes my already weak knees quake and my clit ache. He withdraws his fingers, and I latch on to his wrist. "No, no, please!"

His other hand cups my cheek. "Shower first, then I'll take care of you." He kisses me chastely and gives me an expectant look.

"I should help you out of these." I tug at the loop on his jeans.

"If you'd like." His other hand rises, and his eyes stay fixed on mine as he licks his index finger and hums with approval.

I'm so out of my depth, totally in over my head. I can't decide if I'm more likely to faint, spontaneously come, or turn into a puddle. I fight to steady my hands as I shimmy his jeans over his hockey butt and push them down his thighs.

I drop to my knees on the cold tile and carefully pull them past his wrapped knee. He steps out of one leg and braces his hand on the shower behind me as he does the same with his non-injured leg. And then he's in nothing but boxer shorts and the bandage around his knee meant to stabilize it.

"Should I remove this?" I settle my hand above the bandage.

"I can do it," he says.

"Let me, please." I find the Velcro on the side and gently peel it away. The stitches from surgery have already dissolved, so only a few small red spots mark the incisions.

Once the bandage is removed, I tuck my fingers into his waistband and carefully free his reawakening cock before dragging the boxers down his thighs. He steps out and kicks them aside. I'm at eye-level with his penis. If I lean forward, I can nuzzle it, or kiss it, or suck it. My thoughts must be written on my face, because he bends and slides his hands under my arms, lifting me to my feet. "I'll keep that sweet mouth of yours busy later."

He opens the shower door, and I put my hand under the spray, testing the water before I step in. Hollis follows me and closes the door. Steam billows around us as water cascades over his chest and down his abs. I run my hands over his shoulders and down his inked arm, and then we're kissing, slick bodies pressed against each other. His erection swells against my stomach, and I roll my hips, wanting more, wanting his hands all over me, fingers inside me, tongue on my skin.

He pulls back, eyeing my face before he taps the jet on the wall. "I can see why you prefer my shower."

"My showerhead does the job."

"But it's more work," he notes. "So I should help."

He squirts some of my body wash into his palm and rubs his hands together, creating suds. And then his hands are on the move, sliding down my arms and up my ribs, skimming the undersides of my breasts and smoothing down my back, squeezing my ass before he spins me around, my back to his chest. He turns the rain showerhead toward the back wall and slides the door open. The fan is on in the bathroom, so the mirror is mostly fog free.

I stare at our reflection across the room, and it's like I'm seeing myself for the first time. Hollis is six-three and I'm nearly five-nine, so the top of my head reaches his chin. But he's so broad and thick and so intensely gorgeous, he takes my breath away. His soapy hand eases up my stomach, the tattoos on his biceps rippling as he cups my breast. He kisses a path up my neck. "The number of times I fucked my hand to the image of you naked in my shower is obscene."

"The number of times I fucked myself with my vibrator in your bed last week was equally obscene."

"I know. I watched the videos before I deleted them." He reaches for the detachable showerhead. "Now show me."

His admissions give me courage, as does the hot, expectant look on his face. I spread my legs and lean against him, letting my head rest against his chest as I guide the showerhead between my thighs. It only takes a few seconds to find the spot that makes my eyes roll up and my knees wobbly.

"That's it, Princess." Hollis's arm tightens around my waist, and his lips move along my neck, nipping, kissing. "I've got you."

He toys with my nipple with the other hand, rolling the stiff peak, tugging, pinching. And all the while, I watch our reflections in the mirror while he watches me. My belly flutters, every muscle tightening as sensation builds, radiating through me. And Hollis murmurs hot words of encouragement, telling me I'm gorgeous, that he loves watching me come. When my body starts to shake and my coordination suffers, he takes over, keeping the pressure where I need it. As the orgasm rushes through me, he takes almost all my weight, his arm wrapped tightly around me, his lips on my neck. When the shaking subsides, he carefully sets the showerhead back in the holder and waits until my legs remember how to do their job before he turns me around and takes my mouth in another bone-melting kiss.

I can't get close enough, can't get enough of his hands on me, of mine on him. "Please, Hollis."

He takes my face in his hands, molten gaze roving over me. "Please what?"

"Take me to bed." My stomach is full of butterflies. I want all of him. Every part, even the one I won't admit aloud. Especially that.

He turns off the shower and grabs a towel, drying me off, then himself. He's hard again, thick and ready, and all I want is to know what it feels like to have him inside me. Grabbing his hand, I pull him into my bedroom. I can't get there fast enough, half afraid he'll change his mind about this. About us. About me.

I riffle through the condoms in my nightstand drawer. The one on top is glow in the dark—it must have been the Halloween theme or something. I pick a different one, and when I turn around, Hollis is standing behind me.

He takes the foil packet and kisses me softly. "It's okay if you're not ready for this."

"I'm ready." I want this with a ferocity that verges on desperation. If his guilt takes over and this is the only time I get him, I want to make the most of it.

"If that changes, you say the word, Princess," he murmurs.

"It won't."

A faint smile appears, and then he kisses me breathless before he lifts me onto the bed. I slide back as he joins me.

"Lie down for me, Princess."

"But shouldn't I be on top?" I wish I wasn't so nervous.

An amused grin curves his lips, and his eyes heat. "We'll see." His gaze shifts to the pillow, a silent command.

I love that he can say so much without uttering a word. I stretch out on the cool sheets, cheeks heating as he strokes himself lazily while he looks over my naked body. He stretches out beside me and drags a single finger along my jaw, down my cheek, over my chest, circling a nipple before continuing his descent. "So many things I want to do to you." His tongue sweeps across his bottom lip. "For you."

And then his mouth is on mine, lips soft and sure as his fingers drift lower. I part my legs automatically and he strokes me, circling my clit once before he slides a finger inside. He pulls back, eyes hooded with lust. I whimper as he withdraws his finger, then moan when he slips it between his lips and makes a guttural sound. "Will you let me taste you?"

I nod and manage to whisper, "Yes, please."

He edges his good knee between my legs and props himself up on his forearm, looming over me. His lips brush mine, and then he starts the descent, kissing his way down my neck, pausing at the sensitive spot along my collarbone before he nibbles his way over the swell of my breast. He sucks one nipple, then the other, teasing me with his tongue and making me gasp when he uses teeth. He gives attention to every sensitive spot on his way down. "So fucking beautiful." He settles between my thighs. "Every part of you." He kisses the inside of my thigh and then his tongue sweeps up the juncture—close, but not to where I want his mouth.

And I love it. Love the sure way he touches me, love the feel of his calloused but gentle hands pushing my legs wide, of the softness of his mouth as he explores. He teases me with nips of teeth and soft kisses. His tongue is wet velvet between my thighs, taking me higher, spinning me into orbit. I thread my hands through his hair, unable to tear my gaze from the sight of him with his arms looped around my thighs, holding them open as he French kisses my clit. He licks me up and down, teasing me. Every nerve ending is alive with the heat of his mouth.

His rough palms slide along the backs of my thighs, thumbs hooked into the bend in my knees as he pushes them toward my chest, spreading me wider. His expression is deliciously carnal as he sucks my clit, then drags his tongue through my wetness, fucking me with it before he goes lower. The heat of his tongue causes my breath to catch. No one had ever touched me there, let alone how Hollis is touching me.

"Oh my God, what are you doing?" Even as my cheeks burst with color, unexpected heat floods my center.

"Eating your sweet ass." He licks at my hole again and I whimper at the sensation. I've never felt more exposed or wanted. His tongue wipes and swipes at me, swirling before he moves from my clit all the way back again.

"But—"

My protest dies at the hot feel of his tongue pressing against me, awakening a whole new desire.

"Keep your knees to your chest," he orders.

I quickly hook my arm under them, and he chuckles. "So fucking eager to get your ass eaten, aren't you, my naughty little Princess?"

I nod and bite my lip, then groan when his teeth sink into my ass, followed by a soft kiss. "That makes two of us." He shifts one hand so he can strum my clit, while he alternates tongue-fucking with rimming my asshole. "I will be the only one to touch you here." It's dirty, and hot, and feels so unexpectedly good to feel him fucking me like this.

I'm nearly gasping as he changes position. His rough hands hold me as my legs start to shake. My heart races as his tongue finds every way to bring me pleasure. His fingers penetrate me, sliding in easily. He drags some of my juices down before slicking a thick finger into my ass. I feel the fullness as he moves deeper to his knuckle, pulling back before pushing it in more.

Every thud of my heartbeat is in time with the spasms that have me clenching around his tongue in my pussy, my ass trying to pull his finger deeper. I come so hard the world is a wash of stars.

And then his gorgeous face is right in front of mine, and his huge body is stretched out over me. He frames my face with his hands. "God help me, I want you. I'll be right back."

I stroke his cheek with shaking fingers. Desire makes my body electric. "Please, Hollis. I need you."

"I need you too, Princess." He kisses the end of my nose. "But hold that thought for just a second." He rolls off the bed in one smooth motion and disappears into my bathroom. The faucet turns on and I bite back a smile. I can't believe that just happened. He returns a minute later, nabs the condom from the nightstand, tears open the package, and rolls it down his length.

Anticipation makes it hard to breathe as he fits himself between my thighs. I want him so much, want to be connected to him in the most primal, intimate way, and I'm terrified I won't be what he needs. I'm already in so deep. Completely head over heels for him.

"Hey." He caresses my cheek, his breath is cool mint on my skin. "Stay right here, with me."

I nod and set my palm against the side of his neck, his pulse hammering under the skin.

"You tell me what you need and how you need it, okay?" he murmurs.

"You, just you." He's all I want. This is all I want.

He reaches between us and drags the head over my clit, sliding lower until he nudges my entrance. Our gazes hold as he pushes in, slowly, gently, stretching me, filling me an inch at a time until his hips rest in the cradle of mine. "You okay, Princess?"

I nod. The intimacy of it is overwhelming, but I can't look away. I exhale a shuddering breath, already on the edge of something. "You feel so good." *So right.*

"Like perfection," he murmurs.

"This feels different." It's not a fumbling first time. There's no awkwardness. I don't want to close my eyes to escape his gaze. If anything, I want to drown in the emotions swimming behind his eyes. I run my hands through his hair and down the sides of his neck, addicted to the feel of him. "I just...I can't get close enough? And this is...more?" I feel like I'm connected to him beyond the physical. It's as though everything I feel for and about Hollis is winding around us, through us. Like he's sifting through my emotions and urging them to surface.

His smile softens, and he sweeps his thumb along my bottom lip. "It is more."

My fingers coast down his back, over straining muscles as I luxuriate in the fullness and the weight of his body over mine. In the feel of being surrounded by him, of surrounding him. When I reach his ass, I squeeze.

"I need to start moving," he murmurs.

"Please."

He pulls his hips back, and I groan at the loss. It only lasts a moment, but it feels endlessly tragic until he pushes back in. Each stroke is slow, measured, taking me higher. His hand eases down my thigh, catching in the crook of my knee. He hooks it over his hip, changing his angle and deepening his thrust. I do the same with the other leg, locking my feet at the small of his back, my whole body wrapped around him.

I don't need to tell him what I need or want, because he already seems to know. "It feels so good, Hollis." We've hardly even started, and it's already the best sex of my life. It's everything I wanted it to be and so much more.

"You're fucking perfect, Princess." He brushes his lips over mine. "You were made for me."

Those words settle in my chest, all the months of uncertainty melting away with his conviction. In this moment I feel healed. Whole. Like he's where I belong.

He moves over me, hips rolling, eyes never leaving mine. He murmurs words of praise, telling me I'm his. That he'll never get enough of me.

I want it to be true. It feels like it is—like he's the missing piece, and now I'm finally whole. I want this to last forever, to stay in this bubble with him, where we fit together perfectly and nothing can come between us. Where I'm enough. Worth the risk.

I'm so hopelessly, helplessly in love with him. I'll never want someone else the way I want him, with every fiber of my being, with my entire heart.

The orgasm washes over me, not a crashing wave, but one that drags me down and keeps me swirling in interminable bliss. Hollis's strokes grow erratic, and he pushes in deep and stills, a low, desperate groan vibrating against my lips.

I swear I see everything I feel for him echoed in his eyes. Like we're finally on the same page.

He rolls us over in one smooth motion, still inside me, and I lie on top of him, our bodies slick with sweat. I rest my cheek on his chest, forehead pressed against the side of his neck. His arms come around me, and his lips find my temple.

Fear slithers down my spine. What if the guilt hits him? What if he thinks this was a mistake? What if he shuts me out?

His finger drifts along the edge of my jaw, and he lifts my chin. Anxiety makes my stomach clench. He's still inside me. What if I see something I don't want to in his eyes? What if the best sex of my life becomes the worst?

He kisses me softly. "Hi, beautiful."

"Hi." I'm suddenly shy and uncertain.

"I think we might need another shower."

I laugh, relieved, as I take in the warm expression on his gorgeous face. No regret. No guilt. Just contentment that echoes in my chest. "And a glass of water."

"I'd prefer a beer. And maybe a snack. And then I'd like to get you back into this bed and keep you here for the rest of the day, minus the occasional break to refuel."

I smile and duck my head. "I was okay?"

His eyes flare, and he shifts, sitting up and taking me with him. He waits until my gaze meets his. "*Okay* is never a word I would use to describe you. I have been fighting this since January, and not just because of the attraction we share, Aurora. It's so much more than that. This, you and me, what's happening here." He pauses, shakes his head, and presses his lips to mine. "You are incredible. *That* was incredible. For me, anyway."

"For me, too." I finally understand what the phrase *making love* means. Because that's what it felt like, being filled with his love. But I don't tell him that, too afraid to admit those feelings. Maybe I'm overwhelmed by lust and how good the sex was.

He kisses me one last time. "Shower, snack, and cuddle, and then back to bed?"

"Sounds perfect."

CHAPTER 30
HAMMER

I wake to breakfast in bed. Cinnamon French toast and fresh fruit, and coffee exactly how I like it. Yesterday, last night, and this morning are hands down the best first time I've ever experienced.

"We need to talk about how we want this to look—this thing between us," Hollis says when I'm most of the way through my French toast.

I want it to last. I want this to be real outside of this bedroom and my apartment. "I want more of this with you," I tell him.

He nods slowly. "What exactly do you mean?"

I wished I'd had the nerve to bring it up first, so I know where he stands. I'm scared to put my heart on the line after all the ups and downs since January. For me, this isn't a fling. "More dates, more of you and me."

"For this to work, we should talk to Roman."

I set my fork down, appetite gone. I move the tray off my lap and turn toward him. "He'll be upset." I can't see this going over well. I hate upsetting him. I won't even be honest about my favorite color with my dad. How can I be honest about this?

He'd be so disappointed in me. For breaking his one rule, and with the very last person on earth I should want. For all the lies

I've told him. For the secrets I'm keeping. Thinking about it makes me want to vomit.

"At first, yes. But if he knows we're serious, he'll come to terms with it." Hollis takes my hand in his, eyes on my fingers. "Unless that's not where your head is."

Talking about it makes it all very real. It feels like I'm breaking out in a full body sweat. I see his point, and I'm relieved that we could want the same thing, but what if my dad finding out changes that? "I want to see if we can work as a couple. We've spent the past few months fighting this connection, and I'd like time to explore that. But if we tell my dad now —" I release an anxious breath. What if it doesn't work? What if Hollis changes his mind? What if my dad doesn't forgive me? "—then we'll have to manage that, too. Playoffs are coming up. There are only a few weeks left in the semester, and this one has been harder than I expected."

His brow furrows. "Harder how?"

"The shift back to classes, the workload, taking on the gala. It's been a lot, and I've made the dean's list every semester. But I'm on the cusp right now." I've been powering through, but I need to be honest about this. I want to prove that I can manage the pressure that would come with being Hemi's assistant once I graduate. But if I'm suddenly dating a player and then being handed the job, how will that look? No one will take me seriously.

"Because of me." Hollis squeezes my hand.

"Because of a lot of things. My mom is coming to visit next week." I always have a lot of feelings when I see my mom, and telling her I'm dating Dad's best friend is…not an ideal birthday surprise. I can only imagine how she'll feel about it. "You're still waiting to be cleared for practice. It's a lot for both of us. Maybe we take the next few weeks to just be us?" The biggest worry I don't voice. What if my dad loses it, and Hollis doesn't choose me? Or my dad is so upset it messes up our relationship? He's the most important person in my life and I'm his. My shame bucket is already full enough as it is, I don't want to add my dad's feelings to it, too.

"How will waiting change the outcome?" Hollis asks gently.

I swallow my anxiety. "He'll be upset no matter what... I just don't want it to negatively impact my final grades, or the gala, or the end of your season. It's the potential ripple effect, Hollis. From school, to my potential job, and my dad, and the playoffs. There's so much at stake." I'm on the verge of tears, thinking about how wrong this could all go. But I don't want to cry or give Hollis a reason to question whether I can handle this.

He nods slowly and kisses the back of my hand. "Once you're through exams, we tell him, regardless of my ice status. Okay?"

I exhale a relieved breath. "Okay. I just want a little time to enjoy this." It's only a few weeks. Hopefully, it's enough time to figure out how best to tell my dad. And the gala will be over by then.

"So to be clear, this is us dating," Hollis says.

I press my fingers to my lips and nod. In secret, but we're dating. "I didn't know if we would ever get here," I whisper.

He tucks my hair behind my ear. "I'm sorry it took me this long to figure my shit out, Princess."

"I know I made it hard for you." I lean into the touch, into him.

"No holding the blame. If anyone made it difficult, it was me." He moves me to straddle his lap. "And for that, I'm sorry. But I will make it up to you however you want, as many times as you need me to."

"You can start by kissing me," I murmur, fingers sliding through his hair.

"Everything for you." He pulls my mouth to his.

We end up celebrating our newly established secret-relationship status, which means I'm running way behind. I've never been late for class, but this morning it's inevitable.

"What if I drive you in? Will you make it on time, then?"

Hollis asks as I toss things into my bag, double-checking to make sure I have my laptop charger since the battery only lasts a few hours.

I give him a look. "You can't drive me to school, Hollis."

We haven't even talked about what will happen after we leave this apartment. How will secretly dating look? The sex fest we had last night and this morning isn't about getting each other out of our systems. But he's still my dad's best friend, and I'm still a university student. It's complicated as fuck.

He crosses his arms. "I absolutely can drive you."

He's still shirtless. And I stole the hoodie he wore over yesterday and am currently wearing it and a pair of leggings. I flip the safety latch and shove my feet into my running shoes. "You're sweet to offer, but the subway is faster. I've already emailed my professor to let her know I'm running behind." It's a seminar class, so showing up late will be embarrassing, but at least I've done what I can.

"I'm sorry about this."

"Don't apologize for eating my pussy for breakfast." I give him a quick kiss. "We should probably talk later."

"We will."

I turn and watch in horror as the knob turns. My stomach flips as the door swings open. There is no explanation I can give my dad that will make sense with Hollis standing shirtless in my foyer. I'm suddenly terrified for Hollis's face. And life. I take a protective stance in front of him. I don't know why. It's not as though I could stop my dad if he wanted to kick Hollis's ass. Especially since his knee is still healing.

"What the fu—"

My relief is instantaneous and so overwhelming I almost burst into tears.

Tristan frowns as he steps into the apartment. He's holding a box from Just Desserts. He does this often—leaves cakes or treats for Rix with messages written on them. He sets the box on the entry table and holds up a hand. "Don't say this isn't what it looks like."

"Don't tell my dad," I blurt.

Tristan looks surprisingly empathetic. "I don't want to be on the receiving end of Roman's wrath any more than you do." He turns his concerned gaze on Hollis. "We talked about this."

"It's complicated—"

Tristan holds his hand up. "You think I don't know that? Hiding this isn't going to make it less so. I'm not here to give you two a lecture. You're adults and you can make your own decisions. I need to grab Bea's laptop and get back home before she wakes up." He pauses on the way to Rix's room. "I know it's not the same situation, but please don't make the same mistakes I did." He disappears down the hall to Rix's room.

"It'll be okay. We'll talk tonight," Hollis assures me.

I trust that Tristan won't tell my dad, but he has a point. When shit went sideways with those two, it really went sideways. I don't want that to happen to us. But there's no way out of this without someone getting hurt.

CHAPTER 31
HAMMER

"My calves are so tight," Tally announces. She's lying on the living room floor of Hemi's apartment with her legs stretched against the wall, index fingers wrapped around her big toes.

"You are ridiculously flexible," Rix observes.

"And sore. We practiced for four hours yesterday, and we still didn't get the routine down." She does a backwards somersault and crosses her legs, sitting upright. "But we're close. I just want a strong finish to my senior year." Tally attends an arts school and is a competitive dancer. Outside of attending hockey games, school, and spending time with us, that takes up most of her spare time.

"You've got this," Hemi says with conviction. "We can't wait to see you kill it."

"You don't all have to come," Tally says.

"Pfft." Hemi makes a circle motion with her finger to encompass our group. "We're your Babe Brigade. We will support you one-hundred-and-ten percent, one hundred percent of the time."

"This," I agree.

"Does that mean you'll come visit me in the dorms next year?" Tally asks cheekily.

"Oh girl, we're moving you in," Dred says.

"I'm kind of super excited for you," Rix adds.

"Speaking of university, have you heard back yet about that program you applied for?" I ask Rix.

She shakes her head. "Not yet. But I applied late, and there's a waitlist, so we'll see." After much prodding from Tristan, Rix finally applied to the food and nutrition program at the university in Toronto. "But I am taking another class with Eliza Van Horn this spring, so it's something."

"I hope you get in so we can be in university together," Tally says.

Rix smiles. "That would be a lot of fun."

"Frankly, I can't wait for you to graduate, so you can finally become my full-time assistant." Hemi points a finger at me.

"I still have to apply for the position, though."

"You're the perfect candidate," Shilpa assures me.

I voice one of my major concerns. "I just don't want it to look like I got it because of my dad." I keep the part about dating a player to myself.

"You have literally stepped into the role this semester by handling all aspects of planning one of our biggest charity events. You are so very qualified. But if you think it would be better to work somewhere else, I'll understand," Hemi says gently.

"I looked at other options for my internship, and other job postings, in case the position doesn't pan out, but honestly, I just want to be part of the Terror."

"It makes sense to me," Shilpa says. "I was already married to Ash when I joined the organization, but they're very much your family."

"Yeah." I run my hands up and down my legs, considering what it will be like to work for the team while also being involved with Hollis. It feels impossible that it could actually happen. All the lying and hiding and sneaking around has felt so necessary up until now. And with so many pivotal things happening in my life, I can't imagine how my dad will handle all the secrets I've been keeping from him these past months. The potential fallout makes me feel sick.

"You worried about something else?" Hemi eyes my anxious hands.

I glance at Rix, who gives me an encouraging nod. These are my best friends. If I can't tell them, who can I tell? "You all have to swear on the health of your lady parts that what I'm about to tell you stays here with us."

Rix already knows. Mostly because my bedroom smelled like latex and vagina and there were an unreasonable number of used condoms in my garbage. Also, Tristan talked to Rix after he caught Hollis shirtless in our apartment. She assured me he won't say anything. He doesn't want to be present when my dad loses his mind.

"Is everything okay?" Hemi's unease is evident in the slant of her brow.

"Yeah. No. I just need you all to promise it doesn't leave this space."

They all promise.

I swallow my nerves. "It's about Hollis."

The team is on a two-game away series, due back tomorrow. Prior to them leaving, Hollis and I had sex every day and even fit in a sleepover. Sex with him is a heart, mind, and full-body experience, and I'm totally addicted to the high. My vagina and the rest of me misses him. We've been texting nonstop, and those kitty cams are being used for a lot more than monitoring the kitties.

"Oh my God, are you pregnant with his baby?" Hemi asks.

"What? No! What the fuck? The last thing I would do is repeat that piece of history. My dad would lose his mind if I made him a grandpa at forty."

"You're older than he was, but I understand." Hemi crosses one leg over the other. "Proceed."

"I think he's in love with you," Shilpa announces.

Rix nods in agreement.

"Uh, I don't know about that." He is definitely in deep like and lust with me. I'm for sure a hundred percent in love with him, though. Thinking about him gives me butterflies. He also sent me flowers after our first night together. They're in my bedroom. It's an extravagant bouquet. Yesterday he sent me chocolates.

"He looks at you the same way Ash looks at me," Shilpa adds.

That's news to me—and a bit worrying that other people have noticed this, even though Ash and Shilpa are couple goals. He looks at Shilpa like she hung the moon and stars for him. "Right, okay."

Rix gives me an I-told-you-so look.

"You're finally a thing, aren't you?" Hemi asks. I hear the trepidation in her voice.

"Are you secretly dating?" Tally's eyes are wide.

"Yes, sort of. Just until exams are over, though. Then we plan to date openly." I wring my hands, then sit on them.

"That's what? A few weeks from now? Why keep it a secret at all?" Dred asks.

"I have final projects and exams, and the gala, and Hollis got cleared to practice with the team again." We celebrated that with the team at the Watering Hole and then later, just the two of us. "I want a few things off my plate before we tell my dad." I bite the inside of my cheek, glancing around the room.

Rix has already expressed her concern with this plan. Shilpa makes a face, but Tally nods in understanding. Dred purses her lips, and Hemi sighs.

"It's just a few weeks," I assure them.

"Aside from breaking his no dating players rule, is this because Roman won't be okay with his best friend dating his daughter?" Hemi lays it on the table, as is her way.

"He's a little overprotective," I say defensively. I'm terrified of his reaction. The more I think about it, the worse my anxiety gets.

"But won't he be less okay when he finds out you've been hiding it from him?" Dred asks.

"This." Rix crosses her arms.

"I don't want the stress of him losing his mind when I have exams. I'll have a perfect record if I make the dean's list this semester, which will only help my resume for the assistant position." They sound like excuses, even to me. But I'm half a percentage point from losing my place. My dad is so freaking proud that I've made it every semester. It would feel like letting him down. And me and Hollis will be enough of a blow.

"The dean's list is a nice bonus. But you've already proven you're more than capable of handling the assistant position," Hemi says. "Maybe officially dating before you get the position would be better? Shilps, cover your ears."

Shilpa looks at Hemi as she speaks. "I'm not saying that could be a work around, but I'm also not saying that dating him before you have the job would be infinitely better when it comes to policy and paperwork. Because this is not legal advice and I never said any of this, okay?"

"Right. I never heard you or anyone suggest anything to avoid paperwork or corporate rules." A deep sigh escapes me. "I just don't feel like saying anything right now makes sense. The gala is next weekend, though. I don't want this to overshadow the event. I worked too hard to make this mine to have it all blow up in my face because of who I'm dating."

"You think Roman would be that upset?" Shilpa asks.

"Maybe? Probably. I don't know. But my birthday is this weekend, and my mom is coming to visit. There's just a lot." I love my mom, and time with her always makes me miss her. It also reminds me that I was too much for her to take care of and that my dad had to make sacrifices for my well-being. It's a weird cycle.

"And then the team is heading into playoffs. There's so much going on. What if my dad freaks out and it screws up his game? What if it costs them the playoffs?" I've had terrible dreams the past couple of nights where they lose. Because of me. My dad has given up so much for me, and he's so excited about this season and the potential for Toronto to make it to the end. To screw the team out of a potential Cup win, especially this close to the end of my dad's career... The guilt would be crushing. What if my dad blames me? What if I hurt him so badly he won't talk to me or Hollis anymore? The shame spiral is too overwhelming.

"What if he's totally fine with it?" Shilpa asks.

I give her a look. "Considering I've only ever had one hard and fast rule and that's to never date a player, I just can't see it. Especially because that player is also his best freaking friend."

"As someone who appreciates the importance of rules, I'll also point out that you're an adult. And that the longer you wait, the more difficult it will be," Shilpa says gently, echoing Tristan.

"We just need a little time," I assure them. "We'll get through the gala and exams. Then we'll tell my dad."

CHAPTER 32

HAMMER

"Happy birthday, sweetie!" Mom steps into Dad's penthouse and wraps me in an embrace.

"Hi, Mom." I breathe in the scent of sage and patchouli and lift a hand to wave to North, her life partner, who's standing behind her with their backpacks.

Mom is the embodiment of a hippie, from the waist-length hair braided at the crown to the flowy skirt to the off-the-shoulder oversized Grateful Dead tie-dyed T-shirt that's older than I am.

"I've missed you so much." She squeezes me.

"I've missed you, too." I haven't seen her since Christmas, when I went to visit her at a Reiki retreat.

She inhales deeply, taking my hands as she steps back. "Are you wearing a new perfume?"

An hour ago my dad ran out to pick up a last-minute something or other—he was not specific—and I ran over to Hollis's for a birthday quickie. I probably smell like his cologne. I plan to sneak back over later tonight.

"Oh, uh, I ran out of my usual soap." Lying to my dad is hard enough, but my mom is unnervingly observant.

"Your energy is…" She tilts her head, gaze shifting behind

me to where Dad is standing. Her eyes hold questions when they return to mine, but she's smiling. "There's just so much going on, isn't there? Your birthday, the gala next weekend, finals, graduation, *life*."

"Yeah." I squeeze her hands. "There's a lot going on."

My mom is a lot of things, highly intuitive being one of them. She practices Reiki and teaches palmistry. She's as woo-woo as they come, and I adore that about her. That she and my dad ever ended up together, however briefly, is a mystery. Hormones are mostly to blame, and charisma.

"You'll have plenty of time to fill me in on everything."

I nod. "For sure." My stomach is already roiling.

She lets my dad pull her in for a brief hug while I do the same with North. His long, dirty-blond hair is pulled back in a ponytail, and he's wearing an ancient Beatles shirt, linen draw-string pants, and a pair of sandals with wool socks. He smells like he smoked a bowl right before he came inside.

He pats me on the back. "It's great to see you, Aurora."

"You too, North."

He and my dad hug it out next, because North is all about affection and good vibes. I set up North and my mom in the spare room while my dad pours drinks and makes sure every-thing is ready for the party. Guests are scheduled to arrive in the next half hour.

Mom threads her arm through mine and pulls the bedroom door closed behind North. He always takes a good half an hour to get settled when they visit. He needs to align his energies. "Did you give Roman free rein on the party decorations?"

"I don't know if I gave it to him so much as he took the reins and sprinted with them." My dad desperately wanted to throw me a party, and I couldn't say no.

"Oh wow. That's something else." Mom squeezes my arm as she assesses the pink, white, and silver metallic balloon arch in front of the windows. There's also a banner with HAPPY BIRTH-DAY, PEGGY on it strung across with a place for photos.

"Yup. It really is."

"Aren't your favorite colors blue and yellow?" She gives my outfit an appraising once-over.

I'm wearing a long, off-white tulle skirt that nearly touches the floor and a pale blue, off-the-shoulder shirt. My bra is the same color. "I don't mind pink."

She squeezes my arm. "We'll make a plan once you've graduated to go on a trip somewhere. Just the two of us – anywhere you want. I'll even brave any big city you might want to go to. Plus before you settle into a new job, you can visit me and North for a week. We have a month-long retreat in Arizona next month. I think you'd love it."

"That sounds fun," I agree. My mom is one of the most sincere people I know. Maybe that's why things feel complicated with her.

"And maybe you can bring the owner of the cologne you're wearing," she whispers. My stomach drops.

"Zara, I poured you a white wine." Dad hands her a stemmed glass.

"Peggy, I have prosecco for you." He passes me a fluted glass with BIRTHDAY GIRL etched in pretty cursive. "Oh! And I got you something special." Dad rushes off and returns a moment later. "Ta da!" He holds out a tiara in rose gold that also reads BIRTHDAY GIRL.

"Oh wow! That's just...so fun!" Thank sweet baby Jesus that dinner is coming to us and I don't have to go out wearing a birthday crown.

"I thought you would like it." Dad beams.

"I love it, Dado. So much." I try to match his smile, but lie-riddled guilt gnaws at me. I love him and how hard he tries, but I think he still sees me as nine and not twenty-one.

"Maybe Zara can help you put it on?"

"I can absolutely do that." Mom squeezes my shoulder.

"Great." Dad gives us two thumbs-up. "I'll call the Thai place and make sure we're still on target for a six-thirty delivery. Guests should arrive any minute."

"Mom and I can manage the door. You do whatever you need to," I assure him.

As soon as he disappears down the hall, Mom turns to me. "How many times has he called the Thai place today?"

"Three, I think. But I dropped off a bunch of signed merch yesterday so I could thank and warn them in advance. He just wants everything to be perfect."

"He loves you to pieces." She helps fasten the tiara to my hair. "Although I think someone forgot to tell him you're turning twenty-one, not twelve."

I shrug. "I'm his one and only." The effort he's gone to over my birthday proves that.

She nods thoughtfully. "It would be good if he found someone."

"Agreed. I've been trying to get him to date, but I'm not having much luck. Maybe whoever buys the night with him at the gala auction will end up being the woman of his dreams."

Mom and I laugh. Last year at the auction, he was purchased by a woman who would have loved more than a kiss on the cheek at the end of the night even though she was closer to my grandmother's age than my dad's.

"What's he waiting for?" Mom muses.

"I don't know. Maybe for me to be done with school and on my own? He's really focused on what's coming after he hangs up his skates. He may want to be settled in the next phase of his career."

"Sounds like an excuse not to let anyone into his heart except you," she says. "Does he realize the pressure that puts on your relationship with him?"

"He gave up a lot for me," I say defensively.

Her smile turns sad and knowing. "He's always chosen you, sweetheart. From the moment you were born, you were his first and only love."

This conversation is getting heavy, as it sometimes does with my mom, and I'm already carrying enough guilt. So when the doorbell chimes, I rush to answer it. Rix, Hemi, Tally, and Tristan stand in the hall. Tristan is holding a box from Just Desserts, and the girls all hold wrapped gifts.

"This was supposed to be a present-free night," I say with my hands on my hips.

"Pfft. As if." Hemi rolls her eyes.

"I didn't have anything to do with your gift. I just picked up the cake," Tristan assures me.

They file in one at a time, hugging my mom. Hemi has met her before, but Rix, Tally, and Tristan haven't had the pleasure.

While we're still partially in the hallway, Hollis opens his door, holding a large box. He's wearing black dress pants, a blue button-down, and another tie I gave him. He looks delicious, like the birthday present I most want to unwrap. Again. There are other gifts at his place for me, I know. But those are for later, after everyone goes home and my parents are in bed.

"I like the tiara," he says with a smirk.

"One guess who got it for me."

His grin widens. "Oh, I was there when it was purchased."

I roll my eyes. "Of course you were."

"Hollis! It's been too long!" Mom pulls him in for a hug.

Her brow furrows as her gaze slides my way. Anxiety makes my heart gallop. *I'm being paranoid.* There's no way she knows what's going on.

"Zara, it's always a pleasure. Did North come with you?" Hollis asks as she takes the box he's holding.

"He did! He's just centering himself, but he'll be out shortly."

Dad goes into host mode, pouring drinks, ensuring that everyone knows that there's a vegan, gluten-free charcuterie board. He also makes every new guest stand with me under the balloon arch for a photo. It's ridiculously over the top, and I love him for it.

When North finally appears nearly two hours later, it's very clear that he centered himself with a giant doobie out the window, because he smells like he rolled in a field of burning marijuana. He immediately drinks two liters of water and loads a plate with fifty percent of the vegan charcuterie board.

Almost the entire team is here. Shilpa and Ash brought Dred, Flip, and Dallas with them. Music is playing, and there's a ridiculous pile of gifts in one corner of the room. Yesterday I went out with my school friends for a birthday lunch. It was easy to get out of a club night with my mom in town.

"So is North your stepdad?" Tally sips her mocktail and watches as he chats up one of the team rookies.

"Um, I guess, sort of? He and my mom aren't married, but they consider each other life partners. They have an open relationship." Last year they brought a friend along and invited Flip and Dallas to join them in the hot tub. Dad put his foot down and told North he couldn't entice his teammates into bed with them. "They love each other, but they also love variety. It's not for everyone, and certainly not for me, but it works for them. You should see their communication skills," I explain.

"I would never share Ash," Shilpa declares.

"I feel the same way about sharing Tristan," Rix says. His sex life was prolific and extensive prior to falling in love with her. I can't imagine him letting someone else touch her either.

"I've done it, but I don't think I would make it part of my love life quite like they have," Dred says.

"Really?" Hemi asks.

Dred shrugs. "It was during my university days. It lasted a few months. It was fun, but the dynamics can be challenging."

"You're full of surprises underneath that cardigan, aren't you?" I muse.

"Apparently." Dred smirks.

I find Hollis across the room. His gaze locks on mine for a second before he turns his attention back to his conversation with Dallas and Tristan. "Yeah, I'm not a sharing kind of girl either."

Rix elbows me. "Stop it with the lust eyes."

"Sorry." I down the rest of my prosecco.

Despite spending most of the evening on the opposite side of the room, eventually Hollis and I end up in the kitchen together. Dinner is over and cake is next, but we're taking a short break to refresh drinks. I glance over my shoulder to make sure we're alone.

"You look stunning," he says quietly. "Staying away from you is killing me."

I live for these stolen moments as I pick up his tie and let it slip through my fingers. "We can't even get five minutes alone."

"Later, when everyone's in bed, I'll take care of my birthday girl," he murmurs as he adjusts my tiara. "And this should stay on." He drops his hand in a rush and steps back, gaze shifting over my shoulder. "Hey, Zara, can I get you something?"

I spin around to find my mom standing at the edge of the kitchen. "Just my baby girl." Her eyes move from Hollis to me. "Your dad wants to serve the cake, and you went missing."

"I was grabbing another bottle of prosecco," I say.

"Roman has champagne for you." She holds out her hand, and I take it.

"Don't forget your glass." She nods to the counter, where it sits empty.

I grab that too, glancing at Hollis, but his expression gives nothing away. Thank God I didn't try to kiss him. All he did was adjust my tiara. It was totally innocent.

Mom doesn't say anything, so I cross my fingers.

Everyone sings "Happy Birthday," and I cut the cake. Then my dad makes me open the gifts he bought me, which include two Barbie pink bath sheets that have been personalized with *Peggy* in enormous cursive. "Oh wow, Dado, these are great."

His smile is huge. "They're really soft. I made sure they were like the ones Hollis has."

Tristan chokes on his beer. Rix slaps him on the back. Hollis sips his scotch.

I almost die. "They're perfect."

And then, because I don't have enough pink stuff, my dad also bought me a hot pink robe, matching pajamas, fuzzy slippers, and a new set of metallic pink luggage. It's a lot. He spoils me and it makes me feel so loved, but I'm grateful I don't have to open the rest of the gifts in front of our guests.

The party continues until well after midnight. It's one thirty in the morning by the time my dad and Mom and North finally go to bed. I wait twenty minutes before I sneak across the hall to Hollis's. I promised my dad I would stay with him while Mom visited. It's tradition.

Hollis has fallen asleep on the couch waiting for me, with Postie and Malone asleep beside him.

I quietly strip out of my shirt and skirt, leaving on the blue lace bra and panty set Hollis bought for me and the tiara. His head is back, eyes closed, lips slightly parted. I lean in, bracing one hand on either side of him as I whisper, "Hollis, wake up."

"Princess," he murmurs groggily. His fingers slide into my hair, and his lips move against my cheek. "Time's it?"

"Late." I kiss along his jaw until I reach his lips. "I want to unwrap my favorite present," I purr as I find the hem of his shirt.

"Not yet." He pulls back, eyes already hooded with desire as he gently captures my wrist. "Let me see you." I straighten and feel his eyes like a caress. "So fucking beautiful." His fingers sweep along the outside of my thigh. "Turn around for me."

I give him my back, looking over my shoulder at him as his fingers drift up the outside of my legs and he sits forward. "This fucking ass." He squeezes one cheek and bites the other on a low groan. "Knowing you were wearing this under that pretty outfit tonight was torture." He turns me to face him. "Naughty birthday girls deserve a spanking, don't you think?"

Everything clenches below the waist. Hollis waits—assessing my reaction, maybe.

I swallow my nerves.

"Then I'm going to make you come as many times as you can handle, Princess." He leans back and pats his thighs. "Be a good girl and bring that ass over here."

My heart hammers in my chest as I stretch out across his lap. His erection presses against my side, and he exhales a sharp breath as he gently runs his hand down my spine.

"Princess." Hollis's voice is a deep, gritty rasp that makes my clit ping.

I push up on my elbow and prop my cheek on my fist as I twist my head in his direction. At the same time, I bend my knees and cross my feet. "Yes, Daddy Hollis?"

He runs his tongue across his teeth, eyes narrowed. "You do that to get under my skin, don't you?"

I grin and bat my lashes. "Absolutely."

"Such a little brat." He swats my ass. Not hard. Just a light smack followed by a rough knead.

The smile slides off my face, and I moan.

"Do you like how that feels?" His voice is low, and his expression darkens as he rubs soothing circles on my ass.

"Yes," I whisper.

He pushes my calves down until my feet hang over the edge of the couch, and he runs his hand up and down the back of my thigh. I don't expect the next smack. I yelp.

He presses his palm against the stinging flesh. "Tell me if it's too much, or you don't like it, and I'll stop."

I meet his heated gaze. The look on his face is heady, addicting. "I can take it."

"Fuck, Princess." He takes my chin in his palm and kisses me roughly, then lightly sucks my bottom lip. "You're so perfect for me."

I nod. "Just for you."

"I won't stop until you ask, or you're coming all over my fingers, whichever comes first."

"Yes, please."

Two swift slaps follow.

I suck in a gasp and then moan when his hand slips between my thighs and his fingers graze my clit. "So fucking wet for me," he murmurs.

I groan when his hand disappears from between my thighs and shriek when he slaps my ass. And then his fingers are between my thighs again. I push against them, wanting more. But they're gone, and his hand smooths over my ass. I rest my cheek on my arm and watch his face. His smile darkens as he raises his hand and brings it down. Hard. My gasp turns into a moan as his fingers fill me again, fucking me.

"So perfect." Hollis settles his other hand on my low back to keep me still as he fucks me with his fingers. This time he doesn't remove them when he spanks me.

The rough feel of his pants over his thighs rubs against my skin. Every brush puts me into sensory overload. All I can think about is *him*. Every press of his palm feels like he's molding me into something beautiful and ready to shatter.

I'm so close—right on the edge and he knows it. He massages my clit, then adds another finger, stretching me, and then I'm falling, flying as the orgasm rushes through me.

"That's it, chase it." Hollis murmurs words of praise and encouragement as I quake and shudder.

Panting and sweaty, I melt into the couch, fighting to catch my breath.

Hollis brushes my hair out of my face. "Aurora? You okay?"

"So…" I bite my lip. "It's safe to say I'm a fan of the spanky finger-fuck."

He chuckles and rearranges me so I'm straddling his lap. "Me too." He adjusts my tiara. "Now let me be sweet to you." He gently grips the back of my thighs and pushes to a stand.

I grab his shoulders and wrap my legs around his waist as he carries me to his bedroom.

As he lays me out on the comforter, I look around the space. Electric candles flicker all over the room, and the bed is covered in yellow rose petals.

"Hollis, this is incredible."

"Just like you."

I rub one of the delicate petals between my fingers as he strips out of his clothes and stretches out next to me. "You didn't need to do all this."

"Of course I did. It's your birthday, and you deserve to be treated like the princess you are." He kisses me reverently, then peels me out of my bra and panties. He kisses his way down my body and brings me to orgasm with his mouth before he settles between my thighs.

"I waited all day to be able to touch you like this," he whispers against my lips as he fills me.

"Me, too. I ached to be close to you tonight," I admit.

He makes love to me, sweetly, gently—tipping me over the edge into bliss again and again until we're both delirious with exhaustion. I want to stay the night, to sleep in his arms, but my mom is notorious for being an early riser, so I sneak back to my dad's at five thirty-two in the morning.

I carefully close the door and flip the safety latch. And then nearly die of heart palpitations when I reach the kitchen and my mom is sitting at the island with a mug of tea.

"Holy shitballs, Mom, you scared the crap out of me."

She's wearing a nightshirt that reads *NAMASTE in bed*.

"How long has this been going on?"

My eyes dart around the kitchen. "How long has—"

She gives me a look.

I bite my lips together.

"How long, honey?" Her voice wavers with anxiety and something else.

"Since January-ish."

She nods once and exhales what seems to be a relieved breath. "Nothing happened between you before that?"

I shake my head. "I mean, I've had a crush for a while. But it wasn't until this season that he saw me as more."

"Is this a fling?"

"No."

She regards me for a few long seconds before she asks, "Does that mean you're serious about each other? That he's looking for exclusivity?"

"Yeah. We're serious." The exclusivity goes without saying. He couldn't even handle me going for coffee with someone else.

"And Roman is unaware this is going on. You know his rule about dating players." It's a statement, not a question.

"We're going to tell him. I just want to be done with exams and the gala first. You know how Dad can be."

"You're his baby."

"In three weeks, I'll be a university graduate. I'm his baby, but I'm not *a* baby."

"I know this world you've grown up in has matured you faster than most. But you still have a lot of learning and growing to do." She holds out a hand, and I settle mine in hers. "I trust you to make informed decisions about who you want to be with. Your dad is a fantastic example of a good man. He can be over-protective, and sometimes oblivious when it comes to how he sees you versus who you truly are. But you hiding this concerns me. Why the secrecy?"

I glance over my shoulder to make sure we're alone. "He wants to tell Dad, but I asked him to wait. Dad will be upset. He won't be okay with this. Not at first, but hopefully with time. I just need for this not to affect my exams or the end of his season." My dad's already given up so much for me, and now this. What if it's too much? What if this is the thing that makes him realize that all his sacrifices were pointless?

"You're not even giving Roman a chance to manage his feelings on this."

"It's not just his feelings, though, Mom. It's mine too. I don't think I can handle him being mad at me. Worse, what if he gives me the 'I'm not mad, I'm disappointed'? Thinking about it is just…" I shake my head. "It makes me feel sick. We never ever fight. This is his second to last season ever, and I have to finish the year strong. Plus what if he can't forgive me for this? What if he hates me for it? What if it changes our relationship and I can't fix it?"

"Honey, your dad would never, and could never, hate you. And yes, it could very well change your relationship with him. But you're allowing your fears of what if to dictate your actions. Maybe it would be better to talk to him now."

Panic takes hold. "You won't tell him, will you?"

She gives me a sad smile. "It's not my place. That's for you and Hollis. But it can't feel good to be in the same room and maintain distance. To hide all those feelings you have for him, and him for you. To lie." She cups my cheek in her hand. "Honey, that's so hard on your heart and your soul."

"Hollis has had such a difficult year. He's just been cleared to get back on the ice. I don't want to mess with the team dynamic." It could ruin everything.

"Love is always complicated, Aurora. But if he has your best interests and your heart in mind, he needs to put you first instead of keeping you a secret. I love you so much, my sweet girl. I just want the best for you."

CHAPTER 33
HOLLIS

The benefit of Aurora staying at Roman's while Zara visits means all she has to do is cross the hall once everyone is in bed. The downside is the potential for getting caught sneaking back in again—Zara's already done it once—and the growing awareness that I'm deceiving Roman. It hasn't stopped me from seeing Aurora, though. Or getting inside her. I'm an addict, always looking for a fix, worried the next time will be the last. The last time to touch her, kiss her, hold her.

I'm on my way home from the grocery store, having run out of Postie and Malone's favorite cat food. I also picked up a few treats for Aurora and a bottle of her favorite wine. We have plans for later tonight, when everyone else is in bed.

My phone buzzes, and I fish it out of my pocket, checking the new message from Aurora.

> **PRINCESS**
> I have an hour before I leave for class and I need you.

I check the time. Roman and I head over to Tristan's for a workout in half an hour. I pick up my pace as I round the corner.

You can't wait until tonight?

pouty faced GIF

She follows it up with a picture of Batdick lying on her bed—back in her own apartment, based on the lack of pink.

PRINCESS

Guess I'll take care of myself.

I have enough time to get her off before I meet up with the guys.

HOLLIS

Don't start without me.

I speed walk the rest of the way, and her door opens as I come down the hall. Aurora is wearing a short, blue satin robe cinched at the waist and a pair of team socks, the ends of her hair are damp. "Hi."

"Hi, yourself."

She flips the latch while I shrug out of my jacket, toe off my shoes, and drop the groceries on the side table. As soon as my hands are free, I pull her against me, curving my palm over her ass. "Are you naked under there?"

She nods as she links her hands behind my neck. "I know you have a workout soon, so I wanted to be ready."

"I always have time to take care of you." I grip the back of her legs, hoisting her up, fingers close to all that tight, soft, and wet.

She wraps herself around me, hooking her feet at the small of my back as she nips at my jaw. "I can't get enough of you."

"Feeling's mutual." I carry her across the apartment and into her bedroom, kicking the door shut while she bites my neck.

Batdick is lying on her bed. I climb up with Aurora still wrapped around me.

I tap her thigh. "I can't help you like this unless your plan is to hump my stomach."

She unhooks herself from around me and drops to the bed. Her hands go to my belt buckle.

I catch her wrists in mine and give her a dark look, *tsk*ing. "Such a bratty girl. You think you deserve my cock right now?"

Her bottom lip juts out. "But I want you."

Nothing will ever sound as good as her telling me how much she wants me—needs me. I slide my fingers into the hair at the nape of her neck and hover my lips over hers. "How should I fuck you?" I pull the tie at her waist, and her robe falls open.

"However you want. I just need you to make me come, Hollis. It's never as good when I do it myself."

I skim her nipple with a knuckle, and she whimpers. "Should I fill you with my fingers?" I trail them down her stomach, pausing when I reach the apex of her thighs. "Or maybe my tongue."

"Please, yes." Her fingers lap my wrist, and she tries to guide it between her thighs.

I brush my lips against hers. "Lie back for me."

She complies, falling against the pillows. I skim her clit with my knuckle. "So wet and ready."

"It's like this every time I think about you." Her legs part for me, and I tease her opening.

Batdick rolls into her sock-covered foot, and I snatch it up before she can. "I think it's time I find out why you're so in love with this."

Her eyes flare for a moment, but her grin turns coy. "But you're right here. Why would I need Batdick when I can have you?"

"You get me later." I push my sleeves up to my elbows and note the arrow at the bottom of the device. I twist it, and the vibrator buzzes to life.

"I can show you." Aurora moves to sit up.

"I think I can figure it out." I shift so I'm between her spread thighs and press the buzzing head to her clit. She shrieks, and her knees clamp against my hips.

When she tries to wriggle away, I bar my forearm over her stomach, pinning her to the bed, but dial back the buzzing. Her legs fall open again, and her eyes roll up. She sucks in a gasping breath as I slide the vibrator inside her, watching it disappear inch by slow inch. "Oh, fuck. Yes, please..." She groans when I tilt it up as I pull it back out, slick and coated with her juices.

I start a slow, easy rhythm. The kind that will keep her on the edge, needing more. "Tonight, when we're alone, I'll fill this pretty little mouth with my cock first, and then I'll fuck this greedy pussy until you're coming all over me."

"Oh, God, do it now, please." She snakes a hand between her thighs, but I capture her wrist.

How much would I love to send her to class with swollen lips? But I don't want to rush. I shake my head. "Bratty girls have to wait to get fucked properly." I bend down and bite the inside of her thigh, close to her knee.

"I need more," she whimpers.

"You'll get more when I'm ready to give it to you." I change the angle, finding the spot inside that makes her eyes roll up again and those deep moans I love so much tumble over her lips. I give in to the urge to taste her, pushing the vibrator deep as I capture her swollen clit and suck. At the same time, I drag the thumb on my free hand along the edge of the vibrator, going lower still, until I graze my thumb over door number two, as she likes to call it, while blushing.

She drags in a high-pitched gasp as I gently massage the tight opening. I lift my gaze to hers and press against it, testing her.

"Hollis," her voice is soft and breathy.

"You want more, Princess?" I lap at her clit.

"Please, yes," she whimpers.

I keep fucking her with the vibrator while I circle her clit with my tongue and ease my thumb into her ass, up to the first knuckle.

"Oh God. Oh my God." She grips one breast and arches.

I push in farther, cock kicking at the possibilities. At how fun it will be to show her all the ways I can make her feel good.

"I feel so full. That's... Oh, I—" Her hands slide into my hair, and she moans my name, hips rolling and jerking as her thighs close around my head. She shudders violently and tries to pull my mouth away, but I suck again, addicted to the sound of my name on her lips, the feel of her pulsing against my tongue.

I lick her one last time and lift my head as her hands fall from my hair. I ease my thumb out first, then turn off the vibrator and slowly withdraw it. Her eyes flutter open, and I smile at the dazed look on her face. "Feel better?"

"Immensely," she mutters. "You can fuck me with Batdick any time you want. And do that thing with your thumb." Her cheeks flush pink.

I give her a quick kiss, wishing I could fuck her exactly the way I want to, then glance at the clock on her nightstand. "I have to go. I'll see you tonight."

"But you're rocking a ridiculous hard-on." She flings a hand in the direction of my crotch. The jogging pants don't help my situation.

"Don't worry, I'll calm down." I leave her sprawled on her bed and rush to shove my feet into my shoes and nab my jacket from the floor. I adjust my hoodie so it covers my problem and head for the elevators. The doors slide open, and Roman looks up from his phone.

"Hey, man, I was just texting you." His gaze shifts to the number on the elevator. "Were you at Peggy's?"

I scramble for a good reason to be at his daughter's that doesn't include fucking her with her goddamn vibrator. "Yeah. I ran out of cat treats, and I grabbed Aurora some smoky bacon chips because she mentioned she couldn't find any when she went shopping earlier in the week. I was dropping them off."

The elevator doesn't seem like a great place to tell him the truth, since there's no way to escape his wrath in here, but isn't that what I deserve anyway? I hate seeing Aurora so anxious about it, and it makes me want to fix it. I almost open my mouth to say something, but the words lodge in my throat. She expressly asked me to wait. To hold off. To give her time. I need to trust that *not yet* will become *now*. It's harder than I want it to be. My past creeps into my present, the fear she'll just change her mind sinking its claws in. I could push her away if I say something now. And the idea of losing her...that's a wound I'm not sure I'll heal from. I can't let her go.

He smiles and claps me on the shoulder. "I appreciate you always looking out for her, even the little things, man."

I rub my lips, trying to camouflage my guilt, but my fingers still smell like Aurora. I shove them in my pockets. "It's not a big deal."

"It's just nice to know I can count on you to back me up when it comes to my baby girl. I couldn't ask for a better friend."

Shame is a heavy rock in my stomach as I force a smile. I know it won't be easy, but Aurora and I need to figure out how to tell him before it's too late.

Roman has a couple of errands to run after our workout. He invites me along, but I feel like a bag of garbage, so I head back to my place. As I'm letting myself into my penthouse, Zara pokes her head out of Roman's door.

She's wearing a floor-length skirt, a flowy top, and her long hair hangs over her shoulder in a braid. I see Aurora in her lean frame, dark eyes, and soft smile. "Hi, Hollis. Do you have a minute?"

"Yeah. Of course. Come on in." I step aside, and she crosses into my place.

I've been waiting for this since she caught Aurora sneaking back in on her birthday, two nights ago. According to Aurora, she promised not to say anything to Roman. I suggested maybe now was the time to tell him. But Aurora nearly broke down in tears, worried about how it would affect the rest of Zara's visit, so I relented. I hope Zara hasn't changed her mind.

"Can I get you anything? Something to drink?"

"A glass of water would be nice, thank you." She glances around my place. One of Aurora's scrunchies is on the floor. Malone has decided they're his new favorite toy.

I offer her a seat in the living room and excuse myself to pour us both water. It gives me a moment to collect myself. Zara's easygoing, but I can only imagine how this looks from her side.

Postie has already made himself at home in her lap on the couch by the time I return. Malone is snuggled by her side. I take a seat in the chair across from her, and Malone defects to my lap. Thankfully he doesn't start the blanket humping. It's like he knows it's inappropriate in current company.

"I think you're a great guy, Hollis, and I believe you will treat Aurora well. But I have some real concerns."

We're cutting straight to the chase, apparently. "We plan to talk to Roman."

"Aurora mentioned that." She strokes Postie, who purrs up a storm, oblivious to the tense conversation taking place. "Let me be very clear. I understand that everyone sees me as a free-loving hippie, which I am. But it's the openness of my relationship with North, and our willingness to communicate and set clear boundaries, that allows this. How do you think this will go over with Roman? How will he feel knowing you've been dating our daughter behind his back?" Her tone isn't confrontational or combative; it's a question she wants answered.

I go with honesty. "I think he'll be very upset."

She nods slowly. "Especially since you're intentionally keeping it from him."

"I'd rather take Roman's anger than create more stress for Aurora. Especially with how much she has going on. The idea of her being upset unravels me," I reply.

Zara nods again. "And that's why you're so intent on waiting? Because you think she can't handle more stress?"

These reasons are convenient and hide my own deeper fears —that Aurora will realize she can do better, that the baggage I'm carrying around is more than she's prepared to deal with. I run my hands down my thighs, considering my words carefully. "Aurora is used to taking care of Roman as much as he takes care of her. She's the one who cheers him up on a bad day. She takes care of him when he's sick, or takes a hard hit on the ice. He's as much her world as she is his. She's concerned about Roman's reaction, and how it will impact the team dynamic going into playoffs. Roman's my best friend. I hate to admit, but she's not wrong. It will mess with things on the ice."

She arches a brow. "Do you truly believe that's her sole reason?"

"Fear of the unknown and hurting Roman are at the top of her list." There's a level of codependency between them, but part of that is directly related to Zara's role in her life. I don't particularly want to go there any more than I want to do a deep dive into my own shit.

She rubs Postie's cheek while I do the same with Malone. Thank God for selfish cats who want to be petted. It's the only thing tempering my anxiety.

"I can't force you to tell Roman sooner, and I certainly understand your concern about his reaction. He is incredibly protective of our daughter. I appreciate that you want to support Aurora's needs. I think you can be very good for her, but she's young. You have far more life experience. How will you ensure that she's a healthy person? It's easier to manipulate your partner when there's such a gap between you." She raises a hand when I start to interject. "I don't believe that's something you would do intentionally, but she will look to you for guidance. It's up to you to make sure you're helping her realize her full potential. It would be easy for you to swoop in and take care of her, give her everything she could ever want. But as a partner, you'll also need to make sure she's following the path she wants, and not the one you're setting out for her."

I nod, absorbing her words. These are all things I've thought about, but I want to put her at ease anyway. I want her approval and her support, not just for myself, but for Aurora. "I'm in the last few years of my first career, and she's about to start hers, so we'll be on a new path together. She's ambitious and driven. I want to be there to support her dreams and help her achieve them."

Zara smiles. "Just remember that as her lover, your advice and your words will hold more meaning than most. Aurora has incredibly deep feelings for you, and I sense that yours match. I believe that's why you're following her lead with Roman. But it's up to you to show her she's worth the risk you're both taking."

"She is. Absolutely."

"Right now, I think you believe you're putting her first by honoring her request for secrecy. But who are you really protecting by not telling Roman? Whose heart are you risking? Sometimes by trying not to hurt someone, we end up doing the most damage."

CHAPTER 34
HOLLIS

"You're so good at this. Yes. Dear Lord in heaven. Right there. Ah! Sweet fu—Postie! Not now!" One of Aurora's hands leaves my hair as she pushes Postie away. For the fourth time in the past ten minutes. "Can't you see Hollis is busy with another pussy?"

"I told you we should've closed the door," I mumble against her skin, undeterred by Postie's insistence that he's the kitty I should be paying attention to.

"They just meow at the door. It's distracting," she gripes.

"More distracting than Postie trying to lie on your chest while I tongue-fuck you?" I unhook my arm from her thigh and feel around for the toy mouse Postie loves. My fingers close around it, and I toss it across the room.

Postie meows and launches himself into the air.

I suck Aurora's clit, and she bows off the bed.

"Ah! Shit. Do it again."

"What was that?" I slide a single finger inside her, but don't curl.

"Again, again. Do it again," she demands. I love how vocal she is in bed. Her confidence between the sheets—or in the shower, on the couch, on the kitchen counter—grows every day, and it's sexy as fuck to watch her discover her intensely sensual side. She's not afraid to tell me what she wants and needs in explicit, dirty detail.

She tries to roll her hips, but I push my other forearm across her low abdomen, holding her down. "Do what again?" I lap at her, softly.

"Hollis," she whines.

"Tell me what you want, Princess." I lift my gaze and meet her frustrated one.

Postie jumps back onto the bed and drops the toy mouse beside her head.

I can't help it. I grin.

She glares at me, grabs the toy mouse, and yeets it across the room. Then her expression shifts, softening, along with her voice. "Please suck my clit, Hollis."

I do, but gently.

"More, please, with teeth." She strokes my cheek. "And more fingers, please, so I'm ready for your cock."

We could spend all day in bed, and it would never be enough. Not for her, not for me. The power balance is addictive. Sometimes she's compliant and sweet; sometimes she's demanding and needy. And sometimes she'll push my buttons until I break—which is a personal favorite. I don't think I had this much sex even when I was in my twenties.

I add a second finger, but still don't curl. And I suck, but still not the way she wants. "How's that?"

"Still more, please." I add a third finger and graze her clit with my teeth.

"Yes. God. Thank you." Her hand tightens in my hair. "More, please."

"I'm already using three fingers, Princess," I murmur.

"I can take more. Tristan puts his whole hand in Rix's vagina," she pants.

I lift my head. I could not have heard that right. "I'm sorry, what?"

Her eyes flare, and she whispers, "They do the *Chasing Amy*."

"You mean the Kevin Smith movie from the nineties?" I probably watched it as a teen.

"Yeah." She makes a circle with her thumb and middle finger and then slides her other hand through it until she's holding her wrist.

"That's—his whole hand?" My gaze drops to where three fingers are buried inside her. The physics of that seem...not ideal. Rix is small, and Tristan's hands are like baseball gloves.

"Maybe we should talk about this later." Aurora's face is an adorable shade of red as she tries to push my head back down.

"Or maybe we shouldn't." I curl my fingers.

She gasps. I lick her clit and then latch on, watching her eyes roll up.

She grabs her right breast, tugging roughly on her nipple. "Yes, yes, yes," she chants, back arching as her legs shake and the orgasm rolls through her.

I don't give her time to come down from the high. I roll on a condom, stretch out over her, and replace my fingers with my cock, pushing inside in one smooth stroke. She clenches around me, legs hooked behind my back, her arms winding around my neck.

Her orgasm drags on, her body quaking, a low keening sound humming across my lips. I pull back so I can see her. Aurora's nails dig into my shoulder, the fingers of her other hand tremble against my cheek, my name a nearly soundless whisper on her lips.

"God, you're beautiful when you're coming for me," I murmur.

"I d-don't want it to end," she pants as she writhes under me.

Every time is better than the last. I feel the connection we have in more than just our bodies. I feel it in the softness of her eyes, in the way she whispers my name. I'm about to tell her how I feel, how deeply rooted in my heart she is, but another orgasm rolls through her. Aurora's mouth drops open, and her eyes flutter closed as her body contracts. And then I'm falling with her.

Half an hour later, we're sitting in the living room, Aurora wearing one of my hoodies, her legs draped over mine. I run a hand up her bare calf. "How are you feeling about the gala?" It's just a handful of days away.

"Good. Great, actually!" Her eyes light up. "We have a whole table for the Hockey Academy, which is so amazing. They confirmed that Kodiak Bowman and his wife are coming."

"That's great news." He's the new "it kid" in hockey. He's on track to blow a lot of records out of the water.

"Hemi thinks this will be our best gala yet. I love this side of the hockey world and how we get to give back to the community that supports us."

Her excitement is infectious. "I love your passion for this."

"I feel like I've found my calling, you know?" She runs her fingernails down the back of my neck. "Hemi says the auction is where we usually make the most money."

"I can pull out—tell Hemi I can't participate." I've been thinking about this a lot. In part because Scarlet is attending, and even though I've told her I'm not interested in rekindling our relationship, I worry she'll bid on me anyway.

"Most of the dates usually end up being a hang out with a hockey player night, like the way Dallas ended up spending his at the retirement village with the coach's grandmother," she says. "Besides, if you back out there will be questions. And people might think it's because of Scarlet."

I can feel her apprehension over it, which is the only reason I don't press harder. "I don't want anyone but you."

"Scarlet still wants you, though?"

The only way to set her mind at ease is to be honest with her about my history with Scarlet. If I want this to work, I need to open up. "She knows I'm not interested. I'm not the same person I was when we dated. Her life is very public, and while being a pro hockey player means parts of my life are available for public consumption, I was never on board with my personal relation-ship splashed all over social media."

Aurora hesitates, looking uncertain. "I know how private you are about your life, but will you tell me what happened?"

I should have offered it up as soon as we returned from the away series, like I said I would. But we've been so preoccupied with each other. And talking about this shines a light on how Scarlet affected my views on relationships and love. "Have you been afraid to ask?"

She shrugs. "Your life is already public enough, and I've wanted to respect your privacy. But I'm also aware the media coverage and reality don't always match."

That's a *yes* disguised as nonchalance. Keeping this part of me closed off from Aurora won't help us understand each other. "You're right, they don't." I lace our fingers, needing the connection.

She squeezes my hand, and both our knees bounce. I don't want this to be the thing to derail us, but leaving her in what-if limbo won't make it better.

"Before I was traded to Toronto, I'd planned to ask Scarlet to marry me. I'd even gone as far as buying the ring, but she broke things off."

Emotions flit across Aurora's face. Surprise hits her first, then shock, jealousy, hurt, fear, and sadness. And then finally empa-thy. "But why? Clearly she regrets that choice now."

"It really came down to me wanting my private life to remain private and Scarlet wanting the opposite." I'd been so certain we could get past it. That she would eventually see the benefit of being out of the limelight when she wasn't filming. I didn't understand compromise, or how to listen to what she really needed. It took time for me to see how I contributed to the downfall of the relationship.

Aurora's hand tightens around mine. "Did she know you were planning to propose?"

I shake my head. "Not until later. But she didn't want the

same things I did. So when I moved to Toronto, she gave a statement saying we'd broken up because of the distance. She wished me well, and that was that." It had been gutting to see how easily she dismissed a two-year relationship.

"But really, she broke your heart," Aurora says softly.

"She did."

"And now she regrets her decision." I can't read Aurora's tone or her expression.

"I can't pretend to know how she feels, or if she sees us as a missed opportunity she wants to revisit only because we're in the same city for a few months."

She releases my hand and slides her fingers between her thighs, as though she's trying not to fidget. "Are you over her?"

"Yes. But the way she handled things hurt. A lot." So much that I've avoided talking about it for the past seven years. And the only people who know what happened are my family, and now Aurora. Even Roman only has the barest of details. "It's framed how I've dealt with relationships, and I realize I haven't put my heart on the line in a long time." For fear of having it crushed. I almost proposed to the wrong person. It isn't a mistake I'll make again.

"Whatever feelings I had for her, they're in the past," I add. "I saw her only because I needed closure." And maybe I hadn't seen it at the time, but talking to Scarlet made me realize how invested I am in the woman sitting in front of me. "I want this with you, Aurora." I can see a future unfolding with her. And it's terrifying, in part because she's so young. But I don't want to make the same mistake twice by hiding her from the world. I can make these compromises with her. It won't ever take her autonomy. It will be equal decision making, even if it's hard to walk the lines Aurora wants me to walk.

"I want this with you, too." There's relief in her soft smile.

The things Zara said make so much sense. She's right. I have life experience Aurora doesn't, and I need to be careful to use it wisely and move us forward.

"Maybe I could feel Roman out before the gala, get a sense of where he is." It gets harder every day to lie and keep her a secret —and then it would be easy to remove myself from the auction. Telling him would be something real. Something tangible to assure me she won't change her mind about me yet.

"Before the gala?" Her voice is laced with panic.

What if she's not ready for this the way I want her to be? What if she's on the fence about us and forcing her to make a choice now moves us in the wrong direction? I stroke her cheek. "What are you most afraid of, Princess?"

"The ripple effect for him, and the team, and me, and you, and—" Her bottom lip trembles, and she exhales a steadying breath. "Maybe it should be me instead. I can say something to him. Not tell him, but just...see?"

"I don't want to push you into this." But, God, I want her. I've never wanted anything so much. Her discomfort is a sharp bite, a warning to be careful with her.

"I know."

I pull her into my arms, and she comes willingly. I don't know what the answer is anymore. I don't want to keep hiding this, but I don't want to cause her more hurt, either. And I hate making her cry. But more than that, I don't want to move too quickly and end this before we've had a chance to begin. I couldn't give Scarlet what she needed; I don't want to repeat history with Aurora.

"This has just been so nice, and I don't want to ruin it," she whispers.

"I understand." I tip her chin up and kiss her.

I want to believe this is one of those instances where I have to be careful not to make decisions for her. But it's impossible not to worry about the next few weeks, and how hard it will be to keep this bubble from bursting.

"How you doing, kiddo?" Dad asks as I usher him into my apartment. "Looks like maybe you're a little busy."

My laptop sits open on the couch, surrounded by snacks, papers, Post-it Notes, and my list for the gala. Which is in three days. I still haven't managed to muster up the lady balls to broach the subject of me and Hollis. There isn't an easy way to slide it into conversation. *Hey, Dado, how would you feel if I started dating your best friend?* doesn't seem like the smoothest option. Neither does saying, *What if I dated a hockey player? You know him. He's a really good guy, don't worry.* "Just double-checking all the last-minute details. What's up?"

He produces a gift bag from behind his back. "I got you something."

"For what? You didn't need to do that. I just had my birthday."

"For the gala. Hemi can't stop talking about how you've stepped up and taken the lead. I'm so proud of you. You haven't even graduated yet, and you're already doing all these amazing things. I wanted to get you something to celebrate all you've accomplished."

"You didn't need to." Here he is, buying me presents and

being an awesome dad, and I'm sneaking around with Hollis. The bucket of shame gets heavier with every passing day.

He takes me by the shoulders, expression earnest. "You're my one and only, Peggy. I want to celebrate you every chance I get. I know this world isn't an easy one to grow up in, and it hasn't always been sunshine and roses, but you've turned into an incredible young woman. It's such an honor to be your dad."

I wave my hands in front of my face. "You're making me cry."

He pulls me against him and squeezes tightly.

I want to appreciate his love and support, but I'm deceiving him every day. I have to fix this. Maintaining boundaries with Hollis when we're with the people we care most about is becoming a challenge. I've found myself almost reaching for him more than once in front of my dad.

Hollis is right; we can't keep this secret forever.

"Go on." Dad holds out the bag. "Open it."

My hands are unsteady as I pull the ribbon free and remove the tissue paper and the small jewelry box. I already know what's inside. Any time I've accompanied my dad to one of his suit fittings—which is every single one he's had since I was a teenager—I window shop at the exclusive jewelry store nearby and fawn over a specific pair of earrings. They're ungodly expensive and nothing I ever need. Let alone deserve.

I flip the lid open and try not to cry. Inside are the diamond earrings I've admired for years. "Dad, this is too much."

"Consider it an early graduation gift, if you need to, but I thought they would be beautiful with your dress. You should put them on, and the dress. I've only seen pictures."

"Thank you. I love you. You're the best dad." I wrap my arms around him, and he returns the embrace.

"I love you to pieces, sweetheart. And I know I can be a lot sometimes, but it's only because I want the best for you."

"I know. And I love you for it."

He waits in the living room while I put on my gala dress, shoes, and earrings.

I take a few deep breaths, working to keep my emotions in check. I'm so scared—of his reaction, of the possibility that Hollis might not choose me if my dad isn't okay with us dating. But I won't know if I don't test the waters.

I open my bedroom door, and the expression on my dad's face nearly undoes my composure. His hand goes to his chest, and he looks as though he's on the verge of emotion, like me. "You are just so beautiful."

"The earrings are perfect. I love them."

"They go with the dress okay?" he asks.

"They're amazing, and I'll only ever buy dresses to match them." They're yellow diamonds ringed in white diamonds and unbelievably indulgent.

"You worked so hard for this. I know this semester has been stressful for you, but you're almost there. The finish line is in sight. And I know the PR assistant position with the team isn't quite yours yet, but I'm excited to have you back in the office. We all loved having you there. And while it isn't the job I envisioned for you, I love that I'll finish out my contract with you in house."

"Me, too." Fingers crossed they don't find someone with better qualifications.

"Just don't date any of the players and we'll be fine," Dad adds with a smile.

My stomach lurches. "They're good guys, though. I mean, I know Flip can be an issue, but even he's been there to look out for me."

"They're young and full of hormones."

"You would know, since I'm standing here."

"Touché," he mutters.

This is the chance to lay some groundwork. To plant the seed. To finally be honest with him and alleviate some of this guilt I've been carrying for months. I can be brave. "Look at Tristan. He was a hot mess last year off the ice, and now he's head over heels with Rix. He's desperate for her to move in with him. I know there were some issues with him and Flip for a bit, but they've worked it all out. Now Rix and Tristan are so in love, and Flip and Tristan are still best friends."

Dad's jaw clenches, and his expression darkens. "I would murder Hollis and bury him in a very deep grave if he ever put his hands on you."

My heart feels like it's been put in a vise. Just like that, any hope I had that I wouldn't destroy everything by telling him about me and Hollis goes up in flames.

CHAPTER 36

HOLLIS

Two days before the gala, my younger sister, brother-in-law, and niece stop in for a surprise visit. Mike is a professor and sometimes guest lectures at the local university. Occasionally when he has a trip, he'll bring Micha and my nearly three-year-old niece, Elsa, along. They live a couple of hours away in Niagara.

"Unca Haw-lis, look at my fissy! And my turble!" Elsa holds up a stuffed rainbow fish and a stuffed green turtle.

"They are amazing! Did you have the best time at the aquarium today?" I pick her up and raspberry her cheek.

"Ah! Unca Haw-lis!" She pushes on my chest and giggles. "Do again! Do again!"

I give her another raspberry, and she bursts into a fit of giggles.

There's a knock on my door. I glance at the clock, realizing it's probably Aurora. Roman has taken on training with the backup goalie a couple of times a week, so he's out for a few hours some afternoons. Yesterday, Aurora told me she'd tried to feel Roman out, and it did not go well. She explained what happened through panicked tears. I can't decide if his reaction had more to do with what we know about Tristan's proclivities, or him actually dating Rix. Regardless, telling Roman before the gala is off the table now. I offered, again, to pull out of the auction, but Aurora is afraid he'll connect the dots and I'll be minus a few teeth, or my head.

"Just let me get the door, and then I'll hook you up with something to drink. Can you stay the night, or do you have to head back?" I put Elsa down and cross the room.

"Mike is teaching a seminar back home tomorrow morning. I figured we could visit the aquarium, and then you, before we drive home." Micha thumbs over her shoulder at Elsa, who's rushed over to the wall of windows overlooking the city, pretending to make her fish and turtle swim in the reflection. "And if timed correctly, this one will pass out on the ride."

I open the door and find Aurora holding this week's prepared meals from Rix. She looks tired and anxious. "I brought your dinners for the week and—" Her eyes flare. "Oh! You have company. I'm so sorry."

"Oh my gosh, Peggy?" Micha practically shoves me out of the way and pulls her into a hug.

Aurora mouths *sorry* and gives me her oh-shit face while she pats my sister on the back. "Hey! Hi, Micha. It's so nice to see you."

"Good Lord." Micha's eyes widen as she steps back. "Wow! You are...not a teenager anymore!"

Aurora smiles, cheeks turning pink. "Uh, no. Full-fledged adult now."

Micha takes the bags from her. "Well, come on in. Hollis was about to pour me a glass of wine. You're old enough to drink now, right? By a few years?"

"Uh, yeah, I'm legal to drink in the States now, but I don't want to interrupt family time."

"Nonsense. Mike and Hollis will talk hockey, and I'll nod and smile because I still don't really understand the rules. I think Hollis mentioned you're almost done with university. Is that right?"

"Yeah, just final exams left and I'll be finished with my undergrad."

"That's so exciting. What I wouldn't give to go back and relive my university days. I had a lot of fun during my undergrad."

"And then you met me and traded house parties with cheap beer for fine dining and nice wine." My brother-in-law smiles fondly as he takes a sip of his beer.

"I regret neither," Micha replies.

"Hi! My name is Elsa, and this is my fissy and my turble!" My niece holds up her stuffed toys for Aurora to see.

Aurora crouches, so they're at the same level. "Hi, Elsa. You probably don't remember me, because I haven't seen you in a long time. My name is Aurora."

Elsa's eyes go wide. "I love Princess Aurora!"

"And I love Queen Elsa. *Frozen* is one of my favorite movies ever!"

"Mine too!" Elsa smiles up at me. "Unca Haw-lis, I really like your friend Aurora."

Micha gives Aurora an apologetic smile. "I'm so sorry. I don't know why I thought your name was Peggy."

"Technically it is, but she prefers to go by her middle name," I explain.

"Oh, okay."

"I answer to both, though. And the team calls me Hammer, since it's a last-name world for those boys," Aurora explains.

"But you prefer Aurora?" Micha asks.

"I do."

"Daddy, I have to pee!" Elsa announces.

"I can take her," Micha offers.

"I got it." Mike kisses Micha on the cheek and takes Elsa's hand, leading her down the hall.

I hand Aurora a glass of white.

She takes a small sip and smiles. "It's my favorite. Thank you."

Micha gives me a look. I busy myself with opening a beer.

"If I remember correctly, you're working on a degree in public relations, right? What's your plan when you graduate?" Micha asks.

"There's an assistant posting to work with the Terror's public relations liaison that I'd like to apply for."

Micha nods. "Oh wow, you don't see enough of these guys as it is? You want to work with them, too?"

Aurora shrugs and blushes, eyes sliding my way for a moment. "I completed my internship with the head of team PR last semester, and it was a great fit."

"That's right. Hollis mentioned that in the fall. Did you travel with the team?"

"Some of the time, yes."

Micha's eyes light up. "That must have been fun. Private jets and famous hockey players. How's Roman feel about that?"

"He loved it. The team's like a big, extended family, for the most part." Aurora sips her wine to hide her nervous swallow.

Micha *hmms*. "Wasn't there some drama earlier in the season with one of the players' family members dating another player? Tristan Stiles? That wasn't you, was it?"

"Uh, no. That's my roommate, Rix. Her brother is Flip Madden," Aurora explains, shifting uncomfortably.

"Right! Yes! That must have been scandalous."

"It's all smoothed over now," I interject. Micha has no idea that she's poking at raw wounds. "I'll put this stuff away and we can go hang out in the living room," I suggest. "I should have some coloring stuff for Elsa in the spare room."

"I think it's in the closet. Want me to check?" Aurora offers, probably happy to escape this conversation.

"That'd be great. Thanks, Princess."

Micha waits until she disappears down the hall. "What the hell is going on?"

"What are you talking about?" *Fuck, fuck, fuck.*

She motions toward the hall. "There's a vibe between you two."

I look at her like she has two heads, but my stomach knots. I can't afford to have Micha digging now. Not when Aurora is already on edge.

Micha crosses her arms. "Why does she know you have coloring stuff for Elsa in the closet in the spare bedroom?"

"Because she watches Postie and Malone while I'm away, and sometimes she runs the towels and cat blankets through the wash for me, which go in the spare bedroom closet." I glance toward the hall, needing Micha to drop it.

"You called her Princess," she says pointedly.

"I've always called her Princess, because she's the team princess." I don't realize I'm doing it in front of other people, though, and that's a problem.

"Why do you have her favorite wine in your fridge?" my sister presses.

"Because in addition to feeding my cats, she sometimes watches the game with them while I'm away." Footsteps come from down the hall. "I need you to drop it. And don't grill Aurora. She's got a lot going on."

"Dropping it." She raises both her hands. "For now."

I make a big deal about Elsa peeing in the potty when she comes bumbling back into the living room with Mike in tow. Aurora returns with an entire bin of coloring books, crafts, and stickers. Elsa entices her into coloring with her. She takes a seat on the floor with my niece and keeps her occupied for a good half hour.

I try my best not to watch them. But every once in a while, she glances up at me, and all I want to do is wrap my arms around her and tell her everything will be okay. Hiding my feelings is becoming impossible. I just need her to believe we can do this.

CHAPTER 37
HAMMER

"Bask in the glory of your hard work." Hemi threads her arm through mine, a wide, proud smile on her face.

"I can't believe how smoothly it's going." Especially with how anxious I've been since my failed relationship conversation with my dad. I've been a mess, terrified of the potential fallout. So, over the past two days, I've put all my energy into making sure this gala is perfect. So far, it really is.

"It's all in the planning. You really owned this, Hammer."

That makes me smile. This evening has gone off without a hitch. The silent auction has been a huge success. Dinner was amazing. Yet as wonderful as it is, my dress feels like a vise around my chest, because the night with a hockey player auction is up next. Maybe, I should have agreed to Hollis backing out. I just didn't want the questions or my feelings to get in the way of the success of the event. Regret is a weight in the pit of my stomach that gets heavier with each passing hour.

"Hammer, Willy, you two know how to throw one heck of a party." Dallas passes us each a glass of pink champagne.

Hemi gives him her best death stare and holds up a hand. "I'm not drinking."

Dallas gives her a patient smile. "It's mostly strawberry cordial. There's merely a splash of champagne."

I take a cautious sip. Like Hemi, I'm drinking soda water with a shot of cranberry juice. People think it's a cocktail. We're both on duty, so we'll save our bubbly for when the guests leave. "He's not lying."

Hemi reluctantly accepts the glass but doesn't sip the drink.

Essie and Rix appear, along with Tally and Dred.

"This is one heck of a shindig." Normally Dred wears khaki pants and cardigans in pastel colors. Tonight, she's wearing a siren red evening gown with a slit up the right leg. Hemi brought her as her date in hopes that Dred could help her babysit Flip. It seems to have worked, since he hasn't disappeared into a bathroom with anyone. Although he has been better the past few months.

"Seriously. I've never seen so many hot guys in one room in my entire life," Essie adds. She's Rix's best friend from childhood. She lives in Vancouver and works as a makeup artist and cleverly timed her visit to overlap with the gala.

"Thanks." Dallas winks at her.

"She wasn't talking to you," Hemi snaps.

"Wow, no dickface or asshat attached to that? We're making real progress in our relationship, Willy." Dallas turns back to Essie and Dred. "Have you had a chance to meet Alex Waters and his crew?"

"No," Dred, Essie, and Tally say in unison.

"Well, let's fix that." Dallas motions for them to follow.

Tally threads her arm through mine. "I can't believe I'm about to meet Kodiak Bowman."

"I've heard he's actually super sweet and very shy, and his wife is hilarious," I assure her.

"He always looks so intense."

Essie is scanning the crowd. "Do you think Kodiak might have any single friends?"

My dad and Hollis are chatting with Alex when we

approach. Hollis looks delicious in his black tuxedo. If my dad's reaction had been different, maybe I could have been Hollis's date tonight. Then he could have backed out of the auction. But it's probably best that we put that off. Hollis and I struggled initially because he prioritized his friendship with my dad over his feelings for me. If he does that again, now that we actually have something between us, I don't know how I'll recover. I can't add that to my plate right now. But I can't walk away from this either. I just wish I could see the path forward more clearly.

I've been careful to avoid Hollis for the most part tonight, but it hasn't been easy. His gaze moves over me, familiar and comforting as we close in on them. His smile softens, and I return it.

Hemi elbows me in the side. "Tone it down with the heart eyes."

"Dallas, it's great to see you again." Alex Waters pulls him in for a back pat and a hug. "This event is incredible."

"I'm glad you came." Dallas's smile is bright, like his last name, as he motions to me and Hemi. "And you can thank this duo for putting on such a kickass event."

There's another round of introductions, and I officially meet Kodiak Bowman, who plays for New York along with Flip's nemesis, Connor Grace. I also meet Kodiak's wife, Lavender. She's a tiny thing, but clearly the boss of Kodiak with the way he can't stop making moon eyes at her. Or touching her. I also meet Maverick Waters, who is a carbon copy of his dad, and his girl-friend, Clover, who, if I had to guess, is a few years older than he is.

Hemi and I get pulled into a conversation with Lavender, Clover, and her friend, Sophia, who doesn't have a date.

We learn that Clover and Maverick run a place called Lavender House in the lake district out in Wisconsin. It's where women and families escaping abusive relationships can call home while they get back on their feet. Sophia works with them as their lead psychologist.

"I have a question for you," Clover says to me and Hemi.

"Fire away," Hemi says.

"That man right there." Clover points to my dad and Hollis. "Will he be available in the auction?"

"Clover!" Sophia elbows her in the side. She looks to be in her early thirties.

I grin. "They both will."

Clover's smile widens. "That is fantastic news."

We chat for a few more minutes before Hemi and I excuse ourselves to prepare. I scan the room, and my stomach sinks when I notice Hollis talking to Scarlet. Her hand rests possessively on his arm as one of her castmates snaps photos. I hate how good she and Hollis look together. She's poised and elegant. Refined.

When Scarlet's castmate slides her phone into her purse, Hollis steps back, severing the connection. My heart unclenches. A little.

"It'll be fine." Hemi squeezes my arm.

"I hate that she can touch him, and I have to stand here and watch," I murmur. But that's the tip of the iceberg.

"I know."

We head for the stage, my stomach twisting as we call on the eligible players. Everyone approaches the stage, but Dallas is missing.

"Of fucking course. He asks to go first, and he's nowhere to be found," Hemi gripes.

"Maybe he's in the bathroom. I could send someone to check," I offer.

"It's fine. I'll get him up here." She adopts a smile and adjusts the microphone. "Good evening, everyone, and thank you for being here. I'd like to give a special thank you to Aurora Hammerstein, who has stepped in this year to help me co-run this gala." She turns to me. "I couldn't have done it without you. A round of applause, everyone!"

I blush and wave, embarrassed and elated by the praise. I'm

used to fading into the background unless I'm posting on my dad's social media accounts.

"Now, we all know what everyone is really here for tonight, and do we ever have a winning lineup of eligible hockey players for you!"

The room erupts into whistles and applause. The crowd can get raucous during the auction. Last year Flip ended up ripping off his tuxedo, like he'd joined a male stripper crew, and stood on stage in nothing but a pair of black dress shoes and a team banana hammock.

Once the crowd calms, Hemi walks across the stage to the empty chair and taps her lips. "Hmm... It looks like our first hockey player has a little stage fright. Oh, Dallas!" she sing-songs. "No time for hide-and-seek tonight! Come out, come out wherever you are!"

He bursts through the doors on the other side of the room, red faced and slightly disheveled, buttoning up his tux jacket as he goes. His bow tie is askew.

"There he is! Let's have a round of applause for our fashionably late first date, Dallas Bright!" Hemi smiles, but she looks like she wants to murder him, which isn't unusual.

Dallas pauses to murmur an apology to Hemi, and he hands her a small note card.

"Don't worry, Dallas. I'll make you look good," she tells him.

I've never seen the auction from behind the podium, and Dallas seems to be sweating as he makes his way to center stage.

Hemi glances at the card in her hand. Her smile freezes for a second before she folds it in half, tucks it between her breasts, and her expression turns downright evil. "Some fun facts about our first player. Dallas loves long walks on the beach. His favorite food is sauerkraut pierogis, and in his spare time, he dresses up as a clown and makes incredible balloon animals. He loves all things horses and horseback riding. When Dallas isn't on the ice, he can be found playing Uno with his grandmother, and his favorite TV show is *Letterkenny*. Your night with Dallas will include an evening at a carnival, complete with a ride on his favorite Ferris wheel, and a photo shoot with Dallas's favorite clowns! Bidding starts at two thousand dollars."

Dallas looks like he's about to faint. Paddles rise all over the room as the bidders go wild—at least until Dallas hits fifty thousand. That narrows things down to two bidders. For the first time in three years, the team owner's grandmother is outbid, and one of Scarlet's castmates wins.

"Congratulations, Candice. You've won a night with Dallas! We'll give you a little time to get to know each other!" Hemi's smile is wooden as Dallas is led off stage by the attractive brunette.

My dad is up next. I don't need to look at his bio card. "Roman Hammerstein is our next player," I begin, "starting goalie for the Terror and the most eligible single dad in tonight's lineup!"

The crowd breaks into a massive round of applause.

"If you're lucky enough to win a night with my dad, you're guaranteed the best chicken parmigiana in the city. He's a fan of nineties rock, but don't hold that against him because he's also a secret Swiftie. I would know since I've seen him shaking it to her music. He learned how to sew and knit so he could teach me when I went through a brief, but intense, crafting phase as a kid. He loves the outdoors and adores hiking and romantic picnics. Bids start at two thousand for an evening with this hot, sensitive single dad!"

Clover grabs her friend Sophia's hand and forces it into the air, shouting ten thousand. Other hands raise and bids are shouted, but Dad eventually goes to Sophia (by way of Clover's hand) for the incredible price of forty-two thousand dollars. Her face is bright red as she meets him at the end of the stage, and he escorts her back to her table.

Flip thankfully keeps all his clothes on, but unsurprisingly, he ends up causing a bidding war between the woman who bought a night with him last year and one of Scarlet's castmates. Scarlet's castmate is the winner by five thousand dollars at the cool price point of seventy-seven thousand.

More hockey players are auctioned off—all of them going for more than thirty thousand each—and then, finally, Hollis is up.

My mouth goes dry as Hemi reads his bio. "Hollis Hendrix, number fifty-five. Hollis loves a night in with his adorable rescue tabbies, Postie and Malone, who shower him with their affection. He's a fan of action movies but doesn't mind a good romantic comedy. He makes a mean French toast, and his ideal night out includes a stroll through the city and a romantic dinner at his favorite restaurant overlooking the harbor front. Bidding starts at two thousand for a night with Hollis!"

The worst part about this? The evening I arranged for Hollis is exactly where I would want to go with him. Which, in hindsight, was stupid. I went to that restaurant with him and my dad and some of the team for my nineteenth birthday. What I wouldn't give to be the one raising a paddle...

My mom was right. It's hard to love him from a distance. To want him with this wall between us. I've been so concerned about my dad, school, and my job application that I didn't consider the most important part of me. I didn't think about what lying would do to my heart, or how I would handle tonight without the rationalizing shield of ambition or safety.

My stomach flips as several hands rise in the air. Dallas's previous winner bids, and then someone else across the room, and finally Scarlet raises her hand. It goes around and around, the number climbing until Scarlet outbids everyone by shouting, "a hundred thousand dollars!" The room falls silent, shock clear on several people's faces. All I can see is the back of Hollis's head.

Hemi calls for final bids, but all that follows is a twitter of laughter from Scarlet.

"Going once, going twice, and a night with Hollis Hendrix goes to Scarlet Reed!"

Scarlet pushes out of her chair and smooths her hands over

her hips. She's wearing a sophisticated black dress that high-lights her perfect curves. She smiles and waves, cameras clicking and flashing as she crosses the room to meet Hollis at the end of the stage. My chest feels like it's caving in as she pushes up on her toes to kiss his cheek. And then they pose for photos before he guides her back to her table.

I think I'm about to die.

This is absolutely my worst nightmare. Hemi must sense my panic because she gives the wrap-up speech I was supposed to and thanks everyone for their generous donations. I plaster on a smile, but my entire body feels numb. The lights shining on the stage make it difficult to see the faces of the people in the crowd, but I have a clear view of Hollis and Scarlet sitting at the table to the right of the podium.

Her body is angled toward him, legs crossed, arm threaded through his. She leans in close, so her lips are at his ear. He's smiling, and to anyone else, it probably looks like he's genuinely happy to have her attention, but I notice the stiffness in his body language. It doesn't bring much comfort, though. They have history. Deep history. He planned to propose to her, for fuck's sake. More than seven years ago. And the first I heard of it was earlier this week. Because it was too painful to talk about.

What if she lures him back in? What if he goes out with her and changes his mind? What if he decides he wants to give her another shot because being with me is too complicated? Seeing them like this—her touching him with casual affection, looking at him like he belongs to her—it's not difficult to believe it could happen.

And now my mind is really spinning. Even if my dad could get over it and accept us, would everyone else? How would people react if it was me on his arm? Would they whisper? Say awful things about him? About me? Would they say the same thing Hollis has? That I'm so young. Would they chalk it up to perky tits and a fun time in bed? Will I be compared to her? We

327

look nothing alike, but I'm the same age now as she was when they started dating.

Hemi makes another announcement as the lights dim and music filters through the sound system. I'd forgotten this part. Every year, the players and their dates take to the floor for the first dance of the evening. And it's always a slow song.

Hollis pushes his chair back and rises. He holds out his hand to Scarlet. It feels like my heart is being carved out of my chest with a butter knife when she slips her hand into his. Of course she smiles at him, and he smiles back. Of course he guides her to the dance floor.

"You're okay. Come on, Hammer. Let's get you a glass of champagne." Hemi gently leads me to the bar.

"Why did I do this?" The words slip out of me.

"Because you wanted the most money for charity with the biggest splash." She wraps her arm around my shoulder. "I understand how wanting someone and wanting something for yourself can be so diametrically opposed. It'll be okay."

Rix and Tally meet us there. Tristan takes one look at my face and then the dance floor. I half expect an "I told you so" but he just pats me on the shoulder and kisses Rix on the cheek. "Thank you for dealing with my idiot ass," he murmurs as he walks away with his glass of scotch.

I'm on the verge of a panic attack. What if I've pushed him into Scarlet's arms? What if Hollis won't pick me when it counts?

Hemi passes me a glass. I take it with shaking hands and gulp the fizzy liquid. "I'm so stupid," I whisper.

"No, you're not." Rix squeezes my arm.

I scan the dance floor, where players and dates sway to the music. I want to appreciate how cute my dad and Sophia look, especially with the way she can't stop blushing and how he's smiling so widely the corners of his eyes crinkle. I want to appreciate the incredible success of the auction. How we've raised more money than ever before. Nearly a million dollars from the auction alone. Hollis being ten percent of that. But I can't take my eyes off Hollis and Scarlet. Can't seem to pry my gaze away from her hand curved around his. Or the graceful way they move together.

"That should be me." It's too late to fix it. And I'm terrified of what this means. I can barely watch him dance with her. How will I manage when they spend an entire romantic night together?

Scarlet throws her head back and laughs at whatever he's said. Cameras click and flash. This will be all over the hockey sites tomorrow. That she bought a night with him. How great they look together. That they're getting back together.

I can't watch this. "I need to use the washroom." I down the rest of my champagne and set the glass on the bar.

"I'll come with you," Rix offers.

I shake my head. "I need a minute on my own. Please."

I rush out of the room, desperate to escape this nightmare.

CHAPTER 38
HOLLIS

"I hope you're not upset with me for bidding on you," Scarlet says with a smile. "It's such a worthwhile cause. I know you're not looking to rekindle, Hollis, and I completely understand, but I'm only here for another month, and I didn't want to leave without seeing you again." She looks slightly embarrassed —and hopeful. She did just spend a hundred grand on a night with me.

People snap pictures of the couples on the dance floor. I can already predict how this will look when they hit social media. There will be endless speculation. Are we getting back together? Is this the beginning of Hollis and Scarlet 2.0? How the hell will Aurora deal with it? How can I put her through something like this?

Hindsight is an asshole. I should have told Hemi to pull me from the auction regardless of the suspicions it might raise. We'd been lulled into a false sense of security, believing it wouldn't turn out this way. I should have talked to Roman, admitted I have feelings for his daughter months ago instead of all this sneaking around, let him knock out a few of my teeth if that's what needed to happen. This is the shitstorm I've created. I scan the room for Aurora, but the lights have been dimmed.

Scarlet's hand slides over my shoulder and rests on my chest. "I know I hurt you in the past, but it's been years, Hollis. This could be good for both of us."

I glance down at her. "In what way, exactly?"

"You'll be retiring from hockey in the next few years, moving on to the next phase. You'd be great at sportscasting. Maybe you even want to try your hand at acting?"

Cold realization slithers down my spine. "Is this a publicity stunt?"

She gives me an imploring look. "It could be good for your career to be seen with me, don't you think? We can push the platonic angle if that's what you want. I know the last year has been a challenge. Back-to-back injuries, two surgeries. It can't be easy. I want to help. I want only good things for you. I'm trying to apologize for what I put you through, make it up to you the one way I know how, Hollis."

Of course this is how she sees it. She's the same woman I dated all those years ago, just older and smarter, but still intensely focused on her career. And apparently mine.

I keep searching the room for Aurora. I need to tell her I'm done hiding what's going on between us. I'll deal with Roman and the fallout, whatever it is. I should be on the dance floor with her tonight. She should be the person in my arms.

My stomach sinks as I spot her rushing for the exit, the skirt of her dress billowing out behind her, head down, hand covering her mouth.

When will this fucking song end?

"Hollis." Scarlet's voice drags my attention back to her. Her expression is pained, uncertain.

"I genuinely appreciate what you're trying to do, Scarlet, but I don't want the media speculation this will bring. I'm seeing someone else right now. She knows about the auction, but I can't handle the rumors and press." *Not when I'm deeply in love with her.* If I'd been smart, I would have told Scarlet that when I said I wasn't interested in trying again. "I don't think being around each other is good for me." My voice comes out a lot sharper than I intend.

"I'm sorry. I just...I thought I was helping."

"I know. I appreciate it, truly. It's not..." I sigh. "There are other things going on in my life."

"I understand." For a moment, I see the young woman I'd fallen in love with all those years before she turns on her movie star smile before stepping out of my arms. "I'll see you around."

The song finally ends, thank fuck.

I excuse myself so I can find Aurora and run into Tristan on the way out of the ballroom.

"Whatever you're going to say, I don't need to hear it," I snap.

He holds up both hands. "I already expressed my concerns. Hammer is hiding around the corner trying to keep her shit together, so maybe go fix what you broke instead of worrying about me."

I brush by him and step out into the open foyer. A few small groups are gathered with glasses in hand, others head for the restrooms. I go in the opposite direction and find Aurora tucked into a narrow alcove, her back to me, shoulders shaking.

"Princess?"

She spins around, and it feels like someone punched through my rib cage and ripped my heart out of my chest. This is the very last thing I wanted to happen. I hate seeing her cry. Hate that I could have prevented this. Should have.

She ducks her head. "I'm fine. It's fine. It's my fault. I'm so stupid."

I move in and I wipe away her tears with my thumbs, but new ones keep falling. "It's not your fault, and you're not stupid. You're so smart I don't even know what to do with myself half the time."

"I did this to us. You tried to take yourself out and I said no. And now she'll have you all to herself for a whole night, like she wanted, and there's nothing I can do about it. What if you decide you want to give her another chance?"

"That won't happen, Aurora. You are the only woman I want." I brush my lips over hers. "The only one."

She curves one palm around the back of my neck and fists the lapel of my tux with the other. "I hated seeing you together. I hate that you can dance with her, and you can't do that with me. That you can touch her, that she can touch you. I want to be the one you take on dates."

"I want the same thing." I stroke her cheek. "And I know it won't be easy, or simple, but I'll deal with Roman."

"He won't be okay with it, though. He already said as much." Her voice wavers with fear.

"I'll make it right." Like I should have done weeks ago. "Not being able to celebrate with you has been hell. I can't watch you from the sidelines anymore," I admit.

"I'm just so scared." She's practically shaking in my arms. "What if it damages my relationship with him? Or your relationship? What if we can't fix it and it's too late? I don't want to lose him. He could decide none of the sacrifice was worth it. What if he never forgives me?"

"You're his world, Aurora, nothing will change that. But I'll fix this, Princess. I'll make it better." I sweep her tears away. "When we're alone, I'll make it up to you," I murmur. "I'll take away all the hurt." *And I'll tell you exactly how I feel about you. When we have privacy.* "Does that sound good?"

She nods.

I brush my lips over hers again, powerless against the pull.

"What the hell?" Roman's disbelief-laced voice is a bucket of ice poured over our heads.

I move Aurora behind me as I spin to face him. The person I've been lying to for months. Who I should have been honest with ages ago. Who I've betrayed in the worst way possible.

Of course this is happening now. As if this night wasn't already a shitshow of epic proportions. Everything Aurora has worked for, all she's done to prove herself, will be overshadowed. What kind of lasting damage will that do? What will the ripple effect do to her, to Roman, to us?

His wild gaze moves from me to Aurora, who's mostly hidden behind me. "Peggy?" His voice is low and unsteady.

"Roman." I raise both hands. In surrender. In supplication. "I can explain."

His confusion is replaced with cold realization and simmering rage. "Explain? What did you do, Hollis?" He moves closer, wild eyes focused over my shoulder. "Get away from my daughter."

"Roman."

"Now."

I reach behind me and uncurl Aurora's fist from my jacket, but don't release it as I move two steps to the side. She's sheet white, her chin trembles, and her eyes dart between me and Roman. His livid gaze is locked on our joined hands.

"Peggy?" His shaking voice is full of barely contained fury and fear. "What's going on here?"

Her shaking hand goes to her lips. "We wanted to tell you. We were going to tell you."

"You were going to—" His jaw clenches and he snarls. His dark gaze snaps to mine. "How long has this been going on? *What* is going on?"

I squeeze her hand. "I care very deeply for Aurora." This can't be how I tell her I'm in love with her.

"That's not a fucking answer!" he shouts. "How long, Hollis?"

I swallow the guilt and own the truth. "A few months."

His eyes flare, and he rushes forward. Aurora tries to step in front of me, but I block her. Roman's fist connects with the wall behind my head, and Aurora grabs hold of me. I'm set off balance and go down on my bad knee. The pain is momentarily blinding. I deserve it—for lying to Roman, for falling for his daughter, for keeping her a secret.

"Hollis!" Aurora's hands are on my face.

"Don't touch him!" Roman roars.

"Dad! Stop!" Aurora pleads.

"Princess, please step back. This needs to happen," I murmur.

"You fucker." Roman grabs me by the lapels and drags me to my feet. "You've been going behind my back and—dating my daughter? She's twenty-one years old!"

"We're both adults, Dad," Aurora snaps.

He shoves me into the wall but lets me go as his angry gaze shifts to her. "Then why are you sneaking around like...like teenagers?"

"Because I knew this is how you'd react!" Aurora bites back.

"What did you expect?" His expression turns incredulous. "That I'd be overjoyed to find out my best friend and my daughter have been lying to me?" He scrubs a hand down his face. "For months. He's on my fucking team, dammit!"

"Hollis wanted to say something weeks ago, but I asked him to wait. And then I tried to bring it up with you, but you made it clear you weren't going to be okay with it," Aurora says softly.

"I have only ever asked one thing of you, Peggy. And that was not to date a hockey player. Our lives are too fucking unstable. You deserve a partner who is present for you all the time." He runs a hand over his face. "Is this what the whole Tristan and Rix conversation was about the other day?" His livid gaze shifts from her to me. "You cowardly piece of shit. You put it on my daughter to tell me?"

"I thought it would be better coming from me," she says. "I wanted the gala to be over and my exams finished before this happened." Aurora's voice cracks. "I needed it to be a success so the Terror would want to hire me because I'm qualified and not because you're my dad, or not hire me because I'm dating a player."

Roman's gaze swings back to me. "Do you hear her? You did this." He points an accusing finger at me. "You are the reason my daughter is crying and defending your lying, worthless ass."

"The last thing I wanted was to hurt Aurora. She asked to wait until the end of school and the season. It's the only reason I agreed to wait, but I should have come to you sooner. I should have been honest with you." I search for a way to fix this, to unbreak what I've broken.

"But you didn't, and you weren't." He paces the small hallway. "How this looks—" He laces his hands behind his head. "You're making me question seven fucking years of friendship, Hollis. I should never have trusted you with my daughter."

"I would never—"

He slices his hand through the air. "But you did!" His eyes are wild, chest heaving. "Are you sleeping together?" He glances between us. The answer must be written on our faces because his turns a terrifying shade of red.

"I care about Aurora, Roman," I say softly.

"You care about her?" He motions toward the end of the hall, the thump of upbeat dance music a discordant soundtrack to this nightmare unfolding. "You were just auctioned off to your ex. If you care so much about Peggy, how could you allow that to happen? How could you get up on that stage and let someone else buy a night with you when you're involved with my goddamn daughter?"

"I didn't think—"

"No, you didn't. Look at what you've done." He motions to Aurora, who's hugging herself now, tears streaming down her face.

"I was trying to protect her." The words taste sour, like a bad lie. How am I supposed to explain that I was trying to honor her wishes? That we're both falling in love and scared out of our minds at what that means.

"Fuck you and fuck that. You never should have put her in this kind of position. You put yourself between me and my daughter. You knew how to do this right. You knew how I would feel about all of this. If you'd *asked* instead of doing what you wanted behind my back, I might not have lost my fucking mind. But we'll never know, will we? This is a massive betrayal, Hollis. How could you do this to my daughter?"

"You said you would murder him if he ever touched me," Aurora says softly.

"Days ago. I said that *days* ago. That doesn't account for the months of secrecy before that." His voice shakes with ire. "Like she's something to be ashamed of."

"I know you're upset, and you have every right to be, but this conversation would be better somewhere private," I tell him.

He looks at me like I'm the one who's lost his mind. "I can't have a conversation. I'm livid. I don't feel like you're my friend or my teammate right now." He motions between us. "This. I don't know if it's even fixable. My concern is Peggy. This isn't about you or our friendship. I need to figure out how to help her manage...whatever this shit is." He holds out his hand. "Peggy, sweetheart, we're going home."

"Hollis, please," she whispers, her expression imploring. Torn.

But I don't want to create more dissension than I already have. Her relationship with her dad is the most important thing to Aurora. I squeeze her hand, nodding. "You should go. I'll tell Hemi."

The way her face crumbles breaks my damn heart, but we're not solving anything tonight. I want to go to her. I want to sweep her away and tell her how much I love her. That I would do anything for her. I would sacrifice anything to make her happy.

Instead, I let her go, and Roman puts a protective arm around her shoulder. He shakes his head, disappointment leaching through the anger as he shoots me a hateful glare and guides her down the hall.

Leaving me with a truckload of regrets.

CHAPTER 39

HAMMER

I keep my eyes on the floor and don't say a word as my dad leads me to the car. His protective arm around my shoulder is shaking. I've only ever seen him this angry once before. When I was seventeen, I dated a guy who drove a sports car. He was an idiot behind the wheel and got into an accident with me in the passenger seat. I ended up with mild whiplash, but my dad lost it on the guy. Unsurprisingly, I broke up with him right after.

I'd been embarrassed at the time, but in hindsight, I understand my dad's reaction. It's one thing to be reckless with your own life; it's another to be reckless with someone else's.

But this is so different. So, so different. The very thing I was afraid of has happened. Almost a decade of friendship is at risk, and so is the health of the team—not to mention the damage I've done to my relationship with my dad. I've tried to be so perfect for him, to make everything easier—to not be a burden for him. Now I just ruined everything.

"Are you okay to drive?" I ask when we reach the car.

"I had one drink," Dad grinds out between clenched teeth.

"You're really angry, though." I wish I could keep my voice from cracking, or the tears from falling, but I'm a mess. "And you punched a wall. You should probably have your hand looked at." If he broke anything, I'll never forgive myself. What if he can't play the rest of the season because of me? This is all my fault.

"I'm fine, and my hand is fine. Get in the car, please, Peggy."

I don't argue. It's not like I'm in any condition to get behind the wheel.

I slide into the passenger seat, wishing I'd handled tonight differently. It's like my shame bucket is overflowing and drowning me in the process. If I'd been able to keep it together, this wouldn't have happened.

The ride home is silent. I don't want to set my dad off while he's driving. All he's ever done is love me unconditionally. He sacrificed so much for so long, and this is how I repay him? By fucking his best friend. I'm a terrible daughter.

He parks the car when we arrive but doesn't make a move to get out. "I need you to be honest with me, Peggy. How long has this really been going on?"

"Since January," I admit.

"What about before that? Did Hollis ever do or say anything to make you uncomfortable?"

"What? No." *But I did plenty of stuff that made Hollis uncomfortable.* My dad would be so disappointed in me if he knew.

"Honey, it's okay to be honest. You don't have to lie to protect him." His expression is pained, fearful even.

"Dad, that's not—whatever you're thinking..." I shake my head. It wasn't Hollis I wanted to protect. It was me, and maybe my dad, too. From the anger, from the hurt, from *this*. "It's Hollis, Dad. He's your best friend."

"I don't even know who he is anymore. He went behind my back and put his hands on you." His jaw clenches.

I twist in my seat, stomach in knots as I prepare to tell the truth. Afraid of the damage it will do. "You have it backwards, Dad. He tried to maintain boundaries, but I kept pushing."

"He knows better!"

I jolt at his volume. I unbuckle my seat belt and step out of the car, needing space. He does the same. "I understand that you're upset, but I am an *adult*."

"He's more than twelve years older than you! You spent months sneaking around behind my back!" The hurt on his face is bad enough, but the disappointment is more than I know how to handle.

"Twelve years isn't an unreasonable gap." And while it's a piece of this shit puzzle, it isn't the biggest issue, and I know it.

"You're still in university!" He grips the back of his neck. "That's not even the point! Why lie about it?"

"Because what if it didn't work out? Plus, I knew you wouldn't be okay with it, and you confirmed it when you said you would murder him! How was I going to tell you after that? I didn't want it to mess with the end of your season or my exams!" I head for the elevator, and my dad follows.

"But it took you months to even bring it up! Hollis should have come to me first. Before anything happened."

"Would it have changed your reaction? Would you have said it was okay if he had?" I press my fingers to my temples.

"You didn't give me a chance to be okay with it, did you? Where did I go wrong? Since when don't you trust me enough to tell me the truth? And how clueless am I that this was happening right under my nose and I didn't even know?" He runs a hand through his hair. "What else have you lied about?"

I drop my head, unable to look him in the eye. I don't want to tell him about the pink bedroom or anything else from over the years. That I didn't love living in the off-campus apartments as much as I said I did, because he wanted me to have the full university experience he never had. I don't want to tell him that for the first two years after I moved in with him that I kept a bag packed in my closet with all my favorite things in case he decided I was too much to deal with. But keeping these secrets has been so hard on my heart and it's not fair to him. Or me. Lying to him is what got us here in the first place and my shame bucket is pouring over. Before I have a chance to speak, he lobs another question at me.

"What do you think will happen with you and Hollis, Peggy? What exactly is your plan?"

I shrink in on myself, feeling untethered. Like my whole world is breaking apart and I'm about to slide into one of the crevices. "We were going to date like normal people do." Go out together. Be a couple. Tell our friends. Hope they understand. Hope my dad will eventually understand.

"You have faced none of the challenges that come with dating a professional hockey player. He will be gone half the year, Aurora. What kind of life will you have when your partner is never there?" Dad points out. "And Hollis couldn't even stand up for what he wants when it matters. Neither of you could."

"You lost it on us! You're not even giving us a chance," I argue.

"Like you gave me a chance?" He crosses his arms. "Obviously I've done a pretty shitty job of parenting you if you felt the need to *hide* a relationship from me. I'm just so...disappointed that you felt the need to lie. That you both did. Because it means I've failed you in some way. I didn't protect you the way I should have."

I cover my mouth with my hand, the tears falling faster now at that dreaded word. The one I've always tried to avoid.

I've done this to him, made him question himself. All because I wanted Hollis to choose me over him. Because I wanted everything to work out with school and playoffs before I ruined anything. Because I couldn't be honest with him. "You didn't fail me, Dad. I was afraid to tell you because I didn't want to be the one who failed *you*. I broke your only rule." I wring my hands, wishing I could step out of the shoes I'm stuck in. "I didn't want to hurt you, or upset you, and I knew this would happen. I understand that you're mad, I knew you would be, but how it makes me feel—" I choke on the words, on the fear. "I don't want you to be disappointed in me and you are."

The doors slide open on the penthouse floor, and Dad waits, like he expects me to get off the elevator with him. He puts his hand over the sensor. "We need to talk this through."

"Not tonight, please. Everything is super messed up, and I'm really worried about Hollis." I'm on the edge of a complete emotional breakdown.

Dad's face softens a fraction. "Peggy."

My eyes burn with the threat of more tears. I hate that I can't get a handle on my emotions. Everything I love is slipping through my fingers and I don't know how to stop it. "I didn't mean to fall in love with Hollis, Dad. And I'm so sorry that I did this to you, but right now my heart is in pieces. Please let me have some time to process that and fall apart."

The elevator alarm starts buzzing obnoxiously.

"I love you, sweetheart. That will never change." He removes his hand, and the doors slide closed before I have a chance to say it back.

I manage to make it into my apartment before I start bawling again. I pull my phone out of my clutch. I've been so wrapped up in my dad and his reaction to what was likely the worst possible way for him to find out about me and Hollis, that I've missed more than a hundred messages.

The group chat with the girls has blown up. But there are a few private messages as well.

HEMI

> Hollis told me your dad took you home. He didn't elaborate but the look on his face said it all. I'm so sorry. I hope you're okay.

> And don't worry about the gala, everything was coming to a close. But if you need anything, just message.

> Please provide proof of life at your earliest convenience.

I send her a picture of my feet on my coffee table and move to the next thread.

RIX

> I'm on my way home in case you need moral support/ice cream/hugs.

She sent the message about twenty minutes ago, so she should be home anytime. That brings a fresh wave of tears. Thank God for Rix. She's such a great friend. I move to the last thread, the one that scares me the most.

HOLLIS

> I'm so sorry, Princess. This was the last thing I wanted to happen. Message me when you can talk.

I don't know what that means, and I'm afraid to find out. Everything is falling apart.

Five minutes later, Rix, Essie, and Tristan walk through the door.

Tristan sighs. "Ah, fuck."

Rix points a finger at him. "If you utter the words I told you so, Palmella and Fingerella will be your only source of pleasure for the next month."

He holds up his hands. "I would never drop an I told you so." His face softens as he turns to me and puts his hand on my shoulder. "I know things are messed up now, and it probably feels impossible."

Rix sits on the couch beside me and passes me a box of tissues.

I pluck a handful and blot my face, even as the tears keep flowing. "I haven't had a chance to talk to Hollis since my dad found out what's going on. He's just so angry, and he feels so betrayed. It's such a mess." I explain what happened, how my dad found us in the alcove and lost it.

"Hollis let your dad take you home?" Tristan asks. I don't

like that he's wearing the same disappointed expression my dad did.

"He didn't want to get between me and my dad, and it wasn't an ideal location for a productive conversation," I say defensively.

Tristan runs his hand through his hair and shakes his head. "I thought he knew better."

"What do you mean?"

"He should have manned the fuck up and really fought for you. I screwed that up before, too, though. So there's hope yet," Tristan offers, somewhat helpfully.

But Tristan's words press a wound he doesn't realize has never fully healed.

A knock on the door makes my stomach flip-flop. Everyone looks at me.

Tristan breaks rank first. "If it's Roman, I'm not answering it."

He might not want to give me space, but I can't see him knocking on my door already.

Tristan puts his eye to the peephole, and a moment later, he flips the lock and throws the door open. "Dude."

"I know." Hollis stands on the threshold, his bow tie half undone, his hair a riotous mess. He looks worried and sad and broken, like me.

"Well, your face is still in one piece, so you're ahead of me and Flip there," Tristan says.

No one cracks a smile.

I'm not ready for whatever is coming. I'm terrified.

"Aurora, can we talk?" Hollis asks.

An ominous weight settles in my chest as four sets of eyes shift to me.

I nod, unsure if my voice will crack or not.

"We'll be at Tristan's. Text if you need anything." Rix bends and kisses the top of my head. "Seriously, just text. We've got you."

Essie, who's been mostly a silent observer, hugs me. "Stay strong. We're here when you need us."

They file out, and Hollis closes the door, flipping the safety latch before he crosses over to the couch. He leaves space between us, and he doesn't make a move to touch me. The lack of affection cracks my fragile heart.

"Are you okay?" His eyes close. "That's a stupid question. Of course you're not okay. How are you and Roman?"

"He's upset and blaming himself for being a bad father. I told him we both needed time to process."

He runs his hands up and down his legs. "So he's upset with you?"

"I understand his anger in a way I couldn't before, but I'm an adult who can make my own choices. Even if some of them could have and should have been done differently." My stomach churns, and my mouth is dry.

I wish Hollis would take my hand. I want him to wrap me in his arms and tell me we'll figure this all out. That we'll get through this.

He rubs his bottom lip, expression pained. "I should have been honest with him from the beginning. As soon as I realized I had these feelings, I should have gone to him."

"But that isn't what happened, so where do we go from here?" I ask.

He sighs, eyes on his hands, which are clasped in his lap. "We're both in such transitional places in our lives, Aurora. You're so young, and you have so much growing to do."

The fissure in my heart deepens. I'm losing him. This is a breakup speech. He let me go home with my dad so he could take the time to prepare this. To end this. He's not choosing me. Words like *burden, too much, too hard,* take up too much space in my heart and my head. I don't trust my voice, so all I do is nod.

"The way I feel about you. I can't—" He looks so sad, like he knows exactly what this will do to me. "Maybe in a couple of years when you've had time to settle into a career..." He pushes to his feet and paces the room. "Maybe that's what we need."

I can barely breathe around the pain in my chest. We have years of friendship behind us. We care about each other, and he's not even willing to try to make this work? If he doesn't think I'm worth the effort, then who will? Maybe he's right, though. He knows how hard relationships are. Maybe I'm not ready for this. He would know better. I feel so foolish and empty.

I fight not to fall apart in front of him. "Why did we do all this then, Hollis? What was the point?"

He hangs his head. "I thought... I wanted it to be the right time."

I bury my face in my hands, unable to keep the tears from falling. "Why did you let me love you?" I whisper against my wet palms.

"Princess." He pries my hands from my face as he drops to his knees.

I try to stop the tears, but I'm too weak. They keep falling, and my heart keeps breaking.

"I'm so sorry," he whispers.

I push him away and swipe at the tears. "Keep your sorry, Hollis. I don't want it." I want to be worth it. I want to be his—to belong to him. To be his something real and true. I want him to fight for me, for us.

"Aurora."

"You should leave."

He doesn't move, not right away. And I'm so close to losing it for real. "Now, please." I don't recognize my voice. It's cold, detached, void of emotion.

He pushes to his feet. I keep my eyes on my hands, folded in my lap. It isn't until I hear the soft snick of the door closing behind him that I grab the throw pillow next to me, bury my face in it, and sob my heart out.

CHAPTER 40
HAMMER

All I want to do is lie in bed and cry, but I don't have time to wallow. My final independent project is due—including a presentation outlining my role in the Terror organization and execution of the gala—as well as two group projects. It doesn't matter that I'm sleeping like shit and food tastes like cardboard. I have work that needs to be done, so my broken heart is forced to sit on the sideline until I have time to fall apart. School and the job with the Terror are all that matter now.

I've spent the past couple of days at the library. Mostly so I can avoid dealing with my life. Hollis has checked in twice to see how I'm doing. I haven't responded. The truth is, I'm a mess. I've broken up with guys before and been broken up with, but none of them has hurt the way this does. I thought Hollis was my person. I thought we were starting on the road to forever, and now there's this blank, hollow space in my chest where that dream used to be.

A coffee appears on the table as Jameson slides into the seat next to me. "Hey, Aurora. I figure you could use—" His smile drops, and his expression shifts to concern. "Shit. Are you okay?" He rummages around in the front pocket of his backpack and withdraws a pack of tissues. I touch my cheek and realize I'm crying.

"Oh my God. What the hell is wrong with me?" I accept the tissue and dab at my cheeks and eyes. Thank God for clear, waterproof mascara.

"We're all under a lot of stress these days," he offers.

Last week I learned Jameson had been offered grad school admission in BC and the program in Toronto. Ultimately, he accepted the offer out west.

"Yeah. I still don't make a habit of crying in the library." I shake off the emotions and try to compartmentalize.

"Is it school related? Can I help with anything?"

"It's personal. Family and stuff."

"I'm sorry. Do you want to talk about it?"

"Not really. It just makes me feel shitty."

"That's fair." He reclines in his chair. "The gala looked like it was a huge success. I mean, based on the stuff I saw on social media. You got to meet Scarlet Reed. Like, wow." He makes a mind-blown gesture. "Is she nice in real life?"

"Yeah, she is." *And she wants to steal the man I'm in love with.* Maybe she will now that he's decided I'm not ready for a relationship. "*I wanted it to be the right time.*" I blink away the look on Hollis's face, like he'd realized exactly how not ready I was. I thought I could handle it. I wanted to be able to, but based on how terrible I feel, maybe he's right after all. I can't have it all. No one can.

I drag myself out of my head. "How about you? How was your event?"

"Good. Great. We raised like fifty thousand, which is kind of peanuts compared to the gala. I think I read you raised close to a million for all these charities?"

"We had some big donations from some heavy hitters. Fifty thousand is amazing. You should feel great about that."

Thankfully, two more members of our group show up, and we get down to work. The ache in my chest is unbearable, but at least I have something to focus on besides my battered heart.

On the way home, my mom calls. I've put off a conversation, too raw to deal with anything but my own feelings.

"My sweet girl, tell me what's going on," are her first words.

"Have you talked to Dad?"

"He called yesterday. I wanted to give you time, but I also want you to know I'm here for you, however you need me to be."

I tip my chin up to the sky. It's a beautiful spring day, but I can't appreciate it. Not with how heavy my heart feels. "He's so disappointed in me and that's the last thing I ever wanted."

"Oh sweetheart, he's not disappointed in *you*, he's disappointed in himself." Mom sighs. "Tell me the real reason you hid this from him for so long."

"He had to sacrifice everything for me," I whisper.

She's silent a moment, and when she speaks her voice is thick with emotion. "My poor baby, I'm so sorry I did this to your soft heart."

"What are you talking about?" I push through the doors of my building and head for the elevator.

"I wanted to be the best mom for you, Aurora. Truly I did."

"I know—"

"Let me finish, sweetheart." She takes a deep, shuddering breath. "I was not the best version of myself when you were young. And I wanted to be. I tried to be. But your dad, he was... so lost without you. And you, God, you were so lost without him. Every time I would pick you up and bring you home...you would just be so sad until the next time you saw him. He steadied you and you steadied him. He made you shine in a way I couldn't."

I want to argue, to disagree, but I remember how hard it was to leave him when I was little. How excited I would be for every visit and how crushed I was when they were over. The doors slide open, and I step inside, grateful it's empty because I'm on the verge of tears. "I know you tried, though." I push the button for my floor.

"Giving up custody of you was the hardest thing I have ever done in my entire life, Aurora. But I couldn't bear to see you in pain every time you had to come home with me or leave another set of friends. I felt like I was breaking your heart all the time. Especially after your summers away. I kept taking you away from where you were happiest. It was the most painful thing I have ever done, but it was the right thing, for both of you. Roman could give you all the things I couldn't. He could love you exactly how you needed to be loved. The sacrifice for him was letting me try for as long as he did. And I am so, so sorry that I couldn't be the mom you needed then, but I hope that I can be the one you need now. I love you, my sweet girl. You are my most precious gift."

"I love you. I don't think I realized how much I needed to hear this."

"You are such an old soul, sometimes I forget that you need the same reassurances as the rest of us."

My dad is waiting outside my apartment when I step off the elevator. "Hi Dad," my voice cracks with emotion.

"Talk to him. Be honest. I love you. I'm here when you need me."

"Okay. I love you."

"With all of my heart and more."

I end the call.

"Zara?" Dad asks.

I nod, bottom lip already trembling.

He opens his arms.

I step into them. "I'm sorry I lied to you," I mumble into his chest.

"I'm sorry I made it impossible for you to be honest with me."

We stand there in the hallway for long minutes, me crying and him holding me. When I finally get control of my emotions I pull back.

"I can't leave tomorrow morning without making sure you're okay and having a conversation to make sure *we're* okay," he says. They have a two-game away series coming up.

"I might cry again," I warn. But I don't want him to get on a plane with this kind of tension between us either.

"I can handle tears better than silence," he replies. He looks tired and worried. I did this to him. Upended his world. A bucket of shame isn't big enough, maybe a lake would be better?

He pushes the elevator button and turns to face me. "How are you?"

"I've been better." Might as well be honest since lying is what got us here in the first place.

"I could have handled things with more grace the other night," he says as we take the elevator back to street level.

"You could have," I agree. "But I'm also aware it was a shock."

His expression is sad. "I just want to understand why you felt you had to lie." The elevator doors open, and I follow him back into the warm spring afternoon.

"So many reasons." I look up to the sky. "I was breaking the only rule you ever really enforced. And not with just any player, but with your best friend."

His jaw tics, and darkness clouds his expression. "He should have come to me. It would have been the right thing to do."

"But he didn't. Because I asked him to wait." And it took us months to even get on the same page. When we finally did, he put my wishes ahead of his own, because I told him that's what I wanted. But all it took was my dad's anger for Hollis to change his mind about me, about us.

He holds the diner door open for me. Our preferred table in

the back corner is open, so we grab menus and slide into the booth.

"Just the two of you today?" Rainbow asks as she drops off coffee and waters.

I force a smile. "Just the two of us." We're back to how it used to be.

We order the usual, and she hustles off.

"But why did you ask him to wait?" Dad asks.

I hear the hurt. The still-present anger.

"Because I was afraid. I still am," I admit.

"Of what? Why hide this from me for all these months?"

The bucket tips and the truth spills out. "What if you left me? What if I was too much? What if you hated me? What if all the sacrifices weren't worth it and you should have left me with Mom?" I'm terrified that this could be the thing to break us. That everything I've tried to do to make his life easier will be erased with this one betrayal. "What if you resent me for taking your best friend away from you along with everything else?"

His expression shifts, anger fading into something like horror and then sadness. "Sweetheart, I could never resent you, or hate you. You are my entire world and you have never been too much to handle." His eyes slide closed for a moment and when they open, I see his pain. He reaches across the table, and I set my hand in his. "Loving you, getting to be your dad, to have this relationship with you, to be in your life like I am? That was not a sacrifice for me, it was a sacrifice for Zara. It was the hardest thing she has ever done, and I am so fucking proud of her for it, because I know how deeply she loves you. And she would do anything for you, even if it meant having to love you from a distance."

"I never wanted to be a burden for you," I admit softly. "I thought if I could be the perfect daughter—"

"I don't expect you to be perfect, honey. That's an impossible ask of anyone. You are a gift. You will always be my first priority. Our bond is special. We're a team, you and me."

"I know." I line my silverware up on my napkin, relief over hearing this from him giving me the courage to say the things I need to. "But then I started working with Hemi. And I stopped being a student, and I started being a professional. I stopped seeing Hollis as your best friend, and he stopped seeing me as his best friend's daughter."

"Then that's when he should have come to me."

I swallow down the fears. "I was trying to protect you, Dad. And myself. I thought I could manage it all, have it all." I roll my lip between my teeth. "And when I tried to bring it up, you weren't particularly receptive."

Dad arches a brow. "If Hollis was doing to you what Tristan does to Rix, I would have a hard time not putting him six feet under."

For half a second, I consider defending Tristan, but decide against it. "Okay. Fair. But can you at least see why your reaction scared me from saying something?"

"But it was months of hiding."

"All you have is me—and hockey and your teammates and Hollis, Dad. You're so focused on me that you don't leave room for anyone else. I was so focused on proving myself, to the team, to you, to me. And I was terrified of your reaction, and what the fallout would be."

His expression grows pained. "There is nothing you could do that would make me stop loving you."

More tears leak out of my eyes, and my dad moves from his side of the booth to mine and wraps his arms around me.

"I hate that I disappointed you," I murmur.

"You haven't, honey." He kisses the top of my head. "I wish I'd left room for you to be honest. And it doesn't help that he's only six years younger than me."

I sniffle and wipe my nose with a napkin. "You were a teenager when you had me. Even if I dated someone in their late twenties, you would still be weirdly close in age. And a twelve-year gap is not unheard of. At all," I point out. "Hollis's sister is married to a guy who's fifteen years older than she is."

"You can understand my struggle here."

"Honestly, Dad? It really shouldn't be a surprise that I ended up falling for one of the guys on the team. Just be thankful it wasn't Flip."

His eyes and nostrils flare. It would be funny if I wasn't so emotional. "Dallas is still in his twenties!" he says. "He's a nice guy."

"Uh, he kind of has a thing for Hemi." That's the vibe I get from him, anyway. Why else would he put up with all the weird shit she makes him do?

"You're not the first person to say that," he muses. "And half the team is still in their twenties."

"But they're still hockey players and they're not Hollis. Not that it actually matters since we're not seeing each other anymore, secretly or otherwise." The ache in my chest grows nearly unbearable with that admission. My eyes prick with fresh tears.

He frowns. "What? When did that happen?"

"You haven't spoken to him?"

"I'm too angry to talk to him. Is this because of how I reacted?"

"Yes. No. I don't know."

He's back to looking angry. "Why aren't you seeing each other anymore?"

I fight tears but lose the battle. I pull another napkin from the dispenser and dab at my eyes. "It's not the right time for us."

"Is that what he said?"

"Does it matter?"

"If he's not going to fight for you, he doesn't deserve you," Dad says sharply.

I lean my head on his chest. "I know you're still angry, but my heart hurts, and I just need you to be my dad and love me, and not give me shit for falling in love with Hollis, okay?"

He squeezes my shoulder and kisses the top of my head. "Okay. I'm sorry you're hurting, sweetheart. Is there anything I can do to make this better?"

"Just be my dad."

"Always." He sighs. "I could kick his ass, if you want."

"Thanks, but I'm good."

"I figured you'd say that but, I thought I'd offer anyway," he says softly. "Is there anything else you've been hiding from me that I should know about?"

"My favorite color is yellow, not pink."

He pulls back and frowns. "Since when?"

"Since always."

His eyes dart to my bag, and the hair tie around my wrist. His mouth opens and closes. He sighs. "Can we make a new rule?"

"Depends on the rule."

"No more trying to be perfect. I love you exactly as you are."

"Even if pink isn't my favorite color."

"Even then." He kisses the top of my head. "I love you."

"I love you, too."

CHAPTER 41
HOLLIS

We're playing in New York tonight, and I'm still on the bench, though just for one more game. As awesome as it was to get that news this morning, the fact that I can't celebrate it with Roman or Aurora makes it less of a win. It also stings that I would probably have been playing tonight if I hadn't gone down on my knee at the gala. Thankfully, Roman's hand is fine. I watch my teammates fly down the ice. Like always when we play New York, Madden and Grace are riding each other hard, at least they're staying out of the penalty box, though. The game is tied, but we still have twelve minutes to score another goal. There are only a handful of games left in the regular season. We're heading for the playoffs no matter what, but every point counts. Grace slams Madden into the boards, and New York gains control of the puck.

"I wish I understood why they hate each other so much," Palaniappa mutters.

"They went to hockey camp together when they were teenagers. Something happened there from what I understand," Bright says.

"Must have been something pretty damn bad," Palaniappa replies.

I don't comment. I'm half here, half still in Toronto, wondering how Aurora is doing. Rix came up and got the fob from me before I left and said she would take care of the boys. She told me Aurora was doing as well as could be expected. I wish things were different. That I'd handled this better. That I hadn't imploded my relationship with Aurora and my best friend. I feel fucking lost. I was afraid she could change her mind years down the road, but now I'm scared I've lost her forever.

Bright and Palaniappa are called back onto the ice, and Madden and Stiles rotate off. Stiles takes the spot beside me. "You need to keep your head on the next shift, man," he says to Madden. "I can't hold your hand during playoffs."

"He knows how to push my buttons," Madden grumbles.

"And you let him," Stiles replies.

"He shit talks," Madden counters.

Stiles claps him on the shoulder. "You're better than he is, on the ice and off. Stop letting him get under your skin."

"I'm trying." Madden's leg is going a mile a minute, though, so it's hard to say how effective he'll be.

Palaniappa passes the puck to Bright. He rushes down the ice, toward the net, New York on his heels. Palaniappa gets into position, and Bright sends the puck his way. Spencer blocks another New York player from stealing the puck, and then it's back to Bright, who shoots on net. It bounces off the post, but Palaniappa is ready for the rebound. He slips the puck by their goalie's skate as he shifts to the other side of the net, giving us the goal we need to take the lead.

The arena goes wild—the New York fans freaking out, the smattering of Toronto fans shouting their approval. We keep the lead through the rest of the period and win by one.

Roman is still ignoring me. I figured sharing a room on this trip would force conversation, but so far, my attempts are met with one-word answers and a lot of cold shoulder. After the game, I follow Roman to the hotel room, hoping we can finally clear the air. I'm unable to handle all this fucking nothingness.

"How long is the silent treatment going to last?" I ask.

He drops his coat on the bed. "As long as it takes for me to get over you having a relationship with my daughter behind my goddamn back. Maybe it'll take a month, maybe a year, or maybe I'll never get over it. You knew better. You put Peg—Aurora in a shitty position. It was up to you to do it the right way. My daughter is a fucking mess, and that's on you. Her heart is in pieces because you're a selfish, fucking coward."

I start to interject, to explain, but he cuts me off. "You don't have a daughter, so you can't possibly comprehend how awful it is to see her go through this. The only thing I can do is be someone she can lean on. She's my first priority, which is a hell of a lot more than she is for you."

Everything I did was meant to protect her from pain, but I failed miserably. At least I didn't ruin her relationship with Roman. That's something.

His phone rings. "That's Aurora. I'd like some privacy while I speak with her, so if you could see yourself out, that would be great. One of the guys will text you when I'm done." He crosses the room and opens the door, motioning for me to leave. "Hey, sweetie. How was your first exam? Did you feel good going into it?"

I grab my jacket and my phone and step into the hall. What else can I do? Roman doesn't want to hear my side, and I don't want to upset Aurora more than I already have.

The door slams in my face. I can still hear his voice, but the words are too muffled to make out.

I knock on Flip and Tristan's door. Tristan opens it. He's dressed in his usual uniform of jogging pants and a T-shirt. "You sleeping on my couch tonight?"

"Maybe."

"I've been there more times than I can count, but mostly because Flip has a problem keeping his dick in his pants." He steps aside and lets me in.

"Where is he now?"

"He went to grab some snacks. I already warned him that if he brings a human back with him, he can rent his own freaking room."

"He's been a lot better over the past few months," Ash offers.

"He has, but my couch-sleeping days are over. Yours, however, have probably just started." His expression reflects both empathy and disappointment.

Ash and Dallas are already on the couch. Dallas brought his gaming console, so the two of them are playing. "So, you and Hammer, huh?" Dallas says.

"Shilps called it months ago," Ash says.

"Did one of the girls say something?" I'm aware Rix has known for some time, and Tristan walked in on us once...

Ashish rolls his eyes. "It's the way you look at her."

"Which is how?"

"With longing."

Well, that's not inaccurate.

"I can't believe you've been boning your best friend's daughter. That's ballsy. Pun intended," Dallas says. "And stupid."

"I'm not a douchebag. I was not *boning* Aurora."

"Fine. Having sex." He pauses the game, and his eyebrows pop. "Or making sweet, sweet love to your best friend's daughter."

"I'm going to punch you in your fucking face if you keep talking about Aurora like that."

"Oh, shit." Dallas sets his controller down. "You're in love with her."

"Seriously, can we change the subject?"

"Dude. You're in love with Hammer. Like, Hammer, who basically grew up with the entire team as big brothers-slash-bodyguards." Dallas keeps talking. "Damn. Well, now what happened with Willy yesterday makes sense."

"What happened with Hemi?" Ash asks.

"She signed me up for this photo shoot with a python before we flew out yesterday, probably because she knows I hate snakes, but then she said something came up, and she rescheduled it. She didn't even call me a name or tell me she hates me. She *always* tells me she hates me. But I guess she was preoccupied with whatever's going on with you and Hammer. I thought maybe you wanted a bite of the forbidden fruit. You know, taste that fresh, forbidden apple."

"Seriously, I'm going to strangle you in your sleep," I tell him.

"Similar to how you'd like to bite Hemi's apple," Ashish says.

"Oh no. I don't want to bite Hemi's apple. I want to make a fucking pie out of it."

I look to Tristan for some actual advice, which clearly puts me in the highly desperate category. "You've been through this before, and you and Flip figured things out and Rix took you back."

"Uh, yeah, but only because Bea is the most understanding woman in the universe. I don't think it hurts that I provide multiple orgasms every single time."

"It's a good thing Flip isn't here for this conversation," Dallas says.

Tristan shrugs. "He's aware of my ability to provide multiples, which is another reason Bea should not be interested in being my girlfriend, but here we are. She's the first person I want to talk to every morning and the last face I want to see before I go to bed. I would do anything to be the lucky bastard who gets to love her. Take your own advice, man. If you really love Hammer, why aren't you doing something about it?"

"I don't want to come between her and Roman," I say. "Maybe in a few years, when she's older, we'll be able to make better decisions together."

"She's gonna spend the rest of her life living with her daddy? Being his little girl?" Tristan shakes his head. "Sounds like a bullshit excuse to me. Maybe you need to ask yourself what you're really afraid of, and why you're allowing yourself to be sidelined."

"I hear what you're saying, but you know it's not that simple. I just wanted her to feel safe and supported."

"Safe from what? Roman being rightfully upset? Love is never simple. It's always a risk. You need to decide how far you're willing to go for Hammer, or maybe you don't love her as much as you think." His words hit me harder than any fist ever has.

I spend the night on Dallas and Ash's couch. The following morning, we board the plane and fly to Buffalo for one more away game. We settle into the hotel before practice, and Roman continues to ignore me. I miss Aurora. I'd gotten used to checking the kitty cams for footage of her and having an ongoing conversation via constant text messages. But now everything feels empty.

I change into my practice gear and hit the ice with the rest of my team. Tonight, I'm back in the game for the first time, so I need to make the most of this practice. The dull ache in my knee quickly dissipates these days, and despite my life being a complete shitstorm, the workout goes smoothly.

Coach pulls me aside afterward to check in. "You looked good out there today. You feeling game ready?"

"I'm ready to be back out there with my team."

"This is a good team to be up against for your first night back," he says.

Last night wouldn't have been smart with Madden and Grace all over each other. But we've beat Buffalo every game this season, so we're feeling strong about a win tonight. "I agree."

He nods and rubs his chin. "Everything else okay?"

I'm sure he's noticed the tension between me and Roman.

Unlike Madden and Stiles, we're not duking it out on the ice, but Roman doesn't hide his death stares.

"I'm working out some personal stuff," I say.

"Will that impact how you play tonight? There's no shame in needing a little more time, Hollis."

They're giving me an out, but I'm not inclined to take it. "I'm good. I need to put my focus somewhere, and the ice is the best place for it."

"Okay." He raps on the arm of his chair. "If that changes, you let me know."

"Will do."

I avoid my hotel room between practice and the game and spend a few hours with Flip and Tristan, since Dallas and Ashish are with Roman. I don't like the divide this creates. My unease follows me into the locker room as I suit up for the game. And it doesn't let up when we step out onto the ice, or when I take my place on the bench. What Tristan said keeps rolling around in my head. When I ended things with Aurora, I thought I was doing the right thing after doing the wrong thing for months. Did I step back when I should have stepped forward? Am I allowing myself to be sidelined?

"You got this, man," Palaniappa says. "You played well during practice. Stay out of your head, and you'll be fine." We watch Stiles and Madden pass the puck back and forth, skating toward Buffalo's net. Tonight, they're fighting to stay out of the bottom of the playoffs.

"I'll do my best."

Madden and Stiles rotate off, and I rotate on with Bright. Spencer passes the puck to him, and we skate down the ice, heading for Buffalo's net. I lose speed as I head for the crease, not wanting to repeat history, but I miss an easy pass because I'm being too cautious. We scramble for control. I shake it off and remind myself that I have a decade of professional ice time. I can play better than this.

Bright commands the puck, but Buffalo is playing like their

lives depend on it, and their goalie deflects every shot, keeping the score at zero. We rotate off, and Madden and Stiles rotate back on. They do what we couldn't and score the first goal of the game. Buffalo is desperate to even it up, but Hammerstein shuts them out, and defense is playing tight.

Bright and I take the ice again, and I push aside my fears of another injury and try to keep my head in the game. This time, I don't slow when I approach the crease. I make the turn and the pass, but I almost collide with a Buffalo player. I avoid the hit, but slam into the boards and go down.

"You all right, man?" Palaniappa asks as I get to my feet.

"Yeah, just playing like it's my first time on skates." I test my knee to make sure everything feels fine before I chase the puck down the ice. But that fall cost me precious seconds—the kind we can't afford in a game like this, let alone when we make it to the playoffs.

We're still leading 1-0 at the end of the first period. I follow my teammates down the hall to the locker room, the weight of the truth hitting me. I'm distracted, worried I'm going to do something to screw up my knee—or the game, and then Aurora will feel like it's her fault. We're playing against a team fighting to get themselves out of the bottom position. It will only get more intense. Especially if we keep the lead, or increase it.

"You gotta pull me from the game," I tell Coach Vander Zee once we're in the locker room.

"You need the doc to look at your knee?" he asks, suddenly on alert.

I shake my head. "My knee feels fine, but I can't play the way the team needs me to tonight, and I don't want to be the reason everyone else has to play harder and better. I'm not willing to risk this game for my ego."

"You want me to sit you out this period?" Vander Zee asks.

"I need you to sit me out the rest of the game." This is what Aurora feared, that the rift between me and Roman would screw our chances in the playoffs. But it's me that's the problem, because I fucked everything up. Because I don't have the one person I love more than anyone else. Keeping it a secret didn't stop me from falling for her. It isn't time we need, it's for me to get my head out of my ass. Aurora grounds me, inspires me. She owns my heart, and I've lost her. Because I'm terrified of getting hurt. So I broke my own heart before she could. Like a fucking idiot. I've screwed myself over, but I can't screw my team over, too.

"Does this have anything to do with the personal stuff you got going on?"

I start to shake my head but stop. I can't compartmentalize what's going on with me and Aurora and Roman. I won't be able to play my best until I fix this. It's about having the person at my side who makes me want to be better, do better, live a fuller life. I had that with Aurora. She's been there to lift me up when things were hard. She's been my champion through two injuries. And I want her back. Not in a couple of years, like I told her, but now. I want to navigate the new path *with* her. I don't care if she's just graduating university. I don't give a shit that there's more than a decade separating us, or that people might have opinions. I love her. I'm *in* love with her, and I don't want to wait for the timing to be right. This is as right as it gets. I want her now, and I'll gladly take whatever challenges that brings if I can have her at my side.

"Hollis?" Coach asks.

"I can't be what the team needs right now, and I don't want to put us at a disadvantage," I say again. I don't want to explain it any further. I need to get Aurora back before I can be useful to my team.

He nods. "We'll meet when we're back in Toronto to talk this through."

"Yeah. Absolutely." And I need to call my agent and have the discussion I've been putting off. I need a contingency plan if this season is my last. I need to start planning for my future, and I need it to include Aurora.

I watch from the bench as we win the game 3-2. It's a huge boost for the team, and as hard as it was to sit on the sidelines, it was the right thing to do.

The sportscasters are stationed outside the locker room after the game. I hate interviews, but when one of the young reporters shouts my name, instead of muttering *no comment*, I turn to face him. Shocked, he shoves the microphone in my face. "What happened on the ice out there?"

"I couldn't be what my team needed."

"Is this because of your knee injury? Do you think you'll be able to handle playoffs?"

"It's not because of my knee," I grumble.

"Do you think you'll do better with home-ice advantage? Scarlet Reed has been attending your games. Is she your good luck charm?"

I level him with a glare. I'm so tired of people telling me who I'm supposed to be dating. "This has nothing to do with Scarlet. Despite media speculation, we are not together. And we will never be again, because I'm in love with Roman Hammerstein's daughter—uh, Aurora."

I'm met with shocked silence for half a second before ten microphones are shoved in my face.

"Does Hammerstein know you're in love with his daughter?"

"Are you secretly dating?"

"How does Scarlet feel about you dating someone else?"

"How does Hammerstein feel about this?"

"I'm not taking any more questions." I stomp into the locker room as they shout after me.

As the door closes behind me, Roman is standing there, an unimpressed look on his face. "It's just words if you don't follow up with action." He disappears into the showers.

Dallas claps me on the shoulder as he passes. "Willy's going to kick your ass for that."

Have I dug my hole deeper or built myself a rope ladder?

CHAPTER 42
HAMMER

"Okay. You've finished all but one written exam, your last major projects aren't due for several more days, and you're watching horrible reality TV. We're going out tonight, and you are not allowed to say no." Rix stands in front of the TV with her hands on her hips.

She's spot on about the horrible reality shows. I found some from a decade ago that have zero in the way of plot, and the cast is comprised of the most frustrating humans on the face of the earth. For a show that stresses the importance of strategy, there seems to be none. Unless being an annoying jerk counts.

I drag my eyes up to her face. "I still don't know how to feel, and I'm still sad."

"Of course you are. You're watching the world's biggest assholes vie for a quarter of a million dollars. That would make anyone sad." She drops to the cushion beside me. "And you're allowed to be conflicted."

In a rare, shocking post-game interview, Hollis publicly declared he's in love with me. Well, he said he's in love with Roman Hammerstein's daughter and tacked my name on at the end. I've watched the clip an unreasonable number of times. Dissected it.

Tried to read between the lines. As nice as it is to hear I'm not alone with my feelings, that he referred to me as Roman's daughter first leaves me with a lot of questions. Like how can it ever work between us if my dad is the third party in our relationship all the time? Also, it's one thing for Hollis to tell the world how he feels, but what is he going to do about it? I don't know if this will impact my potential job with the Terror, but I can't worry about that today.

"I miss Hollis." I look up to the ceiling to fend off my tears. He messaged the other night, but I haven't responded. I'm over here working on my relationship with my dad and standing up for myself. I can't do his part as well. I need Hollis to make an actual move. I want him to say those words to my face and tell me how he plans to prove he means it.

"I know." Rix wraps her arm around me. "Which is why we need to dress you up like a thirst trap and go shake our asses on the dance floor. And we should also do shots like they're not the worst idea we've ever had."

"Shots are always a bad idea. And yet I always say yes to them."

"Truth. I'll text Hemi, Dred, and Shilps."

"What about Tally? I feel bad that she gets left out of bar nights."

"She's on a senior-year high school trip, and we'll have a girls' night when she gets back. I'm sure she'll have all kinds of drama to fill us in on, because teenagers."

Rix sends the text message, which quickly turns into a buzzfest. Shilpa and Ash are on a date, so they'll meet us there, but Dred and Hemi come over. I love that Dred has become part of our core group when we're hanging at our apartments or the Watering Hole.

Rix pulls me off the couch and drags me to my closet. Then she decides we need to up my outfit game, so we raid her closet instead. "This skirt." She tosses a skintight pleather number at me.

"Will barely cover my ass." I have several inches on Rix, so this already-short skirt will be something else.

"If you're opposed to showing that much skin, how about this as an alternative?" She tosses a pair of black leather-looking leggings at me. "They're the magic-butt pants."

"How come I've never seen you wear these?" I ask.

"Because if Tristan sees me in them, I don't make it out the door."

"Ah, that makes sense." I rub my chest at the sudden sharp stab. "Less than a week ago, I would have put on magic-butt pants for Hollis." I try to make my breathing even, so the tears won't fall.

"The hurt hits hard, doesn't it?"

"So hard. But it's more than that. I miss how steady I felt when I was with him. How clear the future started to look when we were trying to make this work, and now, I just don't know."

She nods. "We don't have to go out tonight if you're not up to it. We can eat ice cream instead. All the ice cream."

I shake my head. "If I keep it up, I'll need to buy stock in Kawartha. I need to get out of my head." And my aching heart needs a rest, too.

"Okay." She passes me the magic-butt pants and rummages through her closet for a shirt. "Pair it with this." She tosses a cowl neck, backless, rhinestone tank at me.

Fifteen minutes later I'm dressed—if we can call it that—and we're on a video call with Essie, who functions as our live makeup tutorial guide.

"How have you been my best friend since nursery school and never mastered cat eyes?" Essie asks.

"Because you were always here to do them for me," Rix says.

"I really need that portal between Vancouver and Toronto," Essie sighs.

"Maybe you can transfer to Toronto soon," Rix says wistfully as she follows the video tutorial playing on my phone.

There's a lot going on at once.

"I'm contracted here through the summer, but I have holidays banked, so I will be visiting again soon."

We chat with Essie until our makeup is done. Hemi and Dred show up a few minutes later. I do a double take as Dred shrugs out of her oversized cardigan.

"Holy shit."

Dred looks down at herself. She's wearing a black leather corset dress that laces up the front and does an unreal job of showing off all her assets, which are typically hidden under her cardigans. Although the dress she wore to the gala showed a lot of personality and thigh, this is next level.

"Too much?" Her lips pucker. "It's too much, isn't it? I asked Flip for his advice, and he gave me the thumbs-up. I should've known better. It was a Halloween costume three years ago."

"There's nothing going on with you two?" Hemi asks.

Dred makes a face like she's eaten a lemon. "Ew. No." Then she gives Rix an apologetic look. "No offense. I adore Flip. He is a master at Battleship. But like, just no. He's like a brother."

"It's so...interesting that he hasn't tried to get with you," Hemi muses.

"I was honest from day one. He just nodded and said cool. He's never once pushed that boundary. There's also no chemistry. It's nice to have a hot guy friend who doesn't want to find out if this buttoned-up librarian is a freak in the sheets."

"Well, based on this outfit, I feel like we now know the answer to that," Rix says.

"It really is too much, isn't it?"

I direct her eyes to my outfit, then Rix's and Hemi's. "Really? How can you be worried?"

Rix is wearing the skirt that would have been more like a headband on me and a red tank. Hemi is wearing a royal blue dress that conforms entirely to her amazing curves.

"So, I look okay and not like I'm trying to be something I'm not?"

I nod. "You look amazing."

"Phew." Her shoulders relax. "I wasn't one hundred percent sold. Are we heading out right away?"

"I vote for a round of margaritas first," Hemi announces. "It's already been a night, and if you're okay with it, I might leave my car here and get my drink on." She pulls a mostly full bottle of tequila out of her oversized purse.

"Oh, shit. What happened?" Rix takes the bottle from her. "And you can always take my room, and I can sleep at Tristan's."

"I went on the worst first date in the history of first dates."

"Why didn't we know about this date?"

She waves a dismissive hand. "I'm still in the vetting process for my high school reunion in the summer. There is no way I'm going dateless. Hopefully, I'll find a viable candidate soon."

"What happened on this date to make it so bad?" Rix asks.

"You know when you talk to someone online and they seem normal, but when you meet them in person, you realize they are the furthest thing from it?"

"Oh yeah. That's happened to me so many times," Dred says.

"This guy's profile says he's in the entertainment industry, which is pretty vague, right?"

"I feel like there's a but coming." Rix dumps half the bottle of tequila in the shaker.

We're in for a night.

"He's a clown for children's birthday parties. Like, that's his actual job. Which is…whatever. Fine. Being a birthday clown is a legitimate job. But he drives around in a white van. Just a plain white van with no windows. He gave me serious serial-killer vibes. I deleted my profile off the site. I'm so glad we never exchanged phone numbers." Hemi grabs the tequila and takes a swig straight from the bottle.

Rix hands her a lime wedge.

"Yikes. How about next time you go on a date, you let us know?" I suggest. "And we should all do that app tracking thing on our phones so we can friend-stalk each other in situations like these."

Dred nods. "Flip put that on my phone recently, after he found out I had a weird encounter at work. It's also great when I need him to check on Dewey when I work late." Dred has a pet hedgehog, and he is the cutest, stinkiest little guy with a robust social media following.

"Flip monitors your whereabouts?" Rix asks. "He doesn't even do that with me."

"But Tristan does, right?" Dred asks.

"Yeah."

"So Flip doesn't have to. He only started doing it recently. Sometimes I'm at the library until midnight, and it can get dicey when I check the bathrooms."

"Why the bathrooms?" Hemi asks.

"It's a free public space. Sometimes people suffering from addiction use the bathrooms, especially in the winter. Mostly they're harmless and want to be left alone, but I've had a couple of scary interactions. When a security guard isn't available, I'll call a friend or Flip and they stay on the line with me until I'm sure it's all clear."

"Wow. That's—I had no idea. You can call us too." I touch her arm.

"Same," Hemi replies.

"I'm glad Flip does that for you. That's the kind of brother I know he can be," Rix says with a wide smile.

It's kind of him, but it hurts my heart a little that he was such a thoughtless dick when Rix was living with him.

Rix pours us very strong margaritas, and we briefly video-call Tally. She's in a hotel room with three of her classmates, two of whom are attempting to sneak out and meet up with guys. Tally has no interest in joining, since one of the trip chaperones is her mom's best friend. Last year the kids who tried the same thing were sent home by bus at their parents' expense. We promise her we'll get together as soon as she's home so she can fill us in on everything.

Once we finish our margaritas, we head to the club. It seems Hemi's already organized bottle service, so we have a table and tequila as soon as we arrive. It's a busy night, the dance floor full of pulsing bodies. *Just try not to wallow for an evening*, I tell myself. I need to focus on something other than how impossible it all seems.

After a while, we've made our own little dance floor in front of our table. I'm trying to lose myself in the music, but my heart and head are somewhere else.

Dred's eyes go wide. "Oh, shit."

"What's wrong?"

"Remember that tracking app?"

"Yeah."

"Flip is here."

"I told Tristan where we were going," Rix offers with a chagrined smile. "Not on purpose. I was distracted when he asked." We all know what that really means.

I scan the bar, searching for Flip and Tristan in the crowd. They're not hard to find. Both of them are over six feet with broad shoulders, and they look like they own the place. They're wearing black dress pants and button-downs. Dallas appears behind them, and then, much to my surprise, Hollis.

"Fuck a duck. Hollis is here," I mutter. Like the rest of the guys, he's wearing black dress pants, but instead of a light shirt, he's paired it with a black button-down. My breath catches in my throat. I search the space behind him for my dad, hopeful something has changed. But he's not here.

Hollis's gaze locks on me as the guys close in. My palms start to sweat.

"I can tell them to go somewhere else, if you want," Rix says.

"Let's see what he does first?" It's more question than answer. My heart aches in a way that's become uncomfortably familiar. Hemi and Rix move to flank my sides.

Tristan looks like he's mentally undressing Rix as he approaches. His gaze shifts to the right for a moment, and he frowns. "Dred?"

"Hey." She raises her hand in a wave.

. "Fuck. You look...not like you."

"Um...thanks?"

"You look nice!" He gives her an awkward two thumbs-up, then motions behind him. "Hollis wanted to tag along. But if you need him to fuck the hell off, just tell me."

I nod. "Okay, thanks."

"But as someone who fucked up royally not so long ago, maybe it wouldn't be the worst thing in the world to hear him out tonight." He rubs the back of his neck. "That's all I'll say about that."

Hollis is making a move by being here, which is what I need from him. So I nod. "I'll take that under advisement."

"Willy, you look stunning," Dallas says.

"Eat a urinal cake, Dallas," Hemi replies.

"You ladies need anything from the bar?" Flip asks. He high-fives Dred once he's closer to her.

Dred points to the bottle of tequila. "We're probably more than good for now."

Hollis moves around the guys and approaches me, sort of the way someone would a cornered animal. As he gets closer, I notice dark circles under his eyes and uncertainty on his face. He stuffs his hands in his pockets and leans in, his mouth close to my ear, which means I'm huffing his cologne. The music is loud, so we have to shout to hear each other.

He tucks a hand into his pocket, expression full of remorse. "If you'd prefer not to be around me, I also understand, and I'll leave."

"I don't want you to go," I blurt.

"You tell me what you want, and I'll do my best to give it to you."

What do I want from Hollis? Isn't that the million-dollar question? He's here, and that means something, but why did it take until now for him to get to this place? "I don't know what that is right now, but I'm glad you're here."

His fingers brush the back of my hand, and he inclines his head toward the dance floor. "Go have fun with your friends. I'll be here when you're ready to talk."

With a nod, I join Hemi, Dred, and Rix on the main dance floor. Tristan is standing guard against a pole fifteen feet away, watching Rix. She grabs my hand and pulls me into their circle. "What's going on?"

I shrug and take a hefty gulp of my margarita. "He wants to talk when I'm ready."

"Are you going to hear him out?" Dred asks.

"I should." It comes out sounding like a question.

"What do you want?" Rix asks.

I want to be chosen by him. To be put first. For him to own his words and prove he means them.

Rix takes my free hand in hers. "Talking doesn't mean you have to make a decision right away."

"I know. I'm just scared." But worrying about things I can't control won't help.

As I dance with the girls, I'm acutely aware of Hollis's eyes on me. And he doesn't look away when I meet his gaze from across the room. He pulls his phone out.

A few seconds later, mine buzzes with a new message.

HOLLIS

Will you dance with me?

I bite back a smile and nod. That's something I can manage.

He moves through the crowd, eyes never leaving mine. When he reaches me, his hand settles on my waist, and he drops his mouth to my ear. Like he's perfectly comfortable touching me in public. Like I'm his. Like he's mine. His fingers drift down my other arm and slide under my palm. He lifts it and presses his lips to my knuckles. "I've wanted to do this for so long."

It's what I wanted. What I still want. But fear makes it almost impossible to move.

He doesn't pull away, doesn't look around to see who might be watching. Instead, he pulls me closer. "Is this okay, Princess?"

"It's okay." I close my eyes as the endearment hits me right in the chest. I've missed hearing him call me that.

I move closer, until our bodies are flush, waiting for him to back off or tell me it's a bad idea. He doesn't. All this time spent fighting our connection, and now here we are, broken and afraid and still so drawn to each other.

He kisses the tip of each finger. "I miss you."

"I'm right here." But there's an ocean of hurt between us.

"Then why do you feel so far away?"

Our chemistry crackles, but there's still everything else we need to figure out. Wanting him is one thing. Moving forward is another.

He drops his head, his warm breath on my neck, lips at my ear. "It was torture having to watch you out here on the dance floor and never be able to touch you." The hand on my hip shifts to my low back, keeping me close. "I'll never make the same mistake again if you give me the chance, Aurora."

It's all the right words. But I need more. He dips his head, as if to kiss me, but I press my thumb against the center of his lips. His eyes meet mine, and my knees weaken at the emotions in them. Lust and longing are always there, but it's the deeper emotion—the one I haven't dared to address—that makes me wish we could go back and do this over, but better, without the deception and the hurt. But he was still pages behind me. Maybe it's me who's fallen behind this time. All my fears are holding me hostage.

It would be so easy to let him take me home and fall back into bed with him, to connect us in the way that feels so right. But then we're back where we started. "My heart is broken, Hollis."

I need him to prove he won't walk away again, that he sees

me for me, and he'll do what it takes. Because I'm worth the risk. Only then can I do the same. If we're both hiding from our fears, this will never work.

He kisses the back of my hand. "Can we go somewhere and talk? If you're ready?"

If I want all these things, I have to give him the opportunity. "I'm ready."

Hollis waits while I hug the girls and say good night. "I should not sleep with him tonight, right?" I ask Rix.

"Totally up to you," she says. "However, sex and feelings go hand in hand, so it might be better to have the feelings part managed before you go adding the sex back in."

I really love her. "Good call."

"Stay strong." She squeezes my hands. "Batdick will do his job until Hollis fixes his fuckup."

When I'm done with the hugs, Hollis laces our fingers and guides me through the crowded club. It's April, so it's chilly once we step outside. He wraps a protective arm around me while we wait for his car. He does it so casually, like it's the most natural thing in the world. Like it's not the first time it's ever happened in public. And like he didn't break my heart less than a week ago.

"Are you okay to drive?"

"I only drank club soda."

"Oh." That's much smarter than my three-margarita night. I'm definitely tipsy. And horny. And emotional. At least I stayed away from the martinis.

He runs his hand up and down my back. "You look incredible, but this outfit isn't very practical for the weather."

"The plan was thirst trap, not practicality."

"You definitely hit the mark. Everything about you is sexy."

The valet pulls up with Hollis's blue sports car. He opens the door for me and holds my hand while I climb into the passenger seat. My knees go weak as I'm immersed in the scent of his cologne. After he settles behind the wheel, he turns on the seat warmers and reaches behind him to retrieve one of his hoodies for me.

"Oh, thank God." I shove my arms through the warm, soft fabric that also smells like him.

"Do you want to go back to one of our places, or would you like to grab a bite to eat?"

Having this conversation in public will make it a lot harder to end up in bed with him. I could also use some carbs to soak up the tequila. "Food would be good."

"Are you in the mood for anything specific?"

"No, wherever is fine. Maybe just not the diner." It has too many conflicting memories.

"Okay."

It's late, so we end up at a chain restaurant about a fifteen-minute drive from home. The host's eyes bulge as we walk in. He's wearing a name tag that reads *Scott*. "Hollis Hendrix?"

Hollis gives him a friendly smile. "That's me. I'd appreciate if you didn't announce it too loudly, though." He glances around the semi-full restaurant.

We're a little outside the club district, but close to one of the local colleges. In hindsight, this might not have been the best location.

"Yes, sir," he whispers. "It's an honor to have you here. I hope you're able to get back in the game for playoffs."

"Thanks. If you could seat us somewhere private, that would be great," Hollis says, still wearing his professional smile.

"Of course." Scott grabs two menus and motions for us to follow him.

He seats us at a booth in the back corner and rushes off, telling us our server will be right with us. She appears a second later. Pearl is in her sixties, and she doesn't so much as bat an eyelash at Hollis. We both order coffee and water, and I opt for the bananas foster crepes because I need comfort food while Hollis gets the all-day breakfast.

I'm so nervous. I squeeze my fingers together in my lap, waiting to hear what he has to say.

His voice is raw with emotion, and when he straightens, I see anguish in his eyes. "I'm fucking lost without you."

He's so sad and beautiful. My fingers twitch with the desire to touch him. To slide into the booth next to him and let him wrap me in his arms and forget everything that's happened since the gala. But I can't just hand him back my heart after he discarded it. He has to make me believe he wants it. "Then how could you let me go so easily?"

"Because I'm an idiot. A scared idiot. And a lot of other things. But those two top the list." He rubs his bottom lip. "I don't know if I can fix this, but I am going to try, and I'm not giving up without a fight."

Those are the right words. My heart sings, but then stutters. I'm scared to trust him. I hate that my brain goes to my dad right now, but I think he's right. Without action, Hollis's words don't have much meaning. I search for what to say as my heart moves to my throat. "Do you want to talk about the interview?"

He blows out a breath. "That was not the ideal way for you to hear those words from me for the first time, but I meant them." Hollis puts his hand palm up on the table, his expression hopeful.

I settle my hand into his and immediately feel more at ease. "Tell me something real and true," I whisper.

"I'm so fucking in love with you, Aurora. Hopelessly, stupidly, irrationally in love with you."

"And yet, you still walked away from me."

"I let fear stand in my way," he says softly. "But I won't let that happen again, if you give me another chance."

"What are you afraid of?"

"That I was an infatuation for you. That whatever your feelings were, they could change. That they would."

"Because of what happened with Scarlet?" I ask.

He nods. "I thought I was protecting you and your relationship with Roman, but it was my heart I was trying to safeguard. I stood in my own way. You're such a bright star, and I didn't want to hold you back."

"How would that happen?"

"The world is yours, Aurora. Whatever you want, you just have to reach out and take it. I've already hit my peak in my career, and you're just starting." His thumb sweeps across my knuckles, as if the contact grounds him. "I guess I convinced myself that you could, *should* do better than me, and eventually you would see that."

"She really did a number on you, didn't she?" I say.

His smile is sad. "Yeah. I come with scars, Aurora."

"Welcome to life, Hollis. Everyone has baggage. My dad is a professional hockey player. I was the result of a teen pregnancy. I lived in eighteen different cities in the first five years of my life. My mom, who I love dearly and who loves me the best way she can, had to step back and let my dad take over because she couldn't raise me. And then I grew up as the team princess." Thank God for good therapists and my dad being constant. "I'm surrounded by alpha, elite athletes who make more than half a million a year at the very least, and I will never come close to that. Everyone puts me on a pedestal, and I just want to be me, for that to be enough. I can't be perfect."

"You're more than enough, Aurora. I just worried I wasn't."

"Well, we're two peas in a pod, then, because I worried you were going to go back to Scarlet because she's a better fit for you than me."

The hurt in my heart is echoed in Hollis's eyes. He closes them for a moment, as if he's siphoning the pain, absorbing it and making it his. When they open, sadness lingers, but determination prevails. "There is no one for me but you. I should have stood up for us from the beginning. I should have known from the moment we started that you were it for me. I know you don't trust me right now, and words are empty unless they're carried by action. But I keep looking at my future, and all I can see is you." His thumb sweeps along my knuckles.

The life with him I'd been building in my heart and head feels terrifyingly possible again. "How do I trust that the way you feel about me will be enough?" That's what this comes down to. This isn't about my dad or his feelings, or how anyone else will perceive our relationship. It comes down to us, and whether we can stand up for each other when it matters most.

"Time, Aurora. I'm asking for time and the chance to show you I'm yours. Wholly. Unequivocally, eternally yours. I choose you, Aurora. I love *you*. You are worth every risk. Let me prove it."

He's so earnest. My soft, broken heart mends with his words. But I can't say them back. Not yet. Not when everything feels so unsteady. I don't want to set myself up for more heartbreak, but what was the point of enduring this pain if we don't at least see if we can fix what's broken?

I can't make decisions out of fear. I have to choose to be the person—the adult—I want to be. My dad can not love my choices and still love me. I don't need to try to be enough, because I already am. I have to believe I'm worth the risk, too. "I'll let you try."

CHAPTER 43
HOLLIS

Now that Aurora is willing to give me another chance, I find myself very motivated—and not just where she's concerned. Although I'm realizing all parts of my life include her, or at least I want them to. And that means I have some shit to take care of. I meet with my agent to discuss options, including early retirement if my knee can't handle another season on the ice. I tell him I need to start planning my life beyond the ice, because that day is coming eventually, and I want clear direction on where I'm going when it arrives.

He nods. "I'll have a list of possible options for you within the week."

"I want to stay in Toronto. I understand that narrows things down." Roman is here, and Aurora has a solid friend group and is loved by the team. I don't want her to have to choose between me and her support system.

He arches a brow. "This have to do with that interview you gave?"

I bounce my fist on the arm of my chair. "Yup."

He nods slowly. "You know I've got an inbox full of requests now."

"I'm not giving a follow-up interview."

He grins. "If you change your mind on that, let me know."

"I won't." I pause halfway out of the chair. "Unless Aurora wants me to."

"Noted."

With that conversation taken care of, I make a stop at Hemi's office, crossing my fingers that she's in the building. I find her at her desk with Shilpa. "Hey, sorry to interrupt," I say in greeting. "Are you around later, Hemi?"

"I'm around right now. What do you need?" She removes a pair of glasses, folds them, and sets them on her desk. "Apart from some media training. I've already signed you up for a refresher course, FYI." Her smile is pinched.

"Uh... Thanks for that." I realize now that I basically handed our team issues to our competition on a silver fucking platter. A media refresher course sounds awful, but I need Hemi's help, so I'll take it to appease her. "I, uh...I can come back later, when you're not busy."

Shilpa gathers her things and crosses the room, patting me on the shoulder as she passes. "We were literally talking about how long it would take you to get your head out of your ass. I now owe Hemi a pair of Louboutins."

"I'm sorry?"

"Don't be. I'm glad she's right in this instance."

She leaves, and I turn back to Hemi. "You're placing bets on me?"

"Yup." She leans back in her chair, apparently unapologetic. "How are you?"

"Getting my shit together."

"Does this mean you're in fix-things-with-Hammer mode?"

"That's my plan, yeah."

She puts her hands to her chest. Then makes a heart with them. "I am fully on team Hamollis."

"That's a horrible merging of our names, but I'm very glad to hear I have your support."

"Hollimer? Horora?"

"I don't think either of those are much better. But I am looking for some assistance."

She props her chin on her heart-shaped hands. "In what department?"

"First question, have I ruined Aurora's chances of getting the job with that stunt I pulled?"

Hemi flips her pen between her fingers. "If you'd pulled it before the gala, it would have been more problematic. People are always going to speculate. Especially under circumstances like these. But I have the receipts to prove that she pulled that event off on her own, with very little help from me. So aside from watercooler gossip, which she already dealt with during her internship, she'll be fine."

I nod. "Do I need to speak to upper management about my relationship with her?"

"Aside from what you broadcasted to the world, it doesn't hurt to go through the proper channels, and we can pull in Shilps to make it all official once the posting goes up."

"Whatever I can do to make it smoother."

"Does this mean you two are back together?" She arches a brow.

"I'm working on that. Which brings me to the next favor. I'd like to take Aurora on a date. I know her favorite restaurants, but I'd like to take her somewhere special."

Hemi grins. "You want to wine and dine her?"

"Exactly. I'd like to treat her the way she deserves, right down to the dress and the shoes." And going public with her is another way I can show Aurora how important she is to me. I don't want to hide her or my feelings. Not anymore and not ever again.

"You have come to exactly the right person." Hemi shuts down her computer, pushes her chair back, and grabs her purse. "Let's pick the perfect date outfit for Hammer."

"Right now?"

"Do you have somewhere else to be?"

"I guess not." I have things being delivered to the penthouse, but I've already messaged Rix, should they arrive while I'm not there.

"She had her eye on three dresses for the gala," Hemi reports as she heads for the door. "She walked away from her favorite because of the price tag. Since you're in deep-grovel territory, dropping a couple grand on a dress won't be a problem."

"I'd buy her a fucking unicorn, if it would make her happy."

Hemi grins. "Excellent. Let's do this."

On the way, I message Aurora. I feel like I'm asking her to prom. There's real irony in the fact that I took pictures of her with her dad and her date when she attended her high school prom. I also spent most of the night assuring Roman that she could take care of herself. I gave her pepper spray after Roman took her for self-defense lessons beforehand to ensure that.

HOLLIS

Would you go on a date with me?

It only takes a minute for her to respond.

PRINCESS

Like the one we had in your penthouse?

HOLLIS

I was thinking out. Unless you're opposed to being seen with me.

PRINCESS

I'm not opposed.

HOLLIS

Are you available tomorrow night?

I should have enough time to pull this off. We also don't have a game tomorrow night, so it works with my schedule.

She takes longer to respond this time.

PRINCESS

Tomorrow night is good.

HOLLIS

Excellent. I promise you won't regret it.

PRINCESS

We'll see.

Hemi takes me to Aurora's favorite store and shows me the dress she passed up. It's gorgeous, but I spot another one I think she would love more.

"She didn't even try that one on, though," Hemi argues.

I check the price tag. It's more than the one she walked away from. "Did she pause to look at it?"

"For like, two seconds, maybe?" Hemi hedges.

If she looked at the price tag, I guarantee that's the reason she never bothered to try it on. It's everything Aurora loves in a dress, from the color, to the cut, to the fit. She'll look amazing in it. "It's the one."

Three hours and several thousand dollars later, I have everything I need for a date with Aurora, and Hemi has a new handbag as a thank you. She insisted I didn't need to buy it for her; I insisted I did.

Aurora is still at school when I arrive home. I stop by her apartment on the way up to mine. Rix answers the door.

She takes me in, arms laden with bags. "Oh, we are deep in woo-the-woman mode, aren't we?"

"Very deep. Aurora agreed to a date tomorrow night. Did the

flowers arrive?" I ordered a bouquet of yellow and blue flowers for her while I was shopping.

"About half an hour ago. I put them in her bedroom." She steps aside so I can come in.

"And the cake? Does it look good?" It's a pre-final exam treat.

"It is… Well, you should see for yourself."

"Did it not turn out?" I ask, suddenly panicked.

Rix holds up her hand. "Oh, it turned out. Let me show you, and then we can unload all your bags."

I set them on the floor and follow her to the kitchen. Rix opens the fridge and carefully retrieves the Just Desserts box, placing it on the counter before she opens the top.

"It's really fucking corny, isn't it?" I stare down at the elaborate design and the words printed across the top.

"Oh yeah, it is, but it's perfect." She gives my arm a reassuring squeeze. "She's going to love it. This is how you show Hammer that you know her. That you pay attention, and you are exactly the right person for her."

"A cake won't fix what I fucked up," I grumble.

She rolls her eyes. "Why are you guys so damn literal all the time? The cake isn't the thing, Hollis. It's a freaking banana cake with coconut frosting and freaking banana ducks on it that reads *I'm bananas over you.* Is it ridiculous? Ten out of ten, yes. But Hammer is obsessed with things that smell and taste like bananas. And she has an unreasonable number of banana-duck-inspired things, which shows that you know what she loves. If you weren't obsessed with her, you wouldn't know that."

"I'm not obsessed."

"You steal her scrunchies, Hollis. You're obsessed." She pats my shoulder. "And it's okay. That's how it should be." She puts the cake back in the fridge. "Now let's get everything set up for mission Woo Hammer."

"Sounds good." I'd rather do that than find out how Rix knows about the scrunchies.

I follow Rix to Aurora's bedroom and stand at the threshold, feeling like I don't have a right to step inside until I'm invited by Aurora.

Rix gives me a knowing, empathetic smile. "You're okay. She won't be upset with either of us when she sees how much thought you're putting into this."

I cross the room and set everything on her bed. Where I made love to her for the first time. That was so much more than sex. The connection was life altering, but I'd been too afraid to voice it. "I want Aurora to know I'm serious about her, and not just by throwing money around."

"If you bought her a gift card, it would be one thing, but you went shopping *for* her. It's like when Tristan sends me ice cream, or orders groceries while he's on an away series. It's a small thing, but it means a lot." She motions to the array of items. "You know what makes her happy; you know what she needs. Spoiling her is lovely, but by doing all of this, you're showing her she's yours and you're hers."

"Thanks for your help. I appreciate it," I say as we lay everything out.

"I'm glad I can do something other than eat garbage snacks and watch terrible reality shows with her," Rix replies.

"She really does love them, doesn't she?"

"Yeah, she does." She gives me a soft smile. "I know you've had a lot of people giving you their opinion, Hollis. If I let what everyone else thought interfere with my relationship with Tristan, he and I wouldn't be where we are. We wouldn't have worked on the things we needed to be better for each other. You love her; we can all see it. So just love her. Fuck everyone else. Except maybe Roman—his opinion counts, so don't fuck his." She cringes. "You know what I mean. Anyway, that's my unrequested two cents."

I nod. "You're a good friend, Rix. Thank you for being there for Aurora when I was over here fucking shit up."

She shrugs. "She's done the same for me."

With the pre-date stuff taken care of, I head up to my penthouse to start my next project. I glance at Roman's door as I step off the elevator. I've given him space, but I don't want to move forward without talking to him first. So I hit the buzzer.

His voice comes through the intercom. "What?"

"Can we talk?"

Silence follows for several seconds before he finally says, "Talk."

I prop my hand against the wall and make eye contact with the camera. "Face to face."

"I might punch yours."

"It's a risk I'm willing to take."

The intercom goes silent, and a handful of seconds later, Roman opens the door. He crosses his arms and leans against the jamb. "You have two minutes. I suggest you use them wisely."

"I messed up, and I betrayed our friendship."

He blinks at me.

"I'm sorry. I should have gotten over myself and been honest from the start. But more than that, I should never have backed down, and I should never have let Aurora walk away in the first place. You can hate what I've done—and me if you need to—but I won't let her go without a fight. I'm in love with your daughter, Roman. She is it for me. I've made the mistake of not putting her ahead of everyone and everything else once. It won't happen again. You should know I'm pursuing Aurora. I would love to have your blessing, but I won't wait for it. And I understand that might make this relationship impossible to repair." I take a breath. "But she is absolutely worth that risk."

He cocks a brow. "And if she doesn't want anything to do with you?"

"Then I'll back off, but I have to try, Roman. I've asked her to go on a date with me tomorrow night, and she said yes. I don't want to come between you. But I can't let the love of my life go without making a fucking effort, and I hope you respect that." I wait for him to punch me.

He stares me down for a few long seconds. "It's about

fucking time." He rubs his bottom lip. "I'm still really pissed at you."

"I know."

"Just keep showing up for her, and I'll get over it, eventually," he grumbles.

"I won't walk away again unless she asks me to," I promise.

CHAPTER 44

HAMMER

"My stomach feels like an army of butterflies is marching in it." The Badass Babe Brigade is here for moral support. It's like Groundhog Day, except it's me getting ready for a date instead of Rix this time.

"Deep breaths. You look amazing," Rix assures me.

"He was right about this dress," Hemi says grudgingly.

"I can't believe you took him shopping. He hates shopping," I muse. The only time Hollis willingly goes clothing shopping is when he needs a new suit. And he makes an appointment for that, and he and my dad go together. I tagged along, because Hollis getting fitted for a suit is freaking magnificent. I was always jealous of whoever got to measure his inseam. I want my dad and Hollis to get back to a place where they can do that again.

I told my dad I was going on a date tonight. Apparently, Hollis had already spoken with him about it. I'm not sure what that conversation looked like, but my dad seems to want me to be happy more than anything else, and that's progress, since last week he wanted to beat the shit out of him.

Hemi shrugs. "He asked for my help, but I'll be honest, he picked everything himself—from the dress to the shoes. It was all Hollis. I just gave input, and apparently it wasn't always the best input since he called it on this dress."

"It's stupid expensive, which is why I didn't try it on," I admit.

"That's what he said. The man pays attention. I'll give him that," Hemi says.

"He really does. That banana cake was amazing," Rix agrees.

"Banana cake?" Dred perks up. "My granny used to make a kickass banana nut loaf. RIP, Gran." She makes the sign of the cross.

"There should be some left. Everyone except me should have a piece. I've eaten it for every meal since yesterday." I burst into a fit of giggles that quickly dissolved into tears when I found it in the fridge. It was sweet, and cheesy, and everything I didn't know I needed.

"I'm on it," Rix declares.

"He must be taking you somewhere really nice," Tally says. "You're so pretty, Hammer."

"You're so pretty, Tally," we say in unison.

She blushes, as usual.

"Do you know where he's taking you?" Shilpa asks.

I shake my head. "But it must be swanky if this is the dress code."

"Or he wanted to dress you up like a princess," Rix calls from the kitchen.

"I seriously hope I'm not overdressed for this." I wouldn't put it past Hollis to outfit me in something extravagant just because he can.

"I can't see Hollis taking you to the Watering Hole looking like this," Shilpa reassures me.

"Just own it. You look incredible," Dred adds.

I run my damp hands over my hips. It's five to seven. Hollis will be here soon.

A knock at the door has my heart rate spiking. And then my

dad pokes his head into the apartment. His eyes flare when they land on me. "Is it okay if I come in?"

I don't really want my dad here when Hollis comes to get me, but I also don't want to hurt his already big feelings over this.

I nod, and he steps into the apartment, waving to my friends. "I see you have your emotional support team." He crosses his arms, then uncrosses them and lets them hang at his sides.

"Yeah, they're good like that."

"You look beautiful. Hollis must be taking you somewhere nice," Dad observes. "I don't think I've seen that dress before."

"Hollis bought it for her," Hemi says. "He actually bought her entire outfit, right down to the shoes."

The only thing he didn't buy was the underwear I have on. And I'm sure he would have, if it didn't seem a little presumptuous about how he wants this date to end.

Dad almost seems to be fighting a smile. "Of course he did."

There's another knock at the door.

"He's here." I point at my dad. "Please be nice. I know you're still angry and hurt, but he's been your best friend for seven years, and I care about him, and he cares about me."

"I know." He shoves his hands in his pockets. "I'll do my best."

I take a steadying breath as I open the door. And nearly melt into the floor. Hollis is dressed in a black suit. His hair is neatly styled, he's freshly shaven, and he smells incredible. The last hoodie I borrowed has very nearly lost its Hollis scent. I inhale deeply, huffing him from a safe, two-foot distance.

His tie matches my dress, and he's holding a bouquet of blue and yellow gerbera daisies, which are my favorite. His eyes move over me on an appreciative sweep that I feel everywhere, especially between my thighs.

"Hi," I croak.

A grin tips one corner of his mouth. "You look stunning."

"The dress was excessive, but I love it."

"I love it on you." He holds out the flowers. "For you."

"They're beautiful." I take them and bring them to my nose. "I'll put them in water, and then we can go."

"Sure. Do you want me to wait here?" he asks.

I'm intentionally blocking his view of the apartment. I drop my voice. "You can come in, but the girls are here, and so is my dad."

A rare smile spills over the right side of his mouth. "I'll come in."

My stomach flips as I step back.

"Hey, Hollis," the girls say in unison.

"Hey." He raises a hand in an awkward wave.

"I'll put those in water for you." Rix takes the flowers.

"Thanks."

Tally passes me my clutch.

Dad crosses his arms and takes on his bodyguard stance. "Hollis."

"Roman."

This is so awkward.

"I've invested twenty-one years in my daughter. I expect you to bring her back in the same condition you took her out in," Dad says.

"A little strong on the dad game, Roman," Rix mutters.

"Okay. Thanks for that, Dad. That's our cue to leave." I grab Hollis's arm with one hand and the doorknob with the other.

He covers my hand with his and turns to my dad. "I love your daughter. I promise to treat her like the precious gem she is."

"Nice." Dred snickers.

Tally's hand covers her heart.

And now I'm all melty again.

Hemi pats my dad on the shoulder as I usher Hollis out the door. At least he has my emotional support team as backup.

I rapid-stab the down button on the elevator, willing it to come immediately, in case my dad wants to impart any other pearls of wisdom, or punch Hollis in his gorgeous face.

"That went better than expected," Hollis says conversationally.

"You're not bleeding, so I consider it a win."

The elevator doors slide open, and Hollis puts his hand over the sensor, waiting until I cross the threshold before he follows. He pushes the button for the parking garage, and then the doors are sliding closed and we're alone.

He moves into the corner and leans against the mirrored wall. "Are you okay?"

I shrug. "I have a lot of feelings."

"Do you want to share what they are?"

"I'm nervous, excited, scared." *Horny.*

He nods. "I'm all the same things."

"What are you scared of?"

"That I've done too much damage, and you'll decide I'm not worth the challenges this relationship will bring with it," he says.

"We're getting real already, huh?"

"Seems that way." His smile is soft. "What are you scared of, Princess?"

"That you still have my heart, and you'll break it again."

His eyes close, and he exhales a pained breath. "Of all the things I wish I could undo, that tops the list, Princess. I hope to prove I meant it when I said I'll never do it again."

I nod. "I hope you can, too."

We reach the parking garage, and Hollis waits for me to exit the elevator before following. His fingers brush the back of my hand, and I slip mine into his, even though my palms are clammy. He squeezes. "Want to tell me why you're nervous?"

"So many reasons, but mostly because this is our first real date out in public, and people might recognize you."

"Are you afraid of what people will think?" he asks.

"No. I'm afraid that you're afraid of what people will think."

His car beeps as he unlocks the door, and he turns to me. "You think I have a problem with your age?"

"You've said as much."

"You mean every time I've said you have so much growing to do, and that you could change your mind about us," he says.

I guess we're continuing with the hard stuff. "You could change your mind, too. You did."

He takes my hands in his. "I never changed my mind about you, Aurora. I got in my own way, just like you said. I can't take back the hurt I've caused, but you're it for me. My heart is yours."

I can feel his regret and see his sincerity. I pull my hands from his, and his face falls—until I wrap my arms around his waist. His come around me, and I feel his lips against my crown. "I love you so much, Aurora. And I will keep telling you until you accept it as truth."

The words bubble up in me, but I'm not ready. Not yet.

Eventually I step back, and he opens the passenger door and helps me into the car. He takes his place behind the wheel, and we leave the parking garage, heading toward the harbor front.

"How have exams been?" he asks.

"They've been good. I hand in my final project for my social relations management class on Monday, and then there's one more exam at the end of the week. Of course it's on the last day, but I know the material. I'm ready to be done."

"You have been for a while."

"I'm ready to do what I love." I stare unabashedly at his profile. I've missed this easy conversation. We know each other. "You'll be on the ice next game?"

"Yeah. Now that I have my shit together, I can be an asset to the team. I was too distracted to be useful during that Buffalo game."

"Because of what's going on between us?"

"Because I didn't fight for what I want, which is you." He stops at the red light and looks at me. "It wasn't because I didn't want to, Aurora. I did. More than anything. Not fighting was... so fucking hard. But I knew how scared you were, and I wanted to protect your relationship with Roman. It was the wrong choice, but it felt like the right one at the time."

"I understand that. My fear stopped me from being honest, too." And it stops me from telling him how I feel about him now. One step and one revelation at a time.

"You are the missing piece, Aurora. Breaking it off with you was a stupid, reactive decision. One I won't make again."

I smile to myself as he pulls into a restaurant parking lot. *I know this place*, I realize. It's the nicest restaurant in the city, very exclusive, with gorgeous views of the harbor. And Hollis is taking me here for our first date. He's making every effort to show me he's serious. That he wants this. That he wants me.

"Just wait a moment," Hollis says to the valet attendant as he opens the driver's side door. Hollis hops out and rounds the hood, stepping in to help me out of the passenger seat. My stomach, heart, and lady business are all aflutter as he links his arm with mine and leads me up the steps.

The host addresses him as Mr. Hendrix, and we're led to a private table with an incredible view of the water. More than one couple seems to recognize Hollis, but no one approaches or makes it awkward. We order drinks and an appetizer and settle into easy conversation.

We talk about the teams in the playoffs and who we think the top picks for the draft will be. "Tristan's youngest brother is eligible this year," I tell him. "Tristan and Rix always go to his games."

Hollis nods. "Tristan mentioned that he's attending university on a full scholarship. It should give him the time he needs to grow into his skill set."

"I still think you'd be a great coach." I hide a smile behind my hand.

Hollis groans. "You're killing me over here."

"I didn't say anything wrong."

"I can read your thoughts on your face, Aurora." He sets his hand on the table, palm up, and I slip my fingers into his. "And it doesn't help when you look like something straight out of a fairy tale."

My stomach flip-flops as he brings my hand to his lips. I love this version of Hollis—intense, seductive, playful, affectionate. In this moment, he feels like mine, and I want to keep him forever.

"I used to love having your undivided attention when I was a teenager." *I love it more now, though.*

He tips his head. "How do you mean?"

"Remember that math tutoring session you gave me? After I failed that test in grade nine?"

He gives me a questioning look. "I helped you once, I think, right? Then your dad got you a tutor, but from what I remember it didn't last long."

"You're right, it didn't." This time I don't try to hide my smile. "I was actually pretty good at algebra, but I came up with this plan, thinking you'd be my tutor, but it totally backfired."

His brow furrows. "But why?"

"I wanted that time with you. I wanted to smell your cologne, and listen to you explain concepts, and daydream about what it would be like to be right here."

He tips his head. "You had a crush on me?"

"Absolutely, I did. Have you seen you? It was harmless for a lot of years, until it stopped being a crush and became something else." I drag my fingers along the inside of his palm. "This year everything changed. I knew I was stepping over boundaries and pushing down walls. I started really seeing you, like you saw me. You're so dedicated to your team and your profession. So committed to being in the best condition you can be on the ice. I see how hard these injuries have been, how you worry about letting your team down. It's never just about you and what you want; it's about the impact it has on everyone else, too."

"That particular trait has been my downfall recently."

"We're here, though, Hollis. And that means something. Neither of us is perfect, and obviously we won't always get it

right, but we're trying on this new us, and I like how we fit."
Again, I want to say the words, tell him how I feel, really and
truly, but I need more time.

It's like he can sense it in me. He reaches across the table,
palm up and open. "I was doomed the moment I saw you doing
a victory dance down the Terror hall."

I slip my fingers into his. "What victory dance?"

"When you landed your first promo op."

My eyes flare. "Back in September?"

He nods and wets his bottom lip. "I didn't realize it was you
at first. Your joy was so huge, it filled the entire space. And you
were so fucking beautiful and then you turned around and I
knew then that I was a goner. I opened my eyes and saw you,
really saw you. Not Roman's daughter, but *you*. This glorious,
stunning, driven woman who had the world in the palm of your
hand. And I just…fell. For every part of you. For your sweetness.
For that sassy fucking mouth I love so much. For your strength,
and your determination and your gentle, perfect heart. I fell so
hard. And I keep falling. Every day without you has been torture
and every day with you is the most amazing gift. That I get to
love you? There's no feeling that compares to it, Aurora. To
you." He lifts my hand and presses his lips to the back of it.
"And I will tell you this every chance I get, because there has
never been anything more real or true for me than you."

"I didn't know how much I needed to hear that," I whisper.

"I have something for you. I was going to wait until after
dinner, but I want you to have it now."

"Because outfitting me for this date wasn't enough?" I tease.

"Get used to it, Princess. Spoiling you will be one of my
favorite pastimes." He grins as he moves to take the seat beside
me. "I know it will take time to earn your heart back. But when I
can't be with you, I want you to have this reminder that you
own mine. It's yours for as long as you'll have it." He opens the
box. Resting on a blue velvet cushion is a diamond-encrusted

heart-shaped pendant intertwined with a rose gold infinity symbol.

"Hollis." I press my fingers to my lips. "This is beautiful."

"Just like you. Can I help you put it on?"

I nod and turn, my body breaking into a wave of goose bumps as his fingers brush my skin. He carefully clasps it around my neck. It warms, and I face him. "Thank you." I slide my arms around his waist, uncaring that we're in a restaurant as I hug him, my cheek resting against his chest. "For this, for tonight. I needed this with you." It's a taste of what it could be like to be his—not hiding behind closed doors, but outside the walls of his penthouse or my apartment—and I'm addicted already.

"I did, too, Princess." He presses his lips to my forehead.

Soft. Sweet. A promise of what could be if I'm brave enough to let him all the way in.

CHAPTER 45
HAMMER

O ver the week that follows, Hollis and I see each other every day. We attempt a coffee date between classes and practices at one of the local shops, but with Toronto in the play-offs, it's impossible for him to go anywhere without being recognized.

We ended up at the Watering Hole the other night because it's safe, but Tristan and Dallas showed up, and then it became an everyone night out. It was the first time we'd been out with the crew since Hollis took me on the date and I decided to give us an honest shot. No one made a big deal of it. I hadn't realized how hard it was to keep this from the people we care about until we didn't have to anymore. Having Hollis casually put his arm around my shoulder and kiss my temple was freeing in the way I've always known it would be.

The hugs good night are long, and the forehead kisses are sweet. But not giving in to the chemistry is wearing me down. Hollis has set a clear boundary about getting physical again until I'm ready to commit to being his girlfriend. My head is ready— and my lady bits too—but my heart is still bruised and nervous.

He heals it a little more every day with his thoughtfulness, though. He's taken to bringing me treats and gifts. Sometimes it's as simple as a snack from my favorite bakery, or a bag of those horrible but delicious marshmallow bananas. My favorite gift so far, though, is the Terror hoodie that reads *Hollis's Girl* across the shoulders. I wore it to my final exam, which I've just handed in.

I'm meeting Rix, Tally, Hemi, Dred, and Shilpa at the Watering Hole this evening to celebrate my freedom from university life. Next week, Hemi's assistant PR director posting goes up, and I'm obviously applying.

I'm about to send the girls a message when I notice I have new ones from Hollis, asking if I've finished my exam.

AURORA

All done!

I step outside and shiver at the cool spring breeze. We're in that weird time of year where Canada can't decide if she's hot or cold yet. I pause to fish my hoodie out of my crossbody bag.

"Hey! Aurora!" Jameson calls as he approaches. "How'd the exam go?"

"Good. How about you?" I shoulder my bag.

He was still finishing up when I handed mine in. I stopped at the bathroom before I left the building, though.

"Same. I think I nailed the essay question."

I fall into step with him as we round the corner of the building. A parking lot separates us from the quad and the campus pub. I frown when I notice a horde of students gathered in one corner of the lot. "What the heck is going on over there?"

"Maybe a fender bender?" Jameson says.

As we get closer, I recognize the car. How could I not? I've been in the passenger seat recently. It's also a custom shade of blue that stands out. "Oh my God, what the hell is he thinking?" Hollis is ostentatious about two things: his hoodie collection and his car.

As we get closer, I note that most of the excited horde are wearing various Toronto Terror clothing items, like hoodies and ball caps. A few even have patches on their backpacks. It's a cool logo, so it's understandable.

"What the hell was who thinking?" Jameson asks.

"Hollis." I don't know whether to roll my eyes or laugh. "I need to save him."

How would Hemi handle this? We've been out with the team before when one of the guys ended up swarmed by excited fans. She always steps in, and most of the time she gives the fans a minute to take a picture and get something signed before sending them on their merry way. This is a sizable group, though, which means it'll take more than a few minutes. Hollis can handle signing hats, but he gets antsy when there's no crowd control. Which is where I come in. "You want to help me manage this situation?" I ask Jameson. "There are playoff tickets in it for you." I don't have the authority to do that, but Hollis does. And I've learned recently that he'll do just about anything to make me happy.

"Are you serious?" Jameson looks like he's going to pee his pants.

"Absolutely."

"What do you need me to do?"

"Calm this crowd."

A group of screaming girls—judging from the look of them, probably first years—try to push their way to the front.

I channel my inner Hemi as I approach the group, whistling shrilly. "Everyone, please take three steps back," I shout. "Move aside, please," I tell the girls who are freaking out.

"It's somebody famous!" one of them gushes.

"Do you watch hockey?" I ask.

She wrinkles her nose. "Um, no?"

"He's a hockey player."

"Oh." That gets rid of four girls and allows me room to slip through a gap in the crowd.

Hollis is passing back a ball cap when I reach him.

Relief crosses his face when he sees me, followed by concern. He wraps a protective arm around my waist.

I smile. "What were you thinking, coming to a university campus in your flashy sports car?"

His grin is sheepish. "That I wanted to pick you up from your last exam so we could celebrate."

"That was sweet, but you probably should have driven your other car." Before he can defend himself, I curve a hand around the back of his neck and pull his mouth to mine. I even indulge in a few strokes of tongue before I pull away.

"You know that'll end up on the hockey sites," he says, but he's still smiling.

"Yeah. We need to manage this situation you've created. Then we can go celebrate." I pat his chest and turn around, whistling the way Hemi taught me again.

The people closest to us step back. I raise my hand. "Hi, my name is Aurora. I'm Hollis's girlfriend, and I completely understand your excitement that he's here, because I share it."

That gets me a few shocked gasps and some laughter. "Hollis has twenty minutes. He will sign hats, shirts, or bags, but no body parts. Please have your camera phone ready for a photo. Any inappropriate touching or comments, and he will leave immediately."

With the help of Jameson and campus security, who have come over to check on the commotion, we're able to handle the crowd while Hollis signs hats and bags and takes photos with fans. I grab contact information from the security guards and promise Jameson I'll text later this weekend with ticket information.

Once we're in the car and out of the parking lot, I angle my body toward Hollis. "Are you okay?"

"Yeah. That was…unexpected."

"Toronto is in the playoffs, and a university campus is a hotbed for excitement, especially on the final day of exams." We're lucky more than half the campus has already cleared out.

"I wanted to surprise you." His gaze moves over me in that familiar fiery way that makes my toes curl. "You were sexy as fuck back there, by the way."

"Thanks." I beam at the compliment.

"Did you mean what you said?" he asks as he stops at a red light.

I bite back a smile. "About being your girlfriend?"

"That's the part, yeah." His expression is hopeful.

"I'd sort of hoped we'd have a little more privacy when I said that, but there were some thirsty women eyeing you." When his face starts to fall, I rush on. "But yes. I mean it. I choose you, Hollis. I mean, I've been choosing you for a while, and I know you're in this with me. I'm ready for this, for us."

"Yeah?"

"Yeah."

"I am so fucking glad to hear that." His smile is wide and warm and full of so much love my heart gets all gushy, along with other body parts.

"I think we should go back to your place and celebrate our new relationship status and my being finished with university."

"What kind of celebration do you have in mind?"

"Hmm..." I tap my lip. "How about the kind that includes a look at that list of fantasies I have?"

He kisses the back of my hand, and I feel it in my vagina. "I love that idea. Plus, I have a surprise waiting for you at home." The light turns green, and he refocuses on the road.

"Oooh, I love surprises. Except the kind where my dad walks into my apartment unannounced, or when Tristan can't wait for Rix to come over and they end up having a fuckfest in our apartment instead of at his place." They haven't done that without warning since I mentioned to Rix how the walls can be thin. Tristan even apologized for ever making me feel uncomfortable. I think it was more painful watching how awkward he was than accidentally hearing their antics.

"It would be justifiable to return the favor before she moves in with him full time," Hollis muses.

"We're tamer than they are by a long shot, though."

"Yeah. There's no way I'll put my entire hand in your vagina."

"Three fingers are always welcome."

Hollis groans. "Let's hope we make it past the front door."

"I sort of hope we don't."

We hit the next red light, and Hollis taps agitatedly on the steering wheel.

I shift in my seat and slide my hands between my thighs. "I can't wait to get you out of those clothes."

He eyes me from the side. "What else can't you wait for?"

"Mm... So many things. I've missed kissing you."

"I've missed that, too."

"And the feel of your mouth on me. God, I'm dying for your tongue between my thighs."

He makes a deep noise in the back of his throat.

"And that sound. I want more of that." I skim the back of his hand with my fingertips, and he groans again. "I love that so much."

"What else do you want, Princess?"

"I want to be under you. I want the weight of you pressing me into the mattress, your hand on my throat, and your eyes on mine while you fuck me hard and slow."

Hollis nearly misses the turn into the parking garage. The tires squeal as he makes the hard right. He barely has the car in park before he jams the release on his seat belt, spears his hands into my hair, and takes my mouth in a searing, bone-melting kiss.

When I reach for his belt buckle, he covers my hand with his. "As much as I want your hands on me, Roman is finally talking to me again, and being caught getting a handy in my car when we're an elevator ride away from a bed seems unnecessary."

"Fair." I back off, and Hollis rearranges himself before we exit the vehicle. The elevator takes forever to arrive, but it's empty, so he backs me into the corner. "I can't wait to get my hands all over you," he murmurs as he kisses a path up my neck.

The elevator dings, and he puts distance between us as the doors slide open. Which is good because my dad is in the hall, holding a giant gift bag with the word *Congratulations* written across the front in cursive.

"Oh, hey. I tried to drop this off, but you obviously weren't there, and the safety latch was on, so I guess Rix and Tristan are."

"That's a safe bet."

He nods, and his gaze shifts between me and Hollis. "I thought you'd want to celebrate a little, but uh...maybe later?"

My heart squeezes. He's really trying. Do I want to celebrate by getting naked? Yes. But I want to help repair my dad's relationship with Hollis first.

"I was supposed to meet the girls at the Watering Hole in a couple of hours, but we could head over now?" I suggest.

"I don't want to interfere with whatever plans you've made." He looks so unsure of himself, and sad.

"You're not interfering, Dado. This is a big deal and a big day. I want you to be part of it. We both do." I squeeze Hollis's hand.

"Come on, Roman." Hollis pulls my dad into the elevator with us.

I hit the button for the lobby and send a group message about the slight change in plans.

When we step out of the elevator, Hollis laces my fingers with his, and we walk down the street together. We grab our favorite table, but instead of sliding into the seat beside my dad, Hollis takes the spot beside me and stretches his arm across the back of my chair. Our regular server pops by, and Hollis orders me a martini the way I like it and beers for him and my dad.

Dad looks between us. "You picked Aurora up from her exam?" He's started calling me Aurora recently. I'm not a hundred percent sure I want him to anymore. I don't feel like I'm fighting to be seen as an adult the way I used to.

"I did," Hollis says.

My mouth is suddenly dry. I'm not sure where this is going.

"You take your SUV or the Audi?" Dad asks.

"The Audi."

He nods and rubs his bottom lip with his thumb. "How long before you got mobbed?"

Hollis laughs. "As soon as I got out of the car."

"That was a rookie move."

"I wasn't thinking."

"Don't you remember when we picked Aurora up from one of her high school dances in my Porsche?" Dad asks.

I slap the table. It was green and over the top and impossible not to notice. "I was so freaking embarrassed! And then I had to cram myself in the back seat!"

"Shit. I do remember that. You were pissed at us." Hollis laughs.

"You were all my friends talked about for weeks. It was so annoying." I roll my eyes, but I'm smiling. It wasn't long after that when I flubbed my math test and tried to make Hollis my tutor. Never in my wildest dreams did I actually believe we'd end up here.

"I'm sure it was frustrating." Hollis gives me a knowing smile.

I elbow him in the side. "Oh my God, check your ego."

"I gotta use the bathroom. I'll be right back." Hollis kisses me on the cheek and slides out of the booth.

"I can't believe I didn't see it," Dad muses.

"See what?"

"The way you look at each other."

"We were trying to hide it for a long while. And I'm sorry for that."

He shakes his head. "I would have had a hard time no matter what, Pe—Aurora. I know you're an adult, but you'll always be my baby girl. And Hollis is my best friend. There wasn't an easy way around this."

"He's still your best friend?" I ask.

"Yeah. It'll take me a while to get over this, but I see how he is with you. How he feels about you is written all over his face. That he was able to hide it for as long as he did is a freaking miracle. No one was ever going to be good enough for you, but if there's one person I trust to put you first, it's him."

I reach across the table and squeeze his hand. "I love you, Dado."

"I love you, too, kiddo, with all my heart."

CHAPTER 46
HOLLIS

"I remember going to a keg party when I finished my final exam." I take a swig of my beer. It's warm, since I've been nursing it for a good hour and a half. I have plans for tonight, and beer isn't getting in the way of them.

Roman chuckles. "I probably went to all of two keg parties in college."

"I went to way too many keg parties," Flip says.

"I don't like beer." Ash sips his rum and Coke. "Or keg parties."

"They are usually full of bad decisions, vomit, and regrets," Tristan says.

Roman excuses himself to the bathroom, and Tristan glances around before he shifts his attention to me. "Roman seems like he's rolling with things pretty well, though? You never ended up with a black eye."

"We're aware that punching each other won't solve the problem. And yeah, he's coming around."

"Hindsight is a real asshole," Tristan observes.

"That's absolutely true," I agree. "You and Rix doing good, though?"

"Yeah. Bea's a fucking miracle."

"You looking forward to her moving in full time?" I ask.

"She's almost there already, but I'm looking forward to her officially giving up the second bedroom, you know? It's like confirmation that we're on the same page." Tristan scans the room, maybe to make sure no one else is paying attention. "I've been looking at rings. I know it's probably a little early, but Bea's applied to a couple of programs for the fall. She'll have to make a decision soon."

"That's good though, right? That's what she wants?"

"Yeah, and I'm all for it. She's good at the finance stuff—great, actually—but it's not where her heart is. There's no reason for her to stick it out in a job she sort of likes when I can afford to send her to school for something that brings her joy. Hell, I'd pay for courses for the rest of her fucking life, if that makes her happy. But I can't piss a circle around her all the time, you know?"

"The smell would be a lot. And Hemi wouldn't be happy about the public indecency charges," I offer.

"Right? But I can put a huge fucking rock on her finger so all those potential douchebags know she's mine. I figure at the end of summer we'll have been dating a year, and she'll have lived with me for a few months—but not so long that she's totally sick of my shit—so I can lock her in."

I chuckle and pat him on the shoulder. "I don't know that you need to worry about locking her in. She's pretty damn in love with you. I can't see her getting sick of your shit anytime soon."

"I really fucking hope not, because Bea's it for me. I would do anything for her. You know?"

"Yeah, man. I do."

Roman returns from the bathroom, wearing his worried-dad frown. He looks over at the ladies. "How many pitchers of margaritas have those girls had?"

"The last two have been non-alcoholic," I tell him.

"That's a relief."

Roman polishes off the rest of his beer. "You sticking around?"

"Until Aurora's ready to go, yeah." This part is hard to get used to. He's my best friend *and* my girlfriend's dad. I've watched out for her a lot over the years. But her staying at my place, that's new.

"You want to knock on my door in the morning and we can head to practice together?" he asks without looking at me.

It's an olive branch. We've been driving separately.

"Fuck, finally. Let's take your SUV, Hollis, and you two can drive my ass for the next couple of weeks." Tristan shakes his head. "It's been seriously inconvenient for me to drive while you worked your shit out."

"I feel like I had a right," Roman says.

"I'm not saying you didn't. I'm just saying it was inconvenient, and you two can share the responsibility while you're making it up to me." Tristan grins.

I shake my head. "You're an asshole."

"I know."

"See you two in the morning." Roman sets his beer bottle on the table behind us and stops to hug Aurora before he leaves.

"Speaking of people who need a girlfriend, it's about time Roman jumped back in the pool," Tristan says.

"Agreed. Especially now."

"I don't even know what his type is," Tristan muses.

"He doesn't talk to women when Aurora is around," I explain.

"What about the one from the gala? Has he gone on that date yet?"

"Not that I know of. She lives out in Illinois or Wisconsin, so I don't know if that has any real potential."

"They seemed to get along pretty good on the dance floor. At least before shit hit the fan. Speaking of shit hitting the fan—what the hell are you going to do about Scarlet? I can't see Hammer being all that excited about you going on a date with your ex."

"Scarlet saw the interview and gave me a pass on the date. I reimbursed her."

Tristan cough-chokes on his beer. "You gave Scarlet fucking Reed a hundred thousand dollars to get *out* of a date with her?"

"Seemed like the right thing to do. It wasn't her fault I couldn't uphold my end of the bargain. If I'd taken your advice like I should have and manned the fuck up, I wouldn't have been in the auction. Aurora would have and should have been my date that night."

"That was an expensive lesson."

"And totally worth it since I got the girl."

Aurora's eyes find mine from across the room. She's so fucking beautiful, and she's mine. I will spend the rest of my life loving her. She looks around, maybe checking to see who's watching out of habit. Then she rolls her eyes and sashays across the bar toward me.

"And I'm out. I'll see you later." Tristan claps me on the shoulder and walks away.

I drink in the wide smile and impish look on her face as she approaches. "How's it going, Princess?"

"My dad left?" she confirms.

I nod.

She links her hand behind my neck. "I feel weird about being affectionate with you in front of him," she admits. "I don't want to throw it in his face, but also, kiss me, please."

I pull her close and press my lips to hers. It feels damn good to love her without reservation.

She fiddles with the top button on my shirt. "I'm suspiciously sober considering the number of margaritas I've consumed."

I run my fingers down the back of her arm. "I wonder why that is."

Her bottom lip slides through her teeth. "Switching to virgins was smart."

I arch a brow.

She clears her throat. "The number of times I've masturbated to that facial expression is obscene. Take me home and put me to bed, please."

I tap her lightly on the ass. "Go say bye to your friends."

"Okay!" She kisses my cheek and bounces across the restaurant to where the girls are sitting. A round of hugs follows, and then we link pinkies and step outside into the cool evening.

She threads her arm through mine and rests her cheek against my biceps. "As much as I wanted to celebrate today in bed, and I absolutely still do, it was so nice to be *out* with our friends."

I press my lips to her temple. "Loving you out loud feels so much better."

"You are the best boyfriend in the universe." She squeezes my arm. "And my dad seems to be handling things."

"He is." I open the door to our building and usher her in out of the cold. "We're driving to practice together tomorrow."

Her face lights up as I hit the elevator button for the penthouse floor. "Really? Who suggested it?"

"He did." The elevator zips upward.

"I'm so glad to hear that." She runs her hands up my chest. "You and my dad have been so close for so long, and this changes that, but I didn't want the damage to be permanent, too."

"We both love you too much to let that happen." I kiss her softly.

The elevator dings, and I release her as the doors slide open, taking her hand instead.

The second we're inside my place, Aurora drags my mouth down to hers. Unfortunately, Postie and Malone are on us, trying to trip us as they weave between our legs.

"They're adorable, but they're cockblockers," Aurora says against my lips.

"Let's feed them. Then I have something for you."

"You mean orgasms, right? You have lots of those for me."

"I've been willing to provide those all week," I remind her.

"They came with stipulations." Her fingers curl around my belt buckle.

I grab her wrists and spin her around, raising them above her head as I press her into the door. She parts her legs, and my knee slides between them. She sighs and rolls her hips.

"One stipulation." I drag my lips along the edge of her jaw, breathing her in. "And it was reasonable. It still is."

"I know. I can't separate sex from feelings when it comes to you," she whispers, eyes brimming with emotion. "It feels like my heart and soul are on fire when you're inside me."

Her truth soothes the broken parts of me. "I feel the same way." I release her hands and slide my fingers into her silky hair. "That's why I needed you to be in this with me before we got here again."

"Thank you for being patient." She rests a warm palm against my cheek. Everything about her in this moment is soft, open. "I love you."

Her admission unravels me and heals my heart. I memorize this moment: the gentleness of her words, the truth in her eyes, how beautiful she is, hands on my skin, grounding me, tethering me to Earth.

"I've been waiting to hear those words."

"I've been waiting to say them. Now give them back to me, please," she whispers.

I take her face in my hands, emotion making my voice hoarse. "I love you, Aurora."

Her smile widens. "With all my heart," she murmurs and pulls my mouth to hers.

The kiss lasts all of five seconds, though, because my cats are back to being pests.

"Let's feed these two."

"And then orgasms?"

"Surprise first, then orgasms."

She sighs. "I'll get their treats if you get the food."

"On it." I head for the fridge.

Aurora gives the boys treats, which they gobble up in two seconds, while I plate their soft food. Once our hands are washed, I lace our fingers. "Come on." I guide her down the hall, past the spare bedroom, to my home office.

Nerves twist my stomach as I flick on the light and push the door open.

"Hollis," she breathes as she moves into the room. "This is... You redecorated."

The room formerly contained a single desk and an unused exercise bike. As far as home offices went, it was pretty uninspiring. But I usually sat at my dining room table with my laptop if I needed to review paperwork or contracts. If Aurora joins Hemi in the PR office, she'll need space to work outside of office hours, and maybe so will I in the future.

"I want this space to feel like yours, too." I want it to feel like home. Like she belongs here with me.

"This is amazing." She crosses over to the double desks. One side has a black executive chair—that's mine. The other chair is baby blue and plush, designed for function and comfort. The walls have been painted a pale, icy blue and new art decorates them, including a banana-duck print. Two custom lounge chairs face the window overlooking the harbor. "You even picked coordinating throw pillows," she muses.

I wrap my arms around her waist from behind and kiss her cheek. "I thought this would be a nice place to have coffee on work-from-home days."

"I love that." She tilts her head up, and I press a soft kiss to her tempting lips. "Why are you so perfect?"

"I'm far from it." I want to stay wrapped around her, but this is only the beginning, so I step back and link our hands. "There's more. Come."

"More?"

I guide her down the hall to my bedroom. "Eyes closed, Princess." I move her in front of me, covering her eyes with one hand while I open the door with the other. She holds my forearm as I urge her forward. My reflection stares back at me from the full-length mirror across the room. Aurora's cheeks are flushed.

Nervous anticipation makes my chest tight, but I need her to see how serious I am. I drop my hand to her hip. "You can open your eyes."

They flare as her nails bite into my arm in the most delicious way. "Oh, Hollis." She spins in my arms, awe on her perfect, stunning face. "You did this for me?"

"For us," I correct. "It's decidedly self-serving."

"It's incredible." She pushes up on her toes to kiss me, then scans the bed.

"You bought throw pillows."

"I know you like them." She has a ridiculous number on her bed. I've discovered they can be useful and not just a nuisance.

She flits across the room and grabs the one in the middle. "You got me a princess pillow."

"I did."

"You like me a lot."

"I definitely do."

She hugs the pillow to her chest with one arm and follows me across the room to the new dresser. I open the top drawer. I've already folded and put away all the things she's left here over the past few months. "Those are yours. I didn't want to clear a couple of drawers to make room for you. I want this to feel like it's as much yours as it is mine." I skim her cheek, needing the contact to ground me. "I know this is all very new and we need time to figure us out, but I'm also aware that Rix is moving out, and your sublease is only a year. Whenever you're ready to be here, here is ready for you. But no pressure. It's okay if you need more time than that."

She sets the pillow on the dresser top and settles her palms on my chest, her soft smile warming me. "You bought me a dresser."

"You have a lot of clothes," I point out. I hope this isn't too much.

"This is true." She runs her hands over my shoulder. "You're really serious about me, aren't you?"

I swallow past the lump in my throat. "Too serious?"

She shakes her head. "The perfect amount of serious." Her smile grows soft. "Tell me something real and true."

"Loving you is so easy. But hiding that feeling, denying *you*, was the hardest, most painful thing I've ever done, and I'm so glad I never have to do it again." I tuck her hair behind her ear, tracing the delicate shell. "Tell me something real and true."

Her chin trembles as she rests her palm over my heart. "You settle my soul, Hollis. Your heart is my home, and I never want to leave it."

Our lips meet, a gentle brush, a wordless promise. The wash of need is sudden and consuming as we press closer, hands gripping hair as we angle our heads and deepen the kiss.

She untucks my shirt and pulls it over my head, then does the same with hers. "You know what I want to do now?"

"I have a pretty good idea."

She unclasps her bra and tosses it aside, then pops the button on her jeans. "I bet my ideas are better." She shimmies her pants and underwear down her legs and kicks them off, leaving her in a pair of socks with a blue and black stripe around the top.

She tucks her fingers into the waistband of my pants and tugs me toward the full-length mirror.

"You planning to tell me what this better idea is?" I ask as she adjusts my position.

She shakes her head as she slides my belt through the buckle and pulls it free from the loops, dropping it on the floor at my feet. Her tongue drags across her bottom lip as she opens the button and pulls the zipper down. And then she grabs the princess pillow and tosses it at my feet, sinking to the floor.

She smiles up at me. "I'm going to show you with my mouth how much I appreciate your thoughtfulness."

I smirk. "Aren't you sweet?"

"The sweetest." Her grin is saucy as she frees me from my boxer briefs and wraps her palm around my length. I have to close my eyes for a second and gather myself. It feels like I've been without her softness for an eternity, and I'm not adequately prepared for this.

She places a kiss on the tip.

"Fuck, Princess," I groan.

"My mouth, Hollis," she replies.

My eyes open as her full lips part. Her tongue slides along the weeping slit and circles the head before she takes me in her mouth. One hand moves to my thigh, and her gaze shifts to the side—to her naked reflection, kneeling on a pillow, her lips wrapped around my cock.

She pops off, lips brushing the head as she speaks. "I like this mirror." And then her lips are sliding down my cock, pulling me deeper. She moans around me, one hand dropping between her thighs. I stroke her cheek, gaze bouncing between her right in front of me and her reflection in the mirror.

She moves my hands to cradle her face, and her eyes lift to mine.

I arch a brow.

She moans and slides three fingers into her pussy.

I pull my hips back until the ridge hits her bottom lip.

"Yes, please," she murmurs.

I push back in, slow strokes at first, going deeper on every pass, until the head hits the back of her throat, and she moans. Her fingers move between her thighs, eyes darting between my face and our reflection in the mirror. I'm close. So close. I start to pull out, because I'm one thrust away from coming. But her free hand rises, and she grabs my ass, nails sinking in as she pulls me forward until she's swallowing my entire fucking cock.

I come so hard I grab the edge of the dresser to stay upright. Her nails retract from my ass, and I pull out. She sucks in a gasping breath and smiles up at me. "I always wanted to try that."

"For fuck's sake, Princess." I crush my mouth to hers.

And then she's pulling me onto the floor with her. I tuck the pillow under her head and bury my face between her thighs, fucking her with my fingers and tongue until she's fisting my hair and screaming my name.

And then I carry her to the bed, roll a condom on, and settle in the cradle of her hips.

"I need you in me, Hollis," she murmurs, her trembling fingers skimming my cheek. "Please."

"Everything for you, Princess." I drag the head through her wetness.

Aurora arches, canting her hips up as I nudge her entrance. I pause, memorizing the moment, how gorgeous she looks with flushed cheeks and lust-drenched eyes.

And then I push inside in one smooth stroke.

We both moan as I bottom out inside her. "Fuck, I missed you," I groan against her lips.

"I missed you, too." She runs her fingers through my hair. "I missed this feeling."

It's so much more than physical connection. Being entwined with her feels like home. I stroke her cheek. "So did I."

"Let's never take it away from each other again, okay?" she murmurs.

I shake my head. "Never."

"I'm yours." Her hands slide down my back.

"Mine forever now," I promise.

"Every part of you."

I roll my hips, and she moans softly.

"I used to imagine how good it would feel to have you inside me like this. Right here, in this bed. But it's so much more than that." She puts her hand over my heart. "You're inside me here, too."

"I didn't know what I was missing until you," I murmur against her lips.

She wraps herself around me, feet hooked at the small of my back. And we move together, a slow tide rising, until it washes over us, blanketing us in bliss. In a promise of forever.

CHAPTER 47

HOLLIS

A urora glances at the clock on the nightstand and pats my chest. "Ooh, you should probably get dressed. My dad will be here soon." Tonight could be the final game of the season, and if the universe is on our side, we'll bring home the cup.

She grins when I level her with a glare. "You were parading around in your panties."

"I was still deciding what to wear tonight."

"You were being a brat."

"But you're relaxed, aren't you?"

"I am definitely relaxed," I agree and start to sit up.

She leans in and puckers her lips. "I love you."

"I love you, even when you're a brat." I steal one last kiss. "Especially when you're a brat." I roll off the bed and hop to my feet.

She shifts onto her side and props her cheek on her fist. "That was incredibly graceful."

I look at the clock on my way to the bathroom. "We're cutting it close."

"You're cutting it close. I have an hour," she calls out.

"You can't be naked when your dad comes knocking."

"Point taken." She log-rolls off the bed and holds up her

hand as I toss her a warm, damp washcloth. She wipes between her legs and tosses it into the laundry hamper beside her dresser.

The top four drawers are filled with her clothes. Now, whenever Tristan is home and Rix is at his place, Aurora stays here. I'm not pushing for her to move in yet. She still has a few months before the sublet expires, but she's spending more nights in my bed than hers these days.

I quickly put on my suit while Aurora pulls on a pair of jeans, a Terror T-shirt with Hollis's Girl and my number on the back, and her dad's jersey over the top. There's a knock at the door as we finish getting dressed. Roman has stopped letting himself in out of fear that he'll see something he doesn't want to.

He's getting used to me and Aurora being a couple. Nothing has changed in some ways, and in others, everything has. Openly showing her affection in public has been an adjustment, but a welcome one. She's mine and I'm hers, and I refuse to hide those feelings from anyone, especially not Roman. And while our friendship has changed, we both have the same first priority now, and that's Aurora.

We meet Roman at the door together.

"Hey." Aurora wraps her arms around him, then leans back and fixes his tie. "You look great. Feeling good about tonight?"

"Ready to shut out New York." His gaze shifts to me. "How about you?"

"Solid. Ready to get on the ice." I've played every game this series, and I've felt strong. I'm not where I was at the beginning of the season, but I have the entire off season to get there again.

The three of us get into the elevator. Aurora kisses Roman on the cheek as we approach the twelfth floor. "I love you. Good luck tonight, Dado."

He gives her a quick hug. "I love you, too, kiddo."

I reach for her just as she turns to me. It's like that more and more these days. We're in sync. I snake an arm around her waist, and she wraps hers around my neck. It's automatic, and for a second, I forget everything but her.

"You've got this." She kisses the side of my neck and leans back so I can see her beautiful face. "I love you."

I cup her cheek in my palm. "I love you, too. I'll be looking for you out there tonight."

"I'll be cheering for you."

I brush my lips over hers. The elevator doors slide open, and I grudgingly release her. She steps into the hall and blows us both another kiss. "Kick their ass tonight."

Roman laughs, and she winks as the doors slide closed.

"You all right?" I ask once it's the two of us.

He leans against the wall and crosses his arms. "You know, I worried I wouldn't be able to handle seeing you and my daughter together."

I nod. I get that it isn't easy, but she needs to know I put her first every time. "I know it's a transition, but I'd rather you be pissed at me than deny her affection."

"That's exactly how it should be." A hint of a smile tips the corner of his mouth. "She's happy with you. Happier than I've ever seen her. I'm not saying this is easy to get used to, but the way you love her makes the awkwardness worth it. I just want her to be content and loved, and that's what I see when she's with you."

"I'd do anything for her," I admit.

"I know."

The elevator doors open, and we step out into the warm May afternoon. The playoffs have been intense, and this could be a historic night for us. We take Tristan's SUV to the arena, and when we arrive, the energy in the locker room is electric. Everyone is buzzing with nerves and excitement. And that goes with us onto the ice.

When it's time for the game, the girls are all behind the bench tonight. Ashish ends up on the Jumbotron when he blows his wife a kiss. Shilpa catches it and brings her fingers to her lips. Earlier in the season, I would have razzed him for that, but tonight I can appreciate their commitment to each other. This isn't an easy life, and Shilpa is a rock star.

Tristan scans the row for Rix and taps his fist over his heart. Rix makes a heart with both her hands and when the camera pans away, she drops it to her crotch.

Dallas laughs.

Flip glances behind us. "What's going on?"

"Nothing," Tristan and I say at the same time.

Flip gives the girls a thumbs-up, and Tally's face turns red as the cameras return to their row.

Aurora and I do what we always do when she's at games these days: at the same time, we mouth the words *I love you* and make the corresponding hand gestures. Is it cheesy as fuck? Absolutely. But it makes her smile every time. The crowd has gotten wise to this, and pictures of us have ended up on the hockey sites recently. It used to bother me when that happened with Scarlet, but it feels different with Aurora. There's no agenda; we're not on display. And Aurora's grown up in the hockey world, so she's used to it. That makes it easier to roll with.

Stiles and Madden start the game strong, scoring a goal in the first two minutes. But Bowman ties it up at the end of the first period. Grace scores another goal for New York at the beginning of the second period, and then we're fighting to tie it back up through the end of the second period. It's an intense game, with New York working to drag this out to all seven games. But at the beginning of the third period, Madden scores, tying it up again. Everyone is playing hard, and Grace is using it to his advantage. With six minutes left in the game, Stiles takes a hit. It doesn't look like it should take him out of the game, but he's favoring his right leg. And we're set up for a face off at New York's net, putting us in an ideal position.

There's a back and forth with the refs, and Stiles skates back to the bench, shaking his head.

"You all right, man?" I ask as I pass him.

He lifts his chin, a slight smile at the corner of his mouth. "Get that goal, man."

I take my place at right wing, and the puck drops. There's a scramble for control, and Madden flips it to me. I skate behind the crease and pass it back, getting into position. We're back and forth, keeping the puck away from New York, looking for weak spots in their defense. Madden takes the shot on net, but it bounces off the post. The roar of excitement becomes a sigh of disappointment.

But New York's defense misses the opportunity to reclaim control, and Madden snags the pass. Defense is already in position, though, blocking his shot on net. He passes to me as I move in, ready to take the shot. New York's goalie adjusts his position, and at the last second, I scoop the puck and flip it up. It sails over his pads and hits the back of the net.

Toronto loses their fucking minds, and I find myself smashed into Madden and Palaniappa.

We try to compose ourselves pretty quickly. We still have four and a half minutes of play left. We're in the lead, but anything could happen.

New York scrambles to get back in the game, but Grace makes a stupid move during the next shift with Stiles and gets called for tripping. The two-minute penalty attached to that makes it impossible for New York to score the goal they so desperately need to stay in the series.

We win the game 3-2, and the Cup is ours. It's one hell of an end to my comeback season.

The locker room is buzzing after the game, and Tristan claps me on the back, his grin wide. "Dude. You made history."

I shake my head, but I can't stop smiling. "That should have been your goal."

"Who knows what would have happened if I'd been out there instead of you? That could have been any of us. You fought for this, man. I know it; you know it. Celebrate the fuck out of it."

An hour later, we step through the doors of the Watering Hole. Roman is at my side. I don't make it three feet inside before I'm tackle-hugged by Aurora. Her entire body winds around mine. "That was amazing! You were amazing!" She mashes our mouths together. "I've already had two glasses of champagne, so I can't be responsible for the things that come out of my mouth tonight."

"Maybe censor them in front of me," Roman says.

"Oh fu—" She untangles herself from around me. "Sorry, Dado." She dances over and hugs him. "You were amazing, too."

He pats her on the back. "Thanks, kiddo."

She edges between us and links her arms with ours.

In that moment, I realize it doesn't matter what comes next, whether I decide to play next season or hang up my skates and go a different direction. I've done the things I wanted to in this career. Hit all the high notes. This is the win of all wins. And it's that much sweeter because I get to celebrate it with the people who matter the most—my best friend and the love of my life.

Aurora is it for me.

My person.

And she's worth every risk.

EPILOGUE
HOLLIS

THREE MONTHS LATER

I temper my steps as I approach Aurora's office and smile with pride when I see the nameplate that reads *AURORA HAMMERSTEIN, Assistant Director of PR* fixed to the door. She's been in the role for the past four weeks and is quickly proving this is where she belongs.

I pause when I reach the threshold. Today, she's wearing black dress pants and a pale blue blouse. Her hair brushes her jawline and shows off the elegant curve of her neck. She's so fucking beautiful it makes my heart hurt sometimes. And she's mine. I thank the powers that be and the creators of superhero pleasure devices for opening that door and giving her the guts to be the first to walk through it. She's a force, and an inspiration, and I'm lucky to have been worth the risk for her.

When I rap on the doorframe, she looks up from her computer. She wears blue-light glasses, and I love them on her. But then, I love everything about her.

"Hey." Her gaze moves over me in a slow, appreciative sweep. "You look delicious."

I glance over my shoulder, checking to make sure there's no one in the hall before I turn back to her, lips tugging up in a smirk. "You interested in taking a bite?"

"Always, but I'm at work." She motions to her surroundings as she rolls her chair back.

I saunter over and grab the arms of her chair, caging her in so I can steal a quick kiss. I bite the edge of her jaw. "Lots of empty offices, and you're probably due for a lunch break. You should leave the glasses on."

"We have to be at the shoot in less than twenty minutes."

"That's plenty of time to take care of all your needs, Princess." I finger the heart pendant that rests against the hollow of her delectable throat.

"You can't go to an endorsement shoot smelling like vagina, Hollis." She's breathless, though, and she doesn't sound entirely convinced.

"You think it would be better for me to show up to the calendar campaign with a raging hard-on?"

"You're such a bad influence." She laughs and pushes on my chest.

"Is that you saying yes?"

A throat clears behind me. "Hollis, stop pestering my assistant."

I adjust the problem in my pants as I straighten, grateful I'm wearing a suit. "I was just saying hi."

Hemi snorts from the doorway. "Never play poker, Hollis, unless you want to lose your shirt." She holds up a hand. "And please don't use that as an invitation to take it off. You will get to do that soon enough." Her phone chimes with the death march, and she rolls her eyes to the ceiling. "Lord, give me strength." She checks the message and shakes her head. "How the hell can Dallas be late? Didn't he drive in with the rest of you?"

"Tristan said he was driving himself," I offer.

"Do you want me to check on him?" Aurora asks.

"No. He's my problem. I'll deal with him." She points a finger at me. "Be a good hockey player and do not try to lure my assistant into an empty room. You basically live together at this point, so sneaking around like horny teenagers is completely unnecessary." She spins around, but quickly does an about face. "But I do approve of how hot you are for each other, and how often that's captured on social media by literally everyone." Her heels clip on the floor as she crosses the hall and steps into her office, bringing her phone to her ear. "Do you really want to dress up as a clown again, Dallas? Because that's what's in store for you if you keep this bullshit up." Her door closes firmly.

Aurora turns off her computer and leaves her glasses on her desk.

I pick them up and slide them into the breast pocket of my suit.

"I have a spare pair at home. In the office."

I grin at her use of *home* in reference to my place. The only time she uses her own apartment is when she and the girls get together for one of their peen-free nights. I don't call her on it, though. It's all part of my master plan—make her comfortable and happy, move her clothes into the closet and her dresser one outfit at a time, and when November rolls around and her sublet is up, all she'll have are a few boxes of things to move into the penthouse.

I return the glasses to her desk. "Are they the same?"

"They're yellow instead of blue."

I wrap an arm around her waist, pulling her against me as I whisper, "I have some plans for you and those glasses when we get home."

"Ooh." She grips the lapels of my suit jacket and presses her hips into mine. "Should I be a naughty button-pusher this afternoon?"

That's a green light to put her over my lap. "Fuck yes, you should."

"Is nowhere sacred anymore?" Roman's voice cuts through the haze of lust and hormones.

I step back, and Aurora smothers a grin even as her cheeks turn pink. "We were hugging, Dad."

Roman stands in the doorway with his arms crossed. "That's a load of bullshit, based on the color of both of your faces. I always knock now! Always! I even try to remember to message first. I should not have to worry about seeing things I should never see at our place of employment."

"I saw your penis twice when I was living with you last year," Aurora points out.

I give her a look.

She rolls her eyes at me.

Roman's hands go to his hips. "Well, I saw your personal superhero device, and that was not my fault!"

"Um, sorry to interrupt, but we're supposed to be in makeup in like, five minutes," Tally says from the doorway. She's interning with Hemi for the summer.

Roman's face turns the same color as Aurora's. "I'm so sorry." He slowly turns around. "If you could pretend—it's your birthday?"

"It's not until tomorrow." Tally narrows her eyes at Aurora, who taps the top of her head.

Tally closes her eyes and wrinkles her nose, lifting her hand to touch the tiara. "I forgot I was wearing this."

"It looks good on you," Roman says.

I smile and give her two thumbs-up, but side-eye Aurora.

"Hemi and I got it for her," she mutters. "Mine is at home."

That's a fucking relief since Aurora routinely wears her princess tiara around the house. And only her tiara.

"You should leave it on." Aurora shoulders her purse. "This is your birthday week, and we are taking full advantage of that."

Tally sighs. "Eighteen is a stupid age. I'm legal to vote, but I can't do any of the fun stuff for another year unless we drive to Quebec."

"But you are officially an adult, and we can always go to a Montreal game in the fall." Aurora links her arm with Tally's and waves for us to follow. "Come along, my two favorite men. It's time to make calendar history."

"I don't think you should be planning to take the coach's daughter to Montreal so she can drink," Roman grumbles as he falls into step beside me.

"Says the man who knocked up his seventeen-year-old girlfriend," Aurora calls over her shoulder.

"We were almost eighteen," he gripes.

"At least she'll be with the team, and we can keep her safe," I say.

"Of course you're going to side with my daughter." He rolls his eyes but grins.

We run into Rix and Shilpa on the way down to the arena. Today, Aurora has set up a team photo shoot for a calendar for next year. We're donating a portion of proceeds to a number of causes, including Food for Life, a program designed to help families in need, and the Hockey Academy, as well as a local hockey program designed for kids with special needs—Tristan helps his brother with that, and Flip has been involved too.

When we arrive, Aurora excuses herself from the group, taking Tally with her.

Flip, Tristan, and Ash join us as team members filter in.

Tristan adjusts his tie and tucks his hands in his pockets. "Hammer's a freaking boss. I can't believe she organized this whole thing."

"She's amazing," Roman says proudly.

"She sure is," I agree.

Hemi enters the room like a queen, a sweaty, slightly disheveled Dallas following in her wake.

He stops to fill his water bottle before he joins us.

"You all right, man?" Tristan asks.

"Just ate a bad burrito or something. All good." He swipes at his forehead with the back of his arm and proceeds to guzzle the contents of his water bottle.

Hemi whistles shrilly to get everyone's attention, but it's Aurora who steps up to organize us for the group shot. I can't take my eyes off her as she and Hemi take control of a team of hockey hotheads. We change into our uniforms for another team shot, and then we're photographed individually and in pairs, including me and Roman, Flip and Tristan, Dallas and Ashish, and a few other teammates. Then the twelve lucky players who opted to be part of the Special Edition calendar strip down to our boxers, skates, and shoulder pads and grab our sticks.

Aurora gives me a long, heated once-over.

Roman steps up beside me and points a finger at his daughter. "That's unprofessional conduct. Stop looking at my best friend like he's a piece of meat."

"Sorry, Dado. He's my boyfriend. I'm allowed to look at him like that." She snaps a picture on her phone.

"What are you doing?"

"Keeping Rainbow's dream alive."

"She knows you're dating Hollis."

That was a particularly entertaining breakfast when Rainbow found out for certain that Roman and I weren't Aurora's dads, and that I had turned into her boyfriend.

"She still ships you." Aurora tucks her phone in her pocket.

The photographer calls Roman over, leaving me with Aurora. She eyes me from the side.

"Wishing you'd taken me up on the empty-office offer?"

She whimpers, and it's not unlike the sound she makes when we're in bed.

"You're a real problem, aren't you?"

"I know." She rests her cheek against my biceps. "But I'm your favorite problem."

"You absolutely are." I press a kiss to the top of her head. "I love you, Princess."

"I love you, Hollis."

"I can't wait to get you home and show you how much."

Her face brightens with my favorite impish grin. "I can't wait for that either."

The pull is impossible to deny, so I don't. I brush my lips over hers.

"Thank you for choosing me," she whispers.

"Always."

EXTENDED EPILOGUE

HOLLIS

I brush my thumb across my girlfriend's peaked nipple through her shirt. "I thought you said you were ready to go."

"I am."

"We're leaving in two minutes." Despite the number of guesses she's lobbed at me, our adventure today remains a surprise.

"I'll grab my purse."

"And a bra please, Princess," I call after her, then bite the inside of my cheek to stop my smile.

She spins and arches a brow.

I arch one back and cross the room to stand in front of her. She tips her head up, and I stare down at her as she pushes her tits out. I thread my fingers through the hair at her nape and tug. I bend until my lips almost touch hers. "Such a little brat."

Her eyes light up. "The biggest brat. What are you going to do about it?"

I bite the edge of her jaw, skimming the column of her throat with my lips and dipping lower until I can cover her nipple through the fabric of her white shirt, sucking hard.

She gasps and grabs my shoulders. I get my hormones under

control and release her nipple. "Look what you made me do." I swat her ass, untangle my hand from her hair, and rearrange my hard-on.

Aurora's perfect, perky nipples now taunt me from under her shirt. But the look on her face is worth the prolonged torment. Lust and irritation color her cheeks and pull down the corners of her lips. "Why are you stopping?"

"We have an appointment I don't want to be late for. And now you need to change your shirt and put on a bra, and we should be walking out the door right now." I tap my bare wrist.

She props her hands on her hips. "Why do I need a freaking bra?"

"Because of this." I point to my very prominent erection. "We'll be in public for several hours. And while I'm not exactly opposed to fucking you in the back of the car, the potential for getting caught is significant. What if my sometimes-questionable control were to snap because I can't stay away from your perfect, pretty nipples, especially when they're being all coy, peeking at me through your shirt?"

"They could end up in your mouth, and I'll change my shirt." She brushes one through her shirt. Such a little brat.

"Exactly. And if it were documented, and your dad found out, and he goes to prison for murdering me, it would ruin his last season. It would also interfere with my plan to make you my wife, because I can't do those things if your dad ends me."

Aurora rolls her eyes. "Fine. I'll put on a bralette. They're more comfortable."

"Perfect. I appreciate your consideration for me and everyone who might have the misfortune of getting an eyeful of dick print."

"Most people would love to get a load of your dick print," she calls over her shoulder as she disappears into our bedroom. She hasn't officially moved in yet. But it's coming.

"You're a little biased about that," I mutter.

Most of the time I don't give a shit if Aurora's nipples are saluting me in public places. Usually I can hide my reaction behind a suit jacket or the protective cover of a table. But it'll be tough where we're going this afternoon.

She returns a minute later. I'm not sure the wardrobe change has made the situation better. She's wearing a bralette as promised, but the new shirt is pale yellow, gauzy, and has a deep V highlighting her cleavage. She sashays by me and grabs her purse. I keep my mouth shut and follow.

"So…" She waits until we're in the elevator on the way down to the parking garage before she says anything. "How about a hint now that we're going wherever we're going?"

I cross my arms and shake my head.

She loops her arms around my neck; her boobs are now mashed against my crossed arms. I look down into her cleavage. "Pretty please, Hollis. I'll be a good girl for the rest of the day if you give me one teensy hint." She bats her lashes and blinks up at me with her huge, brown doe eyes.

"We both know that's a lie, Princess."

The elevator dings. She steps back as the doors slide open and two guys in their late twenties join us. They're dressed in jeans and T-shirts.

Aurora slides her arm through my tattooed one as their gazes jump from me to her and back to me.

"Hi. How's it going?" Aurora is her personable self, opening the door for polite conversation.

They exchange pleasantries with my girlfriend while I size them up. I smile, though. At least I try to. They get off at the lobby, and we continue to the parking garage. I tug Aurora toward my sports car instead of my SUV.

"Oh, so it's a fun-car day." She bounces as I open the passenger door and offer her my hand.

"I know you love the fun car." It's not usually my go-to for outings like this, but Aurora loves my sports car, and I love making her happy. Once she's seated, I close the door and round the hood, taking my spot behind the wheel.

As soon as we're out of the parking garage, she rolls down the window, frees her scrunchie from her wrist, and pulls her bangs and the hair around her face into a ridiculously cute pony-tail on top of her head. She's all smiles as we drive to the west end of the city. When we arrive, I pull into the private parking lot, secure a ticket, and find a spot. Aurora meets me at the hood. She threads her arm through mine.

"Oh! Are you taking me to vintage stores so I can see all the cool stuff that was popular when you were my age?" She smiles up at me.

"Careful, Princess, unless you want me to put you over my knee when I get you home." The nearly thirteen years between us aren't the big deal I used to think they were, but Aurora does a good job of poking fun at me, mostly just to wind me up.

"I really love it when you threaten me with a good time." She kisses my biceps.

We round the corner and walk the half block to the studio. I open the door and usher her inside. She freezes when she real-izes where we are and grips my hand. "Hollis?"

"I'm adding to my art today. I thought you might like to meet my artist," I explain. Aurora is obsessed with my tattoos. She's constantly taking my shirt off when we're at home on the couch so she can trace the designs with her fingers...and often her tongue.

Her smile is so fucking beautiful. "Thank you for inviting me to be part of this."

She has no idea yet how much of a part of this she is, but she will soon.

My artist is a young woman named Ellie. She grew up in Chicago and moved out this way a few years ago. She went to college in the city and set up a sister shop to her dad's. She's an incredible talent, and despite how young she is, she's making a name for herself for her unique style and ability to create lifelike, realistic designs on three-dimensional canvas. She's done all of my work for the past couple of years.

"Ellie, this is my girlfriend, Aurora. Aurora, this is Ellie, my artist."

"You do such beautiful work," Aurora says as she shakes her hand.

"Thanks. It's great when I get to design so many cool pieces." She guides us to the back of the studio, and we take a seat in her booth. "I know we've been back and forth on color and design, so I wanted to show you a few iterations I worked on this week." She pulls out a folder and exchanges a questioning look with me.

I bite back a smile and nod.

Her cheek ticks and Aurora glances at me, but I don't hold her attention for long. Not as Ellie sets the art in front of us.

"Uh—" Aurora tries to hide her shock. "It's, uh—"

"Exactly what I asked for," I state. "It's perfect."

"I'm glad I got it right." Ellie coughs into her arm, clearly trying to hold it together.

"Where are you putting this?" There's a hint of panic in Aurora's voice.

"We thought my forearm would be good." I tap the inside of my arm. "What do you think?"

"Uh...um..." She licks her lips and looks to Ellie for some guidance. "Are there other places you'd consider? It doesn't really match the rest of your sleeve."

"You don't think so?" That Ellie and I can keep straight faces is amazing.

"I mean, it's really fun..." She drags the word out while fiddling with the scrunchie on her wrist.

Ellie arches a pierced brow. "Should we show her the other design before we go making big decisions?"

"That's probably a good idea." Especially since Aurora looks like she's struggling not to speak her mind about the current one.

"There's another design?" Aurora sounds relieved.

"There is," I say.

"Is it another banana duck?" Her voice is extra pitchy.

"It's a little different." Ellie covers the banana duck with a blue and yellow banana-print scrunchie crown. It's hilarious, and I'm one-hundred percent framing it and putting it on the wall in our home office as a forever reminder of this day.

Aurora's brows pull together. Her mouth opens and closes as she turns to me.

I cough to stifle my laugh.

"You jerk!" She smacks my arm. "I thought you were going to get a banana duck wearing a freaking scrunchie crown on your damn forearm!"

"It's still a strong contender," I argue through my laughter.

Ellie's shoulders shake.

"I love banana duck, I love scrunchies, and I love you and your tattoos, but I don't want to combine the last love and the first one. Ever." She turns to Ellie. "It's amazing. I want to frame that picture, but I don't want it staring at me every time Hollis is wearing a short-sleeved shirt."

"I love me some banana duck, but I totally agree."

"You should have seen your face, Princess." I wipe a tear from my eye.

"That was a horrible thing to do!" She digs her finger into my ribs. "I was trying to figure out how the hell we would explain the meaning behind that without it being painfully awkward all the time." She deflates into her chair. "This one is just so much prettier." She motions to the scene. And then her brows pull together. "Wait. Is this..." She trails off, eyes widening as realization sets in.

"You," I finish for her.

When I came in to see Ellie about adding another half-sleeve dedicated to my other love, we talked through all the things I loved about Aurora, and what made her so special. "You're the light of my life, Princess. You're already in my heart, but I want to wear you on my skin."

"Oh, Hollis." She waves a hand in front of her face, on the brink of emotion.

"I'll give you two a few minutes to talk through which color palate you want to go with." Ellie excuses herself and pulls the curtain closed to give us some privacy.

"You really love me a lot, don't you?" Aurora whispers as she traces the fingers of light swirling in the sky, mountains in the background, pines at the forefront, and yellow gerbera daisies dotting the ground.

"With all my heart," I agree. "Do you like it?"

"I love it. So, so much. It's stunning."

And it really is. It's the embodiment of Aurora: bright colors and a serene setting. It's beautiful and quietly powerful, the threads of the Northern Lights, aurora borealis, streaking across a night sky—rare and precious, just like she is.

"Where are you putting it?" Her bottom lip slides through her teeth as her gaze heats.

"I thought here." I tap the un-inked skin on my biceps. "It would balance out the other side and leave room for more ink as we move forward. I'll want ink for our kids, eventually, when we get there."

She holds up her naked ring finger. "Getting a little ahead of yourself, don't you think?"

"The ring is coming, Princess." I pull her onto my lap and take her face in my hands. "I'm yours. Every part of me. And I want to carry you with me wherever I go, in my heart and on my skin. And when you're ready for the next step, I'll put the prettiest ring right here." I kiss her bare ring finger. "This is to tide me over until you're ready to be my wife and start our forever."

"I've dreamed of being yours for years, Hollis."

I press a soft kiss to her lips. "Let's start it here, then."

Want more bonus content from Hammer and Hollis? Scan this code for access to a steamy bonus chapter.

ABOUT THE AUTHOR HELENA HUNTING

NYT and USA Today bestselling author, Helena Hunting lives on the outskirts of Toronto with her amazing family and her adorable kitty, who think the best place to sleep is her keyboard. Helena writes everything from emotional contemporary romance to romantic comedies that will have you laughing until you cry. If you're looking for a tearjerker, you can find her angsty side under H. Hunting.

OTHER TITLES BY HELENA HUNTING

STANDALONE NOVELS

The Librarian Principle

Felony Ever After

Before You Ghost (with Debra Anastasia)

FOREVER ROMANCE STANDALONES

The Good Luck Charm

Meet Cute

Kiss my Cupcake

A Love Catastrophe

Milton Keynes UK
Ingram Content Group UK Ltd.
UKHW040905040724
445040UK00004B/76

THERE'S NO ONE MORE OFF LIMITS THAN MY BEST FRIEND'S DAUGHTER.

Peggy Aurora Hammerstein. The Toronto Terror's unofficial team princess. I would never do anything to mess with our team dynamics this late into the hockey season, but seeing her work in the front office changed something for me.

I see her as she is now: a powerful woman with ambition for miles. When I hold her against me, she fits perfectly.

Her little flirts and taunts push my buttons, if she doesn't stop—my control just might break.
But I will never cross that line. I will never know what it could be to call her mine.

I've never wanted anyone more than Aurora and no one can ever know.

ISBN 978-1-989185-84-1

90000

9 781989 185841